The River

ALSO BY HELEN BRYAN

The Sisterhood

War Brides

Martha Washington: First Lady of Liberty

Planning Applications and Appeals

The Valley Trilogy

The Valley

The Mountain

The River

BOOK THREE OF *THE VALLEY TRILOGY*

HELEN BRYAN

This is a work of fiction. Names, characters, organizations, places, events, and incidents are either products of the author's imagination or are used fictitiously.

Published by Lake Union Publishing, Seattle

www.apub.com

ISBN-13: 9781542042048
ISBN-10: 1542042046

Cover design by Shasti O'Leary Soudant

Cover image: French river landscape oil painting (1905) by Gabriel Mathieu (1843–1921) via SuperStock/Alamy Stock Photo

Printed in the United States of America

With love for Roger, Cassell and Jonny,
Niels and Lucinda,
and for our dear Bo, Poppy, Jake, and Heath

GRAFTON

CHAPTER 1

1883

In the small hours Katie Marshall slipped out of Wildwood with a carpetbag of clothes and Comfort Marshall's jewelry and set off in a thick spring fog down the path that led through the orchard on the slope of Frog Mountain and ended at the cemetery at the edge of Grafton. Katie knew the Indian legends of shape-shifters and the witch Uktena who prowled in the fog, hunting for victims. Alone on the mountainside in the whiteness, it was easy to imagine the cold damp on the back of her neck was Uktena's fingers. Only fear and her anger drove her on.

Mama Comfort, Katie had called the woman who raised her. Comfort the Quaker, Comfort the saint who'd raised the abandoned baby discovered in her barn. Comfort the liar. Comfort the murderess.

Mama Comfort had shown her the very spot where she'd been found in the Marshalls' barn at Wildwood, wrapped in a dirty petticoat, abandoned by the ragged couple begging for food—an Irish soldier who'd come to fight with the Confederates, and the wife who'd followed him because she had no one else in Ireland. Comfort's husband, Charles, who'd fought for the Union, had been a prisoner in a Confederate prison camp at the time, and Comfort had taken in the orphan baby to raise with her own two children, Priscilla, whom people called Teeny, and Ben. "Thee mustn't judge thy parents harshly, Katie. They were lost and far from home, and couldn't care for a baby so left thee here, trusting in Christian charity," Mama Comfort had explained. Coldly.

People told Katie she was fortunate, being raised at Wildwood along with Comfort's other two children. Comfort was one of the few people with money after the war ended. She was the only child and heir of a wealthy Quaker family in Richmond, Virginia, abolitionists who voiced their support for the Union. This had made her family and Charles pariahs in Richmond during the war. Besides holding fast to their principles, her parents held fast to their money, investing in railway stock instead of the Confederacy, like their southern neighbors had. Comfort inherited a sizable legacy during Reconstruction.

By then Comfort had given up hope of Charles's return, believing he was surely dead. But he had eventually come home, in bad health, two years after the war was over. Yet alive. Katie had called him Pa, like Teeny and Ben did. They turned on her, said she mustn't call him Pa, she wasn't their sister. She was Katie Irish, not Katie Marshall. When Charles heard Ben and Teeny he'd reproved them, said Katie was every bit his and Comfort's child, that she even resembled the Marshall children. Why, in a certain light she even resembled Mama Comfort.

He'd said her name was Katie Marshall now, and she was their sister.

Katie saw Comfort's expression change, heard her sharp intake of breath. Comfort had muttered that no child belonging to her would have such eyes, yellow eyes, how could you say that, Charley. And young Katie had seen that Comfort hated her with a deep, secret hate she hid from Charles, though not from Ben and Teeny.

Yet Katie always had a new frock when Teeny did, she was fed as well, she had her own little bed with her own special quilt, and she got new shoes like Teeny when her old ones were outgrown. None of the children at school could have pointed to any difference. Only Katie knew.

Charles was kind, but within a few years he died of consumption. This left Mama Comfort in charge of the Marshall property and the money she'd inherited, and Katie at the mercy of the Marshalls' hostility.

Aunt Polly Stuart's home had been her refuge from Comfort's dislike and Teeny's teasing. She'd make her way down to Aunt Polly's cabin and play with Aunt Polly's grandson Will, who they said was simple. But Will was sweet and kind, soothing company after Ben and Teeny. He reminded Katie of Charles. At school other boys teased him for playing with a girl, but Will was "slow" in his lessons, and Katie was protective, helping him learn enough to get by. He stuck to her as she stuck to him. "What would I do without you, Katie?" Will would ask over and over, and Katie would smile and say, "What would I do without *you*, Will?"

Comfort, who believed in education, sent Ben to Harvard and Teeny to the girls' academy Comfort herself had attended in Philadelphia. She tried to send Katie too, but Katie grew distraught at the thought of leaving Will, not to mention fear of being marooned at school at Teeny's mercy. She'd cried and begged to stay home. For her part Teeny didn't want the burden of Katie at the academy, so in the end Comfort had capitulated and let Katie attend high school in Grafton.

Ben graduated from Harvard, and Comfort financed the newspaper he wanted. Teeny came home from school and within a year was engaged to Dr. Joshua Vann, an old man, in Katie's eyes, but a prominent one in Grafton. Comfort gave Teeny a generous dowry when she married.

When Katie told Aunt Polly that Teeny was getting married, Aunt Polly said it was a good match and she hoped they'd be happy. Afterward, Will, who had grown into a handsome man with kind eyes whom people continued to refer to as "poor Will Stuart," said they should get married too, and Will held her hand and asked to kiss her and Katie said yes. She was almost swept away by the kiss and the thought of making a home with Will, and being safe for life from the Marshalls.

Once she'd have kept it to herself, but happiness spilled over, and she told Teeny and wished out loud that she might have a small dowry—Will had nothing—and some linen to monogram for sheets and pillowcases like Teeny was monogramming hers. Teeny retorted that Katie wasn't a Marshall and wasn't entitled to anything. Comfort pressed her lips together and shook her head.

Aunt Polly sent Will up to Wildwood with a message that Aunt Polly wanted to see Katie.

"Will says you want to marry," Aunt Polly said, frowning at the two of them. "Is that true?"

"Yes!" cried Katie, turning to Will.

"Yes!" echoed Will, taking her hand in both of his. "I love Katie, Aunt Polly."

"And I love Will!"

Aunt Polly told Will to go and chop wood, she wanted to speak to Katie.

Katie waited for Aunt Polly to say happy things like she'd said about Teeny's marrying.

Aunt Polly sighed. "If I thought this would happen, I'd have made sure you and Will never laid eyes on each other. Guess I was blind, didn't realize a boy like Will would set his heart on marryin'. Much less marryin' you. Well, that can't be helped now. You two can't get married. You'd best go, Katie, leave Grafton."

"*What?* But I know how Will is, Aunt Polly, and it doesn't matter! I don't care! Will needs looking after, I know that. I'll take care of him. I always have, but Will's good, he takes care of me too. I'd never leave Will. It would break his heart," Katie had protested.

"It would," sighed Aunt Polly. "But, child, you don't know what you are, where you came from."

"I know I'm an orphan. But Will thinks I'm good enough for him!" retorted Katie, indignant. "And I'll work hard. Will's strong, and we can have a little cabin and a piece of land . . ."

"No, you ain't an orphan! Your parents weren't Irish and you ain't an orphan, not entirely. You ain't what you think. You're a nigger's child. Comfort's and a nigger's."

"What? No! That's a lie!"

"It's Comfort who lied, all these years," snapped Aunt Polly. "She's your mother. I know, I was there when you were born. It was that no-good runaway slave came out of the woods one day during the war. Called himself Old Sampie, had a limp from his owners cuttin' his leg to keep him from runnin' away, had yellow eyes and evil in his heart. Comfort's husband was off fighting for the Yankees, and there was just Comfort and her two little ones, Ben and Teeny, and Charley's parents, both too old and poorly to do much. They were desperate for another pair of hands to keep them from starving up at Wildwood. And Comfort's a Quaker, didn't believe in slavery. She felt sorry for him, let him have an old empty cabin to live in. He set to work doing whatever needed doing—fixing the roof and plowing the vegetable garden, and seeing to Charley's old pa, who was too bad with rheumatism to walk. Soon's I saw that varmint, saw those yellow eyes, I knew he was bad. I told her send him on his way, don't let him stay here. But Comfort wouldn't believe me. Charley's pa died before long, so it was just Comfort and Charley's mother, Rosa, who was sick herself, and the children. And Sampie.

"I told her to keep Charley's rifle handy and loaded—if she got worried to fire it, and me and the girls would come.

"It was a terrible thing that happened, the night Rosa died. Comfort was by herself, watching by the body with Ben and Teeny asleep in the next room. The man came into the house and he was strong and he forced her.

"Comfort shot him dead the next morning. We heard it, Will's ma and me, and came running up as fast as we could. There he was lying dead in the yard, blood all over the snow and Comfort down on her knees shaking like a leaf and crying, Ben and Teeny cryin' for their mama inside the house.

"We dragged that dead nigger into the cabin where he'd been living and set it on fire. Poured boiling water on the bloody snow, you couldn't tell what happened. Wasn't till afterward Comfort knew she was expecting. She wanted to die. We managed to keep it secret from everyone but my daughter, who looked after Ben and Teeny those last months until the baby came. I helped birth you and I kept you alive. Comfort wanted to let you die. I told her what to say about finding you in the barn."

Katie put her head in her hands. "I don't believe you!"

"No? Just look in the mirror. You take after Comfort, but you got the same yellow eyes as that slave," said Aunt Polly harshly. "Every time she sees you, she remembers."

"All these years, she always hated me. I could feel it. Ben and Teeny were mean because they felt it too. Well, I hate her back! I didn't get myself born! If she was my mother, she ought to have told me! But if it's a secret, that's no reason I can't marry Will."

"But it is. Because Will's ma knows what happened, well as I do, she was with me when we ran up to Wildwood after Comfort fired the gun. She looked after Ben and Teeny when I was birthing you. Will's ma was a good one when she first married, but her heart's hardened since her husband come back from the war with one leg and a mean temper. Wasn't never violent afore he went off, but he's a troubled soul now, bitter about the Cause, his leg, everything. That's why she mostly left Will to me to raise, keep him out of his pa's way. He's hard on Will, hates the way Will is slow, can't understand why he's not more of a man.

"But her heart's got hard too. Behind your back she's laughed about you bein' Will's nursemaid. But try to marry Will, and she won't hold back tellin' what she knows. They'd work on Will, make his life a misery, with you the cause, until Will looks at you like Comfort does. His pa, bitter like he is about losin' the war, he'd shoot Will afore he let him marry a nigger's child. If some of the Marshall money was comin' your way, maybe he'd be different. Wouldn't *feel* different, mind, but he's a poor man."

With a little of her old kindness in her voice, Aunt Polly said, "And Will, I know he'll take your leaving hard. But you got to leave. It's the only way, because I know you two won't keep apart here, and with no money to stay Will's pa's hand . . ."

They heard Will stacking logs on the woodpile, whistling.

"Where should I go?" Katie wept.

"You're smart and you're pretty enough. You'll find your way someplace," said Aunt Polly. "Go quick, before you think on it, or you won't have the strength. Go for Will's sake. Keep him safe."

"Let me say goodbye."

"No goodbyes, just be gone!"

Katie left, slipping away through the back door. Hating Aunt Polly, but hating Comfort more. Comfort might as well have killed her when she had the chance, Katie thought. Comfort the hypocrite! Comfort the liar! And what was Katie to do, run away where? How?

In the distance, an approaching steamer sounded its horn. She recognized the boat, had seen the captain before. He was a grizzled, dirty man who leered and tried to speak with her every time he pulled in, called her missy, and said it got lonely on the boat. She'd dried her eyes, waited while the steamer pulled in, waited for the captain to approach her.

"How long to reach Natchez?"

"Who's going?" He grinned.

"I might be, providing I can work my passage. Haven't got any money."

"Reckon there's ways you could do that, missy. Be here tomorrow mornin', five o'clock sharp."

She'd hurried back up to Wildwood, got through supper somehow, her hatred for the Marshalls growing as Teeny recounted her recent wedding and how it had been featured in Ben's newspaper. Ben's newspaper, Teeny's dowry. Katie had nothing. She felt another wave of hatred for Comfort, who'd denied her a dowry when she was as much Comfort's daughter as Teeny.

When the household was asleep, Katie packed a carpetbag. Slipping out of her room, she contemplated setting Wildwood on fire, but that would bring people up from Grafton, and she didn't want to be seen. Instead she slipped into Comfort's room and quietly emptied her jewel box. Comfort never wore jewelry anyway, not even the things Charles had given her when they were courting. It would be a long time until she noticed her jewelry was missing. And jewelry was more use to Katie now.

By the time she set off for the landing, the fog had come down. Down at the river the fog bell rang as she threaded her path between the dark shapes of apple and peach trees on the way. She hurried. She could hear the faint slap-slap-slap sound of the wheel turning the old gristmill now, the river's murmur, and her own sobbing breath.

The fog bell rang again and she counted "two." She shifted her heavy carpetbag to her shoulder and hastened her steps. She reached the bottom of the orchard and crossed the cemetery, tripping over a leaning gravestone. By the jetty she could make out the bulk of the steamboat, and she broke into a run, reaching the landing out of breath, her shoulder aching, as the third fog bell sounded. The captain was watching.

"Decided to join me after all, did you?" He grinned lecherously as she swung her carpetbag over the railing, then took his hand and climbed on board herself, lifting her skirts to swing one leg, then the other, over the railing in a flash of pantalets and petticoats.

"Well, girlie. Get on in." He held a door open and she slipped through. The cubbyhole with a single bunk reeked of a man's unwashed clothes, whiskey dregs, and the dirty chamber pot. But she had no money to travel any other way. She didn't dare reveal the jewelry. She'd wrapped that in an old petticoat stained by her monthlies—hopefully that would discourage the captain from rummaging to see what she had to steal. Men, she knew, were squeamish about womanish things. And she needed the jewelry. Her knees felt weak and she sank onto the captain's bunk, trying not to think about the trip ahead or she might throw herself into the river.

The captain was leering. "Run away, have we?" He reached out a hand and wound a dark curl round his finger. "From what?" He tugged her hair a little too hard.

Katie shrugged. Her finger gripped the edge of the bunk so she wouldn't bolt. It took all her strength not to push past the horrible man and run back to Will. Only the knowledge she couldn't—because then he'd discover the truth, and that would be worst of all—held her back. No matter what it took, she had to leave. She had to.

And one day she'd come back, rich, so Will's parents would be on their knees for her money. She'd find a way to make the Marshalls suffer, like she'd suffered from Comfort's hate as a child. Like she was suffering now. Comfort the murderess.

Now Katie squeezed her bundle of clothes under the captain's bunk as the captain asked, "Cat got your tongue? Never mind. Don't matter why you're runnin' away. Make yourself to home. We'll reach Natchez in a week or so." The captain pressed against her until she felt his breath hot on her neck. "We go slow in this fog—bad this time of year. Plenty of time to get acquainted."

"Good," said Katie, trying to smile at him. People said she was pretty. Like Comfort! As if she wanted to resemble Comfort! She hoped she was pretty enough to keep the captain interested.

"We'll be off soon. I have to get us a ways down the river in this fog. But I'll be back." He banged the door shut. In a few minutes she heard the mournful fog bell again; men shouted and she could feel the boat moving.

What would Will do without her? What would Aunt Polly tell him, that Katie didn't love him, didn't want to marry him? It was unbearable. She stood and tried the door. She'd jump in the river and they'd find her body and it would be an accident and Will would cry, but it wouldn't be as bad as him thinking she didn't love him . . .

The cabin door was locked from the outside.

Oh, Will, she thought, remembering the captain's breath on her neck. How was she to bear it? How could she survive the week?

Oh, Will! My mother could have given us a piece of Marshall land to farm, a little money to blind your folks. But my mother preferred a lie, and it's robbed me of you.

I'll come back one day, Will. Don't forget me. Wait for me.

HORATIA

CHAPTER 2

In the white clapboard house beside the Bowjay River, the sepia-tinted wedding photo of Ellinder and Josiah Vann was the first thing that Ellinder unpacked to display on the piano that had been Josiah's wedding present. Years later the wedding picture would fascinate their small daughter Horatia. The couple were distant Vann cousins with similar traces of Cherokee ancestry in their dark-eyed good looks. Tightly buttoned into a high-necked wedding dress that showed off her slender waist, the bride held white flowers and appeared to be floating in a lace veil that rippled around her like a wave. Instead of looking directly at the camera, she and Josiah smiled at each other.

Horatia could tell the groom was her father, even though his face looked younger, but she didn't recognize the bride Josiah said was Mamma.

"Not Mamma!" Horatia insisted. "It's a princess, Papa. Like in my storybook!"

"That's Mamma when she was a bride. It's like a princess, only brides are prettier. And what do brides have?"

"'Something old and something new, something borrowed, something blue, and a sixpence in your shoe,'" Horatia recited. She liked rhymes. And she liked the story that Josiah wove around the wedding picture. It was a fairy tale, about a spell being cast on the bride who'd become Mamma. She liked hearing her father tell it, over and over. When Horatia grew older, she realized he'd told the story as much to comfort himself as to ease her nearly motherless childhood.

Her parents had known each other since they were young. Josiah's mother had died giving birth to him, and growing up, he was sent west by steamboat to spend summers with his Vann relatives in Ohio. Like Josiah, Ellinder had no brothers or sisters and welcomed her new playmate. "And we became such good friends," Josiah would say, "that when we grew up I asked Mamma to marry me."

"And how did you ask her?" Horatia would say.

"I got down on one knee and said, 'Oh, beautiful Ellinder, I love you. I beg you, marry me and we'll fly away together and live happily ever after.'"

"Then what?"

"Mamma said she would marry me."

"The next part, Papa!"

"Well, if a man wants to marry a lady, he must ask the lady's father for permission. Remember that, Horatia—you're never to get married without my permission. Next time a young man asks to marry you, send him straight to me."

"Papa! I'm too little to get married! Tell the next part."

"Well, Mamma's parents were in the parlor, reading the paper. I went bravely in and left the door open a crack, in case Mamma was listening. And I gathered up all my courage, in case they said no, and asked if I could marry Mamma. And your grandmother cried"—here Josiah imitated a high feminine voice—"'Good heavens! No! Ellinder's only seventeen!'" And switching to a deep masculine voice, Josiah continued, "Your grandfather said, 'Marry Ellinder? The very idea! Of course not. What nonsense! Consider the matter closed, sir!'"

"Then what did you do?"

"I walked up and down the parlor, and I talked and talked, waving my hands in the air, like this, about how much I loved Mamma and how much she loved me, and how I had this big fine house for her to live in and lots of money from the Emporium to make her comfortable and how we were going to live happily ever after. And all the time Mamma was listening at the door. And finally your grandfather said I could talk the hind leg off a donkey, and your grandmother said, 'Ellinder wanted to be a wife and mother from the time she first pushed her dolls in their baby carriage, Josiah's already like a member of the family, and Ellinder's in love, dear.' Your grandfather sighed and said, 'I suppose Josiah's in a position to provide for her, mustn't forget that either, and there is something to be said for young people settling down as soon as they can.'

"And so, after saying it was impossible, they finally said we could be married. And Mamma almost fell into the parlor because she'd been listening at the door, and she was laughing and crying at the same time, and your grandmother started crying and laughing, and Grandpa went 'Harrumph. Harrumph!' and got out his handkerchief in case he needed to wipe his eyes. And in the end we got married and a man took that picture on the piano. And it's all true."

Horatia thought this was a nice story. "And what about something old, and something new?"

"Oh, Mamma had those things—an old lace veil that had been her grandmother's, new shoes, a locket borrowed from her mother, a blue ribbon on her bouquet, and a shiny penny. That's as good as a sixpence in America."

"And they got married and lived happily ever after," Horatia would finish.

"Almost, child. Almost."

CHAPTER 3

The year before Josiah proposed, his father died, and twenty-two-year-old Josiah inherited Vann's Emporium in Grafton. It was an established business, started before the Revolution by a half-Cherokee ancestor, Gideon Vann, and his Welsh wife, who'd had a trading post to serve the surrounding tribes, trappers, and long hunters who came to sell or barter furs for salt and corn ground at the mill he'd also built. One thing had led to another. The trading post soon had a river landing that drew settlers on flatboats, who exchanged cows and chickens and pieces of excess furniture for iron plows, ground corn, and cooking pots made at the new forge the Drumheller family set up at Rattlesnake Springs.

Out of this, Vann's Emporium had expanded and grown, and by the time Josiah took over, it was stocking everything from nails and farming tools to lanterns, roasting pans, china washbasins and pitchers with flowery patterns, haberdashery and dressmaking fabrics, buggy whips, workmen's boots, petticoats and long woolen underwear, and ladies' and gentlemen's hats and gloves. It was a profitable, solid business, and Josiah was a steady, hardworking young man who was determined to oversee its continuing success. Neither of these facts had been lost on Ellinder's father.

After a wedding trip to Natural Bridge, the couple moved into Josiah's home, across the street from the Emporium. It was a big white clapboard house with tall sash windows and a broad porch on three sides overlooking the river. Josiah's father had built it for his own bride thirty years earlier, but she had died when her only child was born. Her widower had lost the heart to furnish it beyond the basic necessities. He'd devoted himself to business, and despite the ministrations of hired girls, it remained a gloomy, rather dusty home with closed shutters and unused rooms while Josiah was growing up.

He was anxious to banish these gloomy childhood memories. He and Ellinder had both been only children, and they spoke of filling the house with a large, noisy family.

During the first weeks, the couple slept on pallets in the largest upstairs bedroom. Ellinder made do with a single iron skillet to cook meals over the parlor fireplace. They ate their dinner sitting side by side on one of Ellinder's unpacked trunks, discussing shelves and wallpaper, which room was to be Josiah's office, which one Ellinder's sewing room.

Workmen were hired and the house smelled of wet paint and wallpaper paste for weeks. When they finished, Ellinder tied up her hair, polished the oak floors with beeswax, and washed the dusty windows with vinegar and newspaper.

Crates of new furnishings arrived by riverboat. There were sets of carved mahogany furniture and gas lamps with etched glass, and Josiah, who was fond of reading, ordered leather-bound sets of Dickens and Thackeray, Victor Hugo, a Children's Favorite Classics series, a Crowell's New Illustrated Library collection, and a complete set of *Chambers's Encyclopaedia*.

When a shipment of new cloth arrived at the Emporium, Josiah would come to fetch Ellinder to choose materials she liked for curtains or a dress before the fabric was put out for sale. Soon she was spending her days crouched on her sewing room floor with a mouthful of pins as she cut and pinned her new curtains.

Ellinder was proud of her new domain. Insisting she didn't need a hired girl, just a washerwoman, she swept and dusted, practiced her piano, went to the market, and had Josiah's dinner ready in time to be sitting on the porch with her hair combed and repinned and a splash of lavender water on her wrists and throat, waiting for his return from work. After supper she would play the piano and sing for him, or he would read aloud to her in the sewing room while she cranked out curtains on her new sewing machine.

"I fear you're lonely, Ellinder, but the ladies of Grafton will come in droves to pay welcome calls as soon as the signal comes that you're ready for visitors."

"Oh no, I'm too busy to be lonely . . . What sort of signal?"

"Reverend Merriman's wife believes she has the privilege of making the first call on a newcomer. Reverend Merriman is the third generation of clergymen by that name to serve in Grafton, and she fancies this allows her to make rules about how things are done. Be sure to make a good impression."

"Why do you look so amused, Josiah?"

He laughed. "You'll see."

The day Mrs. Merriman came, Ellinder had hitched up her skirts, exposing her long black-clad legs, and was halfway up a stepladder arranging Josiah's books and singing "Girls, Get a Home of Your Own" so loudly she hadn't heard Mrs. Merriman knock. So Mrs. Merriman simply walked in.

Ellinder looked down to see a stout woman in a large hat staring up at her and frowning in a way to make it clear she found such a display of female limbs unseemly. Not to mention the singing. When Ellinder had hastily adjusted her skirts and climbed down, Mrs. Merriman said, "Welcome to Grafton, Mrs. Vann. Here. Made you a Scripture cake, old family recipe," in a tone of voice that left no doubt in Ellinder's mind that a great favor was being conferred, and the cake was less a cake of welcome and more a kind of admonition to read her Bible more and sing less.

A subdued Ellinder made tea and served the cake, but the Scripture cake was dry and not particularly appetizing—Mrs. Merriman tended to scrimp on the sugar and butter. As Ellinder struggled to wash down a mouthful of dry cake with her tea, Mrs. Merriman talked. "I hope we can count on you, dear Mrs. Vann, to join my Ladies' Bible Study group, or assist us in the Mission Society ladies' committee," she said sternly.

"Oh, do tell me about them," said Ellinder, wishing she could think of an excuse not to. She was being subtly reproached, she knew, for her nonappearance at church. Josiah wasn't much of a churchgoer, and she'd persuaded him to accompany her to the Sunday service only a few times before deciding Reverend Merriman's violent sermons were not really her cup of tea either.

Mrs. Merriman leaned forward. "The moral tone, Mrs. Vann! We married ladies must set the female example, demonstrating that the narrow way to heaven lies in good works, godly endeavors at church, the study of the Good Book, and our attention to our families. Otherwise the young people"—she sighed—"give themselves up to singing and dancing. Waltzing up at the Rehoboth Springs Hotel! Midnight suppers! Ukuleles, Mrs. Vann! An instrument devised by the Devil, if you want my opinion, for godless and profane songs. The girls in Grafton think of nothing but beaux and dancing gowns!"

Just in time Ellinder stopped herself from saying "Oh, how delightful" and struggled to arrange her expression in a way that conveyed dismay at this news.

The visitor took her departure after half an hour—a formal call must last no longer, according to Mrs. Merriman—and left Ellinder feeling she and her morals had been subjected to close and not particularly approving scrutiny.

"I feel like I've been sat on by a dragon in a large hat!" Ellinder told Josiah that night as he sampled Mrs. Merriman's cake.

"It's awful," Josiah choked. He was extremely fond of cake and would demolish even very stale cake with gusto. "But at least she's been. Now you must return the visit, and then the other ladies will come."

So Ellinder returned Mrs. Merriman's visit, taking a fruitcake she'd baked from an old family recipe she'd discovered tucked into the Vann Bible, for the church's Christmas Bazaar. Mrs. Merriman invited her and Josiah to a party at the church on Twelfth Night, after Christmas. They would sing hymns and play round games. It was another case of setting a Christian example by declining to attend the Twelfth Night dance up at the Drumhellers' hotel.

In fact, Ellinder and Josiah were looking forward to the Twelfth Night dance. Ellinder had a becoming evening dress as yet unworn in her trousseau, and they were both fond of music and dancing. She racked her brains for a convincing excuse, hemmed and hawed, telling Mrs. Merriman she never accepted invitations without consulting her husband. "And you know what men are, Mrs. Merriman. Sometimes they'll agree to go somewhere, and sometimes, after a hard day at work, they just want to stay home in their slippers and you can't budge them for all the tea in China."

She knew Josiah would refuse to attend a party where they sang hymns.

Nevertheless, the Grafton ladies understood that Ellinder had been approved of and that "young Mrs. Vann was now receiving."

Her first caller after Mrs. Merriman was pretty Hilda Drumheller, who presented Ellinder with a walnut cake and a potted cutting from the rosemary bush in her herb garden, so Ellinder could start an herb garden of her own in the spring. Vivacious Hilda, who was several years older than Ellinder, had married into the rich, prolific Drumheller clan. Her husband was the youngest Drumheller son, the jovial Albert. The Drumhellers, Ellinder gathered, generally did as they pleased, and Hilda confided she fit in well because she also did as she pleased. She made Ellinder laugh.

Every afternoon after that brought another lady or two, with cakes or pies. "There appears to be a sort of baking competition among the ladies," said Josiah, demolishing a third helping of dessert. "Should have married you sooner."

"If we'd married any sooner, I would have still been in school," said Ellinder, brushing up his trail of crumbs. "Everyone's been so kind! I feel quite at home now. Isn't it nice in Grafton!"

By the end of her first year of marriage, she needed shawls to hide the fact she was growing too large in the waist for her trousseau gowns. Ellinder blushed happily when the ladies congratulated her on her "sweet stranger."

She refused to leave the house for the last four months of her pregnancy.

"Is that really necessary?" asked a bewildered Josiah.

"Mother says a woman in my condition mustn't parade about in public."

"But Hilda Drumheller does."

Hilda Drumheller, who already had three children and was expecting her fourth, regularly drove herself down Little Frog Mountain in her own dashing little gig with red wheels to visit her friends or shop at the Emporium, making no attempt to conceal her swelling stomach with a lap rug.

Hilda didn't give a toss for decorum. "I'll be damned if I'll sit home indoors. I told Albert it makes me feel like a fat possum caught in a trap. Where do people think babies come from? Why does everyone pretend they found a baby in the garden? It's silly. Now, do come out for a drive, Ellinder."

But Ellinder was too reserved to follow Hilda's example. She sat on her porch where the sunlight on the water cast cheerful dancing lights on the porch ceiling, humming while she stitched nightgowns for the baby or went up to gaze at the nursery, where the walls had been painted a soft blue, fresh white curtains hung at the window, a Bible verse hung on the wall, cushions were plumped in the rocking chair, and a new baby quilt lay folded in Josiah's old cradle. "Everything's ready," she sighed happily to Josiah, laying her head against his shoulder.

The nurse arrived and unpacked her valise in a bedroom down the hall.

Two days later the nurse hurried across to the Emporium to find Josiah. "Mrs. Vann is confined!" she whispered, to prevent the salesmen hearing.

After a long and terrible labor in their upstairs bedroom, Ellinder gave birth. "A boy!" said the nurse, turning away with the baby. Feeling battered and exhausted, Ellinder watched the nurse swaddle him and felt her heart swell with love. Impatient to hold him, Ellinder held out her arms, saying, "Let me have him now. What a good little darling he is, so quiet."

The nurse turned around. "Mrs. Vann, I'm sorry. He's quiet because he's stillborn. This often happens, with the first baby," said the nurse, meaning to be comforting. "I have to take him away now. I'll call your husband in, and . . ."

"What?" whispered Ellinder. "No! No! Give him to me! Give him to me now!" she shrieked with what was left of her strength. Her cries brought Josiah, disheveled and exhausted himself.

The nurse murmured something to him Ellinder couldn't hear, and Ellinder watched him sink into a chair and put his head in his hands. "Ellinder . . . dearest."

"Josiah, give me the baby!"

He rose, took the swaddled bundle from the nurse, and put it in Ellinder's arms.

The baby looked perfect in every way. He had a dark thatch of hair, a little nose, fat little cheeks, and a small pursed mouth. His eyes were closed. She loosened the swaddling and saw tiny fists curled under his chin.

"He's only sleeping," quavered Ellinder.

"Dearest, no, I'm afraid . . . afraid not."

"No," whispered Ellinder, "no, no, no! Oh, Josiah!"

"Dearest, we'll bear this together, somehow, because we must."

Ellinder laid her cheek against the baby's head and began to cry quietly.

After a long time Josiah said, "Let me take him now."

Ellinder nodded tearfully and pointed to the little nightgown and cap she had laid by. She dressed the baby and kissed him and handed him to Josiah. Through the tearful sleepless night that followed, her heart broke and broke and broke.

The nurse said it was usual just to bury a stillborn baby, but Josiah arranged for Reverend Merriman to hold a funeral next afternoon. It was a hot, bright summer day and the windows were open. Lying in bed, Ellinder could hear the funeral hymns in the cemetery. She imagined Josiah shoveling the first spade of earth into the grave. She wished she were under the earth with the baby.

Two days later Mrs. Merriman paid a condolence visit and told Ellinder it was her duty not to repine in the face of God's will. To kiss the rod that chastised her for the good of her soul.

Ellinder closed her eyes and drew a deep breath. When she opened them she focused a look of such pure hatred on Mrs. Merriman that the reverend's wife stopped talking, gasped, and took her leave.

It was months before Ellinder was "herself" again. Her mother wrote sending her love, saying they were young, they would have other children to fill their hearts and their home.

It left Ellinder gripped by fury.

And yet that was what happened, despite the deep scar left on her heart by the loss of her firstborn. Two years later Ellinder delivered a healthy boy who made a lusty screaming entrance into the world, and three years after him, his sister was born. The two children grew plump and mischievous, their noise and laughter and footsteps and toys filled the house, and the Vanns now had a cook and a hired girl to keep the house, because Ellinder devoted herself to the children.

Her mother came by steamer to visit in the spring, and to help when Ellinder gave birth again. It was a second daughter who kicked and gurgled in a cradle they had put on the porch, which had become the children's playroom. The older two spread toys from the big chest across the porch so that adults had to watch their step to avoid tripping on dolls, blocks, and wooden animals. Josiah secured the porch gate that led to the river path, with special hooks too high for childish fingers to open. He hung two little swings from the porch roof, and Ellinder's rocking chair and worktable and sewing machine were placed there too, because it was a pleasant shady place in summer, and passing neighbors would stop and say hello, or step in to admire the baby. Ellinder sewed for the children and pretended to complain to her mother that they outgrew their clothes too fast.

Ellinder's mother kissed her grandchildren goodbye and left in August. In September, a late-summer heat wave descended on the valley. The sky was a suffocating blanket of heavy gray clouds, and beneath them the atmosphere was uneasy, as if an electrical storm were coming to clear the air. But it didn't thunder or rain. River levels dropped, and the fast-flowing waterway was sluggish and shallow, no longer murmuring or visible from the Vanns' porch. People fanned themselves listlessly, saying they couldn't remember a summer like it. The river was so low that steamers were running aground, and there was a bad smell rising from the riverbed, like something rotten or dead.

Milk soured, meat spoiled, butter melted, and bread rose too fast in the pan. Muggy weather sapped energy, and mosquitoes breeding in the brackish pools and creeks whined irritatingly everywhere. Heat seemed trapped inside the Vann house, and Ellinder was grateful for her riverside porch, where such air as there was circulated while the children played. They were all cranky in the oppressive weather.

Josiah and Ellinder moved a table to the porch to take their meals, mostly corn bread, hard-boiled eggs, cold beans, and tomatoes and cucumbers sliced in vinegar. No one had much appetite. Josiah was allowed to smoke his pipe on the porch to keep mosquitoes away.

Passersby brought news, reported people were coming down with a fever, whole families taken ill. People complained of high temperatures, aching joints, rashes, ague, and shivering. The first casualties, an elderly Hanover couple who lived downriver, were found dead, side by side in their bed. Word spread it was yellow fever again as the stricken suffered horribly, burning with fever, shaking with chills till their teeth rattled, vomiting bile and then blood, and crying from the racking pain in their stomachs. And they died, every day added to the list of the dead. Two Charbonneau servants. A whole family of Pines, the parents and all five children. Mrs. Merriman and her two teenage daughters. Several of the youngest Drumhellers. Poor simple Will Stuart, who'd been the town gravedigger, and his old grandmother, Aunt Polly, were found dead in their cabin on Frog Mountain.

Putrefaction hung in the air. Those who could fled to stay with relatives elsewhere.

With Will dead, the men who were still able-bodied pitched in to dig graves fast enough. The funerals were quick, no funeral meals afterward, no calling to sit with the bereaved. The few mourners didn't stay to sing.

Ellinder's mother wrote that the fever had reached them and Ellinder's father was poorly. Ellinder must keep the children indoors.

The Vanns' hired girls stopped coming, one was sick and one had to nurse her sisters and brothers. The cook complained of feeling poorly, and went home, never to return.

The next week brought a letter from her parents' neighbor. Her father had died and her mother had fallen sick nursing him and was unable to write herself. Ellinder must come and nurse her. Ellinder was torn with indecision—should she risk the trip to go and care for her mother? Or stay with Josiah and her children? In the end the thought of Josiah and the children falling ill without her to nurse them was enough to keep her at home, though she loved her parents and wept to think of her mother suffering alone and untended.

The neighbor wrote again, saying Ellinder had shirked her duty and abandoned her mother to die alone. Grieving, guilt-stricken, and frantic for the children, Ellinder told Josiah they should take the train north to Natural Bridge or Goshen to stay until the cold weather came. Josiah said traveling was too dangerous now; the *Grafton Messenger* reported people fleeing from the sickness were being turned away at gunpoint lest they bring contagion with them.

Ellinder confined her children inside the house with the windows shut. It was close and stifling and gloomy and the children hated it. They wanted to play on the porch with their toys.

She struggled to entertain them indoors, with every game and activity she could devise, but the Vanns' son escaped his mother's watchful eye. When he was supposed to be napping, he crept out onto the shady porch to play with his train, brushing away the mosquitoes.

Three days later he slumped listlessly on the stairs and began to cry, saying the light hurt his eyes. His forehead was burning hot, and Ellinder put him to bed and drew the curtains to keep out the light. She sat by his side all night, sponging his hot brow, soothing his feverish dreams. "Hush, darling. Mamma's here." Next morning, the baby lay limp and hot and quiet in her cradle. Ellinder sent Josiah in search of ice, but he came back to say no one had any. Icehouses were all empty. Later that day, the middle child shivered with chills and she complained her head hurt.

The children's skin took on a yellowish hue.

The terrified parents hovered in a darkened nursery, changing and boiling sheets as the two older children cried weakly with pain and protest at being shifted, vomiting bile over the little nightgowns Ellinder had made them. She wiped their mouths with a dampened cloth, tried to get them to suck a little milk or water from it, but they could eat and drink nothing. The baby lay unmoving except for the little rise and fall of her chest, burning hot.

The weary doctor came but could do nothing except advise them to keep the children as cool as possible and pray they'd come through it.

Then miraculously, their fever abated and all three children felt cooler to the touch. They fell asleep one by one. Ellinder and Josiah were exhausted but weak with relief. The children were on the mend. Josiah put his arm around Ellinder's shoulders and said, "The doctor was right. Rest a little, dearest. You're at the end of your strength. I'll keep watch in case they wake and feel thirsty."

"Just for a little while," Ellinder whispered, and collapsed into the armchair where she read the nighttime stories.

Hours later she was awakened by Josiah's shout: "Ellinder!" She woke to a nursery of horrors. The children were awake, and their skin was hotter than ever to her touch. Their eyes were red. Their small bodies squirmed with pain, and one by one they began to vomit blood, as more blood trickled from their noses and eyes.

Ellinder looked wildly at Josiah. "They were recovered!"

"I don't know what happened. They woke up and . . . and . . ."

The baby gave a feeble wail, shuddered in a fit, and lay still. "No, no, no," Ellinder croaked, slumping on her knees beside the cradle. She prayed her hardest to save the other two, whispering their names, begging them not to leave, Mamma, Mamma loves you so. But she watched their expressions change, and first their son, then their daughter, died within an hour of each other. The small corpses had to be pried out of Ellinder's arms.

Next morning, the three hastily made little coffins were carried across the porch still strewn with toys. "They have to be buried, Ellinder," said Josiah doggedly. He was haggard, pulling the coffins on the children's dogcart to the cemetery. Ellinder stumbled behind him, her hair unpinned, her dress awry, crying, "No, no." Josiah and one of the Pine men dug the graves. Reverend Merriman had survived but was a shell of his former self. He was barely able to whisper a brief funeral service and tried to tell Ellinder to rejoice, the children had gone to be angels.

At that Ellinder collapsed.

Weeks later, when she was finally able to leave her room, gaunt and hollow-eyed, she learned the children's sudden "recovery" had been an ominous sign. A sudden recovery was a fatal harbinger. The reflection that she had selfishly given in to tiredness and not been there when they needed her most ate away at her mind.

Two years passed, and following a sickly pregnancy, thin and a shadow of herself, Ellinder had another son, born two months before he should have been. When the nurse put him into her arms, he seemed tiny as a newborn kitten. The doctor ordered her to have complete rest and feed him as often as possible.

She prayed, bargaining that she would never complain of anything ever, bear any pain, suffer in any way, die herself if need be, if the baby lived. She held the baby and fed him and wouldn't relinquish him to anyone except Josiah so she could shut her eyes briefly without fear of dropping him. He'd been crying, weakly, with a little mewling cry frighteningly like a kitten's instead of a hungry infant. But the crying was a good sign, the doctor said. It meant he was hungry. He was alive. She sang him lullabies. He liked it, she told Josiah, singing settled him to sleep, and the doctor had said if he slept and ate he'd grow strong. And live.

"We'll call him Thomas, after my father," said Josiah.

Josiah had left to attend to something at the Emporium, and Ellinder was singing softly to Thomas, singing his name, when his little bluish eyelids fluttered open to look at her, and then closed. He gave a sigh and, Ellinder insisted later, smiled at her, even though she knew it was impossible a new baby could smile. She took it as a hopeful sign and kissed his head gently, whispering, "Mamma loves you, Thomas." He seemed to sleep in her arms for hours. When she realized Thomas was dead, her screams reached the Emporium.

This time Josiah tried to stop her from coming to the funeral. The doctor advised she mustn't get out of bed yet, it was too soon after the birth for her to be up, but Ellinder was a madwoman in her insistence she would go, she *would* go! The nurse helped her into the black dress she'd worn to mourn her other children.

Ellinder stood beside the baby's grave, hanging on Josiah's arm, listening to Reverend Merriman leading the mourners through the all-too-familiar funeral hymns, "Guide Me, O Thou Great Jehovah" and "O, Sing to Me of Heaven" in call-and-response. They sang "Hallelujah" last. It was a rousing hymn, and the people gathered at the graveside sang it with all their might. Many had lost children to the fever, and singing and the hope of heaven was all that was left to comfort grieving parents. They meant to help Ellinder.

And let this feeble body fail
And let it faint and die
My soul shall quit this mournful vale
And soar to worlds on high.

It didn't help Ellinder. She'd sung all her children to their graves, and now the words stuck in her throat. She listened dry-eyed and silent and spent of everything, willing her body that still held the memory of childbirth, of her babies, to faint and die, the sooner the better. Who cared about soaring?

Oh, Thomas.

For a long time after that she went through the motions of life, vacant-eyed and caring about very little.

Three years later she delivered her sixth child, another daughter, whose lusty howls filled the birthing room at once. The nurse exclaimed what a fine daughter she had. Josiah was called in, and she pointed out to him the baby's rosy color and bright eyes. "Thank God!" he exclaimed. "What a little beauty she is, Ellinder. Just look," Josiah said, the lines sorrow had etched in his face softening a little.

Ellinder turned her face to the wall and lay silent when first the nurse, then Josiah, urged and begged her to hold and feed the infant. Josiah sent for Hilda Drumheller, but Ellinder wouldn't respond to Hilda either. "What can we do?" begged a distraught Josiah. Hilda said there was no time to lose, she could recommend a wet nurse, and after that the baby would have to be fed with bottles, like a calf who'd lost its mother.

Josiah named the baby Horatia and hired the nurse recommended by Hilda. Ellinder lay silent in bed, taking no interest in anything.

The doctor came again and again, and finally, when Ellinder wouldn't talk to him either, he diagnosed postpartum melancholia. "If she doesn't improve, the sanatorium is often the best solution in such cases. No one would blame you."

Josiah said "Never! Ellinder will stay *here* and be cared for *here*" so fiercely that the doctor sighed and prescribed calming drops from a small brown bottle and long periods of rest in a darkened room.

Ellinder was grateful for the medicine, grateful for isolation. She'd take the drops Josiah mixed for her, and when he'd shut the bedroom door she'd sometimes take more to make the darkness come. The darkness where her five little ones waited. She couldn't see them, but they were there when the drops sent her to sleep. Mama loves you, children.

She lost track of time, of day or night.

Occasionally the doctor's voice disturbed her peace like a stone in the water. "How is she today? The same, I see. Josiah, the sanatorium."

She'd tried hard and croaked, "Josiah, Josiah, Josiah, don't let them take me away to the sanatorium. Please! Please!"

"That's good, you're speaking again, dearest." There was a spoon to her lips and she heard Josiah saying, "I'd never send you away! Now sleep and get better." And she slept again.

Sometimes she'd be woken by Josiah saying "Look, here's Horatia," and she'd feel a baby in her arms. She would be confused—where had this infant come from . . . ? She'd blink and look around and hear Josiah pleading with her to grow better and be his love once more, be Horatia's mother—they needed her, and Ellinder would remember that she was Josiah's wife, there was a big white house on the river . . . Horatia? Horatia? Who was that?

"Please try to get better, Ellinder. Please try. For Horatia's sake."

Better, better, better. So she tried. Anything not to be locked away behind the high walls of the terrible place called the sanatorium. Away from Josiah. She loved Josiah with all that was left of her still able to love. With a great effort of will she managed to nod and smile as if she understood, whisper thank you, she was better now. (What was *better*? She had no idea, but it was a thing to say that made Josiah smile.)

She couldn't do anything for Horatia's sake. Only Josiah's.

One day she managed to get up. The wet nurse helped her dress, and Josiah helped her downstairs. Soon she was downstairs every day, sitting at the breakfast table, sipping tea. She did her best to appear "better," going through motions her hands remembered, making cakes and sewing and ordering her household in a kind of daze, numbly, watching from a distance the woman doing these things.

Sometimes the strain was too great, and her need for the medicine bottle and the darkness where her dead children waited would build up and build up until she said she believed she would lie down for a while. Josiah, Josiah, Josiah . . . There would be another interlude . . . then the doctor . . . then Josiah . . . talking . . . Was she better?

Eventually she would manage to get up again, and resume being "better." If asked a question, she gave automatic replies with a sweet smile—"perhaps" was a useful word, or "of course, my dear" to Josiah, that satisfied him, or "we'll see" covered most other eventualities.

CHAPTER 4

1901–1910

As a small child, Horatia never believed the smiling young woman in the wedding photograph was the same as the sad-eyed lady in a black dress called Mamma. If she fell and hurt herself or wanted a story or a hug or a good-night kiss, she went to Josiah or the cook or the hired girls, or Aunt Hilda when she visited. Especially Aunt Hilda, who always had a pocketful of sweets and smiled a lot.

If her mother began to mutter under her breath, "Josiah, Josiah, I must lie down, Josiah, Josiah," it was like having an angry bee in the room. A bee that longed to escape. Horatia knew it signaled a retreat to the bedroom, and the doctor would come soon.

Josiah explained Mamma needed to rest more than most people.

"Why does she say 'Josiah, Josiah'?"

"Mother wants me to take care of her. So that's what I do, just like I take care of you when you have a bad dream in the night."

"Does Mamma have bad dreams?"

Josiah considered that. "I think she does. And you can help me take care of Mother by being good."

So Horatia was good. The hired girls agreed they'd never seen such a well-behaved child. She did as she was told, and they hardly had to watch her at all.

She was an amenable, reasonable child with a sweet, placid nature. Josiah, remembering his own motherless boyhood, was devoted to her. When he came home from work he often brought her some small toy or candy or a hair ribbon. He took her on walks, and pointed out interesting things to see—flights of wild ducks over the river in the autumn twilight, the evening star in the winter sky, the spring sunsets, and the summer lightning bugs. He ordered storybooks and at bedtime read until she fell asleep. And while he was at the Emporium all day he arranged for other children to keep her company. Hilda Drumheller's youngest daughter, Bella, was the same age and came to play nearly every day.

But Bella only wanted to eat cake and play tea parties with their dolls, which Horatia found dull. Horatia much preferred two older, boisterous boys, Frank and Calvert Marshall, who also came to play at the Vanns'.

Bella, who was used to being the center of attention and having her own way, hugged her doll and complained they were bossy-boots. But Horatia worshipped the boys. It didn't matter if they treated Horatia like a puppy, alternating between tolerating her or paying her attention so she'd fetch them cookies from the kitchen or telling her to get out of the way, they were busy doing something too *important* for girls.

Horatia never minded. She was used to being ignored by Ellinder, and it was exciting when the boys were there.

They were orphans, raised up at Wildwood by their widowed Aunt Priscilla, who everybody called Aunt Teeny, her childhood nickname. Teeny had married Dr. Joshua Vann, an older relative of Josiah and Ellinder's, so she was a cousin by marriage. At her husband's death,

Teeny had been left well off, with two teenage daughters and time on her hands. When her widowed brother, Ben Marshall, was dying, she had returned to live at Wildwood to care for him and Ben's two young boys.

It was Ben's last wish that Teeny would run the *Messenger*, the newspaper Ben had founded, after his death until his elder son, Frank, finished college at Harvard and could take over the newspaper. By the time Ben died, Teeny's daughters had been sent to a young ladies' seminary near Washington, and she hired a nursemaid to look after the boys so that she could devote her time to running the *Messenger.*

The nurse brought the boys to play with Horatia at the Vanns'. She often left them with the latest girl hired by Josiah to look after Horatia and went gallivanting off to see her sweetheart, who worked at the mill farther down the valley. Sometimes Horatia's nurse joined her, saying that the cook would keep an eye on the children.

Bella's nurse refused to be left behind, and the three hired girls agreed the Vanns' cook could just as well look after four children as three.

The cook resented having extra work and tried complaining to Ellinder—she had marketing to do and dinner to prepare and refused to carry the extra burden for the shiftless hired girls. But Ellinder responded with her usual vague, smiling detachment and said she'd see.

The cook ground her teeth at this response, the missus was too vague for anyone's good, and the mister was busy at the Emporium all day, and anyway, it was useless to appeal to a man about domestic problems. Nevertheless, the cook felt aggrieved that it was left to her to run the Vann household and watch four children on her own. Bella and Horatia she could manage, but it was too much to have to mind two boisterous boys as well, and she wasn't going to do it!

Thus the four children were often left to entertain themselves, unsupervised.

If Josiah would ask Ellinder if the children disturbed her, she'd wonder for a minute what he meant, before recollecting she'd seen a nurse with some children at the front gate. "No, they're no trouble at all. The nurse keeps them out of the way. I was in the parlor and didn't hear a peep out of them. I even had my nap on the sofa after I had my medicine."

No, Ellinder had no idea what the children were up to. They went where they liked, made mud pies, and dammed the creek that ran through a field next to the Emporium. The little girls were sent to fetch stones and buckets and twigs while the boys did the building. They caught crawdads. They disturbed a rattlesnake that Calvert poked with a long stick until it struck, then slithered away. The boys took a pack of matches from Aunt Teeny's kitchen, and the children started a bonfire behind the barn that they narrowly managed to extinguish before they were caught. They got poison ivy. They got muddy and tore their clothes and skinned their knees, ruining stockings and bleeding occasionally. At the end of the afternoon the returning hired girls sighed and cleaned them up, patched their injuries, put a poultice on the poison ivy rash, washed their clothes, and bribed them to silence with candy.

The children understood that they mustn't mention how they spent their afternoons or the absence of their nurses. Calvert was the ringleader. Horatia adored Calvert. His ideas mostly involved him and the more cautious Frank doing interesting things like building a tree house, while ordering Bella and Horatia back and forth to beg nails and a hammer and a saw from the yardman before sending them up the tree house ladder first, to see if the ladder steps held. Horatia thought the tree house was grand, even though she got splinters in her hands that her nurse had to pick out with a needle.

By the time Horatia and Bella were given their own ponies like Frank and Calvert had, the children went farther afield in search of things to do, secure in the knowledge the hired girls wouldn't notice or care. If they went for a pony ride, they were forbidden to stray from the river path. Instead, once the hired girls disappeared, they would go exploring for hours at a time. They rode over the top of Frog Mountain to search for arrowheads in the valley east of the mountain, where people said there'd once been an Indian village. When they stopped to water their ponies, Frank found a little statue of a lady with a red dress and a blue cloak wedged in the hollow of a rock under some trees. The statue's head had a gold ring around it. "It's a fairy lady," said Calvert. Frank found a metal cross stuck into the rock. He tried to pull it out, but when he couldn't, he told the others it had been stuck in by the magician who left the fairy lady.

They went to see a derelict cabin half-hidden in a tangle of vines and weeds on the edge of Grafton. People said it was haunted. Supposedly, the old man who'd lived there a long time ago had been a freed slave who got rich making whiskey and buried his money nearby. The slave's ghost had been seen walking at night, looking for his money, always accompanied by the smell of burning and the sound of crackling flames and screaming.

They knew that story, from storytelling at the Blackberry Picnic, and Calvert said they ought to investigate. The four children tied up their ponies and crept through the bushes and saplings to look at the cabin from a safe distance. Behind a thicket of creeper and ivy and brambles, a cabin with a leaning stone chimney and a few window-shaped black holes, like eyes watching them, was collapsing. They sniffed and sniffed to see if they smelled burning, but they didn't. It just smelled sort of musty, like wet leaves and old rotted wood.

"We'll have to come back at night—we'd see him then," said Calvert. "At midnight, that's when the Devil walks the earth and dead people crawl out of their graves."

"My parents wouldn't let me go if it was night," Bella whispered to Horatia, relieved Calvert wouldn't be able to make her watch for ghosts and the Devil in this spooky place.

Farther down the river they collected minié balls on an empty field where a Civil War battle had raged. Frank found a rusted sword, and Calvert found a pile of bones, a belt buckle with the letters CSA that Frank said meant the Confederate States of America, and a human skull.

Calvert wiggled his fingers in the eyeholes "like grave worms who eat the dead."

"Ugh!" said Bella.

"Where can we go next?" asked Frank.

"I know, the bear cave where the shape-shifter lives," said Calvert.

Again, thanks to the Blackberry Picnic ghost stories, Grafton children knew about the shape-shifter who lived on Frog Mountain. It was an evil creature, part man and part eagle, that roamed the mountain when fog came down to hide it. It crept up, and suddenly the thing was screeching and screaming and reaching out its bloody claws to grab and eat humans. Back when long hunters with a load of furs had to make their way over Frog Mountain to reach the packet boats at the Vanns' landing, crossing the mountain had been the most dangerous part of the trip. The shape-shifter hated long hunters. It would grab their heads with its claws and scalp them, leaving them to die with a bare bloody head and screaming in pain. On foggy nights you could hear the ghosts of the shape-shifter's victims on Frog Mountain, screaming in pain.

The story gave some Grafton children nightmares for years. It was meant to, to keep children out of the old bear cave.

Bella protested she didn't want to go.

Frank, however, was skeptical. "The shape-shifter's just a story, Bella! Nobody with any sense believes in it. Reverend Merriman said shape-shifters are just old Indian superstition, and anyone who claims he's seen one was probably under the influence of demon drink."

"The shape-shifter is so real!" Calvert protested. "People have seen its handprints in the cave."

"No, they haven't! How could they if there's no such thing!" said Frank, exasperated.

"Is too such a thing!"

"No, there isn't. It's just a story made up! So there can't be handprints!"

"We have to go in and see. If the handprints are there, it proves I'm right and the shape-shifter's real."

"We're not supposed to go into caves," said Frank sternly.

Of course they knew they shouldn't do it, but Calvert liked things they shouldn't be doing. The mountains around Grafton were honeycombed with caves, which seemed like mysterious and wonderful places, but like generations of Grafton children, the Marshall boys, Bella, and Horatia had been warned on pain of terrible punishments that they must never, ever go into them. Caves were dangerous—there were rivers in some of them, deep drop-offs, nests of snakes, and dark winding passages into the mountain. It was easy to lose the way, step into a hole, or drown in some deep dark pool of water. They were certain to get a whipping, even Bella, if the grown-ups found out they'd been inside.

"Don't be a sissy, Frank. Tomorrow we'll go and take a lantern and some matches. We'll be safe then."

Next day, with a growing sense of daring, the children rode past Wildwood, up to the top of Frog Mountain to the deserted Blackberry Picnic ground and the rock called Old Man of the Mountain. The girls expected Frank to say they ought to go back, but he didn't. They tied their ponies to a sapling, and Calvert led the way up the narrow track to the cave entrance.

The children stopped at the cave's mouth, peered into the dark entrance, and felt a breeze on their hot faces.

"Papa says the Cherokees call this the Breathing Rock," Horatia said.

The four of them contemplated for a moment what might be breathing *in* the cave, waiting for them. Bella whimpered they should go home now.

The boys ignored her. Frank lit a lantern he'd brought and went first to prove he wasn't a sissy.

The girls balked.

"Come on," said Calvert, and plunged after Frank.

"I wish we didn't come, don't you?" whispered Bella.

Horatia nodded, too terrified to speak. She wasn't sure what frightened her more—getting lost and having to stay in the cave forever, or disobeying Josiah. Bella wasn't bothered by the knowledge she was being naughty, but she whimpered with fear at the thought the shape-shifter might be waiting inside. But the girls were too accustomed to doing what the boys told them to do to refuse. They crept nervously in behind the boys, not wanting the bobbing light to get too far away.

"Can't we go back now?" quavered Bella. "It stinks and the ground is all slippery."

"Don't be babies. We have a lantern," Calvert ordered. "And shape-shifters don't like lanterns. They don't like little girls either. They aren't tasty enough to rip off their heads and eat. I dare the shape-shifter to come out," he said, striding behind Frank. "Ha, ha, ha, ha, shape-shifter!"

"Ha, ha, ha," the cave echoed back.

The girls squealed that they wanted to leave.

"Not till we see the shape-shifter's hands on the wall," said Calvert.

"But I thought the shape-shifter had claws," quavered logical Horatia, "so why are there hands?"

"It's part human and part eagle, so it can change when it wants to, so sometimes it has hands and sometimes when it wants to catch you and tear off your head and eat it, it has claws," said Calvert. A reasonable if not reassuring explanation. "If we see them, it proves the shape-shifter's real and Reverend Merriman is stupid."

"Don't want to see his handprints," Bella wailed. "I want to go home!"

The boys ignored her. They went deeper and deeper, shushing each other, listening for the kind of sounds a lurking shape-shifter would make. Bella was sobbing now, and Horatia was too scared to speak, but they stumbled after the boys because they didn't want to be left behind in the dark. The smell in the cave made her eyes sting, and Horatia hated to think of the nasty stuff on her boots.

The narrow cave passage widened out suddenly, and Frank cried, "Stop!" The cave ceiling was vaulted here, before narrowing again to a dark passage. He lifted the lantern high, then cried, "I can see them! Look! Up there!"

The children craned their necks to see, and gasped. Over their heads they could see the shapes of hands, many hands, fingers spread white against red on the cave walls.

"The shape-shifter really does live here," Frank whispered in awe.

"I told you," said Calvert.

"A lot of shape-shifters," whispered Horatia. "There're so many hands."

Calvert shouted into the dark, "Shape-shifter! If you're here, come out!"

"Out, out, out" echoed back at them from deep in the cave while Horatia and Bella huddled together, begging to leave before it appeared.

"It doesn't want to come out," said Calvert finally, "but it's there. Look, Bella, there's its eye," he teased as the lantern picked up an eye-shaped piece of quartz that glinted when Frank moved the lantern. "It's watching you."

Bella's and Horatia's screams echoed deep in the cave.

There was a swishing, and then something fluttered jerkily overhead, and Frank dropped the lantern. The flame went out. For horrible long minutes they were stuck in total darkness with things flitting around their heads.

"Hurry, relight the lantern so we can see," said Calvert nervously.

"I dropped the matches, trying to find them. Ugh, whatever's on the ground is squashy and smells so bad it makes my nose hurt."

"What if you can't find them?" quavered Bella.

"Then we'll be stuck here till we die," said Calvert.

"I've found the matches," said Frank, to everyone's relief.

There was the sound of a match striking. The lantern flickered into life, and the flitting things disappeared. "That was just bats that flew over us," said Frank in a shaky voice. "Come on, let's get out." He led the way back until a welcome glimmer of light showed where the cave entrance was.

Back in the daylight, they scraped the nasty stuff off their boots—"Ugh, bat doings!"—uncomfortably conscious they had just done something truly bad, going in the cave and then provoking the shape-shifter, who could have eaten them all.

Calvert bragged he'd been right, the shape-shifter was real.

Frank said he'd be stupid to mention it because they'd all be punished.

"We have to make a pact never to tell we've been inside," said Calvert. "A blood pact. That means you can't go back on your word, or you'll die."

Frank protested he didn't see why blood was necessary, but Calvert took out his pocketknife. "We all have to cut our fingers, and then we put our cuts together so the blood mixes, and that's what makes it so you'll die if you break the pact. I'll do it. Horatia, you first. You're the bravest. Give me your finger."

Being called the bravest didn't help when it came to getting your finger stabbed, but Horatia didn't dare disobey Calvert. She held out her hand and shut her eyes tight. "Ouch!" she gasped as blood welled.

"Bella."

"No!"

"You have to," the others cried. Bella was sobbing again but didn't dare refuse to hold out her finger. She screamed when a few drops of blood appeared on the tip.

"Frank. It's just a prick."

Frank held out his hand. "Ow!"

"Now, me last." Calvert pressed the edge of his knife into the tip of his index finger. "Didn't hurt," he claimed, wincing. "Now we put our fingers together. So the blood mixes." They did. "And say, 'I swear in blood never to tell.'"

"I swear in blood never to tell," they chorused.

"Cross my heart and hope to die, stick a needle in my eye."

"Cross my heart and hope to die, stick a needle in my eye."

"Good." Calvert wiped his knife on his breeches, snapped it shut, and returned it to his pocket.

"Will we really die if we tell?" Bella whispered, following Horatia back down the narrow path.

"Yes," Horatia whispered back. "If Calvert says so, it's true."

"I hate Calvert! Truly, I hate him!"

As they grew older, the boys eventually tired of such adventures in the company of little girls. Busy Teeny shipped Frank and Calvert off to school at a Quaker academy in Philadelphia to get enough education to be ready for Harvard.

Life without the boys was less scary but dull. Bella and Horatia found they missed the adventures.

They waited eagerly for Frank and Calvert to return for Christmas and the summer holidays, but were disappointed when they came. During their months away the boys changed. They grew taller, with deeper voices, laughed at jokes the girls didn't understand, and talked about their new passions, which were of no interest whatsoever to Horatia and Bella. Frank was obsessed with football. Calvert had discovered airplanes. He and a friend from boarding school had been taken by the friend's father to see a flying exhibition, and Calvert could talk of nothing else but the Wright Brothers Military Flyer and how thrilling it must feel to soar away from the earth, and do tricks in the air.

Bella and Horatia were crushed by their indifference. "We have to grow up before they'll be nice to us," said Bella. "I told Mama they just ignore us now, and she said boys that age like young ladies, not little girls. You have to be sixteen before you're a young lady."

"And finish school," said Horatia. "You can't be a young lady until you graduate."

"That's forever. I wish we could just grow up without school," Bella said. She hated school and did as little as possible to avoid learning anything or having to do homework.

Horatia liked school. Josiah had taught her to read at an early age, and she was a quick learner. Her exercise books were neatly written, her sums were usually accurate, and she was always the last pupil standing in the spelling bee.

Bella's parents were constantly holding Horatia up as an example. Over the years Horatia kept Bella from absolutely failing. She made sure Bella memorized her multiplication tables correctly, and as time passed she explained patiently to her over and over how to solve arithmetic and then geometry problems until Bella's eyes glazed over. She checked Bella's geography answers because Bella was often too occupied writing notes to other girls to have any idea what part of the globe they were studying, and she made sure Bella memorized and recited to her the assigned poems from their literature book.

Year after year, at the annual end-of-year ceremony in elementary school, the Drumhellers breathed a sigh of relief when Bella passed into the next class. On those occasions Horatia kept her eyes modestly focused on the toes of her boots while they announced the top girl pupil and tried to look surprised when every year they called her name out to come up to the dais and receive her prize. While it was nice to hear her name called out at the assembly, and of course it was nice to see her father look proud, by her next-to-last year Horatia no longer took any satisfaction in getting the prize. Every year it was a Bible.

A Bible was dull as prizes went, and anyway, in the parlor they already had an old Vann family Bible brought from Wales a long time ago, with births and deaths recorded in the front in faded brown ink. Horatia thought being old and having real names in it made it more interesting and special than the new Bibles with their jarringly bright illustrations. Those she'd been awarded in previous years gathered dust on the bookshelf in her room. She wished the teachers could think of a more interesting reward—a writing desk, or a book.

She liked books, especially ones with beautiful illustrations, like the Lambs' *Tales from Shakespeare*. Bella had a copy, though she never read it, and had given it to Horatia, whose favorite novels were *Freckles* and *A Girl of the Limberlost*. She'd cried buckets over *A Girl of the Limberlost*, never imagining a girl could be so poor or suffer so many trials as Elnora Comstock did with her horrid mother, though it was interesting and even reassuring to read about a girl whose mother wasn't very nice to her daughter. Horatia struggled to love her mother—she knew she ought to love Ellinder—but Ellinder was unpredictable. Sometimes she seemed almost normal, asking Horatia about school, stirring up a cake in the kitchen, or sewing, or talking to Hilda Drumheller when Hilda paid a call. Other times Ellinder looked at Horatia with blank eyes, as if she couldn't remember who Horatia was, which was bad enough, and other times she seemed to think Horatia was a very small child, which was worse.

Horatia longed for a mother like Hilda Drumheller, who made a big fuss over Bella, even though Bella wasn't very well behaved, and always made sure Bella had pretty clothes. Ellinder didn't seem to care about her own clothes or Horatia's. Ellinder only wore mourning, and Horatia was obliged to wear plain dark frocks too, in memory of her dead brothers and sisters.

But *A Girl of the Limberlost* gave Horatia hope. By the end of the book, the heroine Elnora's awful mother had changed and become nicer to her daughter, and everyone was happy. Perhaps Ellinder would change too.

She'd tried to reciprocate for the Shakespeare by giving her copy of *Freckles* to Bella, but Bella wasn't interested in books. She said they had quite enough reading to do in school, and after school there were jollier things to do while waiting to be grown up.

They commiserated about how long that was taking.

CHAPTER 5

1913

Horatia and Bella finally turned sixteen, with only one more year of high school ahead of them, but the age gap between them and the Marshall boys felt bigger than ever. Frank had graduated and come home to learn how to run the paper. Calvert was at Harvard, and Aunt Teeny had arranged for him to read law with a local judge during the holidays until he graduated and the judge took him on full-time. As college men, Frank and Calvert were part of an older crowd and paid attention to girls who'd finished high school and wore long skirts. They took these girls driving. Squired them to parties. Played tennis and croquet and danced with them. And most of the time paid no attention to Bella and Horatia.

But Bella's and Horatia's admiration for them persisted, despite the boys' indifference. They spent a good deal of time companionably buffing their nails, and discussing the delights of young ladyhood once they reached it, and how they would dazzle the Marshall boys *then*.

Between Hilda—who was determined to see her pretty youngest child acknowledged as a girl who, in Rudyard Kipling's words, had "It"—and the articles in magazines like *Ladies' World*, *Housekeeper*, and *Woman's Home Companion*, Horatia and Bella understood that a young lady's purpose in life was to look as pretty as possible, to wear becoming clothes in the latest fashion, to enjoy as many picnics and dances and hayrides as possible, to be popular and flirt, and to keep as many beaux as possible on tenterhooks.

Eventually, the handsomest, richest, most manly of their many beaux would propose, and after a period of deliberation to keep him guessing, they would accept an expensive and exquisite engagement ring and break dozens of hearts as they graduated to the exalted and interesting status of fiancée.

When that happened to Bella and Horatia, Frank and Calvert would be jealous and sorry, which would serve them right.

Being engaged cast a girl in the most lovely romantic glow of all. This delightful state would initiate a new round of clothes to be ordered for the trousseau, the choosing of silver and china patterns, the inevitable piles of wedding presents wrapped in white paper and ribbon rosettes, and endless details about wedding preparations, gowns, and slippers.

They talked themselves into raptures imagining themselves as brides, radiant in white satin and lace, sweetly murmuring their vows with a blush—they had memorized the wedding vows—then exiting the church on the arm of a faceless but adoring husband, and finally slicing the wedding cake, to a background of admiring murmurs: "Isn't she just the *loveliest* thing you ever saw!"

Things weren't imagined much beyond this point, unless it involved what would be the something old, something new, et cetera, how many tiers the wedding cake ought to have, what favors ought to be baked into it, whether it ought to have sugar flowers on top or a little china bride and groom, and the little gift boxes of wedding cake for people to take away afterward. Sometimes they discussed who ought to be invited, and always ended up deciding everyone. Because the more people to admire you as a bride the better. That was the point.

They would "stand up" with each other when the big day came, and they discussed the frocks and flowers they'd choose, depending on the time of year. Horatia wanted to be a June bride and have pink flowers, but Bella had her heart set on a Christmas wedding, which suited her sense of the dramatic. She wanted big red bows on the pews and banks of poinsettias and greens and holly, and candles everywhere, as the background for her in a wedding dress and train.

Bella confided to Horatia, in fits of giggles, "When my sisters got married, they had new nightgowns, really pretty ones. You're supposed to look nice to go to sleep the night you get married, but I think something else happens."

"What?"

"They wouldn't tell me, but I think . . . it involves kissing and spooning. I heard them teasing Jane before she married Wilfred. I don't exactly know, but Jane will tell me eventually," said Bella. "She always does. And I'll tell you."

Getting married was the goal. Neither was particularly interested in what happened after the wedding night. It would involve housekeeping and a husband's preferences for dinner and, judging by Bella's sisters' experiences, getting big and fat when you were going to have a baby—a process that was still shrouded in mystery but painful—and then children to raise and losing your looks if you had too many. None of this featured in their daydreams.

They speculated endlessly about whom they'd marry. They'd tried counting one hundred stars and then looking sharply to the left, where they were supposed to see the image of their future husband. Several times they had tried staying awake and creeping out of bed to look into the old well as the Vanns' clock struck midnight, which was supposed to be a foolproof way to find out. They had put a pan of water under the bed and tried to dream of the man who would bring them a drink of water, who would be the man they'd marry.

So far, no future husband had been conjured up by these methods, and Bella felt quite gloomy at the prospect they'd both be old maids.

"Really, the most convenient thing would be if Calvert married one of us and Frank married the other of us. We know them already, and none of the other boys are as handsome," said Bella as she and Horatia stood side by side in front of Bella's big looking glass, contemplating their reflections and praising each other's good points as they often did.

Both girls had blossomed in their midteens. Bella had restrained her fondness for cake and sweets and outgrown her childish plumpness. She'd grown almost as tall and slender as Horatia. She had unruly brown curls that escaped from every attempt to tame them into a hairdo, large blue eyes usually crinkled in laughter or mischief, and a vivacious personality. Horatia had sleek dark hair nearly to her waist, dark eyes with long eyelashes, heavy brows, and a tendency to be serious. "We look very well together," said Bella as they considered their reflections in her bedroom mirror. "You look interesting, and I look romantic. We'll stick together when we go to dances and have a rule that any boy who asks to dance with one of us has to dance with the other, so we'll have the same number of partners. We'll blaze upon the world!"

"I can't wait to go to dances!"

"We'll show Frank and Calvert! It would serve them right, if they fell in love with us, and we ignored *them* for a change. How can our parents be so vexing as to make us wait until after we've graduated! My cousin in Kingsport says the girls there go to dances at sixteen. She's already been to two."

They spent hours poring over the fashions in the *Messenger* and their mothers' magazines, deciding which outfits in what colors would suit them best.

"It might be too late to show Frank and Calvert anything, by the time we're allowed." Horatia sighed. "What if they fall in love with other girls first? If we have to wait until we're seventeen, we might have to watch them dancing with their fiancées! It will be hard to show them then."

Bella said that mustn't happen. She was the youngest of a large family and used to getting her own way, and, as often happens in large families, she benefited from discipline gradually slipping over the years. Bella's older sisters hadn't been allowed long skirts or dancing or beaux until they finished high school, but the Drumhellers no longer had the patience or the energy to enforce rules where Bella was concerned. Especially since Bella was a good arguer and, when necessary, a good crier.

Her father, Albert, was much involved with making money in the various Drumheller businesses, but he enjoyed playing the indulgent father. Bella, his favorite, had perfected the art of wheedling sweetly for whatever she wanted until he laughed and gave in.

After burying three children and raising six, all of whom except Bella were now married, Hilda was overwhelmed with boisterous grandchildren who lived nearby. The Drumhellers were a prolific family, and they had large houses close to each other on Little Frog Mountain, where the grandchildren spent a good deal of time climbing the fences into each other's yards before heading for their grandparents' house, where they ran wilder, made more noise, and ate more cake than they were allowed at home. Hilda doted on her family, spoiled her grandchildren. She often spoke of Bella being married and settled nearby like her older daughters, after Bella had had her fling as a belle.

If any girl could talk her parents around to letting her go to dances at sixteen, it was Bella.

Horatia often envied Bella her large family and the merry, chaotic Drumheller enclave that was so different from the quiet Vann household, where Horatia and Josiah tried hard not to upset Ellinder. And above all, though she knew it was disloyal to Ellinder, Horatia envied

Bella having a mother who wanted her daughter to have pretty clothes and a good time.

Despite Horatia's protests that she was sixteen and too tall to dress like a child, Ellinder insisted Horatia wear childish pinafores and short skirts with large bows on her twin braids. Her requests for different clothes brought a maddeningly vague response: "We'll see, dear."

Which did not bode well for being allowed to attend dances soon. Or ever.

Horatia reasoned her only hope was that if Bella persuaded her parents, Josiah would agree too, and Ellinder would say, "Of course, dear."

To the girls' surprise, Bella got her way without quite intending it.

One Saturday night that spring, Bella impulsively chopped off her curly brown hair to give herself a "bob."

At breakfast the next morning Bella's parents had fits. Hilda had shrieked, "Your lovely hair! What have you done!" And her father had roared that she was forbidden to leave the house until it grew back. Bella had burst into tears.

As always happened when Bella cried, the parental anger began to abate.

"Church," wept Bella. "I have to go to church!"

"Very well, church but nowhere else . . ."

"C-c-choir practice!" she hiccuped.

She sensed that her parents were looking at each other, calculating what else they shouldn't prevent her going to.

"Choir, but straight home afterward."

Bella sobbed on, understanding from the conciliatory note creeping into their voices that she'd somehow seized the advantage and all she had to do now was see how it materialized.

They told her to stop crying. She didn't.

"Now, baby," commanded Albert. "That's enough. Eat your breakfast."

"You'll ruin your eyes," Hilda interposed. "They'll be all red and you'll look a sight at church."

"I d-d-don't care! I don't want any breakfast! You think I'm ugly!"

"No, no, no, you're pretty as ever."

"No. I'm not!" Bella wailed. "I'm ugly as an old troll!"

Finally, in a complete about-face, the Drumhellers promised if she stopped crying she could attend Miss Edmonia Tucker's dancing classes, and then she *might* be allowed to go with her sister Jane and Jane's husband to a dance at the hotel.

Bella gave a long, shivering sigh, then composed her face and rewarded her parents with a watery smile, astonished at the way things had turned out. "Truly?"

Miss Edmonia's classes were the first step to dances upon graduation from the high school. They were held in the ballroom of the Rehoboth Springs Hotel, where Miss Edmonia, a seventy-year-old spinster, lined the class up—girls on the right, boys on the left—and walked everyone through the steps, one-two-three, ONE-two-three, ONE-TWO-THREE over and over, beating the air with a pointer she used for emphasis as well as for swatting any boys inclined to misbehave. When they had mastered the steps sufficiently, she ordered the boys to choose a partner as she wound the gramophone.

They learned to waltz and polka and two-step, with the occasional Virginia reel for fun, and were reminded to behave like ladies and gentlemen and to avoid making spectacles of themselves with shocking modern dances like the turkey trot. Miss Edmonia taught them ballroom etiquette: how to go down a receiving line, how girls must avoid appearing "fast," how boys must avoid slouching and hands in pockets, must call a girl Miss So-and-So when they asked her to dance, and how a girl should graciously accept, addressing her partner as Mr. So-and-So.

Since her pupils had known each other practically since babyhood, this struck them as ridiculous, and they complained that Miss Edmonia and her rules were too old-fashioned for words. Parents all approved of her strict approach because it was plain that young people's manners and behavior today were not what they had been in the parents' youth. But the young people obeyed Miss Edmonia because only those who had finished her course of lessons received invitations to the dances held at the hotel the last Saturday night of every month.

Since the Rehoboth Springs Hotel was owned by the Drumheller family, no one could complain if Albert's daughter attended the dances a year before other girls.

The hotel, first envisaged by one of the Drumhellers, was a rustic mountain resort offering such wholesome delights as fresh air, spring waters, and mountain walks and views, with diversion provided by prayer meetings and revivals at a nearby church campground. But subsequent Drumhellers realized there was more money to be made from a clientele who wanted gaiety and romance and entertainment as opposed to those wanting to sing hymns and immerse themselves in Bible study.

The original clapboard building had been extended until it was a rambling white structure large enough to be visible across the valley, with a wide porch around three sides, dark-green shutters, tennis courts, a shuffleboard court, a conservatory, a gazebo with benches where a little mineral spring gushed water out of a lion's mouth, and best of all, a ballroom extension.

It had become a popular summer destination for wealthy families seeking to escape the sticky heat and unhealthy air of low-lying cities such as New York and Philadelphia and Baltimore. Some families came for weeks, some for the entire summer, taking suites of rooms and bringing their personal maids and children's nurses, and even dogs. Moonlight picnics, tennis and croquet tournaments, and guided mountain walks featured as attractions in the hotel's prospectus, while dances in the grand new ballroom introduced a note of romance and sophistication.

The hotel had its own little Rehoboth Springs train station at the foot of Little Frog Mountain, where the gaily painted horse-drawn hotel jitney met the guests and transported them up the winding road to the hotel while uniformed servants collected the luggage and pets and followed in a horse-drawn cart.

Hotel guests tended to be of the variety who dressed for dinner and thought nothing of traveling with tuxedos and evening boots and gowns and gloves and dancing slippers in their trunks. For such guests, the monthly dances required both gaiety and a certain *ton*. However, after the hotel had been expanded and the ballroom added, it was discovered that the ballroom, while grand, had been made too large for gaiety if the only dancers were hotel guests. Even with every room filled, the ballroom dwarfed the assemblage, and a small dance in a vast ballroom was a discouraging affair, *ton* or not.

The Drumhellers soon realized gaiety required a crowded ballroom filled with dancing young people, so it was expedient to invite the young ladies of Grafton. That being the case, there needed to be sufficient young men for their partners. Many of the male guests were middle-aged and elderly, and even if they had been an attractive prospect for the girls, their parents would never have allowed them to attend if it meant dancing with grown men who were strangers to the girls' families.

So the young men of Grafton were invited, but to prevent their introducing a rowdy element, Bella's father gave Miss Edmonia free use of his ballroom on Saturday afternoons to teach them how to behave in refined company.

The hotel dances were formal, to satisfy the worldly guests accustomed to city manners, though Albert was at pains to let guests know that, by long custom at the hotel, any respectable young man might attend in a suit if he didn't possess a tuxedo. This relieved Grafton parents of the expense of men's evening wear for their sons, though girls and their mothers lavished time, attention, and money on evening dresses.

Upon arrival there was a receiving line: the hotel manager and his wife, then the chaperones and their husbands, and occasionally Albert Drumheller, resplendent in tails, and Hilda, dressed like a ship in full sail, graced the occasion. The dancing-class girls practiced a curtsey for this, boys a half-bow. Once through the receiving line, girls were given gold-tasseled dance cards for their wrists, with a little pencil attached for boys to fill in their names to claim a dance.

The quartet of musicians who enlivened the hotel dinners also played on dance nights, sitting on a raised platform, surrounded by potted palms and wearing evening dress. The wide porch around the hotel was lined with planters spilling over with flowers and strung with Chinese lanterns. In warm weather the French doors opening onto it were left open to the breeze. From a distance the strings of lanterns were dots of color on Little Frog Mountain, and strains of dance music carried across the valley until midnight, when dances ended because it was now the Sabbath, and it was the decorous custom of Grafton that dancing did not take place on the Sabbath.

When the dancing ended, a buffet prolonged the evening: chicken à la king in chafing dishes, sliced ham, molded salad, waffles, and Russian punch. On warm nights couples took their plates out to the porch where tables had been laid, and afterward, if someone had a guitar or ukulele, the evening ended in singing.

Snatches of "Let Me Call You Sweetheart" and "Any Little Girl, That's a Nice Little Girl, Is the Right Little Girl for Me" drifted across the valley and into the ears of girls too young to attend dances but who lay awake on dance nights, their heads full of grown-up dresses and dancing slippers and of whirling around the dance floor in the arms of someone.

Horatia often lay awake thinking of Calvert. It was easier to dream of Calvert than to actually speak to him. Even at sixteen she was blushing and tongue-tied in his presence. But if they met at dances, things would be different. Calvert would look impossibly handsome in his tuxedo, and she would have a fetching evening dress of pink lawn with a froth of ruffles around the hem and long gloves, and her hair would be up and show off Ellinder's pearl earbobs. As the music started, Calvert would take her hand in his; she would look into his eyes as he pulled her into his arms to dance. She imagined lifting her own hand to his shoulder, felt his arm around her waist, watched his familiar smile become a look of surprise. "Dear little Horatia," he'd say, "when did you become so beautiful? I never noticed before."

And Horatia would look grown up and smile and say, "Oh, Calvert . . ." But here her imagination failed her, and she was unable to think of a sufficiently fascinating response to encourage this interesting conversation, so she'd smile mysteriously—and they'd sweep away round the ballroom in a way that allowed her to kick the ruffles with a neat flourish of her foot, which she'd heard was considered a fetching trick, allowing him to guide her, his arm around her waist pulling her close to him until her cheek was on his shoulder . . . She'd fall asleep smiling into her pillow.

Horatia had never breathed a word of these imaginings to anyone, not even Bella. But to think of Bella dancing with Calvert for a whole year before she could was unbearable.

Bella and Horatia discussed Bella's good luck over and over. Bella was wild with delight—dancing lessons would begin the week after school ended, and would finish in time for her to attend the hotel dance at the end of June. And when Bella started her senior year, all the girls in the class would be in awe of her and want to be her friend.

Horatia, wild with envy, toyed with the idea of bobbing her own hair, then thought better of it. Her parents were used to her being well behaved. Her father often told her what a comfort she was. She didn't want to stop being a comfort, but how utterly horrible if Bella were allowed to go dancing and Horatia wasn't!

"Just find a moment when your mother's better," said Bella. "Mama says she is, sometimes. Then ask them."

The moment seemed to come at supper on the night of the school prize-giving when Horatia had won the top pupil's prize yet again. It had been one of Ellinder's good days. She'd attended the prize-giving, looking elegant with her gray hair neatly fastened in a bun under her best hat, the gold mourning brooch with her dead children's hair pinned at the neck of her best black church dress, and a clean white handkerchief with a lace trim in her hand. She'd applauded Horatia as enthusiastically as Josiah had done, and afterward serenely accepted congratulations from the other parents, and smiled composedly when teachers had praised Horatia's willing attitude, schoolwork, good manners, and ladylike deportment.

However, despite this, Horatia narrowly observed her mother and thought the teachers could have been talking about anybody, any other girl, and Ellinder would have looked just the same. Ellinder never really seemed to recognize the things Josiah praised Horatia for, she thought, watching Hilda beam proudly at Bella, despite the fact that Bella hadn't won a single prize and was supposed to be in trouble on account of her bobbed hair.

At supper that night, Horatia passed her father the vegetables and the biscuits to her mother and, taking a deep breath, said that Bella was going to attend Miss Edmonia's Saturday dancing classes and be ready to go to her first grown-up dance at the end of June. She wanted to be allowed to go too.

"Certainly not, Horatia, not before you finish high school." Josiah laughed. "Next summer when you're grown up."

"Heavens no," murmured Ellinder. "In a few years, perhaps we'll see."

"Oh please, Papa! If Bella may, why can't I? In Kingsport girls go to dancing classes at sixteen, *before* their last year of school. I do think

I ought to be allowed to do that if Bella may. I'm as nearly grown up as she is."

"We'll see," Ellinder said calmly.

Mother isn't listening, Horatia thought resentfully. *She's never listening.* But there was nothing to be gained arguing with Ellinder.

"Next summer," said Josiah. "Men don't want to dance with schoolgirls."

"Frank and Calvert would dance with me."

Josiah said he liked having a little girl, and what good was a young lady who forgot about her poor old father at home because she was too busy gadding off to dances and parties and breaking young men's hearts, and then before you knew it some young fool wanted to marry her and next thing he knew, she'd be gone. So he needed a little girl for at least another year.

Did her father expect a young man would want to marry her as soon as she stepped out the door in an evening dress? Calvert perhaps?

"Next summer is soon enough," said Josiah firmly. "Besides, I expect Frank and Calvert are too busy for dancing and whatnot. Frank's learning how to run the *Messenger*, or he would learn if his aunt Teeny would let go of the tiller. Calvert's meant to spend these summers between college reading law with Judge Evander Marshall. I imagine the judge would rather he studied than danced. I understand the law studies have gone very slowly so far because Calvert has so many young friends." He raised a quizzical eyebrow at Horatia.

"But the dances are on Saturday nights! You can't expect him to study then, Papa! And during the week Judge Marshall sleeps a great part of the time, on the sofa after lunch until either Calvert or his cook wakes him up. Calvert's supposed to be reading lawbooks then, but the judge snores and Calvert can't concentrate. So he goes for a ride or fishing or a game of tennis."

"I'm sure he'll make a remarkable lawyer, given the time lawyers spend fishing and tennising," Josiah said dryly.

"Anyway, Calvert's not really interested in law," said Horatia. "It's just what Aunt Teeny wants him to do. Frank says he's interested in airplanes."

"Airplanes! What next!" Josiah kissed the top of Horatia's head, then took his hat and went off to the Emporium to count the day's receipts and lock up as he did every night.

Horatia scowled.

"Your father's right. A schoolgirl shouldn't go to dances. Whatever is Hilda thinking, to let Bella. Now eat your nice chicken fricassee that we had because it's your favorite dish. And then it's bedtime."

"Oh, Mamma!" Horatia stabbed her chicken with her fork. "I'm too old to be sent to bed at sunset!" Horatia despaired. She hated her mother. She hated her father. She hated everyone. Including Bella.

CHAPTER 6

1913–1914

Horatia was miserable all summer. Bella talked about the dancing class, her new evening dresses, being chaperoned to dances at the hotel by her sister Jane and Jane's husband, Wilfred, and how often she'd danced with Frank and Calvert. At her first dance, Bella bragged, her dance card filled up immediately, even though she was the youngest girl there. As the summer wore on, young men sent her boxes of candy and flowers and wanted to take her buggy riding on Sunday afternoons after church, though of course even Bella's parents wouldn't allow that.

One of her beaux sent her a poem about her cheeks rosy as dawn and her melting eyes. Horatia thought the latter was a stupid metaphor—it sounded like it would make your eyes red and your nose run. Bella didn't know which of her beaux sent it, as the poet hadn't signed his name.

Bella showed the poem to her friends, including Horatia, to see if they could shed any light on the author—and also so that everyone would talk about Bella's loveliness, Horatia thought, handing it back. *I bet she wrote it herself. And no wonder her cheeks are rosy. Bella paints.*

Horatia moped and didn't want to see Bella at all. Bella no longer sang in the choir, as she claimed she was too tired after Saturday evening parties and sat yawning through Reverend Merriman's sermons on Sunday mornings. At the Blackberry Picnic in the fall, Bella was followed around by her latest conquest, Davy Charbonneau, who was five years older and generally regarded as a heartthrob by the Grafton girls. He made a nuisance of himself trying to be her beau, helping the Drumheller ladies unpack their picnic food, and carrying anything remotely heavy for Bella. Horatia sat with her parents and tried not to notice as Davy and other boys vied for Bella's attention.

The winter wasn't any better. They no longer passed notes in class or giggled and whispered in the playground. Bella abandoned any pretense of attending to her schoolwork, saying it wasn't necessary to know history or geography to get married. She had a becoming dark-green velvet evening dress for the Twelfth Night Ball held every year after Christmas at the hotel. The next day Bella came to tell Horatia, who didn't want to know, all about it. Bella said she had danced with Calvert so many times, and called him TDH—a slang phrase Jane used that meant tall, dark, and handsome—until Horatia wanted to slap her. Bella was the envy of all the girls in the senior class.

It didn't help that Ellinder had ordered a new dress for Horatia to attend the hymn-singing Christmas party at church. It was a plain navy silk with a lace collar and skirts only halfway to her ankles—a child's party dress—and Horatia wept with dismay when she put it on. She brushed out her braids and tied her hair back with a velvet ribbon, which helped a little, until Ellinder insisted on rebraiding her hair and fixing the ends with the stupid bows.

Ellinder said she looked sweet. Horatia protested, "I look peculiar, like a giant Alice in Wonderland in a tiny frock. Why can't I have a dress I like?"

Ellinder said vaguely, "We'll see, dear."

Horatia managed not to scream at her mother, and felt miserably self-conscious at the church party. She took refuge in a dark corner and refused to sing or play games, swearing to herself that one day she'd get her hair bobbed. And she'd learn the shocking new dance she'd heard of—from Bella, of course—called the turkey trot, and she'd dance it down Main Street in broad daylight. And get Frank to put a picture of her doing it on the front page of the *Messenger*.

She hated, hated, hated Bella!

Only her seventeenth birthday would end the misery! It was in mid-April, and simply ages away. Ages!

CHAPTER 7

April 1914

The Christmas dress languished, despised, in Horatia's closet. Horatia feared she would never have anything pretty or suitable for a girl her age and would have to stay inside for the rest of her life and die an old maid. Then Hilda Drumheller called to see Ellinder and came to the rescue. She pointed out that Horatia was nearly grown, had developed a shape that required new shirtwaists—she could scarcely button her old ones—and was so tall that her dresses couldn't be let down any farther. Horatia's legs were long, and the short skirts exposed too much of her black-stockinged limbs.

"Really, Ellinder! It's disgraceful!" Hilda said, exasperated. "Send for Miss Willa at once and have some proper clothes made for the girl!"

"We'll see . . ."

"No, we won't see, we'll do it at once," snapped Hilda. "Only look how the child's grown, Ellinder! Horatia has a shape!"

"Oh, perhaps she has."

"Write a note at once, and Horatia can take it to Miss Willa now."

"Tomorrow, perhaps. We'll see. I'm too fatigued at the moment . . ."

"*Now*, Ellinder!" said Hilda sharply, handing her a sheet of notepaper, a pen, and an inkwell and blotter. Ellinder sighed and obeyed.

"Thank you, Aunt Hilda," Horatia whispered gratefully as Hilda was leaving.

"Take that note at once," Hilda ordered.

So Horatia put the note in her pocket and set off for the Negro neighborhood called Hanover, after a colored family who'd owned the land since Grafton was a settlement, and whose descendants were scattered throughout the valley on other property they owned. Miss Willa Freeman, the seamstress, lived in a small brick house with a white painted porch near the river. Miss Willa, who was one of the light-skinned Hanovers, married the much darker-skinned Sam Freeman, who'd worked at the Charbonneaus' stud farm and knew horses. She'd inherited a piece of the Hanover family property in Grafton, and Sam had built a livery stable on it, and by the time they had two small daughters, the livery stable was providing a good living.

But tragedy struck. Sam was killed in Kingsport during a bank robbery in broad daylight. He'd been the only Negro customer present, waiting to ask about the possibility of a loan to expand his business in Grafton. He was standing out of the way, dressed respectably in a suit, vest, and starched collar, his hat in his hand, politely waiting for the white folks to finish their business ahead of him, but the robbers were colored men, and the police assumed he was one of them and shot him dead along with the other two before Sam could say he wasn't.

People in Grafton felt terrible that Sam Freeman had been shot by mistake. They started calling his widow "Miss Willa" even though she was a Negro. The livery stable was bought by one of the Drumhellers, though for less than it was worth, and a collection was taken up for the widow and children in the two white churches as well as the Negro church.

Miss Willa struggled. She used what she didn't spend on food and her daughters' schoolbooks to start a dressmaking business in her front room, and Grafton ladies made a point of coming to her to get their everyday clothes made, to help her out. Soon they were ordering church dresses and even wedding dresses, saying that Miss Willa had magic in her fingers. Her clients had to order the material she recommended—Miss Willa couldn't afford a stock of material—but she knew how to get a dress exactly right. Didn't make any difference if it was only a simple day dress or a skirt whose wearer would be cooking and feeding chickens and weeding her flowers, it would look becoming. Her church dresses meant you could walk to your pew looking nice from every direction because they fit perfectly, and her evening dresses were a match for the gowns that hotel guests brought from the cities.

She could embroider and do fine tucking too, but her special talent was her ability to copy any picture or sketch of ladies' clothing from a magazine or newspaper, make a paper pattern for it, and then, when a garment had been cut and basted, fit it to the wearer perfectly with little darts.

Miss Willa sewed all night sometimes to finish an order.

She raised her girls on her earnings and strict admonitions to work hard and get on in life. By the time they finished Grafton's little colored school, Miss Willa had scraped together enough to send them to the colored normal school in Petersburg to train to be teachers. The girls married fellow students, and both couples had gone on to teach at colored schools. People said Miss Willa and the Freeman girls were a credit to their race.

If Miss Willa heard, she didn't let on.

Miss Willa was slim and seemingly ageless. She wore thick spectacles because years of sewing had ruined her eyes, refused to wear an apron, and carried a neatly organized carpetbag with her scissors and thimbles and papers of pins and samples of tucking. She was soft-spoken and reserved, though look close and there was something formidable in her expression. Her customers were just a little afraid of her, though none had any cause to complain—she was always respectful. She now employed four other Negro women to sew for her, and had enough work that she sometimes refused customers.

The next afternoon, Miss Willa knocked at the Vanns' back door. The cook opened it and said, "Miz Vann waitin' there in the sewin' room, just next to the parlor."

In the sewing room, Ellinder sat twisting her handkerchief in her hands and fluttered. "Oh, Miss Willa, I hope you're not too busy to help me. Little Horatia has grown like a wildflower." Ellinder was nervous around Miss Willa.

"Yes, ma'am. Girls grow up fast, got to make sure they look respectable," said Miss Willa evenly, putting her carpetbag down on the sewing room table and extracting her tape measure, a small pad of paper, and a pencil.

"Mr. Vann particularly wishes her to have a new riding dress, and then she needs a new skirt for school."

"Stand up straight," Miss Willa said in her soft, even voice, "so's I can take measurements."

In her camisole and bloomers, Horatia stood up straight, turned this way and that, and tried not to fidget as she whispered, "Miss Willa, Mamma doesn't realize I need new everything! It's my bosom! Nothing fits over it! Not my church dress, not my summer dresses, not even my school skirts, and my old riding dress is so tight the seams split under the arms. And"—she lowered her voice to an urgent whisper—"Miss Willa, I need an evening dress! Papa says I may go to the hotel dances this summer, so I'll need a real evening dress, as pretty as the one you made Bella at Christmas, and, Miss Willa, I need it to be a grown-up dress. Please! Mamma may tell you different, but she, um, doesn't understand . . ." Horatia was sure everyone knew how odd her mother was, but it felt disloyal to say it.

Miss Willa didn't look sympathetic, or anything but businesslike. "Let's see what's in that material closet we can use."

Josiah had continued giving his wife her first pick of any new material ordered for the Emporium, in case some irresistibly pretty fabric might lighten her melancholy and persuade her into wearing something besides mourning. Over the years the cupboard had filled with a selection of muslin, linen, lawn, tulle, serge, woolens, velvets, even silk, in different colors, all unused, like vanished hopes, and growing dusty.

Ellinder would never leave off black and have her clothes made up in colors.

Now Miss Willa opened the cupboard, and exclaimed, "Glory! It's like a rainbow done burst in here!"

Ellinder hastened to say she'd send to the Emporium for plain cloth, that would be better, but Miss Willa pursed her lips and said firmly, "Waste not, want not."

She fingered fabrics and held up swatches to see about colors and how cloth felt, and Horatia showed Miss Willa, in the latest copy of her mother's *Woman's Home Companion*, how skirts were narrower and that the draped tunic style with a belt was the new shape.

"Hmm," said Miss Willa, taking no notice of Ellinder murmuring ineffectually in the background.

Miss Willa finally chose a length of striped white twill for a skirt and jacket that would do for church and visiting. There was plain white muslin and flowered lawns in pastel colors for summer frocks, navy serge with velvet piping for Horatia's school skirts, and brown serge for a new riding dress.

They mulled over cottons and linens for shirtwaists. Horatia wanted everything done that could be done to shirtwaists—tucks and lace trim and little pearl buttons. Miss Willa nodded in agreement. She liked a nice trim.

"And see, Miss Willa, with skirts narrow, the shirtwaists fit much closer, not such large sleeves. And evening dresses now, Miss Willa, look.

They all have high waists and sashes and"—Horatia's voice dropped to a whisper—"ladies don't wear corsets underneath." Ellinder, who was still firmly corseted into an S shape every morning, would have been shocked if she'd heard. "I was hoping for an evening dress like this one, in pink silk—see the way it drapes at the waist? I've always wanted a pink dress, but Mamma said colors were unsuitable for us because . . . you know, my sisters and brothers. What do you think, Miss Willa?"

To Horatia's dismay, Ellinder interrupted to say they only wanted some school clothes and a new riding dress—a dancing dress wasn't needed, her Christmas navy silk would do for dancing once it was let out on the sides.

The dressmaker shook her head. "No, ma'am, that surely won't do," she said firmly while studying the pictures in the magazine, then Horatia, then making a sketch in her pad. She measured from Horatia's waist down to her toes.

"Miss Horatia got one of the littlest waists I ever seen," Miss Willa muttered approvingly, noting measurements down in her pad.

Horatia slid her hands over her slender waist and turned this way and that in front of the full-length mirror. "Do men really like it if they can circle a girl's waist with two hands?"

"Horatia!" exclaimed Ellinder. "How indelicate! Run along."

Horatia decided this was not the time to ask her mother for some silk stockings, though one of the Emporium girls in the ladies' section had mentioned a shipment had come on the last train. She'd persuade her father to give them to her.

She went upstairs and borrowed a paper of hairpins from her mother's dressing table, then went to her room to experiment with her hair.

She took the fashion magazine from behind the mirror over her washstand and turned it to the illustration of a Gibson Girl. She loosened her hair from its braids, brushed it all forward, then threw her head back and pulled and pinned her hair into a casual pouf on top of her head, with a lock hanging down on each side like the picture. She thought it would become her if she could just get it fixed to stay.

Her dark hair was heavy, and soon hairpins were dislodging themselves and the pouf slid down over one ear. Hairpins were a tricky business! She stuck more in until it held still. No wonder women bobbed their hair.

She examined her complexion in the mirror. It was smooth, but it would be better with powder and rouge. She'd have asked to try Bella's if she and Bella were still friends. She was rather ashamed to have been horrid to Bella for months. She'd try to make amends by asking Bella to come for supper on her birthday. She missed Bella. Nothing was fun without Bella, really.

CHAPTER 8

The following Saturday Horatia's seventeenth birthday finally arrived, as birthdays eventually do. Miss Willa came after breakfast bringing her new riding dress, though Horatia couldn't see why it had been important she have that before clothes for school.

Josiah hadn't left for the Emporium as early as he usually did, and after Miss Willa went home he said Horatia had to come to the stable and meet her birthday present. It turned out to be a pretty chestnut mare to replace the plodding old pony she was too big to ride.

"She's beautiful! Oh, Papa, how kind of you! So *that's* the reason for my riding dress!" Horatia's eyes shone with delight. She hugged her father and kissed the mare's nose and scratched under the mare's chin, murmuring endearments. She found the last of the windfall apples kept in the stable from the autumn harvest and fed her one. The mare nuzzled her cheek.

"Expect you'll be wanting to go out for a ride," said Hiram Pine, the hired man. He grinned as he led the mare out of her stall to saddle her.

"Oh yes! I'll just get ready," Horatia cried.

She flew up the stairs to her room, and before she changed into her new riding dress she quickly polished her boots, which were in a disgraceful state. In the downstairs hall, Horatia caught her reflection in the tall mirror and for once found it highly satisfactory. The skirt was properly long, and the jacket cunningly fitted with little black braid frog fastenings, emphasizing her small waist. The brown serge suited her dark eyes and coloring. She did look older.

She twirled and primped until Josiah told her that admiring one's ensemble in the mirror didn't give the mare much exercise and Hiram had been walking her up and down in front of the house for a quarter of an hour.

Josiah helped her mount, and Ellinder cried from the porch, "Josiah, that mare looks skittish. We ought to wait and see . . ."

Before her mother could decide it was too dangerous, Horatia waved to her parents and rode off out of earshot toward the river path.

The mare tossed her head and trotted. The trees were hazy with green buds, sunlight caught on the rippling river, and the dogwoods had unfurled their white flowers. It was the kind of day when life felt suddenly satisfactory. She'd been promised dancing lessons after graduation, and that meant the dances too. Miss Willa had scrutinized pictures of the new draped skirts and crossover bodices and short sleeves and little trains on evening gowns, and had nudged Ellinder into the right decisions about fabrics and narrow skirts and the placement of tiers and trimmings, saying they wanted Miss Horatia to be the girl dressed "rightest" at dances, didn't they? Ellinder had capitulated, and Horatia's evening dress was going to be a peach-pink silk tulle with a green velvet trim and a raised waist with a wide sash, like the drawing in the magazine. Calvert would surely notice, she thought happily.

"Horatia!" Frank lifted his hat.

She hadn't seen him riding toward her. The mare pranced as she pulled her up. "Hello, Frank! Congratulate me, it's my birthday! How do you like my present? Papa bought her from the Charbonneaus. A beauty, isn't she?"

The mare whinnied, as if to agree.

Frank smiled at her and swung his own horse around and leaned over to pat the mare's neck. "You each look fetching. Congratulations, hadn't forgotten. Calvert and I have a present for you, but unless you want to wait until he comes home in June, I'll bring it this evening."

"Yes, do come for my birthday cake. There'll be ice cream too. I saw the churn on the back porch. Bella's coming. It's not a party, of course. Mamma isn't strong enough for parties, but Papa says a little familiar company gives her pleasure."

His horse fell in step with hers. "I'll be there. I might as well ride a ways with you. I'm meant to be running an errand for Aunt Teeny at the store, but it's not wanted immediately, and it's good to be outdoors. It's not as if she allows me to do anything really useful at the *Messenger*."

"Still? You've been there two years since you left college."

"Still." He made a glum face.

"Do you wish you were reading law like Calvert, instead of having the *Messenger*?"

"No, the paper is what I want, not reading law. Even Calvert doesn't want to be reading law. He's crazy to be flying airplanes. He and his roommate, Terence, went to another air show, and one of the pilots took them up. All Aunt Teeny lets me do is write poky little features about church socials and who visited whom, but I have big plans for the paper when I finally get my hands on it. I've been reading back editions from my father's time, trying to get a sense of what he was like. I was so young when he died that I don't remember him well, but I find that reading the stories he wrote gives me a sense of him. Did you know his father fought for the Union? His wife was a Quaker woman who didn't believe in slavery or in fighting. I found her obituary my father wrote. It said she was a 'shining light of benevolence and Christian charity' who among other things raised an orphaned baby whom a passing soldier and his wife left in her barn. I asked Teeny about that, and she made a face and agreed her mother had raised a girl about her age, but Teeny disliked her, thought she was strange, always hated it when her mother paid the girl any attention or saw that she had as many dresses and bonnets as Teeny. And Teeny was sure her mother didn't really like the girl either."

"What happened to the girl?"

"She stole some things and ran off one day. Never heard from her again. Where was I? Oh yes, I was saying the stories my father wrote show what kind of paper he wanted the *Messenger* to be. Aunt Teeny says he wanted the *Messenger* to be about the people of Grafton, kind of an historical record of life here in the valley. And while she's been running it, the paper's mostly reported what people do here in Grafton but not much about the rest of America, the rest of the world. And she's made a success of doing it that way, of course.

"But I get the impression Father had a broader vision, how what happened in Grafton related to what else was happening in the world, that a newspaper ought to inform public opinion. He'd been to Harvard like Cal and me, you know, after the Civil War.

"He wrote a piece about how the war and then Reconstruction had cast a long shadow. In the old days there used to be a prosperous free black community, the descendants of slaves who'd come here and been given land and made money and been respected. Sophia and Henri de Marechal had taught their white children and the colored children together in the kitchen at Wildwood. But the end of the war brought Confederate veterans to Grafton because land they'd owned had been ruined by the Yankees or their homes had been burned. And that changed things for good. The veterans held on to their wartime grievances, Confederate sentiments. The old Hanover neighborhood with those nice homes became 'Darkie Town,' and colored children and white children had separate schools.

"When I finally take over at the paper, I want to write pieces like that, about bigger things than who attended a tea party. For one thing, I want to cover news from the rest of the world. I think he'd approve of that. The world is smaller today, with trains and fast ships and the telegraph, and what happens somewhere else can come to affect us here too. Take Russia, for example. There's been an uprising, and the power of the tsar is in the balance . . ."

Frank was so earnest about things like that, Horatia thought. As always, when he went off on one of his tangents about world events, she half listened while he told her about a massacre in a distant Russian goldfield and something called *dumas* being formed and dissolved. She said "oh" and "mmm" and "how interesting" before thinking, *Oh, bother Russia, it's my birthday!* "I'll race you to the bridge," she called over her shoulder, and kicked the mare into a canter.

"See you later then," he laughed, passing her with his coattails flying.

That night they were finishing dinner when Frank knocked and came straight in as he always did. "Hello," he said, shaking hands with the Vanns. He held Ellinder's a moment longer, giving her time to realize who he was and stop being anxious.

"Why, Frank," exclaimed Ellinder, relaxing a little, "how nice to see you."

"Happy birthday again, Horatia. Hello, Bella. My, what a beautiful cake! What kind is it?" He patted Ellinder's hand and let it go now that she was smiling.

"Caramel," said Horatia. "Mamma made it herself." She'd been pleased her mother had remembered her birthday—sometimes Ellinder didn't.

"Oh, Aunt Ellinder." Frank sighed, and put his hand on his heart. "Caramel cake is my favorite!"

"Oh, it's just an old recipe of my mother's," she said shyly.

After the cake and ice cream, Frank held out a small package tied up in blue ribbon. "With best wishes for your health and happiness, from Calvert and me," he said.

Horatia opened it to find a small velvet box and inside a gold heart-shaped locket with "HV" engraved on it.

"Ooooh! How pretty!" exclaimed Bella. "You can put your sweetheart's picture in it. When you have one."

"Oh, Frank! Thank you!"

"As you don't have a sweetheart, you can put a photograph of your new mare in it," Josiah teased.

"Open it," said Frank.

Horatia stared, then burst out laughing. Inside were pictures of two small boys. Calvert's eyes were crossed, and he was grinning to show his missing front teeth, and Frank had his arm around a dog wearing a hat that could have belonged only to Aunt Teeny.

"Calvert and I claim the honor of being your first beaux!"

"Where in the world did you have such funny pictures taken?"

"Cousin Evaline May took them years ago. Aunt Teeny gave her a camera for her birthday that time she was having a passion for photography, because she wanted a picture of us for the *Messenger*'s memorial issue for our father's birthday. I remember Evaline May saying people always sat up too stiff and formal, and she wanted Calvert and me to look like real boys. When she saw the pictures, Aunt Teeny was so cross, said what was Evaline May thinking, we should have been wearing our good clothes and had our hair brushed."

"How is Evaline May?" Josiah inquired after Aunt Teeny's older daughter. She was a rather intense young woman with heavy dark eyebrows who'd been away to college. She'd come home five years ago, started teaching school, and then gave it up and used her inheritance from her dead father to buy a house of her own on the edge of Grafton. Where she lived alone! It was one thing for a girl to marry and set up house with her husband, but for a girl to leave the shelter of her parental home if unmarried was shocking. But Dr. Joshua Vann had seen fit to leave each of his two daughters an inheritance, and while the younger daughter, Sarah, had taken hers into her marriage, Evaline May was exhibiting an unbecoming independence.

She was pretty enough, but had always had a brisk manner and a forthright way of speaking her mind that made people feel they were being attacked. She was given to intense "passions" for things—aside from photography, and writing poetry, these included bird-watching (she'd asked Vann's store to order a pair of binoculars), flower pressing, and singing along rather screechily to operas she played on a gramophone.

Her new house was a mess, littered with books and papers and forgotten cups of cold tea, which Evaline May claimed was because she was too busy to bother with housework. She told her mother she didn't want a hired girl to help her either, that it wouldn't be right to exploit a poorer girl than herself, and besides, it would disturb her "work." Evaline May was a suffragette, and a ferocious writer of pamphlets and letters urging votes for women to newspapers, senators, congressmen, and even the president. She would stop ladies in the street and urge them to write too.

Aunt Teeny despaired of Evaline May getting married.

"Cousin Evaline May now has a bicycle," Frank told Ellinder.

"A bicycle! Yes, she rides it in bloomers!" giggled Bella.

"And she talks of getting a motorcar, Bella. She says that if your brother-in-law Wilfred learned to drive a motorcar, she can too."

"Wouldn't it be jolly to drive a motorcar, Horatia!" Bella exclaimed. "We'll get Wilfred to teach us!"

"I don't know. It sounds rather daring."

"Yes! That's why I want to do it!"

Frank was laughing. Horatia turned to him. "When will Calvert be home?"

"Yes," echoed Bella, "when?"

CHAPTER 9

June 1914

Bella and Horatia graduated from high school, and as usual, the *Messenger* covered the ceremony, with big photographs of the graduating class on the front page, boys on one side in dark suits with slicked-down hair, and girls in white dresses and hair ribbons on the other. Horatia had been obliged to share the honor of being valedictorian with Davy Charbonneau's younger brother because, even though her grades were higher, the principal felt the occasion required a boy.

Evaline May was predictably outraged and wrote a blistering letter to the *Messenger* that Frank refused to print.

Horatia had completed her dancing lessons, and the first dance of the summer was fixed for the end of June. Horatia's dancing dress was finished, and her kid dancing slippers and a little brocade evening bag Josiah had sent for arrived at the Emporium in good time. Josiah was to escort Horatia. The girls wanted to make an impression looking beautiful side by side.

But on the day of the dance, Ellinder had one of her turns. Like the Vanns, the Drumhellers had one of the new telephones, and Bella picked up the receiver to hear Horatia in tears on the other end, saying she couldn't go to the dance after all. Josiah felt obliged to remain at home with her mother.

"You needn't stay home, silly! Sister Jane can chaperone us both. There's plenty of room in her and Wilfred's new motorcar. And you know how Wilfred likes to show off. Driving up with three ladies will make him look real swell."

"Oh, Bella, you're a dear!" exclaimed Horatia. "Are you sure Jane won't mind?"

"Of course not! She thinks you're much more ladylike than I am."

So Jane's husband, Wilfred, drove them up to the hotel in his new Studebaker. He had several cars, and this was the biggest and flashiest. He loved the chance to show it off, especially with three pretty female passengers to make him look the gent in front of the hotel guests. Jane sat in front, wrapped in a duster so as not to spoil her evening dress, while Bella and Horatia were in the back, their new evening dresses spread around them like petals on the leather seats. They drew up under the hotel's portico, where a doorman sprang forward to open the ladies' doors. Wilfred declined his offer to park the car in the area near the stables. He preferred to park it himself, especially as a couple of men in evening dress were watching him as they smoked. He drove a lap around the parking area, and the ladies heard him hooting his horn.

It had suddenly occurred to Bella that bringing Horatia might interfere with Bella's hopes for the evening. Tonight's dance was the first since Calvert had come home for the summer. After what had happened at the Christmas dance—which Bella was certain wouldn't have happened if Horatia had been present—she had dreamed of what was bound to happen tonight.

Calvert charmed everyone, even the chaperones. He looked handsome in his tuxedo, danced well, and paid such outrageous compliments to his partners that they grew flustered at first and then dissolved into giggles. Girls agreed Calvert was a great flirt who couldn't be taken seriously for a minute, but half of them were in love with him and all of them wanted to dance with him. And all of them were a little in awe of him.

At the Twelfth Night dance, Bella had observed the other girls whispering and looking eager and hopeful when he walked past. Bella was sure he was aware of the impact he had. He'd swaggered as he approached her and asked her to dance.

"I'm not sure. I might have promised this to Davy," she said languidly.

"Oh, for heaven's sake, Bella! You'd rather dance with me, wouldn't you?" He took her hand and led her to the dance floor. She watched him taking in her new green velvet dress, his grin widening. "Because I'd certainly like to dance with you. Especially as you look ravishing tonight—my, you *have* grown up!"

She'd put her hand lightly on his shoulder as the music began and said, "I saw you walk past, ignoring the other girls. Honestly, Calvert, you're like a rooster parading past the hens!" He'd laughed and said he'd been watching her with her own train of admirers—she was a little minx.

"For shame, Calvert! Is that any way to speak to a girl?"

"Oh certainly, if she's a pretty little minx like you." He pulled her closer.

Bella drew back and made a face to let him know she thought he was impossible, then lowered her eyes and noticed how nice it felt to have Calvert's arms around her. Minx indeed, she thought, she'd show him!

He'd danced with a few other girls while she danced with other men, then came back to dance with her again. Afterward she said airily, "That's enough of you for tonight, Calvert. People will talk if they see us dancing together anymore," and walked away.

As the evening wore on, from the corner of her eye she could see Calvert watching her. Every time she looked up, he was watching her. And he saw her watching him. *Well, well,* she thought. *How intriguing!* She was careful not to look his way again. He'd notice that.

At midnight, when everyone was pairing up to go in to supper, she sauntered past, laughing with her last partner, and Calvert grabbed her and pulled her next to him. "What *are* you doing!" she demanded, but he'd pulled her arm through his, whisking her into an empty cardroom beneath a bunch of mistletoe hanging on a red ribbon, and kissed her. It hadn't been a lighthearted kiss, but a long, lingering one, and it took Bella completely by surprise.

"Oh!" gasped Bella when she could speak. "Oh, Calvert!" She'd kissed a few boys before, more out of curiosity than anything else, but this was different. She tingled all over. She ought to protest.

"Bella, I've been dying to do this," he murmured, before kissing her again in a way that made Bella shiver and cling to him and forget about protesting. The two of them stayed under the mistletoe until the other dancers were heard coming back from the dining room. Calvert sighed and let her go. He'd squeezed her hand and gone to fetch her evening coat. Bella had forgotten where she was. She put her hand to her pounding heart and tried to get her breath back. Around her people were putting on their wraps and coats and exclaiming it had begun to snow.

"Has it?" Bella asked vacantly, wishing they weren't there and Calvert would come back and kiss her some more.

Davy Charbonneau looked at the snow and said, "There's an old sleigh in the barn. I say we get up a sleighing party."

"Oh yes, Davy, what fun!" exclaimed several of the girls.

"That would be splendid!" Bella agreed, imagining herself and Calvert snuggled under a rug in the sleigh.

She went home in a daze, and felt too blissfully happy to sleep. Her lips still felt the imprint of Calvert's. She shouldn't have been so free with her kisses, of course. It would be horrid to be gossiped about as one of the "fast" girls. But Calvert was due to go back to Harvard soon.

What did it mean if a man kissed you like that?

Her sisters had all married at nineteen or twenty, and Bella thought how surprised they'd be if she got married at seventeen. How divine if she could get married now and not have another five months of school.

Bella had dreamed away January and February in class doodling in the margins of her school textbooks, trying out the initials "IDM" in different fonts, for Isabella Drumheller Marshall, just to see how the initials would look monogrammed on sheets and tablecloths. She'd counted the days until he was home from college for the summer. And something told her not to mention the kissing to Horatia. She suspected Horatia was sweet on Calvert too, and since Bella wanted to still be friends with Horatia, she'd best keep her feelings for Calvert to herself.

By the night of the June dance, Bella had seen Calvert only a few times, and always in company, because Calvert was very popular. But he'd called her on the telephone and said he'd see her tonight. She was sure he'd find an opportunity to kiss her again. And perhaps he'd tell her he loved her then.

In the ladies' cloakroom the girls slipped off their evening wraps and handed them to the maid. Bella opened her little beaded bag and took out a small pot of rouge and a compact. She peeled off her white gloves and leaned across the dressing table toward the mirror, rubbing an index finger across the rouge, then spreading it expertly across both cheeks. "Here," she said, handing the pot to Horatia.

Horatia removed her gloves, picked up the pot, and asked anxiously, "How much?"

"Just a dab," said Bella. "You don't want to look like you've got scarlet fever. Or worse, like the girls from Kate Irish's. Here, let me do it."

"What girls? Kate Irish's is a boardinghouse for men," said Horatia innocently. "Why would the hired girls be painting?"

"Oh, Horatia! Don't you know! It's not just a boardinghouse." Her voice dropped to a whisper. "It's really a bawdy house. Jane told me."

"What's that?"

"A . . . a . . . sporting house," Bella whispered. "Men go there to play cards and gamble and drink, and then . . . they go upstairs with the girls. And do what married people do. It's all very wicked and shameful, and you must never, never let on you know about Kate Irish's, not to anybody. Especially not your parents or Frank and Calvert or any of the girls from school. Jane says everyone in Grafton knows, all the ladies know and simply hate it, but they pretend they don't, and they have to put up with it because they say Kate's is good for business in Grafton. Kate Irish spends a lot of money, has people working for her, not just the girls but hired men, and laundresses, and she buys a lot of whiskey and other supplies . . . but people think you're wicked for even knowing! Girls are supposed to be too pure."

"But if it's wicked, how does Jane know?"

"Oh, she's married. And married women know things like that because . . . they're married." She didn't think she ought to tell Horatia more just now, although Bella had pried a good deal of information out of Jane and had an idea what the wedding night involved. Enough that she couldn't stop thinking about it for long. If she were married to Calvert . . . she shivered . . . She *longed* to be married to Calvert.

She dabbed rouge on Horatia, then took her handkerchief and patted and rubbed a little savagely. She dabbed some on their lips and said, "Do this," and pressed her lips together. Then she took the compact and patted powder lightly onto Horatia's face, then puffed her cheeks and blew the excess away. "All done, Jezebel."

"Bella, truly, can you tell?"

"You can, a little. But Jane paints too, so she won't say anything to Mother, and your father's not here to see. Now, my turn."

Horatia patted Bella's face with the puff, then blew away a fine cloud. "There."

Critically they regarded their reflections again, turning this way and that, and resisted the temptation to add more rouge for good measure. They mustn't overdo it. The chaperones had sharp eyes.

Bella patted her bob. She'd promised her parents to grow her hair back, but she liked it short and modern, so she trimmed it slightly every month. Experience told her that her parents would eventually forget she was meant to be letting it grow long.

The two girls gave their evening dresses little pats and tweaks before drawing their gloves back on and taking a last look in the mirror. Bella thought her new high-waisted evening dress with its pale-blue silk underdress and darker lace overdress, with little beads on the bodice, looked particularly fetching. The shades of light blue and deeper blue brought out the color in her eyes. The crystal beads caught the light very sweetly, and Calvert was bound to like it, because it was cut rather low in the bosom. Bella wasn't sure it was ladylike to understand that, but she did.

Horatia's evening dress was simpler, pink with a green sash, a high neck and elbow-length sleeves, and she wore plain flat kid slippers with bows. She'd finally mastered the Gibson Girl pouf so her mother's pearl earbobs showed. Bella gave a satisfied smile at her own fashionably bobbed reflection in the mirror. Her dress was much more sophisticated. All things considered, she felt much more grown up than Horatia now. She was certain Horatia had never kissed a boy. She calculated whether Calvert would try to evade the chaperones to slip outside with her behind the rhododendron bushes. Couples were sometimes found kissing there, but if the chaperones spotted them leaving, it was embarrassing when the chaperones marched the couple back in.

"We *do* look well together," said Bella to their reflections. "Just like I always said."

"What if no one asks me to dance?" Horatia asked nervously. "Except Frank and Calvert. They promised Papa, but . . ."

Bella adjusted her headpiece with a feather in it. She'd have to make sure Horatia's dance card filled up so Calvert would dance with Bella. "You'll have partners. Come on, sister Jane will wonder what we're doing. Follow me, Horatia, and do what I do." They emerged from the cloakroom and found Jane and Wilfred waiting for them by the receiving line.

Jane and Wilfred went first. Jane introduced Miss Horatia Vann.

"Miss Vann, a pleasure," the manager said, echoed by his wife, who hoped she'd enjoy the evening. Horatia curtseyed nervously. Bella followed. She'd been down a receiving line many times by now, and the manager and his wife beamed and called her "my dear Miss Drumheller," said how delightful that she'd come, how lovely she looked tonight, and wished her a happy evening. The chaperones, next in line, scrutinized Horatia so forbiddingly that she was afraid they'd detected the rouge, but they smiled at Bella, saying what a pretty dress.

"They don't approve of me like they approve of you," Horatia whispered as they finished.

"They only approve of me because Papa owns the hotel," Bella muttered back. "And they're supposed to look stern so we'll be afraid to misbehave."

At the end of the receiving line they were taken over by young men who acted as "hosts," a kind of helper, Bella said. Their job was to slip dance cards over girls' gloved wrists and make sure they had partners. Davy Charbonneau, with brilliantined hair and wearing a tuxedo, came forward and said, "Hello, Bella, how jolly you're here at last . . . May I have the first, *Miss* Drumheller?"

Without waiting for her answer, he wrote his name on the first dance. Then Davy did his duty and put his name down for the second dance with Horatia.

Behind the potted palms the quartet was tuning up and there was a buzz of conversation. More girls were arriving in twos and threes with parents or married brothers and sisters, and hotel guests were drifting in from the dining room. Young men crowded round Bella, who smiled and fluttered her eyelashes and let them jostle each other to write their names on her dance card before saying, "I believe you know Miss Vann"—the way Miss Edmonia taught them you must do if you had a friend standing nearby. Good manners then required the young men to put their names on Horatia's dance card too. "See, I said you'd have partners," murmured Bella.

Finally Bella protested she had no dances left, they must ask Miss Vann, calculating that if Calvert didn't come in time to put his name down for a dance with Bella, Horatia wouldn't have a dance free for him either. She cast a sidelong glance at her friend. Horatia was looking prettier than Bella had ever seen her. Would Calvert admire her?

Bella began to wish Horatia had stayed home after all, then felt ashamed of wishing that. It would be hard to have a mother like Ellinder. She much preferred having a mother like Hilda, who wanted her daughters to enjoy themselves. Ellinder didn't seem to know who Horatia was half the time, and the other half she tried to forestall Horatia doing anything by saying "No" or "We'll see" or having one of her "turns," which amounted to the same thing as saying no.

If Horatia ever hoped to get married, Bella thought she'd have to elope, quickly, before Ellinder went into a decline and ruined everything.

Her thoughts returned to Calvert. Surely no gentleman would kiss a girl in that way unless he had what people called "intentions" to marry her. Horatia would be her maid of honor, of course, and then Horatia could get married—perhaps she could marry one of Bella's spare beaux, like Davy Charbonneau. He was quite good-looking and would inherit Chiaramonte, so Horatia would be very rich, or even Frank so they could be sisters-in-law, which would be jolly—and Bella could be her *matron* of honor. Rather satisfying to think of being first to be a Mrs. She'd never beat Horatia at anything else, since Horatia was awfully good at everything.

These thoughts filled her head as she scanned the new arrivals, standing on tiptoe to peer over men's shoulders and around girls' headdresses, but she didn't see Calvert anywhere. Now it was too late, her card was full.

And here came Frank, telling Horatia how pretty she looked, putting his name down for the first dance, the only one still vacant on Horatia's card. Good. Horatia was laughing with him about something, they were talking about Calvert . . . did that mean he was coming or not? She strained to hear, but two boys from her class were vying for her attention . . .

Frank turned to her. "Hello, Bella, do you have a dance for me? No? Unlucky for me you're so popular."

"Isn't it," Bella sighed. She had no dance left for Calvert, and even if she'd had one free, she'd have had to give it to Frank. How she hated these stupid rules!

Why was he so late? Oh, it was too bad of him!

Horatia was saying something to her and Frank. "Look! There's Evaline May talking to Orlando Conway! What a lovely shawl she has! I thought she wasn't fond of dances."

"She claims she isn't, but Aunt Teeny always likes to write up the first dance of the summer for the *Messenger*—the names of guests and the places they've come from—and offered Evaline May her best Spanish shawl if she'd come too, so Evaline May agreed. I think she gets a little bored with ladies' suffrage sometimes—it's not very jolly in the evenings. Look, there's an elderly man making his way over with the manager's wife, who seems to be introducing them. They're going to dance."

They heard the first strains of a waltz, and Davy Charbonneau appeared and held out his hand to Bella.

"Miss Vann, I believe this is my dance," said Frank, holding out a hand to Horatia.

She took it absently. "What's happened to Calvert?"

By Davy's side, Bella strained to hear Frank's answer. "Oh, you know Calvert. Sometimes he's where he's expected to be and sometimes he isn't. Perhaps he's just late. Besides, you're going to dance with me. We'll forget Calvert, not speak of him at all," Frank said firmly. "Serve him right. Now, pay attention or I'll step on your feet," Bella heard him say as Davy swept her away.

Bella was waltzing automatically with Davy, still scanning the ballroom, when she heard Frank say behind her, "Shall we overtake them?" And Horatia protesting, "You can't race on the dance floor, Frank!"

"No, you don't," cried Davy with spirit. "Away we go, Bella! We'll waltz them to the finish! Heigh-ho, Frank!"

And Bella and Horatia were waltzed in great sweeping steps, round the edge of the ballroom, until the girls were laughing and breathless and dizzy, and had momentarily forgotten to mind about Calvert, who had promised to be there to dance with them but wasn't.

Across the room, Evaline May, dancing sedately with the elderly hotel guest, drew back with a gasp, crying, "No!" It startled nearby dancers, who raised their eyebrows at each other. Had the elderly Lothario said something impertinent to Evaline May, of all people?

But he hadn't been impertinent. He was telling her about the telegram he'd just received from a business associate in Vienna. Two days previously, a Serbian lunatic had shot the archduke of Austria, the Austro-Hungarian heir, and his wife in a place called Sarajevo. "There's trouble brewing already between Austria and Serbia. If Austria attacks Serbia, Russia will support Serbia, and the European powers have alliances and treaties that will bring them into the conflict if there is one. My friend in Vienna thinks they're all poised for war—diplomatic communiqués have been flying. A great to-do in Europe is already building, a greater to-do than the wretched archduke deserves. And I hope, Miss Evaline, that you and your lady mother aren't planning a European sojourn. There's trouble coming, my dear, trouble for sure."

CHAPTER 10

It wasn't like Calvert to miss a dance, and Frank was uneasy because he had a good idea where Calvert was and why.

Frank had finished college three years ahead of Calvert and come home for good to find Aunt Teeny distressed by a recent arrival. A well-dressed middle-aged woman had stepped off the train in Grafton, introduced herself as Mrs. Irish, a widow, and hired a wagon from the livery stable and one of the Pine boys to drive it and had herself and her baggage taken to the old brick Stuart house down the river. She claimed to be the new owner.

Eddy Pine was curious. The old place had been built by a family of colored settlers long ago but had sat empty for years. He asked her why a white person would buy a nigger's old house.

She said it was a good size, and in a peaceful spot, some way out of town. She knew it needed fixing up, but she could see to that. She'd paid Eddy more generously than they'd agreed, and he'd come back to town to tell her story in a way that left a favorable impression.

The favorable impression was cemented by the employment she provided. She'd lost no time hiring workmen to repair the place, replace rotten wood and floor planks, mend the roof, and paint the bedrooms and paper the parlors. She placed orders for curtain fabrics and washstands and a full range of kitchen equipment at the Emporium, and before long shipments of furniture, big orders for beds and sofas and tables, were being unloaded at the river landing.

Teeny was one of the Grafton ladies who discussed how soon the new arrival might have her house in order so they could pay welcome calls and take cakes. They wouldn't embarrass her by visiting when everything was in a state.

But then, at the *Messenger* office, Teeny heard more. She kept her pulse on everything that happened in the valley in case it needed to be mentioned in the paper, and working among men as she did, Teeny overheard more male conversation than most women. That was how she learned the new arrival had bought quantities of whiskey and brandy, provisions and cigars. It seemed unlikely that a lone widow would require cigars and brandy. Unless she was a very odd sort of person.

Then young women arrived in groups of twos and threes by train, notably well dressed, with rather free manners and much luggage. Some claimed to be Mrs. Irish's daughters; others said they'd been hired to help with the housework. Before anyone could pay a welcome call, Mrs. Irish hung up a sign that said "Boardinghouse, Men Only" and offered a number of washerwomen steady employment.

Mrs. Irish's new establishment drew local men as well as male boarders. Teeny overheard talk of card games and betting in the boardinghouse parlors. This was bad enough, but ribald comments about the girls there left no doubt in her mind. Whores! She was shocked to her core. A sporting house in Grafton! As a decent woman she had to pretend she hadn't overheard, intended not to listen anymore, when a man mentioned Mrs. Irish's strange eyes. Yellow eyes. More male laughter.

Teeny's expression was indignant. "I felt sick when I heard that, Frank. I never knew a person to have yellow eyes except the girl my mother raised, Katie. We used to call her Katie Irish until my father made us stop. He said she was one of the family and we had to call her Katie Marshall. So we did, but we hated her, and I think Mama didn't really like her either. She had eyes like a bobcat. I remember I refused to ask her to be a bridesmaid at my wedding. I told Mama it would be like a wild animal slinking down the aisle. Mama was a saintly woman, one of the best women who ever lived, people still remember her that way. She set a big store by charity and said it was uncharitable not to have Katie as a bridesmaid. But Katie was trouble. One day, the sly thing stole Mama's jewelry and left. We heard later she'd been seen on board a riverboat with the captain, and people said she'd run off with him. And afterward, Mama didn't want to hear Katie's name mentioned, so of course people were careful not to.

"Nobody knew what happened to her. Nobody heard, nobody cared. Now this . . . this bawdy house and Mrs. Irish with yellow eyes. It has to be the same person. And she does so much business in town that ladies are expected to turn a blind eye. Thank heavens we didn't call on her!"

Frank tried not to smile at his aunt's vehemence and said, "But if it really is Katie, why come back to Grafton?"

"I've no idea. But mind you and Calvert keep away from that . . . place. If it is Katie, she'll be up to some mischief. She was always a sly little thing."

When Calvert came home from college that summer, it didn't surprise Frank that he'd soon made his way to Kate Irish's place. He liked a game of cards, women always liked him, and Calvert, Frank knew, liked women. From what Calvert said, Kate Irish had made herself agreeable when she found out his last name. Calvert had won at cards and came home late smelling of perfume and whiskey and cigars.

At first Frank laughed and shook his head and said Teeny mustn't find out. Through most of their lives Frank had often tried to rein in his younger brother's reckless behavior, or covered up for him. Calvert usually laughed and shrugged it off. He didn't mean any harm, just a young man's lusty male spirits was how Frank tried to rationalize it. When Calvert slept through breakfast, Frank would tell Aunt Teeny he'd been up late reading lawbooks. Still, the amount of time Calvert spent at Kate Irish's began to worry Frank. He'd been off playing cards often since the summer holiday began.

Frank finally remonstrated, "Look, old man, aside from the fancy women, these card games at that woman's place aren't really the thing, though I know half the men in Grafton play there. Even the Charbonneaus, I hear. They're sure to be fixed, and you could lose everything. Leave that place alone."

Calvert said, "Oh, Frank, if only you knew. Fixed? Of course they are. I know how to cheat at cards, so it's easy to spot. The first time I went, Kate was watching me every time I looked up. I wasn't cheating, by the way, but I could tell the dealer was. I still won. When I got up to go, she asked my name, and when I said Marshall, she got a strange look on her face, as if she was excited. When she handed me my hat, she said she knew a Marshall family secret even Teeny didn't know. One that would destroy Teeny's peace of mind forever if it got out. She'd kept the secret for thirty years. She'd tell me what it was if I paid her. If I win at cards, I turn the money over to her, and when she's satisfied I've paid enough, she'll tell me."

"Blackmail!" exclaimed Frank. "Stay away from her, Cal."

"I can't, Frank. Teeny raised us. We need to know what this secret is, then decide what to do."

Frank sighed. "Once she's got her hooks into you, do you think she'll just let go? Just tell you whatever this secret is and leave it at that? Cal, she'll keep blackmailing you."

"She can't do much when I'm not here, Frank. It's nearly the fall term. I'm no use to her unless I'm playing cards at her place, and I'll be gone soon. You concentrate on your newspaper."

"Wish I could," said Frank glumly. "I'd cover more of the war news. Teeny just wants to cover tea parties."

The elderly gentleman who'd predicted to Evaline May there'd be "trouble" following the Austrian archduke's assassination had been proved right. War had broken out in Europe that summer, but it was far away from Grafton. Few people took much notice of it except for the Charbonneaus, who had European business connections. Aunt Teeny thought it was pointless for the *Messenger* to report news from far away. People were mainly interested in local news, births, deaths, weddings, church bake sales, and revivals. They didn't want to read about Europe any more than they wanted to read about votes for women.

The previous November, Teeny's younger daughter in Kingsport had had a fourth baby who was born prematurely, and both the baby and Sarah were so poorly that Sarah wrote begging her mother to come help her. Evaline May, who'd had no success in persuading her mother to run stories in favor of women's suffrage, urged Teeny to go. What if the baby died because Sarah couldn't look after it properly? How would her mother feel if Sarah died too? And what about Sarah's older children?

With such worries playing on her conscience, Teeny decided she had to relinquish control of the paper to Frank, and departed for a long stay in Kingsport.

The paper took a serious turn at once. Frank decided the *Messenger* would carry a piece about the European conflict in every issue. He also published articles written by Evaline May about female suffrage, even writing editorials in favor himself, though he refused to publish her pieces on pacifism. They weren't necessary.

Still, when Calvert came home at Christmas, between parties and dances and spooning with Bella, he reported that up north, people were saying that America would be pulled into the war eventually.

"I doubt that. President Wilson doesn't want war! It's got nothing to do with America."

"America's unprepared," said Calvert. "The army's been run down. And they say there's trouble in Mexico, and the Germans are there helping to stir it up against the US, saying the Mexicans ought to invade and reclaim Mexican territory in Texas."

"What?" spluttered Frank. "That's preposterous! Wilson's made it clear that America's neutral."

"Officially, but we're supplying the Allies with food and munitions. Not exactly neutral."

The rumor America might join the Allies prompted a new song everyone was singing that Christmas, "I Didn't Raise My Boy to Be a Soldier."

It didn't dent the song's popularity when, months later, in May, a German U-boat sank a British ocean liner, the *Lusitania*, off the coast of Ireland, killing over a hundred United States citizens who were traveling on it. The *Messenger* carried a full-page report, and Frank wrote an editorial that America would be pulled into the war sooner or later. Germany was getting too powerful.

People in Grafton were inclined to skip the war coverage. They agreed the Americans killed on the *Lusitania* were a tragedy, but if England was at war, they should have thought twice about taking passage on an English ship. Europe was far away.

CHAPTER 11

Summer 1915

In the summer of 1915, the *Messenger* sent a photographer several times a week to cover what the young people of Grafton were up to. The older generation couldn't remember a social whirl like it. It was started by the Drumhellers, who held a costume ball in Bella's honor at their home on Little Frog Mountain. Bella was in her element as Marie Antoinette in hoopskirts and a white wig with pearls. The hotel organized a riverboat trip with supper and dancing on deck. This set off more parties, hayrides, a fox-and-hounds treasure hunt on horseback, picnics, and barn dances.

Vann's Emporium kept selling out of Chinese lanterns and fireworks.

Up at the hotel there'd been a tennis tournament for the men—Bella and Horatia cheered on Calvert and Frank, and the *Messenger* had a picture of Calvert holding up the trophy and looking particularly handsome in his tennis whites. There was a croquet tournament, where girls and men played in teams against each other, and then mixed pairs had another playoff between guests and locals. There was a photo of Horatia and Bella wielding their mallets, with a caption "Out of the way, fellas! Here come the ladies!" when they and the Marshall brothers played together in the mixed man-and-girl team.

In mid-August, there was a full-page report on the horse show at Chiaramonte, and the supper given by the Charbonneaus afterward with tables laid in the garden and a string quartet from New Orleans who played Italian airs, with dancing and fireworks afterward. There was a large photo of Davy in his dinner jacket, in the receiving line with his parents. The caption beneath said, "Reviving a family tradition from Sicily! Mr. and Mrs. Charbonneau celebrate Assumption Day at home."

Davy tried to get Bella to walk in the garden with him. She laughed and said no, but couldn't help flirting a little when she said it.

That summer, romance seemed to thrive in the warm night air. Most of the young men and all the girls were on the verge of being in love. Horatia wore the locket with the boyish photos of Frank and Calvert and pretended to herself that Calvert was her sweetheart.

The summer was drawing to a close, and the last days of August would see a procession of guests crowding onto the platform of the Rehoboth Springs train station with their luggage, reminiscing with their new acquaintances about the wonderful times they'd had, while waiting for the trains that would take them home. But before that, there was the last dance of summer to look forward to.

Hilda Drumheller had convinced Albert it was plain as day that Davy Charbonneau was in love with Bella and it was only a matter of time before he proposed and his youngest daughter was married. Albert had pulled out all the stops to make the evening extra special.

The evening of the dance coincided with a full moon. A dance band hired from New York had come down by train, and there would be fireworks just before midnight. Supper was to be lobster Newburg—a crate of lobsters on ice was shipped down on the train from Maine—and

Sally Lunn and champagne cup. Miss Willa had been overwhelmed with orders for new dancing dresses.

The evening of the dance, Bella and Horatia were in Bella's bedroom, where they'd been closeted since lunch. They'd lain down to rest with cucumber slices on their faces, washed their hair, and done their nails. Their new dresses were laid out across the chaise lounge under the window, confections of taffeta and tulle in the latest tunic style, belted with a satin cummerbund held in place by a silk flower over a slender, ankle-length skirt. There were headbands to match with a saucy little feather in each.

"You need bobbed hair, to get the right effect," Bella had insisted.

So Horatia stood in her chemise on a sheet in front of the looking glass in Bella's bedroom and clutched a handful of dark hair Bella had just chopped off.

"Bella," she quavered.

"Keep your courage up. I'm nearly done. There! You can look now." Bella had a last snip and pulled the towel off her friend's shoulders. "You'll find it's much cooler in the heat."

Horatia turned her newly shorn head this way and that. "Oh, Bella! Oh dear! What will my parents say? This is bound to give Mamma one of her turns." She sighed. "Good luck I'm spending the night with you after the dance, but tomorrow . . . Oh dear!"

Bella gathered the pile of dark hair into the wastebasket and tossed the sheet in her laundry hamper. "Parents get used to things," she said airily. "After a while they hardly notice. And it does look nice. We'd better dress. Jane and Wilfred will be here any minute. Don't you simply adore our dresses? Miss Willa wasn't sure she could finish them by tonight, which would have been awful considering it's the last dance of the summer before Cal . . . the men go back to college." She shook out a new pair of silk stockings and sat on a little cushioned stool to put them on.

If Bella had been looking at her friend instead of admiring pale silk sliding over her slender calf, she would have seen something wary in Horatia's expression.

"Calvert isn't going just yet, said he wants to stay for the Blackberry Picnic," said Horatia.

"Good!" Bella fastened the garters, smiled at her stockinged toes, and slipped her feet into her dancing shoes.

"Here, you first." She passed the rouge to Horatia, who now applied it as expertly as Bella. They'd perfected a ruse to avoid any close scrutiny, dashing past the Drumheller parents in a rush so as not to keep Jane and Wilfred waiting.

"Calvert taught me the turkey trot when he called on Thursday," Bella confided. "You know, he comes up while the judge has a nap after lunch, and usually there's somebody for him to play tennis with, but last Thursday all the men were busy, so Calvert taught me on the porch. When Papa found out he said if the chaperones catch anyone doing it, they'll stop the orchestra playing."

"Calvert taught me too, when he and Frank came to dinner last week," murmured Horatia. "After Mamma had gone to bed. He says it's all the rage at Harvard. Perhaps we could do it out on the lawn, where the chaperones can't see."

"Mmm," Bella muttered, pressing her rouged lips together.

At the mirror, Horatia leaned over to put on her earbobs. "Calvert keeps talking about the war with Papa. Some Harvard men have gone off to France, to fight for the Allies or be stretcher-bearers or medics. He says if he went, he'd learn to fly an airplane and join the flying corps. I hope he doesn't, don't you?"

Bella stopped fastening the strap on her dancing shoe. She sat up and stared at her friend in amazement. "What? Calvert? The war's in Europe. It doesn't have anything to do with America."

"But some people think it does. Frank and Calvert have been arguing all summer with Papa about it. Calvert keeps talking about the

Preparedness Movement, how the American Defense League speaker he'd heard at Harvard says the country needs a regular army. Papa told him that's nonsense, President Wilson isn't convinced about the army and even if he was, America wouldn't go to war over an Austrian archduke. Calvert said the war may be coming to us, Germans are involved in Mexico on our borders, and there's a revolution there and they'll help Mexico take back Texas. Papa says it's just that Calvert and Terence want to fly airplanes . . . Bella? What's wrong?"

Bella could scarcely draw breath. It felt like someone had knocked the wind out of her. Calvert go to France? He seemed to have said a great deal about airplanes and France to the Vanns and nothing to her.

"Bella? Your expression . . . whatever's wrong?"

"Nothing!" muttered Bella. "Why don't Terence and Calvert just strap on wings and flap them! Airplanes! Fasten me up. There's Wilfred's car coming."

At the dance Bella ignored Calvert and began flirting with the young men who were crowding round her to get their names on her dance card. She went off to dance with Davy, so Calvert danced with Horatia.

Bella was watching Horatia and Calvert over Davy's shoulder. Horatia and Calvert were laughing about something, and then Horatia's eyes were closed and she was smiling as Calvert hugged her. As if she were very happy, Bella thought sourly. Airplanes. Could Horatia be sweet on Calvert? Bella hated them both. She wanted to go to the ladies' room and cry.

For the next dance Bella was staring miserably at her card to see who was her partner when Calvert appeared, crumpled the card, and took her hand. She tried to resist, but he muttered, "Come along, Miss Drumheller. Don't make me throw you over my shoulder like a caveman. The spectacle would be too much for the chaperones."

"Why should I come along? Don't you want to dance with Horatia again? And she says you're going away, off t-to . . . to war . . . in France!"

Bella choked back tears and tried to tug her hand back. "Horatia knows all about it!"

The music started for the next dance, and a young man in a tuxedo was looking everywhere for Bella. "Let me go. There's my partner for the next dance."

"No, he isn't, minx. I am." Calvert put his arm round Bella's waist and half dragged, half danced her out onto the porch despite her protests. All around them the hotel, the lawn, the trees, and the summerhouse were bathed in eerie silvery light. Calvert pulled Bella to the steps and picked her up, carried her across the lawn.

"Calvert, if you please, leave me alone!"

He put her down at a distance from the porch where no one sitting outside could overhear. The moonlight was bright enough to etch their shadows on the grass as sharply as if it were day.

"Bella, there are things I want to say to you. Yes, I am thinking of going to France, only for a while. I want to get away from Grafton for two reasons. First, there's a problem with someone who knows something I have to keep from Aunt Teeny, but with Teeny in Kingsport and me at college, the person can't put pressure on me or do as much damage to Teeny. I can't explain now, Bella, but I'll tell you about it one day.

"And yes, the second thing is, I'm thinking of joining a flying corps. I love airplanes. Terence and I've talked about it many times, and we've decided aviation will be the coming thing and we could start an aviation business after we graduate. I'm not like Frank. He's happy here with the newspaper, in an office all day, but I never wanted to be a lawyer cooped up in an office or courtroom. It's Aunt Teeny's idea, but too dull a life for me. If America goes to war, I'm determined to make the best of it and learn to fly."

"How interesting all that is. I'm going in." She tried to pull her wrist out of his grip.

"But, Bella, I love you. Would you wait for me?"

Bella said "Oh!" in a subdued voice. He'd never actually said "I love you" before.

"Bella." He lifted her chin until she was looking at him in the moonlight.

Bella stared up at him, and a tear ran down her cheek. "How long would you be gone?"

"I don't know. Until the war's over, I expect. But people say that shouldn't be long now."

"And where would you go afterward? With your airplanes?"

"Terence thinks California. Teeny won't like it, and Frank will say it's reckless, and I'll have to put my inheritance into it, but Terence and I've been looking into airplanes for the last few years. And California sounds like a pleasant place. I'm sure you'd love it, and . . ."

"I don't know—first you want to go to war, then you want to go to California. If I moved away, it would break my mother's heart, and I'd hate being separated from all the family."

"Bella, we've known each other all our lives, and I can't do without you now. You can't do without me, can you? Aren't you my girl?" He pulled her closer. "You belong with me. We'll have an exciting life. I promise. And I promise to fly you home to visit your family in my airplane whenever you like."

She sighed and put her arms around his neck. "I don't know, Calvert."

They swayed together, not quite dancing, holding on, slowly across the moonlit lawn. If only the night would go on forever. Just like this, Calvert's arms around her. It was perfect. It wasn't California. If only Calvert didn't hate the idea of being a lawyer!

A shout from the porch made them jump apart. "Yoo-hoo, Calvert! You've been discovered! Everyone's wondering where you two went. Bella, there's a lot of cross young men looking for you. But what a good idea, let's all dance in the moonlight!" And suddenly there were couples spilling out onto the porch, clattering down the steps, laughing and chatting and joining Bella and Calvert on the lawn.

"Oh damn!" Calvert muttered. "Bella," he said urgently, "this has to be our secret for the time being. I shan't say anything to Frank, nor Aunt Teeny. Don't say anything to your mother or Jane or Horatia. I don't want Ka . . . anyone . . . to learn I care for you so much."

"Oh, Calvert! Very well, I won't."

"Cross your heart and hope to die?"

"Cross my heart and hope to die."

It wasn't until she was back home and ready for bed that she wondered, *What exactly am I meant not to mention to anyone? Are Calvert and I engaged? Or not?* She longed to talk it over with Horatia, ask her opinion, but Horatia was asleep already, and anyway, she'd promised. *Bother,* thought Bella, and fell asleep.

CHAPTER 12

September 1915

Between the dance and the Blackberry Picnic, Bella had seen Calvert almost every day, but girls had a very hard time getting away anywhere private with a young man when surrounded by friends, Bella thought, especially when your own home was overrun with little nieces and nephews, Horatia was always by your side, or your mother constantly wanted you for this or that.

The afternoon of the Blackberry Picnic was the last time they'd see each other before Christmas, because Calvert was off on the train next day. Bella had persuaded her family to go early, hoping Calvert would be there. She watched for him as the clearing filled with people and picnics, and a supply of fireworks was stored underneath the long trestle tables that were placed end to end. A group of men had started the bonfire, and Bella marshaled her army of nieces and nephews to carry water from the spring to fill the coffee- and teapots bubbling on the bonfire before distributing pails and buckets for blackberry picking.

Around her, women carried platters and bowls and cakes, enough food to feed an army.

Families with children who'd spent the summer at the hotel had gone home for the start of the school year, but Albert Drumheller had persuaded other guests it would be a shame to miss the Blackberry Picnic, a charming local custom a century and a half old and one of the attractions of the area. The hotel guests arrived by jitney, followed by the hotel wagon loaded with rugs and cushions and picnic baskets of cold chicken, ham in aspic, and charlotte russe. They stood a little apart from the bustle and the children chasing each other and banging their buckets. Albert advised the ladies to taste the iron water from the spring and shepherded the men to observe the view from the top of the Old Man of the Mountain rock, where a jovial group of Grafton men were drinking whiskey from tin cups.

Two spinster ladies from the hotel had brought sketching pads and were settled in folding chairs, drawing the Old Man of the Mountain under the direction of Orlando Conway, a local artist who dashingly divided his time between New Orleans and his picturesque cabin and studio beyond the Charbonneau family's plantation at Chiaramonte.

Albert had prevailed on Orlando to hold sketching classes at the hotel that summer for the hotel guests, and Evaline May had signed up for them. She and Orlando had set tongues wagging in the spring and early summer, often seen out driving together in her nippy little roadster. Evaline May acquired some new hats for these outings, and it had looked as if they were "keeping company." Aunt Teeny had mixed feelings when she heard the gossip that it might be a match for Evaline May at last. In general she disapproved of artists and their loose morals, but Teeny was prepared to welcome almost any applicant for Evaline May's hand.

But that romance, such as it was, came to nothing. The classes had proved extremely popular with the female guests, not least because Orlando was a forty-five-year-old bachelor with a goatee, silk handkerchiefs, a flamboyant manner, and ingratiating manners with the ladies, whose sketches he fulsomely admired. Several of them had remarked on the curiosity of such a charming man not being married, especially Miss Euphemia Joiner, from Ohio, the only child and heiress of a department store magnate in Cleveland. She wondered about it a great deal. Despite Evaline May glowering at her from behind her sketch pad, Miss Euphemia hadn't missed a single lesson the entire summer. She was rude to Evaline May when Evaline May tried to persuade her to sign a petition to their congressman.

Bella idly watched as Orlando stood by Miss Euphemia, pointing out perspectives while she gazed up at him admiringly. The other lady, Miss Martha something or other, was obviously trying to get his attention, and failing. Bella, who was very hungry, swiped up a finger of boiled lemon frosting on a cake Jane had brought. In the process she gouged a lump of cake. She thought she might as well eat that too, when Horatia appeared.

"Horatia, look at Miss Euphemia. Do you think she's setting her cap for Orlando? Look how she keeps calling him to look at her paper. She wants his complete attention. He keeps bending over her sketch, almost like he's bowing. Every time he tries to see what poor old Miss Martha's doing, Miss Euphemia tugs his sleeve so he'll turn back to her. And Evaline May—good Lord, she's drinking whiskey with the men—seems to be looking hard in the other direction."

"Yes, he does look caught between the two . . . Bella, Jane's cake . . . what happened? It looks like a rat made a hole in it!" Horatia exclaimed.

"Hmm, it does a little." Bella licked her finger and tried to smooth frosting over the hole.

"Since you've already ruined it, you might as well just cut a piece," said Horatia. "It wouldn't look any worse, and I'm starving. It'll be ages till the preachers say the blessing and we can eat. They always compete to see who can pray the longest."

"They like having a captive audience," Bella said, sighing. "Stand here so the children can't see, or they'll want some too," she added, locating a knife and surreptitiously cutting out two pieces. "Jane will think it's one of the boys." The two girls ate cake furtively out of their hands.

"I saw you, Bella," said Davy Charbonneau, coming up behind them. "Will you give me a kiss not to tell Reverend Merriman?"

"I'll give you some cake instead. Look over there. Do you think Miss Euphemia Joiner and Orlando Conway are flirting?"

All three young people turned to stare at the couple, whose heads were very close together. Now Orlando's arm was almost, but not quite, draped over Miss Euphemia's shoulder as he pointed to something on her sketch pad. Bella giggled.

"Oh look, there's Frank and Calvert, talking to Mamma, and she's waving me to come back. Calvert promised to say goodbye to her before he goes off tomorrow. It's one of her good days, fortunately. Do I have crumbs?" Horatia rubbed her hand across her mouth.

Bella watched Horatia join her parents and the two Marshalls. Calvert was taking his time saying goodbye to Mrs. Vann, who was sitting in a camp chair.

Davy gave her arm a little shake.

"What?" asked Bella.

"I asked you if you'd eat supper with me—our cook made Brunswick stew and a jelly roll—and watch the fireworks after."

"Oh!"

The fireworks were known to be a courting opportunity mostly sanctioned by parents, provided no one ventured entirely out of sight. During the fireworks, couples sweet on each other would walk a little ways off, hold hands in the shadows, perhaps kiss if they dared.

"Oh, Davy. I don't think . . . No!" Bella stammered distractedly, gazing in Calvert's direction. If only she could find a little privacy with Calvert during the fireworks!

Then it occurred to her—the shape-shifter's cave. It was a climb, but she'd worn stout boots for the walk up Frog Mountain with the children.

She was becoming quite fast, she thought. Well, she didn't care.

Davy was saying something else. "Did you hear me, Bella? Or are you too busy watching Calvert? I said, Calvert was at Kate Irish's place two nights ago. You shouldn't pay him so much attention. He's not what you think he is."

Bella made a mighty effort to keep her expression bland. "Hmm? Where?" she asked, as if she didn't know what he was talking about.

"Kate Irish's! Don't pretend you're too pure to know it's a sporting house. Everyone knows."

"It's horrid of you to speak to me like that! How do you know this? Were you there too?" Bella felt cold with the shock of what he'd just said.

"No, I wasn't, but two of my friends were there playing cards. There's always a game in Kate Irish's front room. Half the men in Grafton go. And Calvert's there most nights. They called him to join the game, but he said not tonight, he had business upstairs."

Bella stared at him coldly. "I don't believe you."

"It's not idle gossip! My friends say one of the girls is expecting. They think it must be Calvert's, and he has to pay off Kate. People have *seen* him paying off Kate."

Bella narrowed her eyes. "How coarse of you to tell me such a vile and wicked story! And insulting!"

"Bella, I care for you. I wish you cared for me, but if you don't, at least take warning about Calvert. Bella, please. Calvert isn't worth it."

"Go!" She stamped her foot. "Get away from me! You're hateful, and I'll never speak to you again as long as I live."

"Bella . . ."

"Go away!" She crossed her arms and turned her back. Davy turned on his heel and went.

Hot tears of betrayal filled her eyes. Calvert had said there was an unpleasant business . . . unpleasant business that would affect his family. What if Davy was right and one of the fancy girls was having his baby? A fancy girl! Teeny and Frank and Evaline May and her sister, Sarah, would be appalled. How could he have asked Bella if she was his girl, said she belonged with him, wanted her to go to California with him! What ought she to do? How should she behave with him now?

The children were coming back, showing her their buckets and wooden pails full and their mouths and hands stained purple. Bella bit her tongue hard to keep from crying. She took pails of berries and pretended to count to make sure no one had been lost in the bushes, but truthfully, she wouldn't have known if half the children had been missing. In front of the Old Man of the Mountain with the two preachers, her father was calling for quiet so he could make the annual speech and grace could be said. Frank and Calvert were still talking to Horatia and her parents.

Bella felt numb. She wanted to run across the clearing and scream and shake Calvert, force him to deny it.

Just then Albert stepped forward and called again for quiet. Torn between misery and fury, Bella struggled to breathe as he launched into what Bella knew would be a lengthy welcome. As he did every year, he reminded the people of Grafton how blessed they were to have lived their lives in this paradise between the mountains, where nature had been tamed so that business and agriculture might thrive. They were all blessed to be citizens of the United States of America, land of the free, and they honored the founding settlers of Grafton who had been led from the Old World to this spot a century and a half ago, to lay the foundations of the peace and prosperity Grafton presently enjoyed. Unlike in the old, unenlightened world of Europe, where the Great War was raging at present. Americans should give thanks they had no part in it.

At the mention of war, Frank shook his head and said something to Mr. Vann. Mr. Vann looked serious and nodded. Probably more about the war. Frank took every opportunity to discuss the war now. Frank leaned over to say something to Calvert and Horatia. Calvert put an arm around Horatia's shoulders as he leaned forward to hear. Bella was prepared to be jealous of everyone, and noticed Horatia was looking at him . . . rather adoringly. As if Horatia herself was sweet on Calvert. It hadn't worried Bella before. Now she thought Horatia and Calvert . . . maybe there was something between them. How could he ask if Bella was his girl when he had a . . . a . . . a . . . harlot at Kate Irish's place! And now flirting with Horatia! Bella felt dizzy.

Calvert looked up and saw her. He raised his hand, smiled, and waved at her to join them.

Bella was in turmoil. She hated him at the moment, but Calvert was going back to Harvard tomorrow and she wouldn't see him for months. For the first time in her life, Bella struggled to control the emotions running away with her. She mustn't be angry. She mustn't cry. Not now. Not now. She made a huge effort to stifle her distress. She told herself Davy was a filthy liar and she didn't believe him for a minute. Calvert loved her. They were engaged. Practically. Calvert was true as anything.

Except . . . Calvert spent time at the Vanns'. Bella was jealous—first the harlot at Kate Irish's place. Now Horatia . . . Bella ground her teeth. She *hated* them!

When the first blessing got underway, Bella picked up the mutilated cake and sidled stealthily around the crowd, whose heads were mostly bowed. She made her way to the edge of the clearing where Josiah had placed chairs for Ellinder and himself, and where the two Marshalls sat on a blanket with Horatia. Horatia smiled a welcome, pointed at the cake, and mouthed, "Hiding it from Jane?" Then Ellinder frowned and nudged her, and she bowed her head again to listen to the droning preacher.

Calvert scooted back to make room for her on the blanket. "I had to say goodbye to Aunt Ellinder," he whispered, "but I've done that now. Let's find somewhere to watch the fireworks away from everyone else."

Bella stopped herself from snapping, *Did you say goodbye to Horatia too?*

Instead she put a finger in the icing and wrote, "S-shift cave?"

The blessing was going on interminably, and the Vanns and Frank had their heads bowed. Calvert raised his eyebrows quizzically and she nodded. He grinned, put his hand over hers, and used her finger to obliterate the words. He looked around to see if their companions were watching, but they seemed to be attending to the preacher. He quickly lifted her hand to his mouth, licking the icing off her finger with his tongue. Bella's breathing quickened and her anger calmed. No, she *would not* believe a word against Calvert. Davy was jealous, that was all. It couldn't be true.

Bella had had no appetite for the picnic, barely spoke to the Vanns, was impatient for the after-dinner speeches and the singing to be over. Never had the sun taken so long to set.

There was a flurry of activity as people packed up food, and children were sent over to the edge of the clearing for their own bonfire and ghost stories, while the fireworks were set up.

"Quick! Before anyone sees us," Calvert said, and took her hand, pulling her through the bushes to the narrow path up the side of the mountain.

When they reached the cave, it was dark. Out of breath, they sank down on the broad stone in front of the cave's entrance. It was still warm from the heat of the day. Bella was catching her breath and trying to think what to say when Calvert turned to her and covered her mouth with his. Anger and jealousy, and a need for reassurance, made her reckless and passionate and soon she was lying down. Neither she nor Calvert took the slightest interest in the fireworks after all.

They lay for a while after the fireworks finished. From below came the sounds of people calling their children, packing up picnic baskets with a rattle of crockery. Calvert rolled onto his elbow and watched as Bella sat up and straightened her clothes. "We have to go back before they miss us," he said, not moving. "But I could stay here like this forever."

"Calvert, it will be all right, won't it?"

He put out a hand and stroked her face, then smoothed her collar. "Of course it will be all right," he said, pulling her to him and burying his face in her hair. "My own Bella?" he whispered in her ear.

"Oh yes, Calvert."

Despite the narrow path that meant they had to walk single file, they held hands and made their way back down to the picnic ground in the dark. People were shaking quilts and collecting their berries, their children, and their dogs, preparing to leave. The hotel jitney had already left. Wilfred and some other men who'd driven up in their automobiles were cranking the motors, and others were hitching up horses to their wagons or carts or lighting lanterns for the walk down the dirt road. Older children were teasing younger ones that the shape-shifter was going to get them in the dark. Many younger ones were crying.

Frank was calling Calvert to hurry, Evaline May wanted to get back. Calvert squeezed Bella's hands and went.

Riding home with her parents and Jane and Wilfred, Bella pretended to doze off so she wouldn't have to join in the talk and could think about what she'd just done. She was uneasy. Had anyone seen them climbing up to the cave? If so, her reputation would be in tatters for going off with Calvert in the dark. A girl was easily ruined by gossip. And a disgraced girl made people point the finger at her family and commiserate, because it meant she'd been brought up wrong or was just "bad" to begin with. The prospect of people laughing snidely at her parents was unbearable, but Bella was torn about how wicked she ought to feel. She was sure she ought to feel remorse.

She didn't. She was sure of Calvert now. It no longer mattered if he had been to Kate Irish's. It didn't matter if Horatia liked him. They'd announce their engagement at the Twelfth Night Ball, and she'd magnanimously renounce a Christmas wedding so they wouldn't have to wait another year. She and her mother and sisters would spend the next six months organizing a June wedding and her trousseau . . . She was happy again. She'd find a way to bear California for a few years. Then they could come back to Grafton. She couldn't possibly be jealous of a pregnant prostitute or Horatia *now*.

CHAPTER 13

Calvert left for Harvard on the morning train. And everything seemed to change as the autumn drew on. Parties and gatherings became fewer and fewer for lack of men. Some were off at college, like Calvert, while others thought it would be an adventure to go train as recruits in the new military camps set up by the Preparedness Movement. People still sang "I Didn't Raise My Boy to Be a Soldier," but there was more talk of the war and German U-boats.

Bella and Horatia saw less of each other. Young ladies who'd finished their schooling were expected to make themselves useful at home until they got married. Horatia dutifully wrote notes for her mother, polished silver, and arranged flowers to put on the graves of her dead brothers and sisters. She persuaded Ellinder to attend a new Bible class. She rode her mare in the afternoons.

These kinds of activities were a dreadful bore, and Horatia sometimes felt she missed school. Just a little.

Bella decided to copy Evaline May and learn to drive. She had Miss Willa make her a new duster, and ordered a fetching hat and veil and persuaded Wilfred to give her driving lessons in his Ford. It was harder than it looked, and Wilfred refused to let her practice anywhere but in the driveway.

Since Wilfred wouldn't let Bella drive his car down to town, Horatia rode up one day for lunch and a demonstration of Bella's driving skills. Bella shrugged when Horatia pointed out that the car had a bad dent in the front. "Well, I am still learning, you know! I can do most of it. It's just that my turns aren't very good. I hit a tree yesterday, unfortunately. And sometimes the car just goes where it wants, whatever I do. And I haven't quite got the hang of making it go backward yet," said Bella, climbing into the driver's seat. "But I'll show you how thrilling it is! You grab the handle and crank a bit, then jump in."

Horatia cranked and jumped in and held on as Bella lurched forward and they went chugging across the lawn.

"Off like a wild herd of turtles! Isn't this fun?" cried Bella.

They went faster and faster. "Slow down!" cried Horatia.

"I'm trying. Oh dear," cried Bella. "Hang on!"

Horatia screamed as the car mowed down a large boxbush in front of the house, but at least it brought them to a stop. They surveyed the damaged bush in silence.

Horatia gathered up her skirts and climbed down, muttering, "Never again, Bella, never again!"

Horatia added a PS to Frank's next letter to Calvert: "Bella's latest pash is driving, and she gave me quite a terrifying ride. She's still learning and has persuaded her father to buy her a little runabout of her own once she's mastered the finer points. Such as stopping. She's seen a picture of a yellow one and fixed her heart on that. It does seem unwise of Mr. Drumheller."

There was another PS in the next letter. "Orlando Conway is married to Miss Euphemia Joiner! He calls her Fanny and she calls him Orly. Everyone is very much surprised."

Miss Euphemia Joiner had never gone home to Ohio but had married Orlando Conway instead, quietly on a Saturday afternoon in the Baptist church a month after the Blackberry Picnic. There was an announcement in the *Messenger* that the nuptials had taken place, saying all well-wishing friends would find them at home at the groom's cottage and studio, where they intended to reside.

"She snatched him right from under poor Evaline May's nose," Hilda said disapprovingly, echoing what many people in Grafton thought.

Albert Drumheller gave the couple a belated wedding reception in the hotel ballroom. Teeny came back to Grafton specially to attend and lend moral support to Evaline May, who she insisted must attend the reception as if nothing had happened. It would never do to look jilted and resentful. So, with her mother beside her, Evaline May attended, in a dashing new hat Teeny had brought her from Kingsport.

"You have to admire her fortitude, don't you!" murmured Horatia. "People are staring to see how she's taking it."

"So embarrassing! I'd hate it if it were me," replied Bella.

The colorful leaves of October gave way to bare branches and cold winds in November without a hotel dance to cheer the girls up. Albert canceled the October dance, blaming the lack of young men and male hotel guests on the hunting season.

Life was rather tedious.

Next time she passed Evaline May's house, Horatia saw someone had pinned a sign to the front door that said, "I Didn't Raise My Daughter to Be a Voter." On impulse she pulled it off, knocked, and handed it to Evaline May.

"Come in, Horatia!" Evaline May cried, ripping the sign in two. "The Daughters of the Confederacy are responsible. They're opposed to women voting! Idiots!" She ushered Horatia into the front parlor crammed with boxes of papers and leaflets.

Horatia stared at the mess and exclaimed, "Oh dear! Could you use some help?"

Evaline May looked around distractedly. "As you can see . . . I could indeed. I wish more girls your age understood how important this work is. All that most of you think about is catching a husband. Do you think you could bring order to this?" She opened the double door to the back parlor, which was even more crammed with box after box of newspaper cuttings, papers, magazines, pamphlets, and books. "The mess has run away with me," Evaline May said, sighing, "until I don't know where to begin straightening. I can barely reach my desk." She pointed to a dining table with a single chair in the midst of the chaos. The table was almost invisible under papers and correspondence and a large typewriter.

"My goodness!"

"Could you organize papers into files, letters chronologically into other files, pamphlets into boxes, and so on?"

"Oh dear," Horatia said faintly. She was a neat and tidy person, but as she looked around her, the task seemed overwhelming. "I'll try."

Evaline May gave her some pamphlets that said "Votes for Women" in big type, and when she took them home Josiah laughed and called her his little suffragette. Who was she so anxious to vote for, the New Dress Party?

"Oh, Papa!" Horatia found this maddening. "Why shouldn't ladies vote?" she muttered rebelliously. "We have brains!"

Josiah disapproved when she told him what she was doing, and Ellinder couldn't grasp why a woman would want to vote. But Horatia welcomed having something to do that got her out of the house, and helping Evaline May turned out to be interesting. She kept stopping while organizing to read things that caught her eye.

She found a story about French nurses at the front in one of Evaline May's magazines. There were pictures of them looking starched and professional and serious in their enveloping aprons with a red cross on the front and their white caps, waiting by field ambulances, assisting doctors in field hospitals, and sitting by the bedsides of wounded soldiers. "Angels of the Battlefield," the article called them.

Horatia wondered what it would be like to be a nurse. It would be nice to feel useful. But that would mean going to a hospital in Roanoke or Kingsport or Bristol to get trained. If you were a nurse, helping to save people's lives, surely it was right to have the vote. But her parents would never allow her to go away from home.

So most mornings, she donned an apron against the dust that coated the mess in Evaline May's parlor and sorted and stacked and dusted and filed things before going home for lunch. In the afternoons she went for a ride, alone, unless she met Frank, as she sometimes did. Sometimes Frank called on her parents in the evening to discuss advertisements for Vann's Emporium in the *Messenger*. And he argued on Horatia's side against Josiah that women ought to have the vote.

Bella fell back in the habit of having supper at the Vanns', just like she'd done when the girls were in school and studied together afterward. With so few evening activities there was little to do, and Bella could now drive well enough to maneuver the twisting road down Little Frog Mountain. She hoped her Christmas present would be the little yellow runabout.

Frank was usually there too, and if he had a letter from Calvert, he'd read it aloud. He wrote mostly about the war in Europe, horrible things that had been done by the Germans in Belgium, the Preparedness Movement, and what Harvard students thought about America joining in.

Bella looked anxiously from Frank to Josiah, her fork poised in midair.

"Calvert won't go to war. He'd have more sense," said Josiah firmly.

Horatia tried to persuade Bella to come with her to help Evaline May, stuffing envelopes with suffragette leaflets and writing letters to influential people about giving women the vote.

"Can't possibly. I'm far too busy."

"Busy? Doing what?"

"I've no intention of ending up an old maid like your new chum, Evaline May. I hope to get married like a normal girl, and if you must know, I'm learning about housekeeping to be ready when the time comes. It was Mother's idea, really."

"Housekeeping? You?" exclaimed Horatia. "Why?" Bella had grown up in a house with a cook and hired girls, and Hilda's idea of housekeeping was telling the cook what dessert to make for dinner. Bella's married sisters had similar households. "Getting married? Did you go and get engaged to Davy without telling me?"

"For heaven's sake, Horatia! Who said anything about Davy? It was just a figure of speech! Mother said after a girl finishes school, it's time to learn about housekeeping so . . . so she can tell the hired girls what to do when the time comes for a home of her own."

If Bella's interest in housekeeping was surprising, it was even less like Bella to decline attending the hotel dance at the end of November. She said she didn't feel well. Horatia decided she didn't want to go without Bella, and besides, the dance didn't promise to be very enjoyable. The guests at the hotel were all older people. Young men of the right age mostly seemed to be away at college learning to be soldiers, or, like Davy Charbonneau, they were visiting friends to go hunting.

"What? Not going to the dance? Are you and Bella withering on the vine?" Josiah teased.

"Oh, Papa! In case you haven't noticed, there's hardly anyone to dance with."

By early December Horatia's spirits were depressed. She had the books and papers and pamphlets at Evaline May's in order on the bookshelves and the sitting room organized and tidy, so she'd come to the end of her usefulness. It had turned rainy, and the fog settled in the valley most days, dull and white.

Bella seemed mopey and wasn't inclined to do anything, and Horatia was longing for the Christmas holidays when Calvert and the other young men would be home and liven everyone up. As soon as the college men started coming home, people began having open house parties to show off Christmas trees, and the Charbonneaus would have all the young people to their annual caroling party on Christmas Eve with champagne and a buffet supper they called Reveillon, a custom brought by Davy's great-grandmother from New Orleans. If it snowed, they'd set up a sleigh ride and bonfire picnic, and there'd be the Twelfth Night Ball at the hotel after Christmas.

Horatia thought of Calvert often. Could he possibly be sweet on her? He'd danced with her several times at the August dance, and then at the Blackberry Picnic he'd sat by her quite a long time and even put his arm around her shoulder for a little while—delightful! If it hadn't been for Bella coming over to join them, he might have asked her to watch the fireworks with him. And possibly have held her hand, or even kissed her.

Christmas might be very interesting indeed.

CHAPTER 14

December 1915

With a week to go until Christmas, Ellinder caught a cold and took to her bed. Josiah and Horatia tramped through the woods looking for the perfect Christmas tree, planning to decorate it and surprise her. But when they had it ready, Ellinder had taken some medicine and was sleeping too soundly to look at it.

Josiah asked Horatia to make the fruitcakes they gave to their friends every Christmas—since Ellinder was too ill, and the cook was grumbling that fruitcake was too much mess and too much hard work, her arms couldn't do all that stirring anymore, she was too old.

Josiah loved these fruitcakes. Horatia thought they were heavy and indigestible but couldn't bear to see her father disappointed, so she retrieved Great-Great-Grandmother Caitlin Vann's recipe written on a yellowing slip of folded paper from the Vann Bible. Horatia had hardly cooked anything in her life beyond scrambled eggs and pulling taffy, but she gamely donned an apron and spent the next day shelling nuts, sifting flour, picking through raisins, and beating what felt like a thousand eggs in a hot and steamy kitchen. The recipe made a vast amount of batter, and soon every surface was crowded with bowls and baking pans threatening to overflow with sticky, heavy batter.

By suppertime, she thoroughly sympathized with the cook, who'd left dinner on the range and gone home early. Stirring the cake batter, stiff with dried fruit and nuts, was like stirring cement. Arms aching, she was still wrapped in the splattered apron, hair disarranged, and shoving pans of cake a few at a time into the oven for their long, slow baking, when Frank popped his head into the kitchen to ask what was for supper.

"Chipped beef, unfortunately," groaned Horatia. She hated that, but the cook had insisted it was the only thing she could make with the kitchen in a state.

Frank came in and shut the door behind him.

Horatia glanced at him. "What's wrong? I've never seen you look so grim! Is it Teeny? Or Sarah's poor little baby?"

"Other bad news, Horatia."

"Oh Lord! What?"

"Calvert's not coming home this Christmas."

"What?" Horatia cried. "Why?"

Frank leaned against the doorjamb. "My dear brother's gone to war, that's why. He's on his way to join up, in France. If he and his college friends don't get torpedoed on the way. You know what Calvert's like, he's restless and has got a daring nature, but this . . ." Frank sank down on a chair and put his head in his hands. "This is rash and foolish beyond anything he's ever done. I should have listened last summer when he kept saying he didn't want to be a lawyer, he wanted to fly an airplane, he wanted to get away from Grafton. But I was busy at the paper, and I thought it was all talk."

Horatia's heart sank.

"He told me he was mixed up in something at that woman Kate Irish's boardinghouse. He talked about his friend Terence and airplanes and California . . . I should have paid more attention. But you know Calvert—he always has some scheme or other for excitement."

Horatia bit her lip. Christmas without Calvert was a very bleak prospect. And whatever he was mixed up in at Kate Irish's . . . it didn't bear thinking about.

Feeling disappointed and dismal about Calvert, as well as tired from the baking, she'd gone to bed early and was sleeping soundly when a thud against her window woke her briefly. She snuggled back under the covers and slept again.

There was another thud, then another.

"Oh, for goodness' sake!" Horatia muttered. She sat up in bed and rubbed her eyes.

Another thud.

She lit the lamp by her bed, went to the window, and pulled back her curtains. Beyond the glass it was snowing. Who was playing a prank in the middle of the night?

Thud. Right before her eyes a snowball hit her window. She put the lamp down and opened it, letting in a blast of cold air and a flurry of snow. "Whoever's there, kindly stop it!"

"Horatia, let me in!"

"Bella?"

"Open the kitchen door and let me in."

Horatia grabbed her wrapper and hurried down the back stairs to the kitchen. She unlocked the door and Bella stumbled in, covered in snow.

"I thought you'd never answer." Bella shivered.

"It's the middle of the night! What are you doing here?"

Bella's teeth were chattering, and Horatia pulled her coat off and pointed to the mat where they left galoshes. She stoked the fire in the range, drew water and set it to boil, fetched towels, made tea, and finally took off her wrapper to put around Bella's shoulders.

"I b-b-borrowed Wilfred's c-c-car."

"You drove down Little Frog in this weather?"

"Yes."

Horatia thought how dangerous the trip down the winding road must have been with the snow making everything slippery. Her driving was still far from perfect. "Why?"

"Because I need your help."

"In the middle of the night?"

In the dim kitchen Bella's eyes were wide with fright in her white face. "Yes. And I hardly know how to say it, it's so terrible." She began to cry.

"Bella! What's wrong?"

"I'm . . . in the family way."

Horatia gasped and stared at her friend. "I don't believe it! How could you be?"

"I haven't had my monthlies since September. I'm sick in the mornings, like Jane was. I'm going to have a baby unless I do something to . . . to stop it."

"Stop it? How do you stop a baby?"

"I don't know exactly, but you have to help me get to Kate Irish's. She knows what to do. And I need to go tonight."

"*Kate Irish!* Bella, for Pete's sake, you know what kind of place it is. You don't want to go near it. What if someone saw you?"

Bella took another deep sobbing breath and said, "I know. But I don't know where else to turn. I heard the hired girls say there's someone at Kate Irish's place who knows how to . . . to get rid of a baby. They said the girls who work for her sometimes need . . . to do that."

Horatia was speechless.

Bella lifted her tearstained face and said desperately, "I mustn't have it! I won't! I'd be ruined! People will point at me and make jokes. No one in my family would ever speak to me again. It would kill my parents. I'd be sent away in disgrace. And I'd never get married . . ."

"Won't Davy marry you? He's truly fond of you, Bella. He's been sweet on you for ever so long. He'd do the right thing."

"Davy?" Bella choked, and looked up with a startled expression. "What's *Davy* got to do with anything? Did you think it was *Davy's* baby? Oh, never!"

"Then whose?"

"It's . . . Calvert's!"

"Calvert's!" Horatia sank into a kitchen chair. "Calvert's! Oh, Bella! How could you?"

"I did wrong. I know that. But we're engaged. Or I think we are—he said he loved me . . . though sometimes I'm sure and sometimes I'm not, and at the dance in August he talked about . . . you know, he spoke about not wanting to be a lawyer and going off to the war to learn to fly and going to live in California afterward. Can you imagine? All my family are here. What would I do somewhere else?

"I wanted to keep him, wanted him to come home, and . . . at the Blackberry Picnic we went off . . . Because I want us to be married more than anything, and we were so happy then, we'd be so happy married to each other." She shrugged helplessly. "If I have this baby, we never will be. I can't ask anyone else to help me, not even Jane." Bella collapsed into sobs on the kitchen table. "And Calvert will be home soon, so I have to get it done now."

"Let's talk this over in the morning. You can spend the night, and tomorrow we'll try to think sensibly what's best. But, Bella, you need to know something. Calvert's gone to France. To the war. Frank told me this evening when he came to supper. He's got no idea where Calvert is at the moment or how to reach him."

Bella gave a hiccup of misery. "Oh God! All the more reason to . . . get it done. Fortunately it's snowing. Nobody will see us. Everybody respectable's asleep, but at Kate Irish's they'll be awake. You have to come with me because I'm scared to death. I don't want to think what will happen, and then if I can't drive home again, I mustn't be found there! I'm sick with worrying how to manage it, and if I don't go now, my courage will fail me altogether and I'll just be ruined and might as well be dead. My family won't be able to hold their heads up for shame. All the girls from school will snicker and gossip, and at church they'll say I'm bad. You'll deny being my friend."

"No, I won't," muttered Horatia.

"Please, Horatia? I am determined. I know it costs money, but I have money. I told Papa I needed new clothes for Christmas. He laughed and gave me this." She reached into her pocket and drew out a wad of dollars. She started to cry again. "Papa spoils me so. It makes everything worse."

"But Calvert," Horatia began. "Perhaps if you write to him? Perhaps Frank will find out eventually where a letter will reach him? Perhaps . . . he'd come home?"

"How? I'd start to show before he got here, and it would be . . . horrid. In church there'll be sermons dripping with disapproval about fallen girls, and people will stare at me. I'd never hold up my head again. It would kill my parents, and all the girls from school would point at me, and their parents wouldn't let them even speak to me anymore. And you know how strict Teeny is—she'd find a way to stop him from marrying me. Even Frank would be scandalized. Calvert might start to hate me. Please, Horatia." Bella blew her nose. "Get dressed, and come with me. This is my only chance."

"Bella, isn't . . . it . . . dangerous?" As well as wicked, she was sure.

The hall clock chimed one.

"I can't think about that now, can I? If we go now in the snow, no one would notice the car, and then . . . when it's . . . done, we'll come back here. I'll say I drove down to see you on a whim after supper. To . . . to look at your Christmas tree."

Horatia thought a moment. Bella was the kind of girl who did things impetuously, so even though the Vanns would disapprove, they wouldn't be surprised if Bella had driven down to see the Christmas tree. Of course Wilfred would be furious she'd borrowed one of his cars, but the Drumhellers were used to Bella's behavior, and eventually he'd forgive her.

"But we have to go at once. There isn't much time. I want to be back before it gets light and people see Wilfred's car and think *he's* gone to a whorehouse. Gossip like that would kill Jane. Please, hurry and get dressed. You're the only person I can count on, Horatia."

"All right," sighed Horatia, against her better judgment. She flew up the back stairs to her room and dressed hastily, not daring to reflect on what she was doing.

They made their way to where Bella had parked at a distance from the Vanns' house. "You crank the car," Bella said, climbing into the driver's seat. Horatia cranked, and the engine spluttered into life. She jumped in, and Bella lurched off down the river road. It was hard to see the road with the snow pelting down. Several times Horatia thought Bella would surely lose control of the car, but she swore and righted it, and finally the lights of Kate Irish's establishment were visible through the snowflakes.

They parked under a tree away from the house. "We'll have to go to the back door," said Bella. "Imagine if some man we know is here and were to see us." They drew their shawls over their heads to hide their faces as much as possible and crept around to the back porch. Bella knocked.

A woman in a black dress and white apron opened the door, letting a gust of warm air out, and stared at them. Bella stammered, "P-p-please, I need to speak to Kate . . . Mrs. Irish." From inside the house they could hear the sound of a piano and men laughing.

"Ah, do you now?" said the aproned woman in an Irish lilt. "Is it work you're after?"

"I . . . not work. No!"

"Pity, we've need of a kitchen maid."

"Ah, who's this, Ida?" said a voice behind the aproned woman. A stout woman in black bombazine and jet beads approached the back door. "Well, step in," she ordered, "before we're ankle deep in snow in here."

They stepped into the warmth. Kate's expression changed. She smiled. "Well, well. Haven't I seen your picture in the papers? Speak up, Miss Vann, Miss Drumheller, what do you want? The house is busy and I don't have all night."

Horatia was gripped with panic. *She knows who we are,* she thought. *We ought to leave at once.*

Bella gulped. "I need . . . I'm going to have a baby. Please, Mrs. Irish, help me. They say there's a woman here who knows how to . . . get rid of . . ." Her voice trailed off, and she held out the wad of dollars.

"Men all the same, aren't they, take their pleasure and do up their pants." She looked at the money and nodded. "Well, well. I suppose it can be done. No sense in wasting time."

The woman named Ida said, "I'll get my things."

"No, Ida, I'll see to it."

"What? Instead of me?"

"I want them gone as soon as possible, Ida. Meanwhile, I need you in front to keep an eye on things."

"Better if I do it," said Ida intransigently. "You don't know how as well's I do."

"I know how well enough. Go on, Ida. See the gentlemen have enough whiskey."

She took the money without counting it and pointed to a doorway. "Be quick. Go in there, and lie on the bed. And you, miss, boil a pot of water for me while I get ready, then wait here for your friend."

She walked briskly out.

They heard Ida say, "Are you certain, Mrs. Irish, you can do this without me?"

"Positive, Ida. Go. We won't discuss it."

"Bella," hissed Horatia, "please, don't do this!"

Bella cast a desperate white-faced look at her friend. "I have to," she said, and disappeared into the side room. Horatia's hands shook as she pumped water to fill a pot and tried to think how to stop this nightmare when Kate Irish returned, enveloped in a white apron to cover her silk dress. Kate opened a drawer, and there was a rattle of steel as she removed an implement.

Horatia shuddered and averted her eyes. She didn't want to know what it was.

Kate took an armful of towels and a basin and whatever she'd taken from the drawer and disappeared into the room where Bella was lying. She returned for the pot of boiling water, and came back for a third time to pour a glass of whiskey. As she closed the door, Horatia heard her say, "Now, girlie, drink this and be very brave."

Horatia sank onto a hard chair and put her head in her hands, trying not to faint.

After a while there was a terrible muffled shriek from behind the closed door, and Horatia started to cry. Kate Irish emerged. There was blood on the apron, and she had covered the basin with a towel. "How did you get here?" she demanded. "Because you need to go back where you came from at once."

"M-my friend d-d-drove a motorcar," stammered Horatia. How were they going to get Bella away? Horatia couldn't drive, and Bella, who could, would be in no condition to do it.

Kate Irish said, "I'll have to send the hired man to drive you."

"But . . . but he'll know where we live, who we are!"

"So do I," said Kate. "But those who work here never gossip."

"Is she . . . able to leave?"

"Yes. Get her to bed and have a towel handy. Give her a glass of brandy to help her sleep. She mustn't do anything strenuous for a while. I'll send for the man." And she went out.

Horatia tried to think on what pretext Bella could stay in bed at her house without the alarmed Drumhellers descending with the doctor in tow.

Kate reappeared, followed by a man with snow on his hat. "She ready to go?" he asked.

Kate disappeared into the side room and came back supporting Bella, who was white as a sheet and barely able to walk. The hired man picked her up like a child. Bella groaned. "You go on now," said Kate as the three went out the back door. "Don't worry. No one will know."

Wilfred's car was only a two-seater, but the hired man deposited Bella in the passenger seat and motioned Horatia to squeeze in beside her. He cranked expertly and drove off. Horatia was grateful it was still snowing, as it would hide them. She looked at her watch. Three hours had passed since Bella had woken her. And everything had changed horribly. She tried to hold Bella steady as the car bumped over the rough road back to town. Bella was moaning.

Horatia's heart felt cold and empty. She must forget her feelings for Calvert. Bella had forgotten herself shamefully, but so had he! One way or another he had to marry Bella and make this as all right as it ever could be. But Horatia didn't think anything would be truly all right again, ever.

CHAPTER 15

The hired man stopped the car away from the Vanns' house. He ordered Horatia to lead the way and open the back door and he'd carry Bella up the back stairs. "Big houses always have back stairs," he said. Horatia ran ahead, thanking her stars she hadn't locked it when they left, and the hired man carried Bella up to Horatia's room and put her on the bed, saying he'd see himself out.

Horatia managed to undress her and, with difficulty, get her into a nightgown. She put a folded towel between Bella's legs. There was a frightening amount of blood. Bella opened her eyes and saw Horatia's expression.

"It's a messy business," she said faintly. "And it hurts, oh, Horatia, how it hurts! But it's done now. I just have to rest, Kate says. And then I'll be good as new, almost. And when I finally get married . . ." She tried to smile and failed. She reached for Horatia's hand. "Thank you, Horatia dear," she whispered, and closed her eyes.

Horatia sank onto her cushioned window seat. She drew back the curtain and looked for where the hired man had left the car. Yes, there it was, barely visible in the dim half-light of a winter morning. She began to think what they'd do to explain themselves to their parents. They would telephone the Drumhellers and say Bella had taken it into her head to go see the Vanns' Christmas tree and give Horatia her Christmas present, so she'd taken Wilfred's car. She reached the Vanns', but when she was ready to go home, the car wouldn't start. Horatia's parents would be aghast that Bella would do anything so silly in the terrible weather, the Drumhellers would scold Bella, and Wilfred would come to collect the car and shout and be very angry with Bella and then go home. The two girls could lie low in Horatia's room until everyone calmed down. By suppertime perhaps Bella would be able to go downstairs. Horatia had no idea how long it took to get over *it*.

She checked on Bella, who was sleeping like the dead. Downstairs the clock chimed seven and she could hear things rattling in the kitchen as the hired girl arrived to start breakfast. Breakfast in the Vann household was at eight.

Horatia felt drained and giddy with exhaustion. She went to her washstand and poured water in the basin. She stripped to her chemise and scrubbed her face and neck and arms, cleaned her teeth and brushed her hair as normal. She put on a clean shirtwaist and an old skirt with a patched pocket that she wore at home on Saturdays. She tried to think how she must behave to look normal. Breakfast would be on the dining room table as usual, with coffee for her father and tea for her mother in case she was well enough to join them, and a platter of sausage and eggs in the middle. Biscuits, jam. Morning light coming through the lace curtains in the dining room. Normal.

At some point she'd casually mention Bella was there. And explain why she was asleep and not at the breakfast table. It was an unwritten rule that Horatia was never allowed to sleep through breakfast, not even on mornings after a dance.

Her head began to ache.

The downstairs clock struck eight, and she went out of the room, closing the door softly.

Downstairs her father was perusing the front page of the *Messenger* and buttering a biscuit. The headline was about the war in Europe again, something about battles in eastern Europe and Russians doing this or that and casualties. Mr. Vann was shaking his head. "Front page is full of war news again. Now Calvert's gone to war himself we won't read anything else!"

Ellinder appeared in her dressing gown, handkerchief in hand, and took her place at the table.

"Oh, Mother, you're up! How nice."

"Yes, I'm better after a good sleep, thank you. What were you saying about Calvert?" she asked, pouring tea.

It was one of her mother's good days. *Thank goodness,* thought Horatia.

"I might as well tell you, Ellinder. You'll hear eventually. Frank stopped by for supper yesterday—you were asleep. Apparently Calvert's left college and gone off to Europe, to fight Huns for the French. You know how young men are, my dear. There's nothing like a war for excitement. And Calvert's always been a law unto himself." Josiah sighed.

"How dreadful! Poor Frank must be awfully worried."

Horatia put her biscuit down. "I need to tell you—please don't be cross—that Bella came to visit rather late last night. She's . . . er . . . had promised me she'd come see our Christmas tree, and wanted to bring my Christmas present, so she, um . . . borrowed one of Wilfred's cars, but it broke down and wouldn't start when she was ready to go home. She's upstairs asleep now. She got soaking wet and chilled trying to . . . to . . . crank it in the snow . . . She's taken a cold from it, is really poorly, sneezing. I told her to stay in bed."

Josiah threw down his paper and demanded, "What? Didn't Bella have more sense than to go driving in such weather to look at a Christmas tree? Where on earth is the car? Wilfred will be beside himself when he finds it's gone, and I don't blame him. Bella behaves like she's a law unto herself. Exactly like Calvert, if you ask me."

Horatia winced. “Yes, she’s very sorry, Papa. She knows she oughtn’t to have done it, and now she’s feeling sick and worried about Wilfred being angry with her.”

“Angry? Of course the man will be angry!” Josiah exploded.

“So, Papa, I was thinking if you telephoned and explained how sorry she is, Wilfred might be more understanding . . .”

“Oh, for heaven’s sake! Girls!” Josiah got up and stormed out of the dining room. They heard him cranking the telephone in the hall. “Wilfred,” he began, one exasperated male to another, “I think you’ll find one of your cars is missing this morning.”

“I’ll just take Bella some tea, Mamma, and see.”

“Good morning, Aunt Ellinder,” said Bella from the doorway. She looked awful, but she managed to smile at Ellinder.

Horatia was relieved, for once, that her mother wasn’t very observant. “You’ve been very naughty, young lady,” Ellinder chided. “Out in the snow late at night. No wonder you took cold.”

“I . . . I know,” quavered Bella, sitting and helping herself to a biscuit, which she began to tear into little pieces.

Josiah returned, looking stern. “Bella, I have to warn you, Wilfred is as cross as you would expect. Your father will bring him down. What possessed you? You could have had a dreadful accident.”

“I’m sorry,” Bella said in a small voice. “I thought it would be all right. It wasn’t snowing very hard when I left, and I wanted to see your Christmas tree.” A tear rolled down her cheek. “I’m very sorry,” she whispered.

Ellinder shook her head.

“Papa, poor Bella isn’t feeling well. We mustn’t be hard on her,” interrupted Horatia, reaching for the dish of preserves. “I’m pleased you’re here, Bella. You can help me with the fruitcakes I made yesterday. I still have to poke holes to drip brandy into them. Wait till you see, a dozen all by myself. They turned out fine in spite of me.”

Ellinder said, "It's an old family recipe, Bella, and very good. Horatia will copy it out for you. It's time you girls started collecting recipes for when you're married with homes of your own."

"Yes indeed, Aunt Ellinder," said Bella. "My mother says the same thing." She forced a crumb of biscuit into her mouth.

Horatia saw Bella's hand was shaking. "I know, Bella. We'll give Wilfred one of the fruitcakes to calm him down."

"Yes. Men love fruitcake. Save one for Papa," Ellinder said softly. "It's his favorite."

Wilfred was indeed fuming when he arrived. He inspected the car, huffed that at least she hadn't dented it again, and told Bella to get in. He was taking her straight home. Horatia gave him a cake wrapped in oiled paper and said Bella had a cold and should stay with her, but Wilfred wouldn't hear of it. Bella climbed slowly and, Horatia could tell, painfully into the car and hung her head as Wilfred drove away, lecturing and still angry.

In the days leading up to Christmas, Horatia debated with herself whether she should brave the telephone party line and the operator, and anyone who might happen to listen, and call Bella to see how she was. Finally she did but got Hilda, who said Bella's cold was terrible and she was in bed, hoarse and unable to come downstairs to talk to Horatia.

Worried, Horatia delivered fruitcakes to the Vanns' friends with her father, admired Christmas trees, drank eggnog and punch at different houses, tried to sing carols at the Charbonneaus', and simply ignored Frank when he tried to kiss her under the mistletoe. Her heart wasn't in Christmas at all—it would always be terrible now, Horatia couldn't help thinking, sadly. Baby Jesus in the manger and Bella's got-rid-of baby at the bawdy house. And Calvert. Wicked Calvert.

All during the holiday the weather remained as grim as Horatia's mood. It snowed, and when it wasn't snowing the lowering skies cast a dull gray half-light over everything. The snow melted into slush that soaked into galoshes and then froze again. She declined invitations, blaming it on the weather. According to Hilda, Bella wasn't recovering well from her cold, and no, Horatia mustn't come visit, she might catch what Bella had. Finally Bella called Horatia late one night—she said she'd waited until her parents were asleep—and whispered she had pain and felt feverish, and the doctor had been and said it might be pneumonia and she should keep well wrapped up and drink plenty of soup.

Bella was still in bed three weeks after Christmas, when a new little yellow runabout came chugging up Little Frog Mountain. It was left under her bedroom window with a big red bow on the roof.

"Bella's father thought that might get Bella up and out of her sickbed," Hilda told Horatia on the phone. "So I expect you'll see her soon, Horatia dear."

In mid-January Frank came over with a letter, not from Calvert but from Calvert's friend Terence, saying that the Harvard men had arrived at Brest without being torpedoed, and they were making their way to the western front, where a unit of volunteer fighter pilots was being formed. They were all looking forward to learning to fly and giving the enemy what for.

Horatia tried and tried to find out if Frank had an address for Calvert in France, but Frank didn't know exactly where he was, just that he was in France, and France was at war and he supposed the mail was difficult. He gave vent to his worry by writing an editorial in the *Messenger* about his brother who'd gone to fight for the French. He compared Calvert to a medieval knight, fighting for a noble cause. Now that Calvert had gone off to fight, more people read the war coverage in the newspaper.

Bella still hadn't recovered and was still in bed, getting paler and thinner. The doctor prescribed various tonics, but they did no good.

Horatia tried again to visit, but Hilda wouldn't let her.

"She keeps saying she's better and would I please just leave her alone to rest," Hilda said, close to tears. "But she isn't better. Oh, Horatia, do you suppose it could be consumption?"

CHAPTER 16

February 1916

When Horatia saw a little yellow roadster chug to a stop in front of the Vanns' house one afternoon, she hurried to open the front door, thinking Albert Drumheller's plan to get Bella up again had worked.

It was Bella, but not for the reasons Horatia had hoped. Bella paused briefly at the parlor door to say Hilda sent love to Ellinder, before hurrying Horatia upstairs. "Let's go to your room. I don't want your mother to see me in the light. I look awful. Mama tells me so constantly."

Horatia hadn't seen Bella since the fateful night, and when Bella took off her hat, she gasped. Bella had grown thin. There were dark circles under her eyes, and her face was unnaturally white. Her bobbed hair was a lank mess.

"You should be home in bed," Horatia blurted out.

Bella shut the door to Horatia's room, took an envelope from her pocket, and said, "I had to come show you. I couldn't tell you on the telephone in case someone overheard. This came in the mail yesterday."

Bella pulled out a folded clipping of an editorial and a note that read, "Does CM know? Another bastard child in the Marshall family?" It was signed, "From a Well-Wisher Reluctant to Speak Out Unless Obliged to by Necessity Which Can Be Relieved for 50 Dollars Left Under a Rock by Will Stuart's Grave."

"CM. Oh no, it must stand for Calvert Marshall!" said Horatia. "Whoever wrote it suspects . . . How would they know? 'Another bastard,' horrid term! What does it mean, 'in the Marshall family'? Oh horrors, a blackmailer!"

"Kate Irish must have sent it. Who else could it be? I didn't mention Calvert's name, but she must have heard Calvert was paying me attention. Several of the girls from school have called him my sweetheart to my face. And then there were those pictures of us at the croquet tournament and at the dances that were printed in the *Messenger*. Kate just put two and two together."

Horatia gasped. "But you paid her such a lot of money!"

"Well, she wants more," sighed Bella, sinking down on Horatia's bed. "Last summer he talked about leaving Grafton, said there were good reasons to leave, he didn't want to be a lawyer, asked if I'd be willing to go with him to California. I stopped him from saying anything more about it. The idea frightened me. I didn't want that life. I wanted to stay, be married, and live near Jane and my mother, the rest of the family. I knew Papa would build us a house—he's done that for all my brothers and sisters—and we'd be so happy! I couldn't imagine anything else. Now I'd go away with Calvert, anywhere he chooses. I wish I could tell him I changed my mind. Horatia, sometimes I'm afraid we'll never hear from Calvert again, now that he's gone to war . . ." Tears trickled down Bella's pale cheeks. Once Bella would have stormed and wept furiously; now she seemed defeated in misery.

"Bella, you look awful."

"I know. Mama says so all the time."

"You've been poorly ever since . . . You need a doctor to, well, see if what Kate Irish did caused a problem. Something must have gone wrong, Bella. It sounded like that other woman, Ida, thought she ought to do it, but Kate insisted on doing it herself. Ida didn't seem to think she should."

"I've felt terrible, weak and sick, and I have a fever and chills and this nagging pain, but I don't know if that's how you feel afterward. Kate told me not to go to the doctor. She said it takes time to get over it. And she said a doctor would have to examine me, and he'd know at once what I'd done. I thought getting rid of the baby would make everything like it was before, but it didn't. And the worst part is, when Calvert finally comes home, what can I tell him? Or not tell him? At night it goes around and around in my head until I can't sleep."

"What will you do about . . . about the note?"

Bella sighed. "I'll have to tell more lies, think of something to tell Papa to explain why I need money. And he's always so good to me, that's the worst thing, but if I don't lie to get the money, my parents will die of shame if this . . . horrible person . . . tells."

"But fifty dollars!"

"It's a fortune, I know. And if I do it once, I'll live in fear of another letter, wanting me to pay again. How horrid life's become." The downstairs clock chimed four. "I have to go. It's getting dark." She rose wearily. Her cheeks were flushed now, and Horatia reached out and felt her forehead.

"Bella, you're burning up!"

"I know. It comes and never quite goes away."

"You have to see the doctor, Bella! You're too sick not to."

"Can you imagine if the doctor in Grafton discovers what I've done!"

"Then we'll see a doctor somewhere else. Look, tell your mother you feel better and we're going to take the train to Richmond and go shopping like we did that time last summer. She'll make Wilfred drive you here. I'll get you onto the train somehow, and once we're there we'll find a doctor and won't give him your real name. You can be Miss Smith. No, *Mrs.* Smith. We'll buy a cheap wedding ring from Woolworth's. If he has to examine you, he'll think you're a respectable married lady. If he's shocked to find . . . what you've done, then tell him . . . tell him something like your husband threatened to abandon you if you had the baby. Dress up in your best traveling costume—you'll feel better if you look nice—and afterward we'll treat ourselves to lunch in a restaurant, before we come back. We'll get you well again. You'll see."

Bella gave a weak smile. "That's a good plan, if I can get out of bed. I'll try to fix myself up with a little paint. But what can be done about this horrid person asking for money? Unless Calvert comes back and marries me and takes me away to California—no chance of that at the moment—there's really no way I can scheme myself out of this. I'm trapped. Oh, Horatia, it goes round and round in my head, and I feel so low!"

"Well, Frank is sensible. I could ask him what to do about blackmail."

"Oh Lord, you mustn't tell Frank!"

"Never fear, I'd think of a way to ask his advice without giving anything away."

They walked downstairs. Once Bella had flown up and down this staircase. Now she clung to the banister, moving slowly.

"We won't give up," said Horatia stoutly. "I won't let you. We'll go tomorrow and you can lean on me all the way to Richmond and back. But we must do *something*, Bella. You know we must or you won't get better. And I'm determined you shall get better."

At the door, Bella kissed her and said, "Horatia, you're my dearest friend in the world. Thank you." She walked slowly down the porch steps, calling to Hiram to please come and crank her new runabout.

In a few moments the car was chugging noisily and Bella was at the wheel. "Goodbye!" she called as she drove away.

"Until tomorrow!" shouted Horatia over the engine noise.

Bella waved. "Goodbye."

CHAPTER 17

Next morning, Horatia was dressing for the train, praying Bella would feel strong enough to go through with the day's plan, when she heard a commotion in the street outside. She pulled her curtains aside and saw a crowd had gathered at the jetty. Men were shouting for rope, and a man was dragging three mules toward the water's edge.

Running downstairs to see what had happened, she met her father coming in the front door. He'd left the Emporium hatless, and he looked shocked. "Horatia, there's been an accident! There's a car submerged in the river. If it hadn't gotten stuck on a rock, the river would have swept it away. I gave them some rope, and they're hitching up mules to pull it out. Fetch some blankets! If there's someone inside . . ."

Horatia ran for the blankets, then followed Josiah outside. She watched from the porch as men in a small boat struggled against the current to fix a grappling hook on a rope to the wheel of an upside-down, partly submerged car. She couldn't see what kind or what color. The hook caught on the wheel, and the men rowed back to the jetty and threw the rope end to a crowd of waiting workmen who fastened it onto the mules. "Pull!" shouted someone, and the mules strained and pulled and fought the current until the car jerked free from the rock. Slowly and still submerged, it was dragged closer and closer until the men could reach and maneuver it onto the bank.

A yellow car. Horatia caught her breath. "No!" she moaned. She shut her eyes and began to pray, please don't let it be Bella's car, please let the car be empty and Bella safe and cross because she looks like a drowned cat, just let her be safe . . .

Horatia watched, frozen with horror as the men grappled with the door and finally pulled out the limp form of a young woman, hat, long scarf, and skirts soaked and plastered to her body. Crying, "No! Oh, Bella, dearest, no! No! No!" Horatia flew down the steps and shoved the men aside. "No! *No!*" she screamed. "You mustn't die, Bella, you mustn't!" She fell to her knees by the body and tried to shake Bella back to life.

She felt Josiah's hand on her shoulder. "Stop, Horatia. There's nothing that can be done for her now. Let them get her off the ground before her mother gets here. We have to send them word of the accident."

"How did it happen? Didn't anyone see? Why didn't they pull her out sooner . . ." Horatia wept as Josiah handed a blanket to someone and forcibly pulled her up and away from Bella's corpse. She hardly heard her father say Bella must have lost control of the car, gone too fast, or felt faint. And that it must have happened in the night. No one spotted the car in the river until early this morning.

The rest was a nightmare Horatia would remember to her dying day. Bella's body was carried into the Vanns' dining room and laid out on the table. Her face was white and pinched, and her wet hair and clothes dripped steadily, making a puddle on the floor. Too shocked to mop it up or fetch a towel or do anything at all, the cook stood frozen at the dining room door, a hand over her mouth. Ellinder retreated to a corner of the parlor, where she shrank into a chair and sat rocking back and forth, hugging herself.

The Drumhellers arrived. Hilda and Albert ran from Wilfred's car, and when Hilda reached the body and saw it really was Bella, she fainted. Behind her parents, Jane screamed, "No!" and wept steadily and unconsolably as the rest of the family crowded round, crying Bella's name.

Hilda was helped to a sofa, and after a while Wilfred turned to Josiah, wiped his eyes, and choked that they'd take Bella's body home. "Terrible to see her this way, with all the life gone out of her. Poor girl. Jane and the others will want to dress her for the coffin so she'll look . . . herself when folks pay their respects before the funeral."

"Funeral!" Hilda shrieked. "Her funeral! I should have been dressing her for her wedding, not her funeral! Oh, my Bella! My Bella!"

All the while Ellinder sat frozen in her corner.

Reverend Merriman arrived clutching his Bible and went straight to Albert, who was sitting bowed with grief, his shoulders heaving. He began talking to Albert in a low voice. Drawing ragged breaths, Hilda clutched her handkerchief to her mouth and returned to stand by Bella's body.

Ellinder stood and went to Hilda. She took her distraught friend in her arms. "I know," she murmured. "I know. Don't let Reverend Merriman or anybody tell you it was God's plan, that he wanted your sweet girl for an angel. It wasn't! It was the work of the Devil, Hilda. The work of the Devil."

Horatia spent the following days up at the Drumhellers' trying to help. It was better than being alone with her misery at home. Ellinder had retreated to her bedroom again, after the doctor came with another little brown bottle. At the Drumhellers' a great throng of people came and went. Miss Willa had been overwhelmed by orders for mourning for the whole Drumheller clan, and had been assigned a back bedroom, where she and her seamstresses cut and stitched piles of black material delivered from the Emporium by Josiah.

The weather was cold, and the visitation went on for several days. Bella lay in her open coffin on the shady side of the porch, her bobbed hair brushed, and dressed in her prettiest church dress. Jane had tried to return a little color to the dead face with rouge, but it looked strange against the pallor of Bella's cheeks, so she tearfully wiped it off again.

By the time the funeral took place, Horatia was drained. She had no tears left.

When the mourners made their way from the church to the cemetery, Horatia clung to Frank's arm, hardly able to drag her feet along. She felt unutterably weary. Handsome Davy Charbonneau walked stiffly by himself, looking much older, his face drawn and grim. As they lowered Bella's coffin, as always the congregation began to sing "Guide Me, O Thou Great Jehovah" in call-and-response, and Horatia mouthed the words. The Drumhellers wept, none of them able to sing.

It was bleak without Bella. It would be bleak without Bella until the day Horatia died, until the day Davy died, until the day Frank and Hilda and Albert and Jane and everyone in Grafton died. And Calvert.

And Calvert. *Damn Calvert!* Horatia thought bitterly. *Damn Calvert to hell!*

After the funeral, there were no more dances at the hotel, even when the summer guests began arriving. Albert was a ghost of his former genial self and wore a black armband, and Hilda was now in the same deep mourning as Ellinder, with a brooch containing a lock of Bella's hair at her collar. She wanted to talk endlessly with Horatia about her daughter. What had happened during Bella's final visit to the Vanns'? Hilda wanted to know, over and over again. What had the girls talked about, how did Horatia think Bella looked? She was getting better, wasn't she? How nice the girls were planning a little excursion—it was just the kind of trip Bella loved . . . These visits always ended with Hilda in a fresh burst of tears, unable to understand how the accident could have happened. Bella had been getting better! She'd loved her new little runabout, said it was easier to manage than Wilfred's car.

No one could understand it. Nor could anyone make sense of why Bella would have been driving at night—Horatia said she'd last seen Bella in the afternoon, the Drumhellers had seen her at supper when she'd told her parents she and Horatia were taking a shopping trip next day, and Horatia had been expecting her after breakfast. No one had seen or heard the accident; no one had spotted the car in the river until people had been up and going about their daily business for several hours.

"I just don't know what to make of it all, Horatia," Hilda would say over and over.

Horatia didn't either. Horatia repeated the same answers every time—they'd just spoken of the usual silly things, dresses and the excursion they were planning to Richmond, to shop, she'd said. She didn't mention how hopeless Bella had seemed. How ill she'd looked. How afraid of the blackmailer. How worried she'd been about lying to her father. How she felt low.

It was horrible to think it possible, but had these things depressed Bella's spirits to the point where she had driven into the river deliberately? The question could never be answered, but it went round and round, nagging in Horatia's mind. Oh, if only Calvert hadn't gone to war! If he'd come home at Christmas, Bella could have told him about the baby, and they could have been married. Gossip about the baby's quick arrival could have been faced down somehow. Calvert never gave a hoot about what people thought, and Bella wouldn't have either with him by her side.

Did Calvert even know Bella was dead? Horatia had taken Frank aside after the funeral to ask if he had an address yet for Calvert. Frank said he'd had an address in Amiens and had written him the sad news, but he didn't know if his letters reached him. There'd been a note from Calvert that he was a pilot now, and he and Terence were going to join a volunteer air corps, called the Lafayette Escadrille. He'd been headed for the western front.

The Drumhellers put up a stone angel over Bella's grave. Horatia often went there early in the morning, to leave a little bouquet of wildflowers or a branch of peach or apple blossoms at the angel's feet. It was quiet then, and with no one about she could close her eyes and pretend Bella could see the flowers, and hear Horatia say she missed her.

Approaching the cemetery one misty morning, she didn't notice a woman standing by a grave off to the side, until she heard her. Her head was bent and she was saying something to the dead, like Horatia often did, and Horatia paused so as not to disturb her.

"Every day, Will, every day, it comes to me that you wouldn't have died if I'd been there to look after you, if we'd got married like we wanted. If I'd had some part of the Marshall money to make your pa give in, but Comfort wanted it all for Ben and Teeny. Said I wasn't a Marshall. I hate them all! Calvert's little by-blow is gone, the girl's dead, and Frank is set to be a bachelor. It's the name they took away from me, Will. I'll see it dies out. That's something."

Horatia gasped, and the woman turned to see who it was.

Even in the mist, Horatia could see the woman's eyes—yellow eyes. Kate Irish!

Kate stared at her, then silently brushed past Horatia and walked away.

Afterward she questioned whether she could have heard aright, because Kate Irish sounded like a madwoman. A madwoman who hated the Marshalls. Had she intended to kill Bella? No, surely it was wrong to think that way, Horatia told herself. She'd misheard. She must have done . . . but that night, Kate had insisted she'd see to Bella instead of the woman named Ida.

She laid her flowers on Bella's grave, told Bella what she suspected, and began to cry, saying she could do nothing, could tell no one, without dragging Bella's name in the mud and bringing yet more grief to her family. "And you wouldn't want that," she said sorrowfully. "I know you wouldn't, Bella. So I can't tell."

CHAPTER 18

May 1916–April 1917

Bored and feeling low, Horatia went back to helping Evaline May, just to get away from the tedium of home. She tidied new piles of papers and filed letters and read the latest suffrage news, surprised how many women were now picketing and demonstrating across the country. Evaline May rubbed her hands together and crowed about the suffragettes' progress. "We'll have the vote soon. They can't withstand us much longer!"

Evaline May had become quite fervid on the subject, would talk of nothing else. Horatia felt inadequate in the face of such intense, single-minded enthusiasm. It gave her a headache.

But she felt sorry for Evaline May, whose house was mostly an office full of newspapers and files and books on every surface. There were no curtains or cushions or novels or anything to make it cheerful or comfortable, and Evaline May didn't seem to have many friends. Euphemia Conway hadn't been seen out in public for weeks, and word got around she was expecting, and Horatia sensed it was a further source of humiliation for Evaline May.

People were beginning to find Evaline May rather odd. She went about in her bloomers, hats that were a bit "much" for Grafton, and wildly colorful shawls that she crocheted herself and were terribly large, as if she hadn't paused the crochet hook in time. She was always chasing people for signatures on petitions or letters to congressmen or the president himself, and her shawls flapped like wings as she ran. People began to avoid her if they saw her coming. Horatia tried to make up for other people by being especially nice to Evaline May, but if Evaline May noticed, she didn't say.

After lunch while Ellinder napped, Horatia would walk over to the *Messenger* office for the latest war news. Frank said the Lafayette Escadrille was fighting at Verdun and showed Horatia on the map. The news mostly seemed to be a never-ending and deadly tug-of-war between the Allies and the Germans with victories and defeats for both sides.

When she left Frank, Horatia could sometimes persuade Ellinder out for a little walk by the river, or if Ellinder was disinclined, she'd ride her mare. If it rained, she flopped on the parlor sofa and buried herself in a book. Averse to company, she turned down the few invitations that came her way. *Goodness, I'm turning into a recluse,* she thought. It didn't matter. She missed Bella desperately. She saw only Frank now.

Frank found living on his own at Wildwood lonely and continued to come to supper with the Vanns most nights. He brought scraps of news about Calvert. There had been a postcard in June saying he hoped it would reach them, that he was well and flying behind enemy lines and giving the Huns what for. The other fellows were splendid and brave. He was sorry he couldn't write, but it was difficult to post letters where he was. Terence had leave and promised to mail the card when he reached a place with a post office.

In July there was a brief letter from Terence himself, postmarked Paris. Terence explained it was because his aircraft had been shot up—he'd been wounded by some shrapnel, had an infection, and had nearly lost a leg and been evacuated to a Paris nursing home to recuperate. He'd promised Calvert to let Frank know Calvert was fit and well and could speak French quite fluently, the best of all of them. He said Calvert was a fearless pilot they all looked up to. They flew planes the pilots nicknamed *bébés*. Calvert sent love to Frank and the girls.

When Frank folded the letter back into its envelope, Horatia sighed. "It's not very reassuring, is it?"

"No," said Frank. "It isn't."

Going through the war dispatches one sleepy September afternoon, Horatia exclaimed, "Frank, here's a mention of Verdun! Heavy fighting, and they mention the 'gallant pilots of the Lafayette Escadrille and their . . .' Goodness, I can hardly read this. It looks like it says 'babies.'" She was squinting.

"It's eyestrain from all the reading you do. You need spectacles, Horatia," Frank told her.

"Spectacles!" Horatia was horrified.

"Look around, Horatia. All of us at the *Messenger* have spectacles."

Horatia groaned. It was depressing. Still, when she finally acquired a pair, they did help as she pored over the dispatches. She was becoming a recluse, with spectacles. Was she going to turn into an old maid like Evaline May? The girls she knew from school were one by one getting engaged, and she was neither engaged nor in love.

"Are you and Frank keeping company?" asked Evaline May bluntly one morning in February 1917 while she clipped reports of the suffragettes holding a silent picket outside the White House. "He's at your house every night, he takes you to the pictures, you go riding. Naturally people think you are—wonder what he's waiting for."

Horatia looked up from the scrapbook she was pasting the reports into, took off her spectacles, and rubbed her eyes. "Oh no, Frank is just . . . an old friend, that's all. He's a bit lonely by himself up at Wildwood since Teeny went to look after Sarah. He comes to us for company in the evenings. We go out walking sometimes after supper to stretch our legs." She smiled at the suggestion anyone would think of Frank and herself that way.

Evaline May stared at her over the top of her own spectacles. "Horatia, I'm over thirty, and I know what people say, that I'll never marry, that I was jilted. Orlando and I very nearly had an understanding. I wasn't in love with him, and he never seemed what you'd call 'in love' with me, but still . . . I was truly interested in his painting, and he claimed to be interested in my work, called me a free spirit, and I thought perhaps a man and a woman could do very well together marrying on interest alone, each having his or her work to talk about over supper.

"But then he married that prig Euphemia and her money . . . such a stupid woman! I consoled myself that, unlike her, I had a higher purpose in life, and now my spinster ways are probably too fixed to make a success of marriage. I have no wish to take up housekeeping or make a man's dinners. But I mind not having a family, children, you know, children. I should have liked babies."

She sighed. "Provided he's not disagreeable to you, you ought to seize your chance before it's too late. Frank is a good man, better than his brother, although I know the girls, like poor Bella, were all after Calvert. But Calvert is reckless and restless. I pity the woman who marries him. Frank is the opposite—steady and kind and, I think, in love with you. Don't wait until it's too late. Don't let *him* wait until it's too late to speak."

"What?" Horatia was astonished. "In *love* with me? Why do you think so?"

"For heaven's sake, just open your eyes, Horatia!" was all Evaline May would say.

That afternoon when she went to the *Messenger* office, she looked up often from the news bulletins, observing Frank busy with his editing.

Once he caught her looking and smiled. He held her eyes for a moment, then raised his eyebrows as if to say "what?" Horatia blushed and told herself not to be an idiot. Evaline May was imagining things. And anyway, how was Horatia supposed to prevent him from waiting until it was too late to speak? He probably had no intention of speaking.

What on earth would she reply if he did?

She turned back to a story Frank had just written about an explosion in a New Jersey armament factory the previous month, suspected to have been the work of German agents. It had caught fire and a huge store of munitions and shells had exploded. The switchboard operator had managed to save the lives of the workers present on the site by sending an urgent message: "Get out or go up."

"She's a gallant woman who deserves a medal from the government, and I'm going to write an editorial to that effect," Frank remarked.

What would it be like to kiss Frank?

"Frank, do you really think German saboteurs caused the explosion? But if so, then it would amount to a German attack on . . . America!"

"Yes, I doubt we'll be neutral much longer. Wilson's shifting. Seems Calvert and his Preparedness Movement friends were right after all."

Calvert. They had a note from him before Christmas saying mail was erratic and uncertain on the western front; he never expected he'd be away so long, losing friends too fast; Terence dead, shot down last month; he'd be thinking of their sleigh rides and the eggnog and Christmas cake, and the Twelfth Night dance, all his friends; special love to Horatia and Bella.

It seemed he still didn't know about Bella, though Frank had written him the news several times the past year. Horatia felt sad and rather weary when she thought about him now.

But was Frank really sweet on her? She and Bella had both been so taken with Calvert that perhaps she hadn't noticed. "Open your eyes," Evaline May had said.

That night when Frank came to supper, Horatia observed him closely. She noticed how gentle he was to Ellinder, saw how Ellinder seemed to relax in his presence more than with anyone else, even Josiah. How well Frank argued with her father about President Wilson's changing his mind about entering the war, whether Americans now thought Germany was dangerous after the explosion in New Jersey.

Josiah thought American opinion hadn't shifted enough to back Wilson going into the war. Frank insisted it was unavoidable—German U-boats were now sinking American merchant navy ships in the North Atlantic.

Listening to their argument, Horatia feared Frank must be right.

As she knew from the war dispatches at the *Messenger*, the fighting at Verdun had gone on and on, battles here and there, won by one side, then the other, before the final battle ended in mid-December. There was still no word from Calvert. There was a mention in the news communiqués that a number of daring Lafayette Escadrille pilots had been shot down. This was terrible news, but Frank said they mustn't assume the worst, that if anything happened to Calvert they ought to get a telegram.

There was now a general air of anxiety in Grafton. People were reading the war news in the *Messenger* avidly.

And there were the newsreels. The Drumhellers had built a moving picture house on Main Street, and Mary Pickford in *The Poor Little Rich Girl* and Jack Pickford in *Great Expectations* offered a temporary distraction. But even there the war intruded. Newsreels were shown before the main features, and there were scenes of the suffragette pickets at the White House and war news, jerky scenes of British soldiers waving from the trenches in France and Tsar Nicholas reviewing a military parade in Russia.

In March, alongside the *Messenger's* report of a German telegram intercepted by the British that promised Mexico help recovering Mexican land lost to the United States was an announcement that Mr. and Mrs. Orlando Conway had welcomed a daughter, Vesta Virginia.

"What a silly name, like it's short for vestal virgin!" said Evaline May to Horatia. "But what can you expect from someone named Euphemia?" She was getting ready to catch the train to Washington to join women picketing the White House. "We've been warned we must be prepared to be arrested," she said, pinning on her stoutest felt hat for the train journey and, possibly, a jail cell.

She returned two weeks later disappointed at not having been arrested after all and reported that the talk in Washington was all about whether America would or wouldn't enter the war. Many men there were for it, and this had created another opportunity for her involvement. She brought back a copy of a petition drawn up by the National Woman's Party urging pacifism. Shawl flapping, she pursued the Methodist and Baptist preachers, the elders of the colored church, and most of the Bible class women until they signed it.

When Frank came to supper at the Vanns' now, he didn't stay long. Developments were moving so fast he ate and rushed straight back to the *Messenger* office in case there'd been another communiqué from Washington about the war. He said pressure was building, something was in the air.

In April the *Messenger* printed a huge headline: "USA No Longer Neutral, a War to End All Wars, Congress Declares War on Germany."

CHAPTER 19

May–July 1917

The movie newsreels now featured Americans lining up to buy Liberty bonds, men lining up to volunteer for active duty, the Soviet Women's Battalion marching in Russia, and even shots of airplanes taking off, with captions about the brave pilots.

In the short time Frank could now spare for supper with the Vanns, the talk quickly turned to the most recent bulletins about the war received at the *Messenger*, which the rest of Grafton wouldn't know until the paper came out the next day. One evening at the end of May, Frank arrived exceptionally hot and bothered, telling them the latest communiqué to the *Messenger* concerned a new Selective Service Act. Not enough men were volunteering to go and fight, and the government announced men would be compelled to register to be drafted into the armed forces.

Josiah exclaimed "What!" and Frank repeated what he said.

Ellinder became agitated and cried, "Go to war! Josiah mustn't . . . Don't go to war, Josiah! I couldn't bear it if you went. Everyone gone . . . !"

"Hush, Ellinder." Josiah rose from his seat and came to put his arm around her shoulder. "Of course I won't leave you," he said. "Don't worry, dearest."

Horatia and Josiah exchanged a worried look. However calm Ellinder seemed, anything that upset her brought on one of her bad spells very quickly. Josiah motioned to Horatia and Frank to leave.

"Come, Horatia. Walk back to the office with me, and we'll read the communiqué again. There must be exemptions or deferrals. I hadn't read it very thoroughly before I came to supper."

At the office Horatia put on her spectacles, and she and Frank bent over the communiqué, side by side.

"Hmm, catches all unmarried men between the ages of twenty-one and thirty. That's me and men like Davy Charbonneau and the Pine boys, but . . . fortunately, your father and Jane's husband, Wilfred, are both too old and married. Temporary deferral for married men between twenty-one and thirty if their wives or children can't support themselves . . . if they support elderly parents . . . engage in agriculture. Seems I'm not exempt."

Horatia looked at him aghast. "Oh, Frank, no!"

"Perhaps Teeny would come back to run the *Messenger.* Though she'd change it back to what it was. Just when people will need the real news." He slapped the desk in frustration and muttered "Damn!" under his breath.

All Horatia could think of was not Frank, not Frank gone too! Bella dead, Calvert gone.

"I should hate you to go, Frank!" she blurted out.

Frank turned to face her. "Horatia, would you mind very much?" he asked seriously.

She nodded.

"Why?"

Horatia dropped her eyes. "I'd be lost without you. I feel so low most of the time. Unless you're there, and I start to feel things aren't so bad after all. I look forward to your coming to our house every night. It would be awful if you didn't."

"Horatia." They were side by side to read the communiqué, and Horatia was suddenly aware how close Frank was. "Would you truly miss me?" He turned her to face him. "I never told you how I feel. I thought your heart belonged to Calvert, even when it was plain he and Bella . . . But now Bella's dead, and I feared perhaps you . . . have hopes of him when he comes home."

Horatia shook her head. "No, Frank. I have no hopes of Calvert!"

"Because he's away in France? When he comes home, nothing could be more natural. You've known each other since you were children. Teeny would be delighted to have you in the family."

Horatia looked straight into Frank's eyes and said firmly, "I hope Calvert comes home safely, but I would never marry him, Frank. Even if he were to beg me on his knees." And it was true now, it had to be. Bella would always be between them. "Calvert and Bella were suited to each other. Calvert and I aren't. I just know that. And," she continued boldly, "you and I have also known each other since we were children . . ."

Frank's hands tightened on Horatia's shoulders.

Horatia felt things were taking an interesting turn. She waited for him to continue, but when he didn't, it occurred to her that if she didn't help things along at this crucial juncture, an opportunity would be lost. Frank would retreat into the reticence of a family friend, and she would be living with her parents for the rest of her life, with Frank merely the man who came to dinner sometimes, until they were both old and gray.

"And would you have liked me as a sister-in-law?" she prompted.

"Horatia . . . dear God! I won't pretend any longer. I couldn't have borne it! I've cared for you for so long, ever since I can remember. I just never thought you'd care for me as more than a friend!"

"Oh, Frank! I . . . yes. I . . . I do," Horatia heard herself say. "I do care for you, Frank," she said earnestly. "So much!" She knew girls were supposed to be shy and yielding, but she didn't feel that way. Dear Frank! She loved him. It was a revelation. She loved him, she thought with surprise.

He took both her hands in his own. "I love you so, Horatia. Would you wait for me?"

"*Wait* for you?"

"If I'm called up. And marry me, of course. I should have said that part. Will you? Marry me?"

Her happiness wasn't going to slip away from her if she could help it.

"Yes, I will marry you, Frank Marshall, on one condition."

"What would that be?" he said, on the verge of kissing her.

"That you marry me at once. And we'll hope your call-up will be deferred. I intend to rely on you as my sole support."

Then Frank was kissing her and she was busy kissing him back. Then, "Ouch!" they exclaimed simultaneously, as their glasses banged against each other and they drew apart.

"Horatia . . . I'll marry you tomorrow if you like," he said breathlessly. "The sooner the better, in my opinion." He removed their glasses to kiss her again.

Well! she thought later as they walked back to her parents' house, side by side in the dusk with Frank's arm around her shoulders. She felt lighthearted and thought how strange that overwhelming happiness could happen all of a sudden.

"I'll go in and ask your father now," said Frank, "in case you change your mind."

"I won't change it, Frank. Let me warn you, when Papa asked for Mamma's hand, her father walked up and down the parlor and ranted and raved and refused at first. If Papa does the same thing, don't be discouraged. Please!"

As they crossed the porch, Frank laughed and said, "I won't. Never fear!" He removed his hat and smoothed his hair. He straightened his jacket and squared his shoulders. "Haven't had much practice at this, but here goes," he said, and marched into the parlor where the Vanns were sitting.

Horatia heard the two men talking but couldn't make out what they were saying until Josiah shouted, "Good Lord! You mean you want to marry *Horatia*?"

A minute later Josiah called, "Come in, Horatia. I know you're listening."

As she opened the parlor door, Josiah sat and put his head in his hands. "This is unexpected."

"Papa, girls do get married."

Josiah shook his head as if he'd never heard such a thing, but after a while he lifted his head and looked at the couple. He stood up and offered Frank his hand and said, "Of course, of course. You just took me by surprise. No one I'd rather she marry than you, Frank."

Frank went over to Ellinder sitting on her sofa. "Congratulate me, Aunt Ellinder, I'm going to marry Horatia! As soon as we can."

Ellinder exclaimed, "Oh, Horatia . . . married . . . oh . . . oh dear. And soon? Oh dear. How are we to do that . . . how soon . . . the wedding dress . . . oh dear."

Horatia dropped to her knees by Ellinder's chair and said, "Mamma, might I wear your wedding dress? Do you think it will fit me?"

A distracted Ellinder said, "We'll see."

"Let's see now, Mamma."

Before he took his leave, Frank helped Horatia lift down the dress in its box at the top of Ellinder's sewing cupboard. Horatia unfolded it from its layers of tissue paper, and a creamy waterfall of silk and lace tumbled to the floor. Horatia held it up to herself. "Oh, Mamma! I shan't look as beautiful in it as you look in your wedding picture, but I'd love to wear it."

Ellinder stroked the silk and nodded.

"I'll leave you and your mother to it," murmured Frank, and left.

Trying it on, Horatia couldn't get the buttons on the bodice to fasten. "Mamma, goodness, what a slender waist you had!" She sucked in her breath and made a cross-eyed face as she struggled to do up the buttons. Ellinder startled her by laughing. She never laughed.

"Miss Willa can let it out. You will look beautiful, and you will be happy."

"Thank you, Mamma!" Horatia bent and kissed Ellinder, something she rarely did. "I'm glad you approve."

"Oh yes," Ellinder murmured, "I've always liked *Frank*."

So Miss Willa was sent for, and after she marveled at the dress, she carefully unpicked the seams and let it out. Then she and Horatia persuaded Ellinder to have a new dress of dove-gray silk made for the wedding, convincing her that "dove gray" was an acceptable compromise between "half-mourning" and a color suitable for the mother of the bride. To their surprise, Ellinder nodded with pleasure and put up no resistance.

When Frank wrote Teeny he and Horatia were engaged, she wrote back:

> My dear Frank! How delightful! Horatia is a fine girl. You must hunt down the ring that your papa gave your mother when they married. There was a jewelry box among Great-Aunt Martha Washington Marshall's things when she died, and I remember that among them, your father found a very pretty old ring to give Marietta, who always preferred old things to new.
>
> Now, my dear nephew, you must hunt out that same ring for Horatia. If it belonged to Sophia de Marechal, it is one of the oldest family treasures, but I will leave it to you to judge which spirits, if any, you need to seek

> permission from to give it to your bride. I packed your mother's things away after she died. The third trunk from the window in the attic, I believe, has the box with her jewelry, which was intended to be divided up between you and Calvert for your wives when you married.

So Frank went rummaging in the trunks and boxes that crowded the attic and found the box of jewelry—some pearls and a few filigreed gold bracelets, some gold earbobs, a collection of brooches, and the blue velvet box with a little gilt clasp that did indeed hold a pretty, old-fashioned ring with a large garnet surrounded by seed pearls. It would suit Horatia, he thought. He would divide the rest of the jewelry with Calvert when he came home, but he didn't think his brother would begrudge him the ring.

In the same box wrapped in tissue was a long piece of fine lace that looked like a kind of bib, with a note that said, "Brussels lace that belonged to Martha Washington Marshall," as well as an old prayer book, leather bound and frayed, with gilt-edged pages. Inside on the frontispiece he could make out a faint inscription in faded brownish ink. "Lady Catherine V" . . . something, he thought one said, and the other "Lady Burnham." Beneath the names in bolder letters were the words "Duty Before Inclination" in old-fashioned elaborately flourished handwriting.

He left the prayer book and put the box containing the ring in his pocket. He was about to shut the chest when the thought occurred to him that perhaps Ellinder might like the lace. He was no expert in ladies' finery, but it was finely worked and might look nice on Ellinder's new dress.

The wedding took place at the end of July, at sunset. The Vanns' wide porch overlooking the river had been transformed into a wedding bower with vases and urns of white roses and hydrangeas and ivy. From inside came the sound of hymns played softly by the minister's musical wife on Ellinder's piano. Rows of banqueting chairs from the hotel had been supplied by Albert Drumheller to seat all the guests, and there was a hum of conversation from a host of Drumhellers; Davy Charbonneau with his parents and his new wife, Charlotte, from Baltimore; various Pines who were related to the Drumhellers; various Stuarts who were related to the Marshalls; and a few distant Vann relatives related to almost everybody.

Ellinder sat in the front row in her new gray silk, which showed off the beautiful piece of lace perfectly.

Looking upright and distinguished in his tailcoat, Frank waited patiently beside the Methodist minister, a Merriman great-nephew of the old Reverend Merriman, whose wife had called on Ellinder with a Scripture cake years before.

Upstairs, Josiah tapped on Horatia's bedroom door. "It's time!" Inside, Evaline May and Teeny, who were to stand up with Horatia, wrestled with hairpins and her long lace veil. "Nearly done, Papa. Remember? I can't be married without something old, something new, something borrowed . . ."

"Something blue, and a sixpence for your shoe," finished Josiah.

"I have the old ring from Frank, the new locket from you, Evaline May lent me her handkerchief, and Teeny brought a blue ribbon for my bouquet."

"No sixpence. Will a dime do?" Josiah called.

"Here," said Evaline May, "it's a 'Votes for Women' button. I've removed the pin so you can put that in your shoe."

Teeny rolled her eyes.

"Perfect," said Horatia.

"Please, come on!" Josiah begged. "My collar is choking me to death."

Finally, Reverend Merriman's wife began to play the wedding march. There was a rustle of skirts as everyone stood and Evaline May and Teeny walked slowly to the spot where the minister and Frank stood. Ellinder caught her breath as Horatia came through the double doors on Josiah's arm, looking lovely in Ellinder's wedding dress and veil. "It's like seeing the ghost of myself," Ellinder murmured to Hilda Drumheller at her side.

During the ceremony the sun began to set, and by the time young Reverend Merriman pronounced Horatia and Frank man and wife, the dusk was settling on the valley. The candelabra were lit among the flowers, and the double parlor doors were flung open to reveal a white-draped table with silver platters of food, bottles of champagne topped with gold foil, decanters of whiskey, and a tiered wedding cake.

Before the wedding reception could begin, they all had to wait while a photographer tried to replicate Ellinder and Josiah's wedding picture. He fussed, arranging Horatia's veil to swirl around her feet just as it had swirled around Ellinder's, and positioned her hand on Frank's arm to show off her ring, like Ellinder. And like Ellinder and Josiah had so many years ago, Horatia and Frank smiled into each other's eyes.

"My dear Mrs. Marshall, I plan for us to live happily ever after," Frank said.

"I expect we will, Mr. Marshall," said Horatia, "I expect we will."

CHAPTER 20

July 1924

"What do you say, Eugene?" Horatia admonished her four-year-old son, who was delightedly trailing a wooden duck on a cord behind him up and down the porch.

"Quack!" cried Eugene.

Horatia smiled. "No. Say thank you to Grandpa for your birthday present."

"Thank you, Grandpa!" crowed Eugene. "Look how it follows me! Look!"

"Quack," went the duck, "quack, quack, quack," turning its head faster and faster as it rattled along the floorboards. "Quack, quack, quack."

"You let him choose his birthday present and he picked the loudest toy in the Emporium," Horatia said, laughing.

"Little boys like noise," said Josiah. "I told him he can choose more tomorrow, no use doing it all on one day. We've more toys in stock than usual. It used to be we couldn't stock enough balls and toy boats and doll carriages in summer, when the children played outside all day. Wagons and sleds and games in the winter. But you saw how things have piled up in the toy department. He can have whatever he likes."

"Mustn't spoil him, Papa. Frank says there's a trend for people to buy less of everything these days. They're putting their money into stocks. He says people think they're getting richer by magic. He had a piece about it in the *Messenger*. Davy and Charlotte Charbonneau came to supper last week, and the men talked of nothing else until Charlotte and I insisted we play bridge. Davy said he's pulling out of a lot of his stocks—he's going to sell, then wait and see what happens. He advised Frank to do the same. Frank agreed it might be a wise move."

"Don't think I'll go that far, Horatia." Josiah laughed. "Your husband and I've been disagreeing about things for years. The market's served me well." He patted his stomach with a satisfied air. He'd grown stout.

They went inside where Ellinder was resting on the sofa. Horatia bent and kissed her. "How are you today, Mamma?"

Ellinder looked up with a vacant, polite expression. *Oh dear,* Horatia thought with a pang of alarm. "Horatia? I hear poor Teeny died. I hope the end was peaceful. Frank must feel it terribly, she was like a mother to him . . . like a mother . . . dead. Dead . . ."

Horatia saw the warning signs and hurried to distract Ellinder.

"Mamma, I've brought Eugene to say hello." Ellinder's face broke into a smile. She opened her arms. Eugene cried "Grandma!" and left the duck and flew into them. Ellinder hugged him until he got restless. "That's enough, Grandma. I have to play with my duck now." He struggled away and raced off. Soon the duck was quacking loudly up and down the porch again, and Horatia sat down to talk with her parents. She thought her mother looked paler than usual, and when Ellinder turned away for a moment, Horatia sent her father a quizzical, raised-eyebrows look.

Josiah shook his head and shrugged. "Your mother takes deaths to heart. Remember Calvert." Horatia winced. She did remember. A few weeks after the wedding a telegram came that Calvert's plane had disappeared at Verdun, though the French authorities thought his fate had been uncertain. The telegram informed Frank that the French and American military authorities now presumed him dead. Remembering him as a little boy, Ellinder had cried for days. Calvert's death reminded her of her own lost children.

"Perhaps Mamma would like a cool drink. Is there lemonade in the icebox? I'll fetch some. Goodness, it's gone quiet on the porch. Let me see if he's broken the duck already," said Horatia, stepping out of the open double doors.

At the end of the porch, Eugene was standing with his back to her, looking at something. Someone. There was a person partly hidden by the pillar at the end of the porch. "Eugene Marshall," she heard him say. "It's my birthday. I'm four. I can't come with you. I have to stay on the porch. Mama says."

The person, a woman, was wearing a hat and playing peekaboo. Horatia started toward her. "Hello, Evaline May, come on in and have a glass of lemonade and some birthday cake with us," she began, and just as Horatia reached Eugene, she stopped dead. "Oh!" The woman had moved from behind the pillar and looked her full in the face. Yellow eyes. Kate Irish.

"Eugene, go on inside. Grandma has some birthday cake for you," said Horatia as calmly as she could manage. "Take your duck. Go on."

Eugene ran off calling, "Grandma! Is there cake?"

Horatia stared at Kate, all her senses alert to danger. When she described the episode to Frank later, Horatia said Kate made her think of a rattlesnake before it strikes.

"You've no business here!" Horatia said as coolly as she could manage. "Why did you come?"

Kate said, "Good day to you, Mrs. Marshall. What a fine boy. Is he the last of the Marshalls?"

"My son is no concern of yours."

"Mama," came the cry from the parlor, "come! I want my cake!"

Kate said softly, "Another Marshall child. Sweet little Eugene."

Horatia's eyes narrowed. "Stay away from my child, do you hear."

"Oh, nice respectable Mrs. Marshall," Kate sneered. "If only people knew why you and your friend came to me for help. She was no better than the girls who worked for me, but"—Kate's eyes narrowed—"I would have done nothing if it hadn't been a Marshall by-blow. I would have sent her home to disgrace. But better to put a stop to a Marshall baby. And no possibility of more from that quarter. The Marshalls are dwindling fast." Kate smiled.

"Go away!"

She stayed upright until Kate had gone. Then she sank to her knees, shaking like a leaf. Hearing Kate call Eugene the last of the Marshalls terrified her. She remembered the long-ago morning when she'd been to the cemetery to put flowers on Bella's memorial and overheard Kate muttering at Will Stuart's grave about the Marshall money and the Marshall name—"the name they took away from me, Will. I'll see it dies out." What did that mean? She'd known Bella was pregnant with Calvert's baby. Could Kate have—Horatia hardly dared think it—could she have done something to make sure Bella would be permanently injured even if Calvert came back and married her? So no more Marshall children there. And . . . and Eugene . . . a Marshall child . . . Was he in danger? The woman was surely insane. And dangerous.

CHAPTER 21

Ever since the afternoon of Eugene's fourth birthday, Horatia had been haunted by worry about what Kate Irish might do. But when she told Frank about it, she'd half expected he would brush the threats off as nonsense.

It increased her alarm when he said, "Kate strikes me as a dangerous woman. She blackmailed Calvert about some awful secret about the family that Teeny didn't know, but then Calvert went off to France before he learned what the secret was. Teeny died, and the secret's still a mystery."

Horatia told Frank what she'd never told anyone, about Bella's abortion and her suspicion that Kate ought not to have done it herself, the blackmailing note Bella had received shortly before her death, and what she had overheard Kate say in the graveyard.

"She wants revenge, Frank. Have you any idea for what?"

"No."

They agreed Kate Irish must be insane and to never leave Eugene alone.

And for years they didn't. During the day, Horatia walked him to and from school, and at home at Wildwood she kept him in sight at all times—if he went to play on the swing hanging from the oak tree or rode his bicycle in the yard. She kept a large knife in a sheath in her pocket.

When the strain began to tell on Horatia, Frank would take his son to the newspaper office to spend the day there, telling his employees that Eugene was getting a taste of newspaper life. It would be his someday.

By the time Eugene turned eleven, he chafed at his parents' protective ways. He complained he was too old to have his parents take him to and from school. He wanted to join his classmates who rode their bicycles, went canoeing, and played baseball in the big field beyond the Emporium. Horatia and Frank agreed it was awkward for a boy his age, and to Eugene's delight, they got him a companion. They acquired one of the big hunting dogs the Charbonneaus bred up at Chiaramonte. It went everywhere Eugene did and slept in the upstairs hallway in front of Eugene's bedroom door. This was massively inconvenient, as the dog would wake at night if it scented a possum or fox or polecat and then howl at the door to be let out. But it was devoted to Eugene.

Frank came home from the *Messenger* every night looking worried. Ever since the crash two years earlier there had been nothing but bad news for the *Messenger* to report—worthless stocks, runs on the banks. Foreclosures on homes, businesses, and farms. Bankers and stockbrokers were committing suicide by leaping from New York skyscrapers. People were out of work. The banks couldn't meet the demand for cash by liquidating now-worthless securities. Frank said it felt like the country was dying on its knees.

Horatia saw what was happening to her parents. Business at the Emporium had all but halted, and Josiah was letting the salesgirls go one by one. He tried to keep the knowledge from Ellinder, but she sensed something was wrong and it made her anxious and unsettled. Now Josiah's investments were almost worthless. He confided to Frank he had trouble sleeping at night.

Thanksgiving was approaching, and with her parents and Evaline May coming to Wildwood for dinner, Horatia had stayed up late to make pies and stuffing, anxious to make the holiday as cheerful as possible. Josiah had barely managed to keep the Emporium running, and Ellinder seemed to be retreating more and more often from the present. Upstairs the dog began to bark and she heard him thudding downstairs. She wiped her hands and opened the kitchen door. As the animal swept past her, a strange light in the dark valley caught her eye. She went out on the porch to see. It grew bigger . . . then she saw flames. Some big building . . . the Emporium! Not far from the Vann house, the Emporium was on fire.

She ran to telephone her parents but got no answer. She raced to wake Frank and Eugene. In a few minutes Frank was driving them as fast as he could down the rough dirt road to Grafton. By the time they reached Horatia's old home, they could see Josiah directing the men from the volunteer fire department, who'd begun pumping water from their fire engine as hard as they could. The water seemed to have no effect, as the flames leaped higher and the roof caught.

"Your mother, take care of your mother!" Josiah shouted to Horatia.

With Eugene between them, Horatia and Frank pushed the porch doors open. "Mamma!" cried Horatia.

From somewhere in the back of the house came a plaintive voice. "Josiah, where are you? Why is there smoke?"

Horatia ran up the stairs, calling, "The Emporium's on fire, Mamma. He's with the fire department. Where are you?"

Smoke from the Emporium billowed across the porch.

"Josiah . . ." Ellinder's voice came from somewhere.

"She's gone down the back stairs," said Horatia, running down and heading for the kitchen. When she opened the kitchen door, there was a rush of cold air, and smoke blowing in made the three of them cough and choke. They could hear the fire now, crackling above the noise of the men and the fire engine. "Mamma?" The back door stood open, and Ellinder had disappeared.

Horatia squinted into the yard, half-blinded by smoke. Then she spotted a white figure running toward the burning building.

"Josiah, where are you?"

"Mamma! Come back!" screamed Horatia.

"Josiah!" came her mother's cry.

Eugene was doubled up, choking and gasping from the smoke, saying he couldn't breathe and where was Grandma? Horatia pushed him into Frank's arms and cried, "Take him somewhere safe, I'll go after Mamma." She hastily wet her apron under the faucet, threw it over her mouth and nose, and ran after Ellinder. "Come back! Papa's not inside the Emporium!" From a distance heat scorched her face.

Ellinder stumbled and ran on, calling Josiah's name.

"Mamma!"

There was a boom, and the burning Emporium seemed to move and sway. The men shouted and ran back. "Mamma!" screamed Horatia, beaten back by the heat as Josiah and several of the men also saw Ellinder and dropped their hoses to run after her. But it was too late. The flaming roof shifted and fell, and Ellinder disappeared.

Hours later the fire was extinguished, but the Emporium was a smoldering ruin. Frank put Eugene to bed before the firemen found Ellinder's body, burned and bloody beyond recognition, beneath part of the roof. They carried her back, and, numbly, Horatia indicated they should lay her on the dining room table. She fetched a sheet and spread it over the body, so Eugene would not see it in the morning.

Josiah collapsed into a chair by the table. "Oh, Ellinder," he groaned. He refused to go to bed. He sat with her while the doctor came in to lift the sheet long enough to pronounce her dead.

The doctor laid a hand on Josiah's shoulder. "Terrible tragedy, Josiah. I'm sorry."

Horatia sank into a chair by his side. She was briefly aware that Frank put a shawl over her shoulders.

Dawn broke, and the smell of smoke stung the air. Horatia felt heavy and sad and hardly able to move, but Eugene would be up soon. The morning light filled the house. Everything looked the same. But everything was different now.

She rubbed her eyes and turned to her father. A haggard old man in Josiah's clothes sat with his head bowed. He was awake. "I'll make some coffee, Papa," she said softly.

"Yes," said Josiah dully. "That would be good."

When Horatia came back with his cup, Josiah was staring at the wedding picture. "Remember your mother like this," he whispered. "I do. I always have and I always will."

After Ellinder's funeral, Frank and Horatia begged Josiah to come live at Wildwood.

He refused, insisted he would stay in his house. He had things to see to. Insurance, if that was worth anything. He had to see to that. The Emporium smoldered for days, and the smell of smoke lingered for weeks. Horatia came to see him most days, after dropping Eugene off at school or on her way to pick him up. She brought Josiah meals she'd prepared and showed him Eugene's pictures he'd drawn at school, or little stories he'd written about how one day he'd be a newspaperman like his father and take over at the *Messenger*.

"Papa isn't seeing to the insurance or anything else," Horatia told Frank. "He just sits on the porch with the picture of them getting married and stares at the river for hours."

Frank came to help with the insurance, and Josiah roused himself enough to tell him where to find the papers if he wanted them.

Josiah lost track of time. One day was like another, one season like another.

He often asked what day it was, asked why you never heard what President Wilson was doing. They told him patiently over and over that it was President Roosevelt now. "Don't you remember, Papa? He was elected after the stock market crash."

"The stock market crashed?"

"Yes, Papa."

"I don't remember that!"

Horatia thought it was just as well.

They told him the Drumhellers had lost a lot of their money. Hilda Drumheller had died. Albert had closed the hotel—after the stock market crash, people couldn't afford to come. The Rehoboth Springs train station closed. Many people were out of work. Frank tried to explain how the new president, Roosevelt, was working to get the country back on its feet.

Josiah nodded, as if he understood and approved. He did neither.

The Vann house grew shabby, but Josiah wouldn't let the hired girl or Horatia do much. He insisted Ellinder's things be left as they were. Her black dresses continued to hang in her wardrobe. The brooch with their dead children's hair lay gathering dust on her dressing table where she'd left it. Josiah refused to let anyone touch it. He spent good days on the porch, and when the weather was cold or wet he sat in the parlor. Wherever he sat, he kept the wedding picture of him and Ellinder by his side.

One day blended into the next, punctuated by visits from Horatia, with something for his dinner and bits of news.

"The men's boardinghouse down the river, Papa, do you remember it?"

"Mrs. Irish's place? She did a lot of business at the Emporium . . . good customer."

"Was she indeed. Well, she's gone." Horatia tried to keep the elation out of her voice. "Her boardinghouse burned down last week. They think one of her boarders was responsible. Mrs. Irish is gone."

Josiah just nodded at these bits of news. It was all the same to him. He occasionally said that Eugene seemed to grow taller with every visit. *Yes, Papa, he's going on fourteen . . . fifteen . . . sixteen.*

On a warm September afternoon in 1938, Horatia woke Josiah from a doze. Josiah blinked at the man with Horatia, standing with his hat in his hands. "Why, Frank, nice of you to visit an old man," said Josiah as he always did.

"It's not Frank, Papa," said Horatia gently. "It's Eugene. He's eighteen now, remember? And we're on our way to the station to wave him off."

"Wave him off where?"

"To college, Papa. He's going to Washington and Lee. His luggage is already at the station, and Eugene's come to say goodbye."

Eugene shook Josiah's hand and said, "Until Christmas, Grandpa."

"Goodbye, my boy," said Josiah. "You'll make us proud. I don't know how long it is till Christmas. Forever probably. You've grown up so fast! Why, I thought you were your father! Next thing we know, you'll be bringing a bride home . . ."

His eyes wandered to the photo at his elbow. Horatia's eyes filled with tears. She was trying not to let Eugene see how heavyhearted his departure made her feel. Life went so fast, so fast, she thought. It was only yesterday Eugene was running up and down the porch with his duck. Images flashed through her mind of Eugene in his football uniform at school, laughing with the boys he'd formed a jug band with, Eugene nervously asking her how to ask a girl in his class to dance with him at the prom. She thought he'd be growing up forever, and now he was a young man going away. Oh, she would miss him. And eventually he would come home with a wife. A wife! She ducked her head so her hat brim shaded her face while she composed herself.

When she lifted it again, she was calm and dry-eyed. "That will be something to look forward to, won't it, Papa? Eugene's bride."

Josiah nodded. "Find a good one, my boy. Find a good one," he said after a while. But Horatia, with her arm through Eugene's, was walking down the porch steps, turning to laugh at something her son had said, and the two of them were soon out of sight, hurrying to catch Eugene's train.

PRIMROSE

CHAPTER 22

RICHMOND

June 1949

The morning after her graduation from Miss Leachwood's Academy for Young Ladies, eighteen-year-old Primrose Murray sat down to breakfast with her parents and braced herself. As soon as the maid poured her coffee, Primrose produced the letter of acceptance from Vassar College offering her a place in the class of 1953. She took a sip of coffee, then announced she'd applied to Vassar and was going in September.

Her parents, Mamie Maud and Pemberton Murray III, had stared at her aghast over their ham and eggs. Mamie Maud exclaimed, "You did what? Without saying anything to us about it? You will do no such thing, young lady. Vassar is up north!"

The argument began, as Primrose had known it would, and continued for the next two hours as she pleaded and reasoned that any other parents in the world would be thrilled if their daughter wanted to get more education. The Murrays were not. Before long, voices were raised, the law was being laid down—she wasn't going, and that was final. Primrose stormed from the breakfast nook. A minute later the violent slam of her bedroom door threatened to shatter the two-hundred-year-old windowpanes in the Murrays' home.

"College! Of all things! And one of those bluestocking colleges! I know who's responsible, Pemberton, it's that English teacher at the academy," Mamie Maud raged. "I hear she went to Vassar and kept telling the girls about it, and now look what's happened! What were they thinking, hiring a northern girl with that awful accent to teach in *Richmond*! She must have encouraged Primrose. And I bet Primrose told her she'd do it secretly, she wanted to surprise us, got her to write a recommendation without saying anything about it to us."

This was a shrewd guess on Mamie Maud's part. There were some things she understood about her daughter.

Primrose was a trial. She had always been a trial, willful, the kind of child who had her own ideas about everything. "Go talk some sense into her," said Pemberton as he rose to escape to his office. Mamie Maud drained her coffee cup and sighed and went upstairs.

In her bedroom Primrose sat at her window seat, checking off things on a sheet of paper. "The summer reading book list, for Vassar. I've bought half of it already," said Primrose calmly.

Mamie Maud looked around. Primrose's bedroom was indeed full of books, which spoiled the effect of the pink toile de Jouy of the curtains and bedspread and ruffles. Books everywhere—on the chaise by the window, a stack by the bed, another pile on the dressing table. There was something hard and decisive and unfeminine about all those piles of books. There was such a thing as too much reading.

"Vassar is simply not the kind of place a refined Richmond girl belongs," Mamie Maud began. "There was a *terrible* scandal at the college years ago! A mulatto girl applied and was accepted because she tricked everyone by 'passing' for white. She actually managed to get through four years before they found her out! And to make it worse, the girl had even had the nerve to claim she was descended from Thomas Jefferson and one of his slaves! And worse than that, Vassar went ahead and gave her a degree! You'd think Vassar had learned its lesson, but no! A Negro girl has actually been given a full scholarship to attend Vassar this very fall! I saw it in the papers."

"So what?" Primrose looked up at her mother and shrugged.

Shrugged!

"Over my dead body will a daughter of mine go north to be educated by Yankees who hate the South! Who knows what lies they'll try to drum into your head about your Confederate heritage. I'm an officer of the local United Daughters of the Confederacy because I'm descended from three Civil War generals, and you are too. What if people heard my daughter had a colored girl in her class! And if you came home spouting Yankee nonsense about colored people being as good as whites, well, I might as well resign from the UDC committee! No, you are not going someplace where they pretend Negroes are on a level with white girls. That is final."

Primrose said, "I'm going. Leave me alone, Mama."

"You are a selfish, undutiful, ungrateful child. And I hope you realize you'll be the death of your father!"

Primrose shrieked, "Go away!"

Mamie Maud shrieked back, "Don't you dare speak to your mother like that!"

Downstairs the servants discovered reasons to disappear on errands.

"Mama, if you keep on at me, I refuse to be in the Cotillion this summer!"

"You have to be in the Cotillion! All the girls from Miss Leachwood's go when they graduate! People would talk and speculate about why, and say, 'Well, if you remember, Primrose Murray was always a bit funny'! Think of the gossip and the embarrassment! And no man in his right senses would ever marry you."

It occurred to Mamie Maud that if that happened, Primrose would be at home with her and Pemberton forever. Dear God!

"Well, I won't! Wild horses couldn't drag me to be in the Cotillion now. I don't care what Miss Leachwood's girls do, they're boring. I don't care if you and Granny were in the Cotillion, it's a stupid tradition. In fact, not being in it will give me time to write a story about dumb girls paraded like cattle in white dresses in front of young men. In fact, I'll compare the Cotillion to an old-time slave market, like the one in Richmond, and send the story up north to the papers and magazines . . . They'd probably love it. And it would get published. With my name as the author. From Richmond . . ."

"You'll be in the Cotillion if I have to tie you up and drag you in by your feet!"

The threat made Primrose howl with laughter. "I'm going, Mama. I'll pack my suitcase and run away and take the train to New York."

"When they find out Papa won't pay for it, they'll make you leave."

"I'll tell them Papa's been bankrupted and ruined, so I need a scholarship. They have scholarships. If I do, the part about Papa might get into the papers. Just think of the ruckus that would cause at the club if it did," replied Primrose coolly.

"Bankrupt! That's not true!"

"I know, but he's rich and they'll write about it. There'll be a scandal." Primrose smiled.

Girls Primrose's age were supposed to be sweet. Primrose, thought Mamie Maud bitterly, was horrible.

Mamie Maud stormed off to her dressing room. None of her friends had daughters who acted this way. Those girls who'd gone to school with Primrose went shopping with their mothers, and asked their mothers' advice about clothes, and accompanied them to church on Sunday mornings. *They* played bridge and tennis at the club, and those who had an ancestor who fought for the Confederates put their names down to join the Daughters as a matter of course. *They* would tea and party and dance and be sweet and charming until they got engaged to some nice local man. *They* would have a pretty diamond ring to show off, and *they* would have their prominently displayed, softly glowing pictures in the Engagements sections of the Richmond papers. As brides-to-be, *they* would be in the social pages being honored with bridal showers and luncheons. *They* would choose silver and china patterns, with their mothers by their sides, which their mothers would pretend to despair of because their daughters' choices were so modern, and not the slightest bit traditional, and be guided by their mothers about what was in good taste at their wedding receptions. *They* would shop, with their mothers, for a trousseau, and defer to their mothers' taste and would all be eager to join the Junior League as soon as they could. Like their mothers had been at their age.

Mamie Maud and Primrose didn't speak for a few days. Then Primrose grew bored with the drama.

"Mama, let's make a pact. If you stop trying to prevent me from going to Vassar, I'll agree to be in the Cotillion. I'll wear a white dress and gloves and learn to curtsey. I'll smile at the chaperones and be nice, and everyone will say, 'Do you think Mamie Maud's daughter holds a candle to her mama? Mamie Maud, why she was a beauty. Pemberton practically had to fight off her other beaux.'"

Mamie Maud's shoulders sagged. It was true—she had been a beauty. Pemberton Murray had been smitten and chased off all her other young men. And he had threatened to shoot his most persistent rival—it had been a little scandal in Richmond at the time. Her portrait in the living room, painted when she was a young matron, was a reminder of why this had been so. In it she wore her luxuriant hair piled high, a cloth of gold tea gown with a draped neck and pearls, and a haughty expression—the embodiment of languid beauty. Three-year-old Primrose was painted in a lacy party dress with a wide sash, and an angelic expression, leaning on her mother's knee.

Suddenly Mamie Maud felt too old to continue the battle. If a truce was what it would take to get Primrose into the Cotillion—attendance had to be confirmed by tomorrow—she had to agree.

"You can go for two years. That's all. Absolutely all!" Any longer and the most eligible bachelors would have been snapped up by Primrose's friends. But Primrose would surely get bored with Vassar before that and come home of her own accord. No normal girl could stand four years of college. And then she'd get married to somebody and go live in her own home.

Primrose went to her bedroom, then flopped facedown on her bed and kicked her heels. She screamed into her pillow with delight. "I'm going to Vassar! I'm going to Vassar!"

Then she got up and went to her desk and took out her Vassar material with pictures of the quad and the theater and the student building and Sunset Lake and the Cider Mill. Girls with their bicycles, girls in the laboratory, girls in blue jeans and men's shirts, girls listening attentively in class, the Night Owls singing group, the offices of the two student newspapers and the girl reporters, girls walking with their male callers around the campus, the girls in the Daisy Chain. Real life! She tossed the Cotillion invitation into a drawer and picked up the summer reading list again and checked off the books she'd need to order.

Once she got to Vassar, wild horses weren't going to drag her home after two years. Vassar would be a new world. At Vassar she planned to *live.*

The thought sustained her all summer.

When she finally stepped out of the taxi from the train station on a blazing day in mid-September, Primrose stood amid her pile of suitcases and gazed at the campus, heaving a deep sigh of satisfaction and relief. She was finally here! In front of her was Main Building. Around her, girls rode bicycles and called greetings to each other and that they were all having coffee in so-and-so's room later.

Primrose eyed what everyone was wearing—mostly rolled-up jeans and saddle shoes and men's shirts. Some girls, in what looked like their brothers' cast-off jackets and tatty scarves, could have passed for hoboes. The contrast with the summer's pastel frocks, hats, pearls, and white gloves in Richmond was startling.

She joined a line of freshmen waiting to get their room assignments. One by one they gave their names and were warmly greeted by older students. A girl came to help Primrose with her suitcases. "Welcome to Vassar! You look scandalized by us!"

"Er, well, it's just . . ."

The older girl laughed. "It's all right. My mother is as well. Most of the parents are. But really, it's quite refreshing not to have to dress up all the time. It allows us to concentrate on 'higher things,' as the dean says. We still have to wear dresses or skirts to dinner, but we throw on any old thing in the daytime, and that passes. Come on, I'll show you where your room is."

She led the way to a small single room in Davison, with a bow window where her desk was, a single bed, and a sagging armchair with a floor lamp. Her guide explained about mealtimes, warned her the food was too utterly awful for words and that she must get her family to send provisions for dorm feasts. There was a 10:30 p.m. curfew during the week and a later one on weekends. She told her that men were allowed to visit, and how all the girls were required to do an hour of housework in the building or waitressing in the dining room.

"We get assigned a job, and we all do it, no one complains," she said firmly.

Primrose thought of her mother's staff in the Richmond house—three maids, a cook, and a chauffeur. "Oh, certainly," she replied airily, as if she hadn't been waited on by colored servants all her life. "Why, I'm used to helping at home . . . I'm really good at . . . at . . . well, practically all housework."

"And I have to warn you, sometimes you'll hear a lot of shrieking in the hallways, and I do mean a *lot* of shrieking—you'll think the building's on fire or someone's being murdered—but it usually just means a girl has got engaged. Then there'll be a sort of buffalo stampede when her friends race for the telephone on each floor to pass along the news. It's sort of a Vassar tradition. There's a lot of noise. The dean disapproves because it disturbs girls trying to study. But engagements are engagements.

"Now, there are lots of extracurricular activities—singing groups and drama groups and dancing—but I went for the weekly campus newspaper, *Miscellany News*. It's fun being a reporter and writing stories and learning to edit—same things real reporters on the big city papers do. Of course I want to get married, and have a family, but I thought experience on the college newspaper would help me get a part-time job maybe on a local paper—that would fit in with being a wife and mother once the kids are in school.

"Here's the list with your daily housework assignment—cleaning the bathroom."

"When do I . . . er . . . begin?"

"Oh, tomorrow."

Primrose had no idea how to clean a bathroom but knew better than to say so. Next morning she copied a practical fellow freshman from the Midwest who'd helped out at home, and she was soon gingerly scrubbing a bathtub with Ajax. She thought how shocked they'd be in Richmond if they knew a Cotillion girl was scrubbing rings of dirt out of the bathtubs like a colored maid. No, like a Vassar girl, she reminded herself.

She attended chapel and bought a bicycle and blue jeans and saddle shoes with her allowance. She drank coffee with the new friends she made and signed up for as many English classes as freshmen were allowed. A few times she went with a group of girls into New York City, where they had lunch at Schrafft's and went to a museum or the ballet.

And everybody at Vassar talked and talked, over coffee, after class, at meals, and late into the night, but not like the girls she knew in Richmond, who seemed to babble about nothing more interesting than clothes and what some young man had said to some girl. They read the *New York Times* and knew what was happening in the world. Primrose quickly learned she'd better read the papers to keep up. It wasn't "cute" to play dumb.

A frequent topic of discussion centered on the Peekskill riots that had taken place only a few weeks earlier at the end of the summer. A concert organized by the Civil Rights Congress featuring the Negro singer Paul Robeson and white singers Woody Guthrie and Pete Seeger erupted into a confrontation between concertgoers and angry local people who objected to black and white performers sharing the stage and who called Robeson a communist.

When trade union members stepped in to make a barrier to ensure the concert went ahead, there was a confrontation with a mob of furious locals screaming about "dirty commie lovers, nigger lovers, and kikes." Rocks were thrown, people were injured, and cars were damaged while the police stood by, laughing.

The way the other girls spoke of this, they were outraged by the attitudes of local people. Primrose listened and learned. She'd heard her parents and their friends talk about the evils of "agitators" and "communists" and "trouble-making colored people" and "uppity" Negroes. She'd never heard of the Peekskill riots or Pete Seeger or the Civil Rights Congress, never experienced anything like the physical or verbal violence that was described to her, never heard white people saying Negroes ought to have rights and be equal. She'd never heard anyone talk about these things before. Her mind was busy, trying to understand things and absorb ideas so different from everything she'd been taught. She wanted to fit in, so she'd better learn to think like a Vassar girl. This meant changing her Richmond ideas. Primrose made up her mind that the Civil Rights Congress was a very good thing.

Mamie Maud wrote Primrose to watch out and steer clear of the Negro girl who'd been accepted in Primrose's class. If she was uppity enough to act friendly, Primrose must make it clear she wanted nothing to do with her. But Mamie Maud added that the Negro girl wouldn't be at Vassar long. Negro brains just weren't big enough.

Primrose put the letter down, feeling as she wouldn't have felt in September, that this was a bad thing to say. There were divisions between the races—she'd grown up that way. It was like a river, and you were on one side or the other. How different things looked up here at Vassar. If people in Richmond knew how she felt, they would call her a dirty nigger lover, maybe a communist too. If her friends at Vassar knew how she'd been raised, she'd be an outcast. She didn't dare risk anyone else seeing the letter by accident—she and her housemates were often into each other's desks to borrow pencils or books or lecture notes. She held a match to her mother's scented notepaper and watched the letter crumble to ash in her coffee cup.

The world hadn't come to an end because the Negro girl, who everyone agreed was perfectly nice, was in some of the same classes and occasionally joined Primrose and her friends drinking coffee. It had felt daring at first, and then she got used to it and it didn't. They all studied together and rode their bicycles to the lake and worried about their term papers not being written yet and lent each other their good scarves and gloves for dates. The Negro girl was just like the rest of them.

This was not a view she could possibly voice at home. At Vassar she was constantly being told that if things were wrong, it was your duty as a Vassar girl to help change them for the better. Primrose longed to change something. But if she went back to Richmond to live, she wouldn't. Richmond would overwhelm her. Her mother would overwhelm her. She'd wind up married in a big house with colored servants.

Primrose went on a blind date with the brother of a friend. They went in a group of other girls and their dates to hear Pete Seeger and his group the Weavers sing at a local café. Afterward they all applauded madly and went to discuss the concert over beers. She learned the words to Seeger's new song "If I Had a Hammer." She wrote a story about the experience, how a Vassar girl might have a hammer and swing it, and nervously submitted it to the *Miscellany News*. The editor said it was very good and put it on the front page. She said Primrose ought to write more stories, that she had an original point of view.

Primrose had just read *For Whom the Bell Tolls* in her English class, and all the students were rapturous Hemingway fans. But Primrose had come across a profile in the *New York Times* about the former Mrs. Ernest Hemingway, the war correspondent Martha Gellhorn. It didn't sound like Martha Gellhorn had a part-time job at a local paper, writing up weddings and the latest frocks, to fit in between running the house and taking care of her family. She was a woman reporter who didn't take no for an answer and did things like travel to China to report on the war in the East. She'd lived with Ernest Hemingway in Cuba, reported on the Spanish Civil War with him *before* becoming Mrs. Ernest Hemingway, and after that she smuggled herself on board a ship to make her way to Europe in time for the D-Day landings.

Martha Gellhorn appealed to Primrose immediately. She didn't sound like someone who'd participate in the Cotillion. She looked up some of the war reports Gellhorn had written for *Collier's*. On impulse, to coincide with the essays her English class was writing about Hemingway, she wrote a profile of her for the *Miscellany News*. She titled it "She Had a Nerve."

The editor was surprised but loved it.

At last, thought Primrose, a woman who was exactly like Primrose wanted to be.

CHAPTER 23

June 1950

Primrose returned to Richmond for the summer vacation. She didn't want to go. She told herself to pretend she was going into a war zone, like Martha Gellhorn. Maybe she could find something to write a story about, as if she were "reporting" from Richmond.

A week into the summer and that idea evaporated. She felt swamped by Richmond. She told her parents she wanted to attend the Vassar Summer Institute.

"What on earth's that?" her astonished parents wanted to know. They'd expected Primrose to be fed up with studies by now. Any normal girl would be.

Primrose explained the Summer Institute ran courses to improve a girl's homemaking skills, for when she got married. "And Vassar girls do get married, Mama! Someone's always running up and down the hall screaming she's engaged, and we all go out and congratulate her. The Summer Institute teaches you about . . . children and running a home and . . . how to keep up your personal appearance, grooming tips, so you'll always look nice for your husband. How to volunteer if you want to help people, how to be a useful committee member, how to help your husband's career by being a good hostess, menus, things like that. Really, the Summer Institute at Vassar is like the finishing school in Charleston that my classmate Dabney at Miss Leachwood's went to." Primrose reasoned that if Martha Gellhorn were in her shoes, she would use any excuse to get away from Richmond.

In the end Mamie Maud and Pemberton agreed she could go.

Primrose waved a white-gloved hand from the train window and tried to look sorry to leave. As the train gathered speed going north, she took off her hat and lowered the window in her compartment, feeling she could breathe freely again. Richmond had been suffocatingly hot and humid, as it always was, but it wasn't just the heat.

After her year at Vassar, she was uncomfortable about things she'd never noticed before. She heard her parents ordering the maids and the yardman to do this or that. She heard the cook talking about the Negro school's bake sale to raise funds to fix the school's leaking roof because the state wouldn't give them the money. When she asked the cook why it wouldn't, the cook had looked embarrassed and said, well, theirs was a colored school, like that explained it.

In Richmond she'd never thought about colored schools or even white ones, because if you went to Miss Leachwood's you thought only about Miss Leachwood's. In Richmond "separate but equal" was what people—people Primrose knew—said if they discussed public schools at all. At Vassar they said that separate white and Negro schools meant the white schools got all the money and the Negro ones were terrible.

She watched the yardman ask for a glass of water from the cook before he took his brown paper lunch bag to eat out of sight behind the garage. She wondered if their uniformed chauffeur ate his lunch there too. Servants were always colored. She'd never before wondered what colored people thought about things like eating their lunch out of sight. Did the colored people in Richmond think their schools were bad?

And the worst thing was, if Pete Seeger and Paul Robeson wanted to put on a concert in Richmond, she'd be afraid to say it was a good idea. No one she knew would go. They'd make fun of it, sneer at whites and Negroes sitting together. Maids and drivers and waiters—you wouldn't go to the same places they did.

She probably wouldn't dare go either.

She didn't like the effect Richmond had on her.

It was easier at Vassar.

"When I go back it feels like I get packed in a tight box," she confided later to a friend at the Summer Institute, "and I can't climb out until I leave Richmond."

They were whipping egg whites for meringues in a cooking lesson. "But you'll have to go home eventually, when you graduate," said her friend, whose family lived on a ranch in Colorado. She was occasionally homesick for her horses. "I mean when you get married." Primrose added sugar by spoonfuls and beat her egg whites so hard her meringue mixture stiffened fast. *What if I don't go back?* she thought. *What if I go live in New York? I'll do what Martha Gellhorn did and ask at magazines and newspapers and not take no for an answer until one of them gives me a job.*

That fall and winter she continued to work at *Miscellany News*, where she became a junior editor as well as a reporter. Now she had a story published almost every week. She read the *New York Times* every day. She wrote another piece about Martha Gellhorn, and when it was published she cut it out and sent it to her parents.

Her mother wrote back, "That Martha Gellhorn was a divorced woman! And she behaved scandalously! She carried on with that Hemingway fellow before they were married! While he was still married to another woman! Next thing we know you'll be wanting to write about that awful Mrs. Roosevelt! Write about a nice lady!"

All during Primrose's second year at Vassar, Mamie Maud's letters had been full of news of Primrose's classmates, their engagements and weddings and choices of interior decoration for their new homes.

She disclosed the fact that several of Primrose's friends were already expecting.

And she kept reminding Primrose she'd be coming home for good in June. Her father thought she should sign up for golf lessons at the club that summer. A lot of the young married women had taken up golf.

It was plain from the tone of the letters there was no point asking her parents to let her stay and graduate. She sensed she'd never talk them into it.

Primrose went to see the student officer who dealt with scholarships. The woman in the scholarship office was surprised. Primrose was one of the "gold bobby pin" set. Primrose felt embarrassed, but she filled out the application and said only that there were "circumstances at home."

"Ah," said the officer, understandingly.

The telegram came the first week of May, just after Primrose was told she'd been one of the sophomores selected to carry the traditional Daisy Chain at commencement. This was a coveted honor, and she and the other chosen sophomores had gleefully ridden their bicycles off to the pub to drink a celebratory beer. She'd returned to find a slim yellow envelope waiting for her at the message desk. She ripped it open and read:

Father heart attack serious return immediately.
Mother

When Primrose alighted from the train in Richmond a day and a half later, her mother was waiting on the platform, dressed in black.

"Oh, Mama, no!" Primrose exclaimed as the tears welled up.

Mamie Maud muttered, "Not in public."

Their chauffeur waited, holding the car door open. He was wearing a black armband. "Miss Primrose, I'se so sorry," he said, touching his hat respectfully.

In the car Mamie Maud said, "Your father's gone, I'm all alone now," and started to cry. Primrose had never seen her formidable mother cry before. Mamie Maud took two handkerchiefs from her purse and silently handed one to Primrose.

Primrose dried her eyes and said, "I'm home now, Mama. I'll stay with you." She reached out and put her hand over her mother's black-gloved one. "You have me."

"Only until you get married." Mamie Maud sighed.

Primrose looked out the window as they drove down the familiar Richmond streets. She felt the Daisy Chain—her friends, her classes, the possibility of a scholarship, and *life* itself—slipping from her grasp.

But at first there was too much to do to think of that. Mamie Maud gave in to grief and depended on her. Primrose got through the funeral, kept track of who'd sent flowers and letters of sympathy, wrote acknowledgments, and disposed of funeral flowers to the hospital. There were people to see when they called. There was a gravestone to arrange.

She had a letter approving her scholarship application but had to write back and turn it down. The house felt sad, but the idea of going out depressed her. She had a few invitations to dinner and tennis, but said she didn't feel up to it. Girls she'd gone to high school with got married. She attended the ceremonies and stayed at the receptions long enough to shake hands in the receiving lines, then left early.

The fall term started at Vassar without her, and then the steamy Richmond summer turned autumnal. She tried not to think about crossing the Vassar campus to classes with fall leaves crunching under her bicycle wheels and the library that always gave her a shiver of delight to enter, walking to Sunset Lake for a picnic, gathering for coffee or cards in someone's dorm room, reporting on campus events and getting her story in on time, the last-minute rush to get *Miscellany News* out on Thursday. She missed discussions and arguments and being able to wear blue jeans and men's shirts, even missed cleaning the bathroom.

At Vassar she'd *lived.* Now life's possibilities were ebbing away, out of reach. She was stuck in her old pink bedroom with its chintz and piles of books, like she'd never been away.

Primrose went to the drugstore that had newspapers and ordered the Sunday edition of the *New York Times.* She picked it up herself after church, enjoying its heft as she carried it home. It reminded her that life went on elsewhere, even if she wasn't part of it. This made her feel both better and worse.

Mamie Maud scolded her for getting newsprint on the upholstery.

She fell into the habit of spending the morning in her dressing gown after her bath. She took up smoking. She lost her appetite. Her mother complained she'd become too thin.

Mamie Maud decided Primrose needed to "get out and about." She asked her friends to include Primrose in their little dinners or parties or dances at the country club to "get the young people together." And nagged Primrose until it was just easier to go than argue with her mother about why she didn't want to. She always left early and came home.

One morning in December, Mamie Maud told her to get dressed after breakfast, they had to go to see Pemberton's lawyer, John Avery, about Pemberton's will. Primrose made a face at herself in the mirror as she pinned her hat on. Mamie Maud was waiting at the door, with her marten fur piece around her neck. Little marten heads with their teeth clamped on each other's tails. Little glass eyes glinting beadily.

"They always look like they'd bite you if they could," Primrose observed.

"Don't be silly, dear, they're dead. I'll take you to lunch at Miller & Rhoads Tea Room when we're finished," said Mamie Maud, pulling on her gloves. "And we can do our Christmas shopping afterward."

"How nice," said Primrose dully, climbing into the back seat after her mother.

At the lawyer's, she had a surprise. Mamie Maud had put off telling her, but it turned out that under the terms of Pemberton's will, Primrose would inherit a fortune from her father at the end of her twenty-first year, on the eve of her twenty-second birthday. "Unless, my dear, you get married first. In that case you come into your inheritance at once. Then your husband can look after the money for you, no need to worry your pretty little head with dull finances and investments and bonds and things like that," said John Avery archly.

Mamie Maud nodded approvingly.

Mr. Avery explained a lot of things, about taxes and the income she could expect. When it sank in that Primrose would actually have her own money, and quite a lot of it, she stopped listening to the legal details. She was used to having an allowance from her parents and had vaguely gathered from her mother that once she was married she would continue to have an allowance from her husband. Now she was going to be a rich young woman!

For a minute her spirits had risen at the thought she could go back to Vassar now, but almost at once she decided she couldn't. She wouldn't have control over her money for another eighteen months. It had been a painful break when she'd resigned herself to staying home, but it wouldn't be the same if she went back years behind her class.

But, if she had money of her own, there were other possibilities. She could fly somewhere in an airplane. She could go to Europe and see the places Martha Gellhorn had written about. She could live in Paris and learn to speak French properly. She could listen to jazz in nightclubs and wear all black if she wanted, smoke French cigarettes and go to art galleries.

And money or not, she'd find a job on a newspaper, in New York or maybe even . . . Paris! She could try, she could . . .

She was pulled from her reverie by Mr. Avery, who was standing up and saying call him anytime. Her mother was rearranging the furs round her neck and getting up too, asking how his wife and son, John Jr., were. The lawyer ushered them to the door, talking about John Jr. Primrose said goodbye and strode into the hall. Mr. Avery detained Mamie Maud another minute or two while Primrose smiled at the secretary and said, "What a lovely day it is." She hadn't noticed a lovely day in months. When she had her money, she could do anything she liked. Anything! Her heart soared.

In the Tea Room afterward they ordered club sandwiches held together with little cocktail sticks topped with glossy colored fuzz. Primrose devoured her sandwich in a flash and ordered another one, with french fries, hardly paying attention while Mamie Maud was saying it was time Primrose got out more, she was turning into a recluse and her father wouldn't have wanted that. "We'll go shopping after lunch. You'll need a new cocktail frock. The Averys are giving a party on New Year's Eve. Mr. Avery just invited you personally, and said John Jr. would be delighted if he could escort you. You know one another from the Cotillion."

Primrose unraveled her toothpick fuzz into a long strand of blue cellophane and crossed her eyes in irritation. John Jr. was as pompous as his father.

"Oh, for heaven's sake! Stop looking that way! Don't be so gloomy!" snapped Mamie Maud.

Primrose remembered this couldn't go on forever. Paris was there ahead of her . . . "Fine," she said, resigned to shopping for a cocktail dress if it made her mother happy.

By the time the store closed, Primrose had a whole new wardrobe that filled the car with boxes on the homeward drive—day dresses, church dresses, cocktail dresses, suits, hats, an evening stole, and pumps to match everything. She was ready for luncheons, teas, bridge parties, cocktails, dinner parties, and dances at the club. Their last stop was the beauty parlor. Primrose submitted to having her hair waved and a manicure.

The shopping extravaganza made it clear what her mother had in mind. She was about to be trotted out in Richmond like a prize heifer. A rich one, with its hair and nails done. To attract a bull.

What would Martha Gellhorn do?

Get the hell out of Richmond, she suspected. She just had to hold her nerve for a year and a half.

CHAPTER 24

Mamie Maud mobilized her friends, and from Christmas on, invitations for Primrose came thick and fast. Mamie Maud insisted that eight months' mourning for her father was enough and encouraged her to accept. Primrose accepted rather than argue. It was painfully clear that her mother was desperate for her to get married before she turned twenty-two, so her husband could take charge of her inheritance, and given that girls in their circle of friends usually had yearlong engagements, Primrose needed to get engaged as soon as possible. Otherwise there was no telling what Primrose would do if she got her hands on her money.

Primrose knew her departure for Paris was going to come as a terrible shock, and she bore with Mamie Maud's efforts to push her into the social swim. She tried to drop some hints about her intention to travel, and talked more about her stint on the college newspaper and becoming a reporter. Mamie Maud dismissed the idea. It wasn't what nice Richmond girls did. Once she had a pretty engagement ring to show off, she'd be too busy with wedding preparations and her trousseau and lose interest in a newspaper career and forget such "bohemian" ideas.

"If you want to see Europe, you can go on your honeymoon," said Mamie Maud knowingly.

"What honeymoon?"

"A little bird told me"—meaning her friends were gossiping—"that the banker's son and John Avery Jr. are both crazy about you! They say everybody's just holding their breath to see which it's going to be. Of course, a girl has to tell her mother first." Mamie Maud smiled coyly.

Primrose, who couldn't stand either young man, rolled her eyes.

In April, as her mother continued to direct her social life, she found herself at a dinner party given by their banker. She'd been seated with the banker's son on one side and a tall man, a little more disheveled than most of the Richmond men she knew, on the other. He had a shock of hair that kept falling over his forehead, and he wore glasses. They made him look like a rather handsome owl. When he told her he owned a newspaper in the southwest part of the state, she sat up and took notice. "Do you? Oh my! Tell me all about your paper," she demanded, ignoring the banker's son for the rest of dinner.

It was called the *Grafton Messenger*. He'd inherited it when his father had died the previous year, and he was in town trying to persuade Richmond bank managers to lend him the money to expand.

His name was Eugene Marshall. He was a little older than the young men she knew, a war veteran who'd spent time in Europe. He could even speak French. He wasn't married.

He was a good talker. He told her all about the *Messenger* and his grandfather who founded it, how he'd studied journalism at Washington and Lee so he could make a success of the paper when it came time for him to take over from his father. Primrose told him how she'd worked on the college newspaper and learned about editing there. They talked about what made a good news story. He knew who Martha Gellhorn was and said she was one of the best war reporters ever, that she had an eye for detail that conjured up the reality of war. He knew all about the

Peekskill riots. Encouraged by that, she told him about writing about Pete Seeger's concert, curious what he'd say.

He said he'd wished he'd been there.

They sat huddled over their coffee in the living room afterward. They talked about Paris, where Primrose wanted to live one day, and President Truman and Korea. He recommended a new book, the diary of a girl named Anne Frank who'd lived in Holland during the war, hiding from the Nazis before her family was betrayed by an informer and sent to a concentration camp.

She told him he had to see Humphrey Bogart's new movie *The African Queen*. It had just been showing in Richmond. She understood exactly how Katharine Hepburn's character felt about her adventure on the river. She'd taken her mother and her mother had hated it, she said, smiling. Primrose had gone to see it alone three more times, just for the scene where Katharine Hepburn's character steers the boat over the rapids.

He promised to see it when it came to Grafton's movie theater. They looked up to see that the other guests had left and their hostess was stifling a yawn. He said he'd see her home in a taxi. Primrose slipped out and telephoned her mother she didn't need the car to come pick her up, tell the chauffeur he could go to bed.

Primrose didn't care if he thought she was "fast." She let him kiss her in the taxi. Rather a lot. Eugene ordered the taxi driver to drive around the block many times.

When they finally pulled up in front of her house and they let go of each other, he asked her to lunch at the Jefferson Hotel next day. She accepted, thinking it was stupid to play coy and pretend she couldn't go anywhere on such short notice.

She lay awake thinking about her new acquaintance all night. Was this her chance? She'd been planning to use her inheritance to run away to Europe, but that was over a year away, and it was beginning to feel like forever. She was impatient for what she thought of as Life. What if she invested in Eugene's newspaper instead, if Eugene would let her write stories for the *Messenger*? She could wire them down to him in Grafton, couldn't she? By dawn she'd decided to ask him. Maybe he'd say no.

Maybe he'd kiss her again. She badly wanted him to kiss her again.

She got up early to wash and set her hair.

She spent hours getting dressed and arrived for lunch a carefully calculated fifteen minutes late. The way he smiled when he saw her made her heart leap. After they ordered, emboldened by a glass of sherry, she blurted out, "There's no point beating around the bush. I'm going to inherit quite a lot of money, and I'd like to invest it in your newspaper. Only there's a condition. I want a job as a reporter on your paper. I could cover what's happening in the General Assembly and maybe some of the other national news stories. And I plan to travel; I could write stories and wire them to you. The only thing is, you'll have to wait until my twenty-second birthday a year from June. The inheritance won't be mine until then. Unless I get married. Which I won't."

Eugene stared at her, astonished, and didn't speak. Well, she had been bold. "I can see you don't agree to my terms, Mr. Marshall. Too bad, but I understand. Enjoy your lunch. It's been nice meeting you. Unfortunately, I must dash, and—"

"Primrose, those are your terms? Here's mine. I'll agree, but only if you marry me."

Now Primrose's jaw dropped. "Goodness, that's sudden," she said. "Do you often go around asking girls to marry you over lunch? Of course you're not serious!"

"I am serious. You have a lot to say for yourself." He grinned. "So do I. Can't you see we'd make a good pair? I've never met a girl I thought I'd like to talk to for the rest of my life. I've never asked a girl to marry me before. As I'm going back to Grafton soon, I thought I might as well seize my chance."

"But, I hardly know you!" Marrying someone she'd only just met was cockeyed crazy. And if she did, she'd be trading Paris for something that sounded like a log cabin on the Appalachian Trail. Still, he was awfully attractive and interesting. And she'd be able to write for his newspaper.

Martha Gellhorn had been adventurous enough to go live practically in the jungle in Cuba. And if she, Primrose, didn't do something soon, her mother would finally nag her into marrying the banker's dull son. Or John Jr.

She thought about kissing Eugene in the taxi. And if she married him, she could have her money right away.

"I have to warn you, the *Messenger*'s a local paper. We cover practically every move people make in Grafton, birthday parties and receptions and weddings and funerals and church socials—you'd be reporting local doings, but you could write about anything else that took your fancy."

"Hmm. Say if I wrote a story about a concert with a white singer and a Negro singer, would you print that?"

Eugene didn't hesitate. "Of course. If you write it, I'll print it."

"Or about the Civil Rights Congress?"

He whistled with admiration. "For a Richmond girl you're one in a million."

"I know. What do you say, would you print that?"

"I would."

"Even if people didn't like it, said it stirred up colored folks?"

"Especially if people said that. And anything else you thought needed writing about."

Primrose remembered how they had urged Vassar girls to make the world a better place. Perhaps she'd find a way to do that writing for Eugene's paper.

"Promise?"

"Promise."

Primrose hesitated a moment longer. The thought crossed her mind he was marrying her for her money. She thought about the kissing in the taxi, and said, "It's a deal."

Eugene toasted her with his sherry glass and said, "Wonderful! Now, since your father's passed and you don't have any uncles, I'll have to ask your mother for your hand in marriage. When can I call on her and—"

Primrose put a cautionary hand on his arm. "*No!* Better let me handle that side of things. And by the way, aren't you supposed to kiss me? I did just say I'd marry you."

Eugene laughed and stood up. He tapped his knife on his water glass to make it ring until he had the attention of the startled lunchers around them. "We're engaged!" he announced to the room at large. "I just proposed, and she just agreed to marry me. Isn't she wonderful!" He held out his hand and pulled a surprised Primrose to her feet and kissed her in front of everyone. There were gasps from the surrounding tables.

"As I live and breathe, what a nice-lookin' couple!"

"I declare! That's a romantic fellow!"

"I declare . . . isn't that Mamie Maud's daughter?"

Oh dear! thought Primrose.

Before the news could reach her mother's ears, Primrose told Eugene she had to fly. She went home and surreptitiously took the phone off the hook to forestall any calls. Next day she hurried Mamie Maud out of the house and out of reach of the telephone, to Miller & Rhoads to choose a new hat and then to its Tea Room for lunch.

Over plates of chicken salad she announced that Eugene Marshall had proposed and she was marrying him and investing in his newspaper and going to live in a log cabin called Wildwood on a mountain that was almost but, her mother would be relieved to know, not quite in Tennessee. She was going to write stories for his newspaper. And keep chickens. Eugene was so original, sort of bohemian, really. Just like Primrose herself.

Mamie Maud stared at Primrose like her daughter had suddenly started speaking in tongues. Her jaw and the muffin she was buttering dropped, and for a moment she was speechless. This silence was unlikely to last long, so Primrose babbled, "Eugene's grandfather started the newspaper. It's called the *Grafton Messenger*, and one of his ancestors was an English countess, or something like that. He's been to Washington and Lee. He was in the army during the war. He grows vegetables and goes dove hunting in the fall, and he plays in a jug band with three of his old high school friends. It's called the Hog Wallers . . . no, Hog Hillers . . . Hog Callers . . . anyway, the Hog something. Isn't that just the cutest name! You'll love him when you get to know him. We want to get married right away. It doesn't matter there's no time to pick out silver and china patterns, Eugene says they have lots of those already."

It wasn't ladylike to make a scene in public, so Mamie Maud lowered her voice to an angry hiss. "What's got into you? Over my dead body would my daughter, who comes from a lovely old family and who's had every advantage, run off with Johnny Hayseed she's just met and go live in the back of the beyond with chickens and hogs and jug bands and digging in the dirt like white trash—what would everybody say?

"And a newspaper man! Is that your idea of bohemian, the way you learned at Vassar? Because why else would you even think of such a crazy idea? Who on earth marries a newspaper man?"

"Well, I'm going to, Mama."

"Oh, no you aren't!" said Mamie Maud. "I'll see to that. I'll tell Mr. Avery a fortune hunter has latched on to you and wants to get his hands on your money! We'll figure out a way to keep you from touching a cent of that inheritance until you come to your senses."

Primrose hissed back, "If you do that, we won't bother having a wedding. We'll just run off together and live in sin. Like Martha Gellhorn and Ernest Hemingway did. That would be really *bohemian*,

Mama. And people can say whatever they want, but I won't be there to hear it. I can either be bohemian or married."

"That Gellhorn woman may have written for the big papers," Mamie Maud fumed, "but everybody knows she was nothing but a tramp. Just because you want to get your name in this man's newspaper, it doesn't mean you have to copy her. You've lost your mind!"

Primrose suppressed a sudden small niggling worry that her mother was right. It was a crazy thing to do. But if she didn't seize her chance, when would she get another? And Eugene . . . the memory of their torrid session in the taxi made her blush. She couldn't bear to think of John Jr. or the banker's son kissing her.

"Y'all want some dee-sert?" interrupted the waitress.

"NO!" Mamie Maud fanned herself with her napkin. "I need smelling salts. I feel faint!"

That afternoon Mamie Maud disappeared into Pemberton's study and made frantic telephone calls to her Richmond friends. The first was to berate the banker's wife, who'd given the dinner party where Primrose had met Eugene. Who on earth *was* Eugene Marshall, and what was the banker's wife thinking by introducing him to Primrose? The wife protested that the Marshalls owned a lot of land, somewhere down near Tennessee. Something to do with one of those old royal land grants.

What about the place he was from? It sounded like the back of the beyond. The banker's wife didn't know, but she called back later to say a friend of hers said there'd been a big resort hotel down there years ago, two presidents had stayed there. Another friend said her husband and his friends went fishing in the Bowjay River down that way.

While her mother was trying to gather enough ammunition to forbid the marriage, Primrose took matters into her own hands. Before second thoughts could creep in, she rushed to the photographer to get her engagement picture taken and persuaded him to develop it right away. Next morning she dropped the picture and the engagement announcement off with the Richmond papers. The announcement on the social pages the following weekend left Mamie Maud furious but unable to issue a denial without more embarrassment. She was already mortified by the fact the paper said the marriage would take place shortly.

Everyone was going to think Primrose was pregnant!

A session with the vicar to discuss the wedding confirmed this. He didn't approve of short engagements, lectured Primrose on the perils of "marrying in haste," and made no secret of the fact any girl marrying as quickly as Primrose must have fallen off the path of virtue. Mamie Maud finally leaned over to whisper in Primrose's ear that it was best not to disabuse him if she wanted a quick wedding.

Because if there wasn't a quick wedding, Primrose would just run off with the fellow.

Being a fiancée meant a girl enjoyed a certain status. To enjoy it to the full, girls in Richmond usually had yearlong engagements, which allowed lots of time for planning their weddings, attending bridal showers, being honored at cocktail parties and dinners, choosing their silver and china patterns, and collecting recipes. Primrose and Eugene married within three weeks of meeting. "Shortest courtship in Richmond since the Civil War," Primrose would tell her granddaughter many years later. "Girls I knew had long ones, to prove they weren't expecting a baby."

Eugene said his widowed mother, Horatia, was longing to meet Primrose and would come to Richmond for the wedding. Learning that she lived at Wildwood with Eugene, Primrose had her first qualms about what she'd gotten herself into. She imagined Eugene's mother was likely to be terribly clingy and dependent on her son. And would probably hate the woman who took her son away. Perhaps disapprove of her working on the newspaper.

Primrose and Eugene went to meet Horatia's train at the station. Adjusting her hat and patting her hair, Primrose asked nervously, "Should I call her Mother Marshall?" as the train pulled in.

So far Eugene hadn't called Mamie Maud anything but Mrs. Murray, and Mamie Maud referred to Eugene as "that fellow." Primrose suspected there was little chance he'd ever call her Mother Murray.

"Certainly, you can call her Mother Marshall if you want," said Eugene, his eyes crinkling with amusement. "But her name is Horatia, and I think she'll surprise you, despite your worst expectations." Primrose blushed. He always seemed to know what she was thinking.

A tall, attractive gray-haired woman in a linen suit and pearls was looking around. Then she waved a gloved hand. Eugene waved back and grabbed Primrose's hand to pull her through the crowd. He kissed his mother, who patted his shoulder affectionately, then held out both hands to take Primrose's and said, "You're even prettier than your picture in the paper, Miss Murray."

"Thank you, I . . . Please call me Primrose . . . Goodness, how you and Eugene resemble each other . . . er . . . Mother Marshall," Primrose blurted out.

"Yes, people say we do. Now," Horatia said, drawing Primrose's arm through hers, "while Eugene gets my suitcase, I want to hear all about your wedding plans. Eugene says your mother will hold the reception at home. I had a home wedding myself, and I always think they're the nicest. And I look forward to meeting your mother."

Eugene shot Primrose a humorous look and raised his eyebrows.

"Well . . . she's . . . um . . . looking forward to it too, Mother Marshall," said Primrose, wondering how to tactfully warn Eugene's mother about the minefield she was stepping into.

"When Eugene was just a college boy, my father's last words to him were that he looked forward to the day he'd bring his bride home," Horatia was saying as Eugene disappeared to the baggage cart.

"You must think we decided very quickly, Mother Marshall, but . . ."

Horatia turned to smile at her. "It can take very little time to know your mind. I made up mine to marry Eugene's father in a matter of hours. We'd known each other all our lives, of course, but when I think back, the decision to *marry* was surprisingly sudden. Sometimes that's the best way."

By the time Eugene joined them at the car with his mother's luggage, they were calling each other Primrose and Horatia and talking animatedly about whether Primrose ought to start a books column in the *Messenger*. Horatia was an avid reader.

A week later Primrose and Eugene were married. A photo of the smiling newlyweds, looking smooth faced and young, was taken on the steps of St. John's Church in Richmond. Primrose held a huge bouquet of gardenias and wore a wedding gown with a long train, borrowed from a friend, a lace veil that had been her grandmother's, and a pearl-and-garnet necklace.

Another photo showed the couple, flanked by their two mothers, cutting their wedding cake at the home reception at a table draped in white and decorated with flowers and a pair of silver candelabra. Wearing a pale silk suit and smiling broadly, Horatia stood beside Eugene. Beside Primrose, Mamie Maud had a face like thunder, grimly clutching a champagne flute and dressed in black like she was in mourning.

Eugene would always claim it was his favorite.

CHAPTER 25

August 1952

Primrose had been nervous about living under the same roof with her mother-in-law at Wildwood, but before the wedding Horatia set her mind at ease, saying she intended to move back to her old home by the river where she'd grown up.

"I inherited it when Papa died, and Frank thought, as it's such a big house, we'd do better to turn it into apartments than try to sell it. It needed repairs by then anyway, and Frank said if he had to spend money to fix it up for sale, he might as well spend it turning the house into apartments and rent them for the income. The top two floors are two smaller apartments, mostly rented by young married couples saving up for a house of their own. The biggest apartment is the ground floor, and it's vacant now."

"Oh, Horatia! I don't want to drive you away!" Primrose assured her. And meant it.

"You aren't, my dear. I'm very fond of my childhood home, and the ground-floor apartment is just right for me. It has the biggest rooms, and the big porch overlooks the river. When I married and moved up to Wildwood, I missed the porch and I missed hearing the river. It has a sound that you get used to when you live near."

By the time they returned from their honeymoon in Sea Island, Horatia had moved and Primrose and Eugene had Wildwood all to themselves. Primrose was a slow riser and found it hard to adjust to Eugene's habit of getting up before dawn—especially since Eugene was an enthusiastic lover and neither of them got much sleep. But yawning, she'd get up, start the coffee percolating, and make breakfast—the Vassar Summer Institute had emphasized this was an important wifely duty—slightly impeded by Eugene kissing the back of her neck under her bathrobe.

In the early days, presented with a plate of something that wasn't his usual ham and grits, a bemused Eugene would ask, "What *is* this?" and she'd reply, "That's shirred eggs" or "Eggs Benedict" or "*Pain perdu.* I learned to make it at the Vassar Summer Institute. Do you like it?" Eugene loved his food.

"Oh, Primrose, men should only marry Vassar girls!"

Four months after the wedding, Primrose had settled into a daily routine. When Eugene left for the *Messenger* office, she'd leave the dishes and cleaning to Ruby Pine, the hired girl, and sit at her half of the big old double desk Eugene had bought as a wedding present—"for both of us, so we can work face to face." She'd been thrilled with that. And with the typewriter he'd bought her.

She'd work on that day's piece for the *Messenger*'s "Round the Valley" column. This was mostly about weddings and engagements and church socials, or a cake sale at the local hospital that wanted donations of baked goods, or who was visiting or going to visit elsewhere. And when there wasn't anything happening, she would put in a recipe or a thought for the day or write a feature about a piece of local history—the oldest graves in the cemetery below the orchard, or how a trading post and then Vann's Emporium had once done business on the land where the post office now stood.

It wasn't exactly Martha Gellhorn reporting the war, but people would stop Eugene in the street to say how much they'd enjoyed it.

The *Messenger* had subscriptions to a range of papers, and Eugene brought an armload home every night for her. Over supper they'd discuss the relevance of Eugene's editorials to national and international news.

Within a week of Primrose's arrival, ladies began to visit, bringing coffee cakes or cookies they'd made. They usually stayed long enough for a glass of iced tea and filled her in on who was related to whom in Grafton, which Primrose, an only child with no cousins, found bewildering and soon lost track of.

They also shared an old scandal they seemed to think Primrose ought to know about because it concerned a close friend of Horatia's and a relative of Frank's. "Has anyone mentioned Evaline May Vann yet?" one or another would ask. "Frank's cousin? A spinster lady who was a good friend of your mother-in-law. Well, a man with a foreign accent, Mr. Zoltan or something like that, from Savannah came to Grafton selling encyclopedias. Horatia had little Eugene by then, so she bought a set and Evaline May did too, and Mr. Zoltan would deliver their supplements a couple of times a year. We used to see him sitting on Evaline May's porch enjoying a glass of lemon shrub and cookies, the two of them talking like anything.

"Then another salesman came, I believe Mr. Zoltan wasn't well. Evaline May told Horatia she was going on a trip. But she didn't just pack her valises—they say she packed up all her books, and a truck came and carried everything away. The bank manager's wife said she'd wired instructions to the manager to sell her house, and asked for the money to be sent to an account in a Savannah bank. Some people said she married Mr. Zoltan, though surely we would have seen it in the papers if she had. Evaline May never came back, and Horatia said she died in Savannah! So we all wondered what Horatia knew about it."

Primrose, who heard the story several times, realized that she was being let in on the juiciest scandal to happen in Grafton in a generation and that, if she could learn more from Horatia, she was expected to share the information. Primrose decided the best strategy was to look dumbfounded and say, "Well, I never!"

She asked Eugene about Evaline May. He grinned. "I remember my cousin being a talkative woman, kind of odd, but Mother liked her. She left her encyclopedias to me in her will. We still have them here, in the attic."

Sitting at her desk racking her brains for a story to write for the *Messenger*, Primrose was tempted to write up the Evaline May saga, but she decided against it, to spare Horatia's feelings.

When she was finished with her "Round the Valley" column, she would have her daily walk down to Grafton on the old orchard path. She'd take a few vegetables from Eugene's garden or eggs from their chickens, or sometimes she'd stop to buy a comb of honey from Miss Nettie Stuart, who lived in a little cabin farther down Frog Mountain and kept bees to support herself. Eugene had explained Miss Nettie was a distant cousin—half the people in Grafton were cousins of some variety—and he'd played with her as a child. Now she'd got rather strange in her ways. She spent a lot of time singing to her bees, and she told Primrose she hoped that now Eugene was married, there'd be a new crop of Marshall boys or the name would die out. She always protested when Primrose insisted on paying her for the honey.

After dropping off her column at the paper, Primrose would stop by Horatia's to chat over coffee on the porch that Horatia had furnished with wicker chairs and patchwork cushions. She'd leave the eggs or honey or vegetables and ask if her mother-in-law needed anything from the little grocery store with the slamming screen door by the Pines' gas station.

When she'd fetched whatever butter or bacon or bread she or Horatia wanted, she'd pick up the mail from Wildwood's box at the post office and head back up the orchard path for home. The routine was agreeable, but Primrose struggled not to find it a little . . . dull. She thought it would be less dull when she had babies.

One day at the end of August, a large pale-blue envelope arrived. Primrose recognized the handwriting at once, and after she read it, she turned around and walked back to the *Messenger* office to tell Eugene what it said.

"Mama's coming to visit us," she announced in a voice she would have used to warn of an impending tornado.

CHAPTER 26

"Mama!" said Primrose, stepping forward to kiss Mamie Maud as she alighted from her train. "So nice of you to come!"

How are we going to survive a month together? Primrose was thinking.

"Hello, dear!" Mamie Maud gave her surroundings an appraising stare. To Primrose's relief, her mother's expression said the station's white painted ironwork and flower boxes of petunias met with her approval.

When he'd wrestled Mamie Maud's luggage into the trunk, Eugene and Primrose took her on a carefully planned tour through Grafton, past the haberdasher's and a grocery, the *Messenger* office, the Charbonneau law offices, the post office, and the small courthouse. There were churches—Eugene was at pains to point out the Methodist, saying that was the Marshalls' church. There was a disapproving snort from Mamie Maud—the Murrays were Episcopalians—but the snort wasn't very loud.

Mama's trying, thought Primrose.

Eugene said there had been ministers there from the Merriman family, an *old* family in Grafton, he hastened to add, "Ever since the church was established in the eighteenth century. Many of the *old* families in Grafton attend worship there."

"Ah," said Mamie Maud.

He pointed out the new American Legion post and drove through a neighborhood full of old brick houses with dark-green shutters and white trim and boxbushes next to the river. "This part is called Hanover, after the Hanoverian kings, since before the Revolution, actually when the Hanoverian king was George II. He's the one who made the land grant to my ancestor Viscount Grafton."

"That's a handsome place," Mamie Maud remarked, pointing across the river to the Chiaramonte estate with its neat white fencing and horses in the pasture. "Reminds me of the plantations on the James River."

"Yes, the Charbonneaus own most of that side of the river. John Charbonneau and I've been dove hunting together since we were boys."

"Oh, family friends? My husband wasn't fond of hunting."

They finished the tour at Horatia's, where Horatia served iced tea and ham sandwiches. Mamie Maud approved of the ham. It tasted like Smithfield.

As Primrose and Eugene were getting ready for bed that night, Primrose said, "It went better than I expected. Everything is nicer than she imagined. She told me she'd pictured Wildwood as sort of a sharecropper's cabin. She's impressed it's so big."

"Your mother was impressed by the viscount in my ancestors and anything that happened in the eighteenth century."

"And the portraits. Mama says that's how you can tell the really old families. They have portraits."

Eugene grinned. "We've got those all right."

"*Your* ancestors?" Mamie Maud had exclaimed when she glimpsed the portraits hanging between the living room bookcases. Eugene explained these had all been painted by local artists Rembrandt Conway and his son, Angelo, and that Angelo had gone on to paint a number of senators whose portraits now hung in Congress; that his son, Orlando Conway, had painted local landscapes; and Orlando's daughter, Miss Vesta Conway, the fifth in the family line of artists, had taken over his studio in Grafton after his death and painted interpretive scenes from local history. A picture she'd done of one of the founding settlers was featured in school history books. It was of Gideon Vann, his Indian mother, and a long hunter with red hair leaning on his rifle, who was Gideon's father, around a campfire. The original was hanging in the little local history museum down at the post office. If she wanted to see it.

Mamie Maud had brought along a family silver tea and coffee service and a set of blue-and-gold Lenox china for twelve, partly as a peace offering, partly so that Primrose's rustic neighbors would understand who Primrose's Richmond people *were*. She was nonplussed to see the quantities of silver and china that had belonged to Eugene's great-great-great-aunt Miss Martha Washington Marshall. Still, she couldn't resist observing that the Murray silver teapot was larger than Miss Martha Washington's.

Mamie Maud discovered that the third-generation proprietor of an independent southern newspaper was more important than she'd realized. Eugene knew senators and congressmen and was in demand to give speeches at civic gatherings across the state, as well as commencement addresses and talks to college students.

"What sort of things does he speak about, dear?"

"Oh . . . quite often it's about . . . er . . . relationships between the races."

"I do approve, Primrose!" Mamie Maud exclaimed. "White people should remember it's their duty to keep Negroes in their place, especially with all these agitators trying to stir up trouble."

"Hmm" was Primrose's noncommittal reply. She steered the conversation to another topic. There was no point in her saying that Eugene spoke about the duty of white people to ensure Negroes were given the same advantages enjoyed by the people he was speaking to.

There was a last outing to the Blackberry Picnic, before Mamie Maud went home. There were colored people setting up tables and spreading white cloths in the clearing, and she assumed they were waiters and waitresses. Before Primrose could tell her they were Hanover residents who came to the Blackberry Picnic like everyone else, Mamie Maud had told a young colored woman talking to another to stop chattering and fetch her some iced tea.

The startled young woman said, "Excuse me, ma'am?" politely, but her friends gave Mamie Maud such a cold stare that Primrose winced and hurried to say, "There's iced tea over here, Mother. Let's see what they've done with the sugar."

"I wondered at first why you didn't have colored help, but I can see why," said Mamie Maud afterward. "There's something uppity about the colored people here. And that place they live, Hanover, I thought it looked so refined and historic. But it's a colored neighborhood! Practically *next door* to white people? Horatia's old home is only a stone's throw from Hanover."

Eugene interjected, "Those colored families have been here as long as the Marshalls and the Drumhellers and the Charbonneaus, since before the Revolution."

"As slaves, hardly the same thing as settlers who were white," Mamie Maud said dismissively.

"No, they were free black settlers," said Eugene easily.

Mamie Maud was taken aback. "Free blacks? I hope you didn't have any abolitionists here. Talk about dangerous! They tried to stir up a slave revolution!"

Primrose and Eugene exchanged a look that told Mamie Maud there had been abolitionists.

But Primrose was married, and if she'd married into a family that had been on the wrong side of the war—however unfortunate that was—it was too late to do anything about it. Primrose was bound to have a baby soon, and it would be so embarrassing to have a divorce in the family. The best thing to do was keep it quiet.

Next day Eugene deposited Mamie Maud at the train station. "It's been lovely, thank you," said Mamie Maud, surprising Primrose by welling up with tears. "Thank you for having an old lady like me." She couldn't continue.

"Oh, Mama!" Primrose found herself welling up too. She hugged her mother tight.

Primrose waved until the train was out of sight, and then the two of them collapsed into each other's arms right there on the platform. "Oh Lord!" groaned Eugene.

"It went better than I expected"—Primrose sighed into his shoulder—"considering. We didn't have a single fight. But poor Mama, I could tell she's lonely, because she was on her best behavior. She kept dropping hints about when we'll have her back."

Back home in Richmond, Mamie Maud took out a subscription to the *Messenger*, showed people Primrose's name under the column called "Round the Valley," and her thank-you note to Primrose and Eugene said she enjoyed telling her Richmond friends about Wildwood and the land grant given to her son-in-law's ancestors by King George himself, *before* the Revolution.

"I love Mama, of course I do," Primrose said to Horatia over coffee a few days later. "But now that I'm married and she's gotten to know Eugene—and you, Horatia, she thinks the world of you—I find I like her more than I used to."

"Mamie Maud means well, dear. Mothers usually do." A shadow passed over Horatia's face. "My own mother was . . . troubled when I was growing up, so it took me a long time to understand that. A number of her children died before she had me, and I never realized how that could affect a woman so badly, until I had Eugene. Then I saw her in a different light. And began to like her better."

Horatia sighed, and Primrose put down her coffee cup and prepared to get on with her day. "Helping us entertain Mama has worn you out. You look tired. Eugene and I are sort of exhausted too. Have a little rest this afternoon, Horatia."

A week later Horatia was still feeling tired. Primrose told her, "Resting doesn't seem to have helped. You look a little pale."

"I haven't been sleeping well," Horatia confessed. "It's this hot spell since the Blackberry Picnic, when it's meant to be getting cooler. Hard to get to sleep, the bugs are bad, daddy longlegs and mosquitoes and moths buzzing and hitting the screens. I just sit in the dark here on the porch with a glass of iced tea and a fan to get cool enough to go to bed."

"I know. I thought it was just Mama's visit, but we're feeling hot and lazy too. I don't even want to eat anything when it's so hot and close."

Primrose also began to feel queasy in the mornings. At first she put it down to food having gone off in the heat, but when it got worse after the heat wave passed and it had been weeks since she'd had the monthly affliction, it dawned on her she must be pregnant. Eugene was delighted. "Have you told your mother?"

"I won't say anything just yet," Primrose said. "She might come straight back, and I'm not sure I could take it."

But she told Horatia, to cheer her up. Because Horatia appeared a bit down, still too listless to move from her sofa on the porch. One morning when Primrose came with a basket holding the last of the squash from Eugene's garden and a few apples she'd picked on the way through the orchard, Horatia was actually asleep on the porch sofa. Primrose quietly put down the basket and the copy of the book everyone was talking about, *The Catcher in the Rye*, that she'd just finished and was tiptoeing away when Horatia stirred and said, "Goodness, I must have dozed off." She sat up with an obvious effort, then said, "I've made the coffee. It should be perked by now."

"Don't move. I'll get it," said Primrose. A minute later she was back with two cups, cream for her, black for Horatia, as usual, when all of a sudden the smell of coffee, which she normally loved, seemed disgusting. And the yellow globules of cream floating on the surface . . . "Ugh!" She clapped her hand over her mouth and raced for the bathroom to be sick.

When she came back Horatia raised her eyebrows inquiringly. Primrose nodded and patted her stomach. "This has been going on since Mama left. I feel awful!"

"Babies," said Horatia. She shook herself and smiled at Primrose. "This is such happy news." She reached over and patted Primrose's hand. "They take good care of girls in your condition these days. You know, in my mother's day, ladies were supposed to stay inside the house once they started to show. I think part of it was ladies' clothes back then didn't suit pregnant figures. Now they have all these cute maternity smocks, and girls just carry on going to the store and to church and driving around like normal. Well, I'm so happy to think of being a grandmother. I can't wait to babysit."

Horatia cut up scraps and started making a baby quilt right away, and Primrose, who could cook well enough thanks to the Summer Institute at Vassar but wasn't good at sewing, was touched.

When Primrose paid her morning visit now, she was often fighting nausea, and Horatia would finish her coffee beforehand so Primrose didn't have to smell it. Horatia was sensible and reassuring and kept a box of saltine crackers on the table by the sofa because they calmed morning sickness. They discussed morning sickness and Dr. Spock and how soon Primrose could expect to "show." Primrose munched her way through quantities of crackers and, to Horatia's amusement, sliced lemons, for which Primrose had developed an insatiable craving.

"If the baby's a girl, I want to name her after your mother," Primrose said to Eugene.

"Hmm, might be more diplomatic to name her after *both* grannies," said Eugene. "Horatia Maud?"

"Would you like Pemberton Vann, if it's a boy?"

"Horatia Maud Marshall? Pemberton Vann Marshall? Can you arrange to have twins, a boy and a girl?"

"I don't think so . . . Oh Lord, I'm going to throw up again!"

By Thanksgiving Primrose's nausea had subsided and she cooked a huge Thanksgiving meal despite the fact it was just for Horatia, Eugene, and herself. Primrose was suddenly ravenous, ate seconds, demolished a large dish of cranberries with a spoon, and ate half a pumpkin pie.

Eugene asked, "Don't you think we ought to tell your mother now?"

"Just wait until after Christmas, Eugene, or she'll want to come for the holiday, and right now I feel like that would drive me crazy."

One night shortly before Christmas, Primrose shook her husband awake. "Eugene! Something's wrong! Call Stillman Read!" By the time Dr. Read arrived, Primrose had miscarried.

Horatia came to see her in bed at Wildwood. "Dr. Read could tell it was a little girl," said Primrose dully. "Poor little Horatia Maud . . ." She closed her eyes, and tears streamed down her cheeks.

"Oh, my dear!" said Horatia. "I'm so sorry. It's a terrible thing. I know a baby takes hold in your heart as well as your womb."

"I hated it when Stillman said I'd have more children, as if that makes this less awful," Primrose choked. Horatia took her hand and sat with her quietly until Primrose fell asleep. Horatia left as Dr. Read was coming in with Eugene to check on his patient.

The doctor looked at Horatia for a moment, then took her pulse. "You look as peaky as my patient upstairs. And she's peaky because she's lost a lot of blood."

"Of course she's peaky! It's a terrible thing to happen."

"Have you been feeling breathless again?"

"Only a little."

"Humph! I expect to see you in my office tomorrow. We need to check that heart of yours."

"Oh, I'm fine. It's just that this has been a terrible strain for all of us."

"Tomorrow," said the doctor and Eugene in unison.

"No arguments, Mother."

"I'll see you at eleven tomorrow!" said Dr. Read firmly.

Horatia smiled faintly. "Oh, all right. But it's nothing. Can you drive me home, Eugene? The walk up left me rather winded."

Next afternoon the doctor called Eugene at the office to say Horatia hadn't kept her appointment. He sounded exasperated.

Eugene said he'd bring her himself.

Fifteen minutes later Dr. Read's telephone rang. A choking voice said, "Stillman, I'm at Mother's. Come at once. I found her in bed. Mother's dead."

CHAPTER 27

December 1952–July 1954

Primrose missed Horatia as much as Eugene did. At the funeral Dr. Read told them he'd warned her he suspected heart trouble, but Horatia always insisted it was nothing.

Primrose got pregnant again in the spring, but told Eugene if it was a girl, she wouldn't name her Horatia, because that name belonged to Horatia Maud. But that pregnancy and the next one later that year ended in late miscarriages, and Dr. Read advised waiting awhile before trying again for a baby. Primrose found the loss of the babies hard to bear and found she didn't want to tell her mother. She wished Horatia were there to be sensible and kind and willing to talk about books to distract her.

She would also have liked to ask Horatia's advice about Eugene. Eugene had taken it harder than she'd thought men did. He masked his own sadness with jokes and stayed later at the paper. When he was home in the evening, he would go to his vegetable garden and work until he was exhausted. The long, light summer evenings kept him working there till very late, so she often ate her supper by herself with a book for company and left his plate in the oven. He seemed short-tempered, something he'd never been before. Perhaps it was the loss of the babies, she thought despondently.

Primrose felt things had somehow gone backward in her marriage and was at a loss what to do. The "Round the Valley" column could almost write itself, she thought. She was bored with it—bake sales and church socials were nothing she could get her teeth into. She'd made several trips to Richmond to see her mother, but they just underlined how little she'd made of her adventure. Most of her former Richmond classmates had children, which made her feel her own lack of them. Still, she'd gone to Richmond again in July 1954.

Mamie Maud seemed glad to see her. She talked incessantly of the iniquity of the Supreme Court, who'd recently ruled that segregated schools were unlawful, and that all public schools in the country were now required to integrate with all due speed. Everyone Mamie Maud knew in Richmond was up in arms. There was talk of closing the public schools. Primrose didn't keep up with the news as avidly as she'd once done, so she just said, "Oh, how terrible."

As always, Richmond was sultry in the summer heat. Mamie Maud said Primrose mustn't leave her husband by himself for too long. She dropped unsubtle hints about when she could expect to become a grandmother and come help out with the baby, and even dragged Primrose into the stifling attic to inspect the items kept from Primrose's old nursery, saying she'd bring them to Primrose and Eugene when the time came.

It made Primrose feel worse.

A disconsolate Primrose was packing to go back to Grafton on the next day's train when Eugene called her on the telephone.

"Prim, I want you to stay in Richmond with your mother until this mess over the Supreme Court decision dies down. Some fool shot out the window at the *Messenger*'s office last night."

"What do you mean, they shot the window? Were they drunk? Oh, Eugene, are you all right? Were you hurt? Why would anyone do that?"

"No, fortunately, nobody got hit, but while you've been away, I've written some editorials about the Supreme Court decision on integration."

Primrose felt guilty she hadn't read her mother's latest copy of the *Messenger* and suspected her mother didn't read it often either. "Here, they're talking about closing down the schools."

She could hear Eugene sigh. "I bet they are. I've read the court's decision. Unlike your mother, I agree with it. No one who's seen the colored schools can argue that 'separate' schools for white and colored means an equal education. The colored school is just some tar paper shacks behind Hanover, with no toilets and no gym and no cafeteria and a pittance from the school board to run on, while the white schools are nice brick buildings with music rooms and an auditorium. It's plain wrong, and the *Messenger* has to hold up what's right even if people don't like it.

"I went to see the Drumhellers, the Charbonneaus, some of the Hanovers, and Stuarts personally, to let them know what the *Messenger*'s position would be and ask for their support. It wasn't always so segregated like it is now. Some of the first settlers in Grafton were runaway slaves who lived side by side with the white settlers, and way back one of the Marshall girls married one of the colored Stuart boys, and there're Stuarts all over the Bowjay Valley now. They've all got some Negro blood. Some Stuarts are out-and-out colored, and others passed for white for so long nobody even knows who's what anymore. Mother always said there was a rumor that one of the Charbonneaus married a mulatto girl way back, and nearly everybody whose ancestors lived here before the Civil War has some Indian blood.

"Folks run a mile from admitting mixed blood in their family, but we can't turn our backs on our own history. The *Messenger* will take a stand in support of integration, but it'll help if the leading families back it. They agreed it was important to fight this massive resistance school closure thing they say Senator Byrd's talking about. Nothing good will come of that. I figure Grafton can set an example for the whole state."

Primrose drew a sharp breath. She dreaded Mamie Maud's reaction.

"But it could get dangerous. Tempers are rising. The Virginia General Assembly's behind closing the public schools down. We had a town meeting about it last week. I stood up and said we had to abide by the law and spoke against closing the schools, but people shouted me down. So I published an editorial repeating what I'd said, and that's why last night some hothead shot out the office window. Glass everywhere this morning, bullets in the walls.

"It's likely to get worse too. I spoke to Governor Stanley, who was prepared to adopt a moderate position, but Senator Byrd's whipping people up, saying Virginia is a key state in this, that if Virginia goes down on the integration issue, all the states will follow. Byrd is powerful, and he's got the *Richmond News Leader* editor on his side. Governor Stanley isn't the man to hold out against Byrd for long. They're talking about finding every way to hell and back to avoid integrating the schools, passing laws that any district has power to close down any integrated schools in its area, or the state giving individual tuition grants to white students so they can go to a private nonintegrated school.

"There's bound to be trouble, even if we have a lot of support. Stay at your mother's until things cool down."

"I'll do no such thing, Eugene! People will say I stayed in Richmond because I don't support you. But I do, and I'm damn well coming home."

"Under no circumstances, it's too dang . . ." But she'd hung up. Primrose threw the rest of her clothes into the suitcase. She slammed the suitcase shut and called a taxi. She'd planned to go the following day, but there was an afternoon train, and if she hurried she'd make it.

The taxi was outside already. She rushed past Mamie Maud and said, "That was Eugene. I have to get home, Mama." She gave Mamie Maud a hasty kiss and dashed for the taxi.

She felt alive again, and she couldn't wait to see Eugene.

CHAPTER 28

Winter 1954–Spring 1956

During the winter of 1954–1955, the *Messenger* office felt dangerous after dark. The windows had been shot out or shattered by a rock several times, but Eugene refused to board them up. He said if he did, it would look like they'd been intimidated, and he didn't plan to be intimidated. His Ford had had its tires slashed. Primrose insisted on working at the office with him every day, hoping a woman's presence would deter attacks.

They continued working at home in the evenings. Eugene lit the fire while Primrose made sandwiches and a pot of coffee, and they ate facing each other at their double desk, while they dealt with the swelling mailbag and decided how to slant editorials.

In the spring of '56, the collection of flimsy buildings that was the colored school caught fire and burned to the ground before Grafton's volunteer fire department could mobilize.

Just before graduation in June, the white high school was destroyed by a fire traceable to an electrical fault. But there was a rumor that

Woodrow Hanover, the colored janitor and handyman at the school, had set it by pulling wiring out of the walls and loosening sockets and connections until sparks flew and caught. Woodrow was arrested on suspicion of arson.

Woodrow was arrested for his own safety, the police chief told Eugene. Tensions were running high in Grafton and the whole valley. Both men agreed they'd known Woodrow all his life and he was unlikely to have caused the fire. But Woodrow's wife found a dead raccoon hanging by a noose on her front door. She took their five young children and went to stay with her parents in Kingsport. When Woodrow was finally released without charge, the police chief said the best advice he could give Woodrow was to leave Grafton and join her.

The *Messenger* published the commission's recommendations that state funding be cut to all public schools, and in its place a tuition grant given to individual pupils to attend the private school of their choice, and that new legislation could be passed allowing the governor to close any integrated schools. Eugene and Primrose worked out a robust editorial condemning these recommendations, saying segregation was outmoded and backward. Eugene called on his readers to apply common sense and forward thinking, to remember this was Virginia and not Mississippi.

"That's a good line, has a nice ring to it. Virginians like to feel superior," Primrose said, nodding approval as she handed the draft of the editorial back to him.

The atmosphere turned ugly. For two years the Marshalls were targets.

At night Primrose dealt with the *Messenger*'s mailbag, angry and threatening letters, and copies of petitions to Governor Stanley and the General Assembly, urging them to make a heroic stand against integration in defense of the white race and state sovereignty. There were letters declaring America was under the heel of the communist National Association for the Advancement of Colored People. There were letters praising the leadership of Senator Garland Gray, for setting up the commission to investigate legal ways to maintain segregation in Virginia schools. There were letters threatening to horsewhip Eugene. There were letters calling Primrose a nigger-loving slut.

Mamie Maud wrote a furious letter saying people in Richmond were horrified by Eugene's editorials. Didn't Eugene and Primrose realize that the Richmond papers called integration an outrage to every right-thinking white southerner? She herself had signed petitions to Governor Stanley and the General Assembly to do everything in their power to resist and keep the schools *segregated*.

Why didn't the *Messenger* write that? Instead it took a shocking stand *against* the governor, with Eugene writing that Grafton, one of the oldest settlements in the state, had a long history of *integrated* education dating back before the Revolution. Then, all the children in Grafton, black, white, and Indian, had been educated together by Lady Sophia de Marechal in her own kitchen (Eugene was canny enough to know that nothing was as likely to sway the hearts and minds of Virginians as the mention of an English aristocrat, so he added "Lady" to his ancestress's name for good effect), then later at Grafton's mission school started by the Quakers and the Congregationalists. He pointed out that it wasn't until after the Civil War that their white and Negro schools were separated.

In support of his argument that the integration of schools would not inevitably lead to trouble, Eugene referred to his wartime experiences of fighting alongside Negro units, and the fact that Europeans didn't share the American military's racial prejudices. He pointed out that, as a veteran himself, he could confirm that when American troops were stationed in England during the war, the general opinion was that the only American soldiers with any manners were Negroes. And added that he would have no hesitation in sending his own children to an integrated school when the day came.

Mamie Maud wrote him another angry letter, refusing to believe he would do such a thing, no matter how misguided his views. She wrote that while it was necessary to be polite to colored people, especially when they worked for you, you didn't go to school with them for the good reason that they weren't very smart and they would forget their place and get uppity. Only communists acted like whites and Negroes were *equal.* Was Eugene a secret *communist*? She could hardly hold up her head in her United Daughters of the Confederacy meetings.

She telephoned Primrose and said enough was enough, Primrose must leave her husband and come home to Richmond at once, the man was a dangerous subversive. Primrose laughed. Mamie Maud begged and cajoled and threatened and appealed to Primrose's sense of duty, her heritage, and what was just plain right. But Primrose wouldn't budge. "I'm behind Eugene every step of the way, Mama. One hundred percent. And I help write the editorials," she added.

"Mother lost her temper again on the phone this afternoon." Primrose sighed, putting down a platter of sandwiches and switching on her desk lamp for their nightly routine. "She called me a traitor to my people, called you 'that man,' and said she'd never set foot in our house again. Then she hung up."

She bit into a ham sandwich, then opened the mailbag and took out the first envelope. "Another death threat." She tossed it across their double desk to Eugene.

"Could be from your mother," said Eugene companionably.

"Is this ever going to end?" she muttered, slicing open one ugly missive after another between bites of her sandwich. "Let's see, this one says to bring back tarring and feathering for traitors like Eugene Marshall. This one says you and your paper are a disgrace to Virginia . . . This one says the Bible and the law of the land prohibit comingling the races . . . The NAACP is the jewel in Satan's crown . . . This says communist nigger lovers ought to be shot . . . et cetera, et cetera. That's going in the threat pile for the police." Not that the police were going to do anything.

She ripped open another. Then she sat up and exclaimed, "Eugene, listen to this! It's from a Mrs. Belmont in Petersburg." She read:

> Dear Sir,
> I am an ordinary housewife and mother of three children whose school has been shut to avoid having to educate white and colored children together. I see your paper from time to time and have thought seriously about what you wrote about accepting the Supreme Court judgment. I have talked to many neighbors and fellow parents who wish it were not necessary to integrate the schools, but who desire above all that their children resume their normal education, and if accepting integration is what we have to do, then so be it. Speaking for myself, I experience no undue worry about my children attending school with colored children, and I find the prospect of colored teachers teaching my children does not alarm me.
>
> There has been so much anger and trouble over this, and I welcomed the calm good sense of your editorials. I saw you printed some of the vile letters you have received. These are what prompted me to write, and I trust that you will hear from other Virginians of moderate views, of whom I believe there are many.
>
> Yours sincerely,
> Mrs. Carter Belmont

"Well! You've reached someone who sounds like a nice, normal lady. Maybe there are a lot of people like Mrs. Belmont whose voices just aren't being heard. You have to keep going, Eugene. Or the nice, normal people won't have a voice."

He stopped typing and held out his hand for the letter. "I was beginning to think there weren't any nice, normal people left in Virginia."

"Mrs. Belmont gives me hope, Eugene. Just print it and see what happens."

He did.

Letters agreeing with Mrs. Belmont trickled in. He printed them all and continued with his editorials about common sense and goodwill. He learned from his contacts everywhere that, across the South, a few schools had integrated but the school boards and principals did it quietly, under the radar, as Eugene put it, because they didn't want coverage in the press. He found this encouraging.

And he constantly reminded readers this was Virginia and not Mississippi.

CHAPTER 29

Christmas 1960

Primrose told Eugene it was a sign things might be changing and they were over the worst when they received the invitation to the Charbonneaus' Reveillon party at Chiaramonte. For the past six years, feelings had run so high over integration that some people in Grafton had stopped speaking to the Charbonneaus on account of their support for the *Messenger*, and the Charbonneaus had ceased to hold their annual Christmas party. But somehow, with the federal desegregation order now passed, and the governor's last attempts to think up ways around the federal requirement to integrate all public schools fizzling out, the fire had mostly gone out of the fight against integration, at least in the Bowjay Valley, if not everywhere in Virginia. People were just plain sick of it.

There was a general feeling that everyone was ready to get back to normal. Grafton's children, colored and white, had been educated in makeshift classrooms in churches and the community hall for the past four years and didn't seem to be learning much. Foundations were being dug for a new integrated elementary school and a new integrated high school on land the Marshalls had donated. A bond issue would raise most of the building costs, and the Charbonneaus and Drumhellers had made substantial contributions for facilities like gyms, auditoriums, cafeterias, and music rooms.

The issue of segregation wasn't entirely dead. As the Reveillon party got underway, people agreed with each other that the new schools were a big improvement over the old ones and kept repeating to each other this was Virginia and not Mississippi.

The Charbonneaus had another excuse for the festivities. Their son, John, had married Miss Claire Benedict from Baltimore in November, and Charlotte and Davy Charbonneau were using the occasion to introduce their glamorous new daughter-in-law, who'd worked on a fashion magazine before her marriage.

Eugene was talking to John, so Primrose turned to Claire to say how pleasant she'd found Grafton when she'd first come as a bride, and she hoped Claire would too.

"I'm sure I will, Primrose, but"—she looked around and lowered her voice—"help me out here, do you always have such a, um, mixed crowd at parties? I mean, you look at the Drumheller ladies and their jewelry, and I swear the tall lady there's wearing Christian Dior, and looks like she just arrived from Paris, but then Eugene pointed out those fellows over there are in a band called the Hog Callers, and he said he's one of them. But the colored people! I thought they were the help at first, but then they were so well dressed I realized I was mistaken, but I mean, do they usually come to parties here? White people's parties, that is? Because in Baltimore"—she gave an embarrassed little laugh—"if white people had integrated parties, people would say they were communists or something. I've certainly never been at a party *with* colored people in my life."

Primrose stared at her for a moment, then said, "Try to look on the bright side, Claire, your new in-laws are so rich they can do what they damn well please. And if you want to get off on the right foot with them, be pleasant to their friends. Come along, and meet the Hanovers and the Stuarts." And without waiting for an answer, she took a firm hold on Claire's arm, steered her toward a well-dressed older Negro lady with a head of white hair and some nice pearls, and said, "Miss Willa, how are you doing tonight? I'd like you to meet John's bride, Claire. Claire, this is Miss Willa Freeman. She's had a business making beautiful clothes for ladies in Grafton for many years. In fact, Miss Willa, Claire thought that Mrs. Tom Drumheller bought her dress in Paris, but I happen to know it's one of yours. Claire's worked on a fashion magazine, so she'll know how to appreciate you."

Primrose was relieved to see Claire had the good manners to hide her surprise and shake hands with Miss Willa and say it was nice to meet her. Miss Willa started telling a long story about the party dresses she used to make for Primrose's mother-in-law and her friend back when they were girls when a tall young man leaned over to give her a cup of eggnog and said, "Mawmaw, why are you keeping these ladies all to yourself?"

Miss Willa said proudly, "I'd like you to meet my grandson, Freeman, who's come to keep an old lady company at Christmas."

So Claire shook hands with Freeman, and he congratulated her on her marriage. She asked what he did, and he grinned and told her he was in law school at the University of Virginia.

"I'm thinking about setting up a law office here in town, after." Primrose could tell Freeman sensed the surprise Claire tried to hide, and that it amused him.

Eugene and John joined them. "Are you fellows still talking about hunting?" Primrose asked.

"I haven't been hunting in years, Prim. Davy and I used to take John every year, but I've been too busy and John's been getting married."

"If you're ready to pick up a gun again, Eugene, what do you say we go out the week after Christmas? I'll ask Harold Pine over there to come too. He's a good shot. Wild pigs are digging up the fields, and my dad would take it as a personal favor if we got rid of as many as possible before planting season. You come too, Freeman, help us out here."

Primrose could tell from the expression on Claire's face it was a brave new world when her husband invited a colored friend on a hunting trip.

Primrose was trying not to throw up. She'd taken one sip of eggnog and gagged. She'd bitten a cheese straw and thought it tasted strange. How could a cheese straw taste like metal? She picked up a miniature patty shell stuffed with crab and mayonnaise, looked at it, and put it down untasted on her plate, though crab was one of her favorite things. Yet she was hungry.

She looked around the food laid out everywhere, then spied a platter of cheese and crackers. Crackers! She abandoned Claire. She ate crackers and more crackers. Then she picked a lemon garnish off a platter of sliced ham and ate that. Delicious. She ate the rest of the lemon slices on the platter and went looking for more. She suddenly craved, craved, craved the sourness . . . and it dawned on her.

She went to find Eugene. "See you next Thursday, 6:00 a.m.," he said to John and Harold and Freeman as she pulled him away.

"What is it, ready to go home?"

"Eugene, I hope it's not a false alarm, but I think I might be . . . pregnant!"

"What?"

"Aside from my being very late, the eggnog made me gag. All evening I've been feeling nauseous, then I saw the crackers set out with the cheese and I went crazy and ate them all. Then I ate a whole lemon. By itself. And you know how I love crab? I nearly threw up just now, looking at the crab things." She shuddered. "Ugh! Makes me feel sick just thinking of crab."

"Oh, Prim, we were starting to think it wouldn't happen."

"I know. I hope so much it will be all right this time, but I'm almost scared to hope."

Eugene put his arm around her shoulders. "Let's hope. We have to hope. We want this so much."

"I'll hope, while you find me another lemon. I need a lemon, Eugene. This minute!"

CHAPTER 30

October 1961

When the baby was born, a week late according to Dr. Stillman Read, Primrose and Eugene were both too traditional not to give her a family name. Eugene suggested either Sophia after Sophia Grafton de Marechal, who was buried in the cemetery, or Catherine. Sophia had had a daughter named Catherine who'd married one of the Stuarts.

He liked the first, Primrose liked the second, so they named the baby Sophia Catherine. And from the first called her Sophy.

Mamie Maud came from Richmond for the christening with gifts for the baby—a pair of old-fashioned nursery lamps with a shepherd and shepherdess and china lambs Mamie Maud's mother had given Primrose when she was little and a silver christening cup that had been in the Murray family since before the Revolution, at which time it had been melted down to make officer epaulettes for one of the Murray ancestors before being melted down again and refashioned as a cup afterward.

"And this is for Sophy's hope chest," announced Mamie Maud, unfolding something with reverent hands.

"But, Mama, it's a little early to think about Sophy's hope chest—she's only a month old! What is it? It looks a little stained."

"It's a quilt pieced from the remnants of the Confederate flag your great-grandfather was carrying when he was killed. That's his blood on it. Your great-grandmother sewed it with her own hands and put in pieces of her wedding dress. It will be a piece of history for Sophy to treasure. A reminder of her Murray heritage. Of our Richmond *values.* Of our Southern pride."

"Good Lord, no!" muttered Primrose.

"That quilt is positively morbid," Primrose said to Eugene later.

Mamie Maud had also brought a family christening gown she'd dug out of the attic and insisted Sophy wear. It was a bit moth-eaten and yellow with age and the lace had holes, but Primrose stopped herself from protesting that it looked like an old rag.

Mamie Maud let it be known that while a Methodist baptism was better than nothing, she was sure the minister at St. John's in Richmond would be willing to have a second, Episcopalian one.

Finally, she insisted on hosting a christening lunch at the old Grafton Hotel for all the guests after the ceremony.

"Mama's taking everything over! It was a mistake to ask her to come for the christening!" Primrose was feeling teary and cross and hormonal.

"Let her. Your mother's thrilled to have a grandchild. It would be cruel to stop her, especially since the two of you have been getting along so well, and there's no denying your mother's good with Sophy, can get her to sleep when she's crying."

So Sophy wore the christening gown, and the lunch afterward went ahead. Mamie Maud immediately plunged into a discussion with Claire and Charlotte Charbonneau about girls' schools and how the ones in Richmond compared with those in Baltimore. Mamie Maud said Miss Leachwood's in Richmond was one of the oldest—she and her mother and Primrose had all attended, and Sophy would be a fourth-generation girl.

Overhearing this conversation, Primrose sat up and muttered to Eugene, "Oh no, what's Mama up to?" Mamie Maud, Claire, and Charlotte were all nodding agreement that single-sex education was preferable for girls, just as Eugene responded to a question from Senator Cy Charbonneau that Sophy would go to the integrated Grafton school—how could they do anything else after the stand the *Messenger* had taken?

"What?" demanded Mamie Maud. "*What* did you say?"

"Sophy will go to the Grafton school," said Eugene, puzzled by her angry tone.

Mamie Maud stood up and said loudly, "Sophy will do nothing of the kind! When she's old enough she'll come live with me while she attends Miss Leachwood's! I don't want my granddaughter absorbing her parents' communist ideas!"

There were shocked gasps round the table.

"That's a kind offer, Mamie Maud, but Sophy is our daughter, and she'll go to school here."

By his side Primrose nodded her agreement. "Please sit down, Mama," she begged.

Mamie Maud glared at him, threw down her napkin, and said they were a disgrace, both of them, that she would never forgive Eugene for poisoning Primrose's mind, betraying the family, and ruining first her daughter's, then her grandchild's life. She stormed out and took the next train back to Richmond, leaving the lunch party sitting in stunned silence and Primrose in tears.

Next day Primrose folded the clothes her mother had left behind and packed them back into their suitcase to send on to Richmond. Primrose was torn. Partly she was furious about the lunch debacle and the awful scene in the hotel, but she also felt terrible. Mamie Maud had tried, and she'd thought the two of them had forged a bond over Sophy, even if Mamie Maud had been bossy about what Sophy ought and ought not to do.

"Everything was going so well . . . then Mama sort of blew up. She ought to apologize!" Primrose had been up several times in the night to feed the baby, and she was very short-tempered. Mamie Maud had dealt with the night feeds to let Primrose sleep.

"Stand back and give her time," Eugene advised. "She'll come around. She'll have to if she wants to see Sophy again. Don't get overwhelmed by postpartum emotion, Prim." And it was true that Primrose still felt very down after Sophy's birth. Dr. Read had dismissed it as "the baby blues," not very sympathetically.

At the moment Primrose thought she hated men, and she especially hated Dr. Read and Eugene, who didn't know how it felt to have stitches that still pulled and twinged and exhaustion from getting up nights and a figure so misshapen that most of her clothes didn't fit and a weird sense of being on the verge of tears all the time for no good reason. Her mother had understood all that and been sympathetic and understanding. Now her mother had gone off in a huff.

If only Horatia were alive!

Primrose refused to be the first to get in touch, but she kept hoping her mother would call or write . . . or something. But she didn't, not even when Primrose relented and sent her pictures of Sophy looking fat and adorable in a smocked dress beside a birthday cake with one candle on it. After that she sent snapshots of Sophy with an Easter basket, Sophy in a sunbonnet, and Sophy next to a carved pumpkin.

Maybe the pictures would do the trick eventually.

Eugene tried calling Mamie Maud, but she'd hung up on him. He'd written a letter, but it was returned unopened. He told Primrose the best thing to do was to keep sending the photos. She'd respond eventually.

She didn't.

When Sophy was three there was a terse letter from Mamie Maud's lawyers, informing them Mamie Maud had had a stroke and died suddenly. She'd left her entire estate to a distant cousin, expressly cutting Primrose and Eugene off in her will, citing her wish to prevent any more of the Murray money supporting a cause that would have her southern ancestors turning in their graves.

Primrose was surprised by the grief she felt. She kept the lamps with the shepherd and shepherdess, which she put in Sophy's bedroom, and let her use the silver cup for her milk. She thought the quilt with the Confederate flag was rather poisonous and told Eugene she'd like to burn it—the world didn't need old Confederate flags with blood on them. But it reminded her of her mother. In the end she stuffed it in the back of her linen closet.

In the years that followed, as Sophy grew older, Primrose often reflected on her tempestuous relationship with Mamie Maud. Motherhood wasn't as easy as it looked, she found, no matter how much you loved your child. She'd thought she and Sophy would have the kind of relationship she and Horatia had enjoyed. But they didn't. Sophy seemed to become more secretive and perplexing with every birthday.

"Could Sophy be a changeling?" she asked Eugene after one terrible row.

"Possibly," said Eugene.

Primrose often wondered if mothers and daughters were always bound to misunderstand each other. Were daughters bound to drive their mothers crazy to get something they wanted or needed from life? Were mothers bound to try to take over their daughters' lives like Sophy accused her of doing?

After one particularly trying episode with a teenage Sophy, Primrose snapped, "I hope you have a daughter and see how you like it."

"Careful what you wish for," said Eugene, who'd overheard. "It often comes true, Prim."

And in the end, it did.

ROSE-LINDA

CHAPTER 31

1986

I don't remember much about my life with Mama—Sophy Marshall—before I came to Wildwood. Just snatches of things, like waking up in different places, on a bed or a sofa, even in the car, covered with a blanket or sometimes somebody's coat. Or different people, except for Mama.

We were never anywhere long. For a while there was a room in a city, where the air outside our windows was thick with the noise of cars honking, sirens, and sometimes people shouting. Then a desert, where we lived in a trailer and hot winds blew dry underbrush scratching against the trailer's metal side, like animal claws. There'd been a house by the sea that I'd liked best, with a big porch all around it where I'd sit and peel curls of paint off the railings, and listen to the ocean rolling onto the shore with a thump, swish, thump, swish, thump, swish. I remember cold, milky foam covering my bare toes when I played on the sand with my bucket and spade, and peanut butter sandwiches that were gritty with sand, so I swallowed them almost whole.

Mama told me we were looking for Lamarr Hamilton. He'd disappeared hitchhiking. We had to find him.

I can't really remember my mother. She occupies a shadowy corner of my memory I can't quite reach. I can almost see and hear her, packing the two suitcases, giving me stuff we didn't need anymore, like nearly empty boxes of Kleenex and mostly used shampoo, to throw away. I remember her heaving the suitcases into the trunk, and driving away from wherever we'd been.

I remember best what happened just before we came to Wildwood. Mama caught me in the bathroom shaking Johnson's baby powder on my wrist, and before she could stop me, I'd sniffed it up into my nose. Baby powder comes out fast, and there was lots of it on the back of my hand. I remember sneezing and choking and I couldn't breathe. Mama was pounding me on the back, saying baby powder was just for after my bath, and for crying out loud, Rose-Linda, what did I think I was doing?

If I'd been able to talk instead of choking, I'd have said I was copying her and the people who said we could stay with them while she looked for Lamarr.

"You were supposed to be in bed," said Mama, wiping my face with a damp washrag.

The light had still been on in the room with the kitchen part at one end and the sofa at the other, and I could hear everybody was still up, so I'd gone to tell her I'd had a bad dream. There were a lot of green bottles and glasses, and they were all sniffing the backs of their wrists after they dabbed powder on. They'd been laughing.

It wasn't until years later I understood about drugs.

Mama tried to clean baby powder out of my nose, then said it was time to take me to Wildwood. She'd talked about Wildwood so often I'd formed a picture of a wild wood in my mind. I didn't have many toys, but we'd get books from the library in the places we stayed, and Mama read me stories. Many of them involved woods. We'd read a book about big hairy wild things with claws dancing in a scary way. Woods in books were one thing. Going to the woods for real was a terrifying idea. They were a dark and dangerous place, full of tall trees where wolves and child-eating witches lurked to get you.

"I don't want to go to Wildwood!"

"We have to. You're almost old enough for kindergarten."

"I don't want to go to kinnergarden!"

But Mama packed up our stuff again and I threw out the trash.

We drove for day after day, eating hamburgers that smelled too oniony from drive-through places, pulling off the highway to sleep in the car. Every time I thought about Wildwood, my heart thumped. The last night in the car we'd driven up a windy road in the dark and stopped. Mama bent forward, with her head on the steering wheel and her eyes shut.

"We're here. Just give me a minute, Rose-Linda."

I sighed and hugged my sweater around me, wishing there were a bathroom with a light so I wouldn't have to go brush my teeth with water from a thermos and then pee in the dark.

I opened the car door and got down to wait for Mama's minute to finish, and when I looked up, there were ghosts all around us. I climbed back into the front seat, slammed my door, and locked it, screaming at Mama to drive away.

"What!" Mama raised her head.

"Before the ghosts get us!"

"What ghosts?" Mama's voice was shrill.

"Those white things! Look!"

Mama let out her breath. "You scared me. Those aren't ghosts, they're trees. Dogwood trees. They aren't scary. They're pretty. Lots of dogwood trees in the mountains around here. They have white flowers in the spring. It's OK. Come on, let's get inside. Can't put it off any longer."

Then I saw what I hadn't seen because of the ghosts. There was a big house, with lights in the windows, and when I got out of the car I could smell smoke. While Mama pulled our suitcases out of the trunk, I kept a wary eye on the white things, to be certain they weren't coming toward us in case Mama was wrong.

My heart was still pounding when a loud screech ripped the air and a dark and shadowy form whooshed above us.

I screamed again and grabbed Mama. "I want to go! I don't like it here!" Who knew what else was lurking out there to get us.

Mama shook my hand off. "For Pete's sake! It's just an owl, Rose-Linda! Hunting for its dinner. There're lots of owls around here, but they don't want anything as big as you. They like mice. And you'll like it here, I promise."

I will not, I remember whispering under my breath.

We bumped our suitcases up the porch steps. Out of the corner of my eye, I saw something run across the grass into the trees. I told Mama. "Probably a fox, maybe even a coyote," said Mama. She hadn't even seen it.

It had been a little dark shape about my size, on two legs. Two legs, not four. But Mama sounded like she'd get her mad voice in a minute so I kept quiet.

The porch went from outside into the house. "They call this a dog-trot so the dogs can come in and out and straight into the house when the weather's warm."

I didn't like dogs.

Mama pushed open a door. There was music playing and the room was warm. "Mother," she said. "Dad? Surprise!"

A man poking a log onto the fire snapping in a big stone fireplace turned around, and a lady with heavy eyebrows and white hair who was reading a book looked up like we'd startled her, gasped, then exclaimed, "Sophy? Oh, Sophy!" She dropped her book and got up fast, arms out to hug Mama, as the tall man with round gold glasses that slid down his nose crossed the room to hug her too.

"Sophy? Welcome home, darlin'!" Then he looked down and threw up his hands like he was surprised to see me. "Well now, who have we got here? I bet this young lady is Rosalind that you wrote us about. Ah, fair Rosalind! '*From the east to western Ind, no jewel is like Rosalind.*'"

"Dad! Don't tease her. She's only five. She hasn't read Shakespeare. And it's Rose-Linda. It's Rose-Linda Hamilton Marshall."

"Hamilton, huh?" muttered the tall man. He made a quick face. "Well," he said, stooping down, "Miss Rose-Linda Hamilton Marshall, I'm your granddaddy. And that lady"—he pointed to the woman with white hair—"is your grandmother. Her name is a bit like yours. She's Primrose, and you're Rose-Linda. I think you should call her Granny, don't you?"

I nodded.

"And you can call me Gramps. How about that?"

I nodded again. I asked if there were any dogs, and the tall man threw his head back and made a face like he was thinking, then said, "No, I don't believe there are. We have chickens, though. You can help me feed them in the morning if you'd like to, and we can find the eggs."

The last thing I remember was having a bath and then a glass of milk and some cookies while the grown-ups talked.

The next morning I woke up in a bigger bed than I'd ever slept in, way high off the floor with pillows and covers made out of different cloth pieces. The walls looked like brown-and-white stripes, and when I went outside later I saw the cabin was all like that, inside and out, not stripes but logs with white between. Mama was still sleeping, and I was wearing a nightgown that had little flowers on it. It felt too big for me.

Sun was shining under the curtains at the windows, and I sat up and looked around the room. We'd never stayed in a room like this before. There were little tables on either side of the bed with a cute lamp each. Opposite our big bed there was a chest of drawers with a white cloth and silvery things on top. There was a tall mirror on one wall, pictures on another wall, and a rocking chair holding more folded covers.

By the door stood a box painted with a girl and a boy, and the top was open. Toys!

Careful not to make any noise, I slipped out of bed to investigate, hitching the nightie up so I wouldn't trip.

I squatted down with the nightie billowing around me and lifted out a baby doll in pink baby clothes and a lacy cap, lying with its eyes closed in a doll-sized wicker cradle. The doll was holding a miniature baby bottle and was covered with a doll blanket. There was a stuffed bear and a stuffed rabbit, a box with a tea set, a big wooden painted boat with lots of wooden animals inside, a jumping rope, and some coloring books in a rubber band. They'd been colored in some but still had pictures that were just black and white. I wondered who the toys belonged to and whether it was OK for me to play with them.

I rocked the doll some, then opened the tea things and set out little plates, one for me, one for the doll, and one for Mama. I opened a big flat wooden box at the bottom of the chest and found miniature china food—elaborate cakes, a roast chicken, a fish on a platter, a bowl of fruit. I put some on the tea set plates, and all of a sudden I wished it was real food. I was really hungry.

Right then I smelled cooking. I looked to see if Mama was waking up, but she wasn't. I went to her side of the bed and whispered loudly, "Mama, they're cooking bacon here! Can we buy some? I'm hungry!"

Mama groaned and rubbed her eyes and asked if I was awake already, but she didn't get mad.

And we got dressed, went to the kitchen, and found bacon! Gramps lifted me into a chair, and Granny gave me a plate with a lot of bacon and scrambled eggs and toast with peach jam. I ate until my stomach hurt. Afterward Granny went to the market and came home with a big box of crayons and a white parcel of cut-up chicken. She put the chicken to soak in buttermilk. Mama and I sat at the kitchen table, and I colored pictures that she told me she hadn't got around to when she was five.

I bent over the coloring books. Mama and Granny drank coffee and talked over my head about Lamarr Hamilton, who I knew we wanted to find. Mama's voice had dropped. "You don't understand! I've tried and tried to tell you, but you just refuse . . . I'm not crazy . . . Lamarr understood when I told him . . . I don't make it up! I don't!" She stood up and walked out. Mad. Granny sighed and put her head in her hands. After a minute I went on with my coloring. It seemed like the best thing to do.

I remember having supper that night, Mama carrying dishes to the table, pouring my milk, cutting up my chicken, and whispering that the slimy green stuff I'd spat out was called okra and she didn't like it either but we both had to eat three bites for manners' sake. Mama winked at me as she pushed the rest under the mashed potatoes so you couldn't see it.

Tucking me into bed later, she said, "You're my good girl, Rose-Linda." I remember she said that and pulled the quilt over me. "Good night, be safe," she said at the door, her shape dark against the light in the hall.

I've gone over and over that arrival, that supper, that bedtime so often, trying to relive it, trying to see her clearly, hear her voice, but things you don't know you'll need to remember later slip away, blurred.

Next morning Mama wasn't there sleeping. Granny was at the stove making pancakes for breakfast, saying I could have all the syrup I wanted because it was Sunday. Gramps put his coffee down and said I was just the person he needed to help him wash his car after breakfast. Was I big enough to hold the hose all by myself? Then we'd go down to Grafton and pick up all the Sunday papers, and after that we'd go to the gas station to fill 'er up and see if there was an Eskimo Pie in the freezer there with my name on it. "I'll ask Mama," I said, hoping we didn't have to leave right away.

"She said to tell you you can," said Granny, with such a sharp tone in her voice that I wondered if I was in trouble. "She had to go off."

"To the store?"

Granny put my breakfast down in front of me, kind of banging the plate. "The Lord only knows, Rose-Linda. Lord only knows."

I had fun playing with the hose, washing the car and getting soaking wet. An Eskimo Pie turned out to be ice cream sandwiched between chocolate cookies. The pile of Sunday papers from different places had comics that Gramps called the funny papers. He pulled them out and Granny read them to me. Gramps showed me his garden, and I helped make a scarecrow with straw and some old pants and a shirt from a box in the attic. We found a hat. I wanted to show it to Mama, but she didn't come back.

I missed Mama, but Wildwood was nice. I had a room with the big bed to sleep in and other nice things in it. Besides the toys, there were shelves of children's books, and I could choose one every night for a bedtime story. On one side of the bed the lamp had a china shepherd boy with a crook guarding some sheep with nubbly china fleece. On the other side the lamp had a china shepherdess hugging a lamb. Granny said they'd been hers when she was my age. Then Mama's when she was born. Granny said they could be mine now.

Granny went through my suitcase, frowning and holding up one thing after another, saying what on earth is this? Before, if I needed more dungarees or socks or outgrew my T-shirt, we'd go get more from places that had old clothes, and Mama and I would look through them and find what I needed. At Wildwood clothes came for Granny and me from Miller & Rhoads in Richmond, all folded up in boxes with tissue paper. I had new pajamas and a bathrobe, underwear, dresses and sandals, and seersucker shorts in blue and white, and sweaters to match. Granny put them away in the chest of drawers in my room.

Wildwood had big furniture too, to sit on or eat dinner at, not just plastic tables and broken chairs that wobbled and old toys like where Mama and I'd lived. There were books on some walls right up to the ceiling, and on other walls pictures of people from the olden days. Pictures of people related to me, Gramps said. Some of the pictures made me nervous, because the people in them had eyes that would follow you around the room. I'd try to fool them by moving fast, but it never worked, they still watched me from their frames. A big desk with drawers and a place for a chair on each side, so two people could sit facing each other, stood near the fireplace. Granny said it had been a wedding present from Gramps.

After breakfast, when Gramps had gone to the newspaper, Granny sat at her side of the desk writing for the paper about town meetings and church socials and weddings and guest preachers and who was visiting family in Grafton. Gramps told me that his great-aunt Teeny used to write about things like that in the paper but now that Aunt Teeny was dead he'd married Granny so she could do it. That made Granny say, "Oh go on, Eugene!"

While she worked I'd sit across from her in Gramps's chair, coloring or looking at the pictures in one of the old children's books and pretending to work too. I was supposed to be quiet. Being quiet was hard sometimes.

One rainy day when I kept humming because it was so quiet, Granny looked up from her writing and said, "Why don't you go play in the attic? There are some trunks of old clothes and you could play dress-up."

The attic smelled like sour apples and dust and leather, and the trunks held all sorts of interesting things—papers and books and clothes, a riding habit and a battered hat and fans and tennis rackets and, in a corner, an object Granny later told me was an old sidesaddle.

I found a shoebox full of pictures of a girl. There was a laughing toddler with a raccoon on a string, a long-legged girl halfway up a tree wearing a checked shirt, jeans, and tennis shoes swinging her legs, a teenager in a ponytail and sunglasses grinning at the wheel of Gramps's Ford. I brought the box down to show Granny, and she turned sad. She said the photos were of Mama.

"That's your mother too, when she was eighteen." She turned a silver frame on her desk so I could see it. In it a beautiful girl with her hair swept up wore a long white dress, gloves that went up above her elbows, and a necklace. She was holding a bouquet of white roses.

"Mama doesn't look like that!"

"She's all dressed up, because she was going to a ball."

"Like Cinderella?"

"Sort of. It's called a Cotillion. My mother, my grandmother, and I were all in the Cotillion when we were young. All the girls I knew were in the Cotillion. Maybe you will be too when you're old enough. You can have a pretty dress all the way to the floor. See. There's me." It was a picture of another girl in a different princess dress with long gloves, the same necklace, and white roses. "I had a time getting your mama to do it. It felt important somehow, at the time. Don't know why now."

The young woman in the picture didn't look anything like Mama, who'd fixed her long hair in a braid or ponytail every morning and wore jeans with men's shirts that she bought for a dollar in old-clothes shops, with lace-up boots, or sneakers if it was hot. I thought Granny must have mixed her pictures up, but she might not like it if I said so, so I didn't.

Gramps put up a tire swing in an oak tree and let me help feed the chickens and collect the eggs while they were still warm. I helped pick tomatoes and found the yellow squash hiding under the big squash leaves. Granny pulled out an ice-cream maker from the back of the pantry, and Gramps brought up a load of rock salt, and I helped churn peach ice cream until my arms ached from cranking the handle. It tasted really good.

Mama didn't come back.

My grandparents said fall was coming and I'd go to kindergarten, but first there'd be the Blackberry Picnic. They told me I was going to love the Blackberry Picnic—there'd be a big picnic dinner, and music and fireworks, and the children would toast marshmallows and get to hear stories.

Granny let me help mash up the yolks with mayonnaise for the deviled eggs the day before. The next afternoon we set out in the car with a big basket of the eggs, fried chicken, and potato salad and a whole watermelon in the back seat, and turned left out of the driveway to go up Frog Mountain, instead of right to go down to Grafton, on a little dirt road with bushes on either side that brushed the car. We had to go really slow because there were a lot of people walking to the picnic and they had to get out of our way. There were some people on horseback and a few other cars, because like us, they were transporting picnics. Some of the older girls and boys were holding hands as they walked.

We parked on the edge of a big flat place where you could see the valley a long way down. Gramps pointed to a rock and said, "That's the Old Man of the Mountain. Can you see his face?" It was sort of a squashy face, with a chin that jutted out over the valley, but once you saw it looked like a man's head, it kept looking that way.

Some men who'd gone up early had a bonfire going and a huge coffeepot already perking so you could smell it. There were trestle tables set up, with cakes in plastic containers already on one of them, and a spigot container of lemonade with paper cups.

When we'd put everything from the car on a table and spread our quilts on the ground, Granny gave me a bucket and sent me to join the other children who were in the bushes picking blackberries. My fingers got pricked and turned purple from juice, but Gramps said it was the best bucket of blackberries he'd ever seen.

Afterward I copied the other kids lining up to get a drink of water from a tin cup chained to a rock wall where water was trickling out. The water tasted funny, and when I made a face an older boy named

Ricky said, "That tastes like iron 'cause there's iron in the mountain. It's good for you."

By now people were busy putting out their food on the trestle tables, and a big stack of paper plates was weighed down with a rock so they wouldn't blow away. There were platters and bowls of all different sizes, full of fried chicken and deviled eggs, sliced ham, slaw, baked bean casseroles, barbecue and tuna salad, and sliced watermelon and piccalilli, all covered in plastic wrap to keep off flies.

Mama and I used to eat jelly sandwiches a lot, and even at Wildwood I still felt anxious when breakfast finished there might not be any lunch, or after lunch that there might not be any supper, even though there always was. But so much food in one place made me kind of dizzy. I was hungry right away and dying to eat.

But Granny was walking around with her little notebook, jotting down who was there and who'd come from out of town, and chatting with people to see who had any other news to report for her piece in the *Messenger*.

People got quiet while Gramps stood up and made a speech to welcome everybody, and people laughed at things he said and clapped at the end. Granny said we couldn't eat until the preachers said the blessing. The preachers took turns. They didn't just say bless this food amen. The blessing was really long, about olden times and lots of boring stuff about people and how the valley had been blessed. People called "amen" when their family or business got mentioned. I scratched a mosquito bite and my tummy rumbled.

Granny caught Gramps's eye and rolled her eyes, and Gramps snuck each of us a deviled egg.

Later there were hot dogs cooking on the bonfire. I loved hot dogs, but I'd already stuffed myself with fried chicken and slaw and baked beans, so I wasn't hungry anymore. But when a grown-up handed me one, I automatically ate it. I'd learned to eat when food was offered, and who knew when I'd get another hot dog. Then I went over to the trestle table with all the cake. It was surrounded by children helping themselves without any grown-ups telling them to stop.

My stomach hurt, but . . . cake! I got a paper plate and took a lot of cake when Granny wasn't watching.

After supper Gramps and the Hog Callers played their jug and washboard and spoons and kazoo, and sang songs that made people laugh or sing along. People clapped in time, and the Hog Callers stamped their feet and acted like they were dancing with each other.

"Gramps is funny!" I told Granny, and she said, "You have no idea, child."

When they stopped, the sun had almost set and the sky had gone red and orange. They put more wood on the bonfire, gave the children sticks with a whittled point, and passed around a bowl of marshmallows. I took one and nibbled the edge. By then I was really, really not wanting to eat anything else. The boy named Ricky said, "Ain't you done s'mores before?" and showed me how to catch my marshmallow on fire to wave in the air like a torch, then how to push the blackened marshmallow onto a graham cracker and stick a piece of Hershey's bar on top to melt. The graham cracker and the hot marshmallow and melty chocolate stuck my mouth together. I was full and it was kind of sickening. "You want another one?" asked Ricky. "It's always a competition to see who can eat the most." So I nodded. "Attagirl," said Ricky, sticking a couple more marshmallows on my stick. I hoped I wouldn't throw up. It would be embarrassing to throw up in front of a bigger boy like Ricky, but he'd said *attagirl*, so I put my stick with the marshmallows back in the fire and let them catch on fire and burn up to nothing while he wasn't looking.

When it started getting dark, old Vann Drumheller, who'd lost most of his teeth and smelled bad if you got too close, called the children to come away from the bonfire to where it was dark if they wanted to hear him tell stories. Ricky whispered to me Vann was supposed to be a moonshiner and dangerous, had been in jail. When we were all sitting cross-legged around him and quiet, he switched on a flashlight under his chin to make his face weird and asked how many of us knew Frog Mountain was haunted.

"I knew that," several kids said.

Vann's voice got low and creepy. "There's creatures all around humans can't see unless the creatures let them. Things that lived there forever, before people. These things are everywhere, might be sitting next to you right now. They let you see them when they want to. Or when they're hungry. Or when they're fixin' to *grab* you and never let you go. That's what the drowned people who live at the bottom of the river do.

"There's a place down the river, near the shoals, that, when boats pass over, people on 'em hear singing below the water, and sometimes, they see people who'd drowned having a party down on the bottom dancing and singing, having a fine spread of dinner, just like we had tonight."

"Did they have barbecue?" piped up a girl. "Because you need a fire for barbecue, and if it's underwater, the fire would get put out."

"Yeah," said several voices.

Vann turned his weird face toward her. "It was demons having the party, and demon fire in the barbecue. Demon fire burns underwater. These drowned people would look straight up through the water at the people on the boat and call, 'Come down, come down, join the party,' and travelers passing above them on the river would look down and see how nice it looked, how much fun everybody was having under the water, friendly folks waving and calling, 'Come have some supper, and dance a little.'

"Boat captains would call 'No, no!' to warn them not to do it, warn them the Devil set that table, that's the Devil playing the fiddle . . . but some people jumped in the water anyway. And got pulled down . . . down . . . down, struggling for air, as the water around them got darker and the table and fine food and drink disappeared. And the people who jumped in couldn't breathe anymore. The music stopped, and then they wished they hadn't jumped in so fast. It was just cold and wet, and they wanted to go back to the boat, to go home to their families, get on with their business. And they cried and begged to go back to the boat, but once they jumped in, it was too late. They were drowning, doomed to stay under the dark water forever. They'd never go home again."

"Are they still down there?" asked another child. "Only my daddy has a speedboat he takes us on, but we never saw no drownded people."

"They're still there all right . . . waitin' to lure travelers down. Been doing that since before your daddy was born. Before motorboats was even invented. Bidin' their time. I wouldn't go hangin' over the side of that boat if I were you. And if you hear fiddle music out there on the water where no music ought to be . . . beware! Devil's playin' his fiddle! Comin' to see can he catch you."

There was silence while Vann drank from his beer can.

"And you know, when there's fog on Frog Mountain, watch out! There's a dangerous creature lives up there, comes out of its cave when it gets foggy, looking for human meat. It's a shape-shifter, the Eagle Man with a man's face and an eagle's beak and wings and claw. He hides in the fog, looking for prey to snatch up in his big, sharp bloody claws. So if you're on the mountain and it starts getting foggy, run home. Fast as you can."

He took another drink of his beer.

"And do any of you kids feel a cold breath of air on this hot night? If you do, it means the witch Uktena is creepin' around. Can't see her either, but she's horrible. Has a long, cold stabbing finger, and she creeps up real quiet behind you, and before you know it she stabs your innards out with her fingernail, and eats them. Then she . . ."

One of the children started to cry, "I want Mama!"

I didn't like these stories.

"I want to hear about the rabbit girl on Frog Mountain!" yelled Ricky. "Who's got evil red eyes and follows people home. If you hear her call your name, you'll die."

"No, I can't recall that story," said Vann. "But hey . . . what's that noise?"

From the trees something gave a horrible loud laugh. "Watch out!" a spooky voice called in the trees behind me. "Watch out!" called a voice from higher up the hill in the bushes. "The shape-shifter's watching . . . so're the ghosts and haunts . . . wooo, wooo."

"Ha, ha, ha, ha, ha!" went a horrible voice close by.

"Ha, ha, ha, ha, ha!" echoed another voice.

I asked Ricky if that wasn't really one of the men at the bonfire, but Ricky said it was the shape-shifter. It could change its voice to a human one when it wanted, and it was probably waiting in the trees right now, watching us, wondering which child to grab and eat.

"Shape-shifter ate a whole lot of kids once, long time ago," Ricky whispered. "They were havin' a school picnic and pickin' blackberries, and the teacher was settin' out the picnic and looked up and the kids was all gone, all of a sudden. They never found a one. Shape-shifter musta been pretty hungry to take so many, but you know what I think?"

I shook my head.

"I think he killed those kids, ate a few, and hung the rest up to dry like jerky in his cave. So when he got hungry he could grab one down and eat it."

Back home and in my pajamas, I wouldn't let Granny turn off my bedroom light, because demons and shape-shifters and the Uktena were hiding under my bed, waiting to get me in the dark. It didn't matter how many times Gramps checked under my bed.

"They're just stories, Rose-Linda," said Gramps, exasperated, straightening up after looking under the bed for the tenth time. "Old legends. Indian superstitions. Fairy tales, like Snow White—you know she isn't real. They always tell ghost stories at the Blackberry Picnic, but there's no such things as demons or shape-shifters. There's no Uktena, whatever Vann says. And for the last time, nothing's under your bed." Gramps sounded cross, which he'd never been before.

"They come out in the dark! They can get real if they want. I might see the rabbit thing with red eyes! It follows you home! It might know my name! I want the light on," I wailed.

They went out, leaving the bedroom door open and the lamps on either side of my bed on. "Where'd she hear about that Indian girl story? Vann swore he wouldn't tell that one anymore, after we told him how it gave Sophy nightmares so bad we had to take her to that doctor in Atlanta about it," I heard Gramps say.

"I know we should've stopped Rose-Linda eating all those s'mores on top of the hot dogs," Granny was saying. "All that trash! Give anybody nightmares about red eyes."

I was supposed to start kindergarten the week after the Blackberry Picnic. My grandparents said I was going to love kindergarten. They'd said the same thing about the Blackberry Picnic, and I now lived in terror that red eyes watched me in the dark when I went to bed, that an evil thing was just waiting to call my name, and I still wouldn't sleep without the light. Gramps said that was OK, if the light was on, it meant the shepherd boy and girl were watching out so nothing bad would get me while I slept.

And when Gramps said he and the Hog Callers were going on a weekend fishing trip to the Shoals, I screamed and cried and begged him not to go, because the drowned people would make him jump in the water and we'd never see him again.

Granny calmed me down with sugar cookies and ice cream while Gramps snuck off. But I was still wary of kindergarten.

"Be good." Granny hugged me goodbye at the kindergarten door next day. She said she'd see me at lunchtime, and left me in a room full of strange children and a teacher. What if Granny forgot to come back? Like Mama forgot to. I knew by now that when Granny was at her desk writing, to get a piece done by the time the paper needed it, she'd forget everything. I sat pretending to color pictures at the crafts table, too anxious to play with anyone as the morning dragged on.

A few lonely days passed, worrying whether or not Granny would forget me today, when a redheaded girl plopped down beside me at circle time. Evvie Stuart gave a gap-toothed grin and said, "Mom says you're my cousin and we should be friends, OK?" I nodded. "Good. Look," she whispered, and showed me a packet of M&M's in her pocket. We weren't allowed candy in school. She giggled, slipped me a handful, and whispered, "Eat them like this," then bent over so the teacher couldn't see her raise her hand to her mouth. I copied her.

The teacher caught us with our mouths full of chocolate and said, "Evvie Stuart, I'll take those!" and held out her hand for the M&M's.

"Now go sit on the naughty step." Punishment in front of the whole class, who would probably stare and point, would have reduced me to tears. But Evvie was unconcerned, tossing her head and mouthing "Go sit on the naughty step" and sticking out her tongue at the teacher when the teacher's back was turned. The other children seemed to admire this.

Evvie had sneakers with Snoopy on them, a sassy mouth, and a daring approach to life. I'd seen her in the playground, swinging hand over hand from the highest monkey bars and pumping her legs on a swing till she was higher than any other child dared to go, almost horizontal to the ground, and then hurling herself through the air and onto her feet, shrieking she could fly. Until a teacher saw her and screamed, "Evvie Stuart, get down from there this minute! How many times do I have to tell you not to do that!"

She'd defend any child getting picked on, putting hands on her hips and acting fierce, yelling at kids bigger and older than she was.

She wasn't afraid to fight—she'd bite if she had to—and she knew more bad words than anybody else. She would call kids names they didn't understand, and she had to sit on the naughty step a lot, because the teacher did understand and told her that kind of talk wasn't allowed, do you hear me, Evvie?

She didn't care. She'd sit and make cross-eyed fish faces at the teacher when her back was turned.

Mrs. Stuart often had to come to school to talk to the kindergarten teacher about Evvie's behavior, but Evvie shrugged and said it didn't matter. Her father was dead and everybody felt sorry for her, so she never got in trouble really. I was in awe of anybody so sure of her leeway to be bad but didn't dare try to copy her. My mother might have been gone, but something told me my grandparents didn't feel sorry enough for me to let me get away with misbehaving.

Granny agreed Evvie was a distant cousin and we had to be nice, but I could tell Granny didn't approve of her manners or her sass. And she said Evvie was headed for trouble after she overheard Evvie telling me there was a hole in the wall where you could spy on boys in their locker room changing after football practice. "You can see their willies." Evvie giggled. After Evvie went home, Granny complained to Gramps that, cousins or not, the Stuarts lacked refinement.

"Prim, you know who you sound like?" I could tell from his voice he was laughing.

"Eugene!" I could tell from her voice she was mad that he said that, and knew what was coming next.

"From beyond the grave, Mamie Maud Murray speaks," he chortled.

"I do *not* sound like my mother!"

CHAPTER 32

1987–1994

Growing up, I heard about how Granny had gone to college even though her parents were against it, and how she and Gramps got married over her mother's dead body—as Granny put it. I gathered Granny and her mother had a lot of fights. I think the reason Granny told me about the hard time she'd had with her own mother was because she wanted me to understand that mother-daughter relations were complicated. She was saying, look at her and Mamie Maud. Look at her and my mother. And she didn't have to say look at my mother and me, because Mama was gone.

When I was small Granny or Gramps were always saying "when your mother comes back." But time passed and she didn't and they stopped saying it. At first there'd been an occasional phone call. Cards on my birthdays. Then nothing.

I tried not to think about her because it never did any good. And anyway, I loved living at Wildwood. Who wouldn't?

My grandparents spoiled me, but they were particular about two things: good grades in school and manners. Fortunately I liked school and got praised for being a conscientious student and always on the honor roll. I was also constantly told to "act like a lady" by Granny, which seemed to mean different things at different times. It meant sitting up straight at the table, shaking hands when I was introduced to their friends, and writing thank-you letters for my presents after a birthday party. But mostly it meant "not like Evvie Stuart," who wasn't fond of school and was always in trouble for messy homework or passing notes in class and who, when she came to supper or spent the night, would say if she didn't like something on her plate.

"It's more ladylike just to eat it and say nothing," Granny warned me.

Gramps turned to me and said, "You can take a girl out of Richmond, but you can't take the Richmond out of the girl."

"Oh, go on, Eugene!" Granny would say indignantly. "If I let Evvie Stuart set the tone, who knows what we'd have on our hands."

Because Evvie and I were inseparable. We sat next to each other in school and attended Vacation Bible School at the Baptist church where the Stuarts went. We went to Brownies and then Girl Scouts every Tuesday after school at the American Legion until Evvie got bored, said badges were stupid, and we both quit. We giggled through "The Talk" about getting periods, struggled in the bathroom learning to use Tampax, and started the junior high part of Grafton High School when we turned thirteen.

I was the one who paid attention in class and did my homework and got praised by the teachers, and Evvie was the one who painted her nails black, shot spitballs through a straw at the boys when the teacher's back was turned, and got sent to the principal's office for calling her teacher names under her breath.

But Evvie was desperate to be cool and persuaded me I was desperate too. She had us hanging around the high school, watching the older girls so we could copy them, checking out how they wore their hair and makeup, how they walked and talked, how short their skirts were, how their ripped jeans (Granny wouldn't let me out of the house in torn jeans) had to be worn with gold ballet slippers, plaid flannel shirts over a T-shirt, and big hoop earrings. We pierced our ears with some little pointed rings called "sleepers," and when we tried to wear the hoop earrings we bought at the Winn-Dixie accessories aisle for a dollar a pair, our earlobes swelled up and got red and infected. Evvie stole cigarettes from the purse of a friend visiting Mrs. Stuart, and we practiced smoking behind the chicken house, until we both threw up. Above all, we observed the girls who dated the two baddest senior boys. Because we'd decided we were in love with those boys.

Or Evvie had. Until we got to the eighth grade, Ricky Pine, who'd once showed me how to make s'mores, and his best friend, Guy Charbonneau, were just boys. Ricky's parents, Loretta and Harold, were older parents. Ricky had been a late baby. They owned the gas station, the little grocery store attached to it, and Grafton's only motel. The Charbonneaus were very rich, and Granny told me their big house across the river, Chiaramonte, had been featured in *House Beautiful.* Guy was their youngest child and only son. He and Ricky were just boys whose dads went hunting with Gramps. No big deal until Evvie got into being in love. It wouldn't have occurred to me to be in love, let alone with boys who were seniors, but hey, Evvie was, and I went along for the ride.

Men in Grafton nearly all hunted. They'd go out in twos and threes for doves and wild ducks in the fall, then deer and wild boar. Gramps, Harold Pine, John Charbonneau, and Freeman Hanover Stuart, the only black lawyer in town, who Gramps said had added a middle name so he'd sound like a whole law firm instead of one lone lawyer, had been hunting together for years. When they went out, they usually took several of the hunting dogs they bred up at Chiaramonte. These dogs are called trikklers—they're big and strong but dumb as heck, and they need field training before they're any use. Trained, they fetch a lot of money, and Guy's dad, John Charbonneau, had continued to breed them as the family had done for generations.

Once they were old enough to handle a gun and keep quiet in the woods, Ricky and Guy got taken hunting too, to make some pocket money helping with the dogs. Ricky was wild and kind of crazy, and Gramps said he thought it might be a mistake to let him anywhere near a gun, but he was good with the dogs. They'd mind him in a way they wouldn't mind anybody else. I knew from my grandparents that Guy should have gone away to boarding school, but John Charbonneau got diagnosed with cancer and they'd decided to let Guy stay at home. Guy and Ricky hung out together all the time.

They'd both say hi to me because of Gramps, but that's about it. They were five years older, handsome and swaggery and tough from deer hunting with the men, who'd let them have a beer after they'd been out with the dogs. They drove around in Guy's red Mustang, cut classes, and smoked in a casual, cool way. They had bad reputations for drinking and getting girls to do unthinkable things. Teachers complained they had an attitude problem, but they didn't get expelled because they were stars of the football team, and also the Charbonneaus' timber business—just one of many businesses they owned—employed a lot of teachers' husbands and sons.

Ricky had the worst reputation in high school. He'd crashed two cars and walked away. He and Guy had been caught doing an illegal whiskey run with Vann Drumheller and some guns in the car. There was a high-speed chase, and Vann tried to outrun the police and wound up crashing. The car was totaled, but Vann and the boys crawled out. They arrested Vann, but the police let Ricky and Guy off with a warning. They probably shouldn't have. Ricky and Guy claimed later they'd been trying to shoot the tires out on the police car when Vann ran off the road.

Word got around. Gramps said boys would be boys. Granny said the boys would be felons in the penitentiary along with Vann before long, and the only reason they hadn't been arrested too was on account of Guy's father being who he was and Guy's uncle being a senator.

To Evvie, badness like that was part of their allure. We nursed crushes on both of them, indiscriminate about which one either of us was in love with at any given moment. We hung around them as much and as close as we could. We acquired cheap makeup that neither of us dared put on at home. I bought foundation and blusher and Evvie invested in mascara and a bargain box of multicolored eye shadow for two dollars, complete with applicators. My grandparents were surprised I insisted on getting to school early. This was so Evvie and I could meet in the girls' restroom to pool our makeup and slather stuff on our faces.

Then we hung around anywhere Ricky and Guy were likely to be—the sidelines at football practice, lurking in the hall at school, waiting for them to walk past, watching from the next table at the cafeteria. We said things like "Don't look now but I think they're looking at us . . . oh no, oh gosh, they're *actually* looking at us! How do I look? Do you guess they'll come over?" while giggling like idiots. We told ourselves we were "firecrackers." Looking back, we were really stalkers in braces and training bras, with complexions that looked like we'd been to the embalming parlor. We had to scrub our faces with pungent green liquid soap from the school bathroom dispensers and brown paper towels before we went home with raw red cheeks.

Sometimes the only things dumber than young dogs are fixated young girls.

Despite their total lack of interest in us, we moped dramatically when Ricky and Guy graduated from high school and went off to college. "Thank the Lord!" Granny said. "You girls get sillier every day over those no-good boys, neither of which I'd trust with either of you for five minutes. Be careful what you wish for."

For a while we dropped by the motel after school, casually hanging around with a Coke from the motel vending machine, for a chance to say brightly, "Oh hey, Mrs. Pine, tell Ricky we said hi," in case Ricky's mom, Loretta, felt like telling us what they were up to. She never did. Our passions subsided. Imaginary relationships are hard.

Like mine with my mother. I had missed her at first. Then I missed the idea of her. By now I could no longer remember what she looked like. Granny gave me the picture of her in her Cotillion dress, but that image was as unreal as the one I couldn't quite remember.

I could tell by the way my grandparents talked that they loved her, but at the same time I sensed there were things they didn't want to say in front of me. A couple of times something slipped out about Mama's vivid imagination. She'd had an imaginary playmate called Dora, with red eyes. Dora followed her everywhere. Sometimes Dora was a girl and sometimes Dora was a rabbit. Mama claimed she was scared of both of them. It got so bad her teachers called Granny up about it, so they'd taken her to see a doctor in Atlanta. He gave her some tests but couldn't find anything wrong with her, said only children often invent imaginary companions. She'd outgrow such nonsense.

"Did she?" I asked Granny. "Come on, you never tell me about Mama."

"Maybe you're old enough to know." Granny sighed. "We thought she was coming out of it. She stopped talking about Dora by the time she got to high school. She didn't talk to us about much of anything, but she was a cheerleader, her grades were good, her light would be on all night, she'd fall asleep studying. She applied to Vanderbilt, and she got accepted. We were so proud. Gramps gave her a secondhand Mustang when she graduated. Which makes the rest of it stranger."

Mama didn't go to college after all. She didn't come home one summer evening, and they'd thought she was spending the night at a girlfriend's house. She hadn't spent the night. She didn't call or come home next day either, and they found out nobody else had seen her. They panicked and called the police, and on the third evening Mama called from Kentucky to say she had picked up a hitchhiker, she hadn't been abducted, and she was going to Oklahoma with him, a fellow named Lamarr Hamilton, who was a medical student heading to a job with VISTA on an Indian reservation in Oklahoma. She'd be home when she was ready, and not to worry about her. She had to get away from Dora, and Lamarr could help her. Or his relatives could. They lived on the reservation where he was going. Lamarr was the first person to understand her.

They thought she was having a breakdown, some kind of mental episode. They were frantic to find her, but the police wouldn't do anything because she was eighteen. They couldn't find Lamarr Hamilton in any VISTA program, but postcards came from Mama postmarked different places out West, so they knew she was alive. When I was born a year or so later, Mama wrote them the news in a letter, but there was no address on the letter, just an Oklahoma postmark. Granny showed it to me. It said she and Lamarr were fine.

Not long after that, Mama called in a state to say that Lamarr had disappeared while hitchhiking somewhere. They begged Mama to come home with me and without him. But she wouldn't. By now they didn't believe in Lamarr Hamilton's existence any more than they believed in Dora's, and I overheard them wondering who my father really was.

I think that the worry and frustration wore them out, and little by little, over the years, they concentrated on me and let Sophy go.

Besides, they had new worries.

CHAPTER 33

1994

The new clothes from Miller & Rhoads stopped coming by the time I was a teenager. I was relieved. The dresses and patent-leather strappy pumps Granny chose were too little-girly. Evvie and I were now wearing jeans and sweatshirts carefully accessorized with cheap jewelry and sneakers. Gramps no longer had shirts sent from Brooks Brothers. By my last year in junior high, the hired girl left, and no one came in her place. Granny cooked and dusted and polished the silver herself, even managing to write a funny piece for the paper about her chores.

I gathered the *Messenger* was losing money. Granny explained people were starting to get their news on TV after work, and the advertising at the paper dropped off. Gramps made light of it to me when I finally asked about it, said the Marshalls were land rich and cash poor, "like George Washington and Thomas Jefferson," which made it sound not too bad. And he'd found a solution. He was selling a big piece of Marshall land on the east side of Frog Mountain. The buyer was a developer from Richmond whose father had known Granny's father.

Granny said he should wait and consult Freeman Hanover Stuart before he agreed to anything. But Gramps said that Freeman, Grafton's only black lawyer, had gotten too successful since the network of Hanover relatives in southern Virginia all employed him for their legal business and was currently in Washington testifying about something or other in Congress. He'd become too important to bother with a little transaction between gentlemen. Gramps hadn't bargained hard over the sale price because he didn't believe the land was worth much. Even though a new interstate highway was planned, connecting Grafton to Atlanta, Kingsport, Richmond, DC, and the world, he thought land anywhere on the east side of Frog Mountain was a long way from everything, in a part of the state with bad roads, a railway line falling into disuse, and only some slow barge traffic on the river. He came home gleeful from a meeting where he'd signed the deeds for the sale, saying he'd got a good price for land that he had no use for.

But it turned out Granny was right—he shouldn't have done the sale without Freeman. The buyer knew something Gramps didn't, that a loop of the interstate was coming, and thanks to that, two big plants were relocating to the east valley on the other side of Frog Mountain and there was sure to be a demand for homes. His company built homes.

The developer cut down most of the trees on the east slope of Frog Mountain, and soon homes were going up everywhere. The plainer three-bedroom homes were lower down the mountain, while the ranch-style executive homes, painted in different colors with wooden decks and pools and concrete driveways, were higher up, with better views over the east valley. The bare mountainside was dotted with puny saplings propped up on wooden supports. It looked hideous.

The housing development was named Cherokee Ridge, and it overlooked a sprawling new township, Enterprise, which had sprung up, with an elementary school, high school, a few churches, and a small shopping mall, all surrounded by industrial parks. The developer made a fortune.

Gramps regretted the sale for the rest of his life. He hated the way the mountainside had been stripped of trees to make way for an ugly development. "Cherokee Ridge" became my grandparents' shorthand to describe anything new and tacky. The sale raised enough capital to keep the paper going only another few years. The main benefit he got out of it was that the old winding dirt road skirting the orchard up to Wildwood wasn't suitable to access the new houses on the east slope, so they built a new road up Frog Mountain, and Gramps managed to negotiate that the developer would pave a fork of the road to Wildwood on the west slope at the same time. Granny said it was a small victory.

If the land sale left them feeling bruised, there was a worse blow around the corner. I was fourteen when it came. Granny answered the phone. I heard her say, "Yes, this is Mrs. Marshall speaking," then, "Police from where?" Her knees sagged suddenly, and she leaned against the wall for support. She whispered, "What? When?" Her face had turned gray. Somebody talked on the other end, and Granny finally hung up and sank into a chair. "Go call your grandfather in," she told me, her voice hoarse like it hurt to talk.

We hadn't heard from my mother in years. Now the police in California had called to tell us she'd driven a car off the coastal highway in California, into the sea.

I stayed at the Stuarts' while my grandparents flew out to bring her body home, along with the box containing all her personal possessions they'd found in her rented room. By the time they got back three days later, the news had spread. Evvie then came over to stay with me. We found a bottle of blackberry wine in the pantry and got drunk on it. I remember crying and confessing to Evvie I couldn't remember my mother, and that when I was little I used to hope she wouldn't come back to get me and take me away. And now she never would. I felt awful. Like just saying that helped kill her. And angry too. Why had she just left me? I'd never know.

At Mama's funeral my grandparents looked like two old wood figures. Granny, dressed in black and hanging on to her composure for dear life, had deep wrinkles I'd never noticed before. She wore a set expression that made her resemble the old photo of Great-Grandmother Mamie Maud in the wedding picture. People patted her shoulders and said things like "Sophy's with her Lord" like they thought it was helpful.

I could tell from the way she and Gramps tightened their lips that it wasn't.

The preacher read the scripture verses about everything having a season, and the choir led everybody in "Shall We Gather at the River?" and "Beulah Land," and I can't remember what else. The three of us left the church behind the casket, and everyone followed the pallbearers carrying it to the Marshall plot in the cemetery. The preacher talked about a troubled soul flying home to God and finding peace. We sang "Guide Me, O Thou Great Jehovah" the old-fashioned way people sing it, with the preacher singing a line to people and people singing it back, and threw flowers on the coffin when it was lowered into the grave. Granny held my hand tight, and I squeezed back and tried hard to remember what Mama looked like.

Weeks later, when her gravestone was ready, the three of us went to see it set up among the leaning headstones in the Marshall plot and leave more flowers. It read,

Sophia Catherine Marshall
September 7, 1961–November 12, 1994
Home at Last
Rest in Peace

I laid our bunch of chrysanthemums on it. I wanted to scream at the headstone, "Serves you right for leaving me!"

I cried, "Now I'll never know why she just went off," and gave my eyes an angry swipe with my sleeve.

Granny put her arm around my shoulders, shook her head, and said, "I know, child. I've had a lot of practice trying to understand Sophy, and I never succeeded either. All we can do is think the best of her, Rose-Linda. Try to do that. There was real good in her." Gramps nodded and didn't say anything. He looked terrible and old.

The box of Mama's things stood in the upstairs hallway for a few weeks, and finally Gramps carried it up to the attic unopened. None of us had the heart to look at what was inside. "She traveled light," he said when he came down.

CHAPTER 34

1994–1998

Gramps changed. The fire went out of his editorials, and Granny stopped writing pieces about anything except Grafton's doings. Meals were silent, and the atmosphere felt poisoned, heavy with unspoken recriminations. I caught snatches of arguments behind their closed bedroom door. What should they have believed, what hadn't they seen, what should they have done earlier?

Evvie came to spend the night and said it felt like the curse of the unsaid.

There was more bad news after Christmas the year my mother died . . . After years of treatment and holding off cancer, John Charbonneau was in the hospital, dying, and at the same time Guy and Ricky got expelled from college for getting drunk and shooting beer can targets in their dorm rooms.

At the funeral Guy was a pallbearer, and the bishop, who was a family friend, came down from Richmond to officiate. Ricky and the Pines went home after the burial, didn't go to the gathering at Chiaramonte afterward. Evvie and I sat off to the side on the living room sofa with plates of ham and potato salad while uniformed caterers went back and forth to replenish silver trays on the dining table and refill the coffee- and teapots.

Gramps joined the men in Mr. Charbonneau's study to drink whiskey. Going past the study on my way to the bathroom, I heard a man say they didn't make them as tough as John anymore—he'd refused to give in or give up, and it was time for "that damn fool son of his," Guy, to "grow up and step up."

Claire Charbonneau and Guy's sisters sat with their children and older relatives and the bishop, until the sisters' children, who had been good and quiet for as long as they could stand, started annoying and punching each other and got sent outside. Evvie said the Pines must have left early because they felt bad about the boys getting expelled from college, they probably felt like it was Ricky's fault. "Probably was," I agreed. "He's the crazier one."

Going home after the funeral, Gramps told us Guy and Ricky had surprised everybody by signing up to join the army. Granny said she hoped the army would straighten those boys out before it was too late.

The winter after Mama and John Charbonneau died was long, and spring was gray and rainy most days, with fog hanging over the river. I felt blue a lot of the time. I finished ninth grade struggling to remember Mama so I could argue with her about why she hadn't come back for me. It made me cry that I couldn't. I hardly knew what to say to my grandparents. Evvie said I was a misery.

Our freshman and sophomore years, Evvie devoted her efforts to her social life and cheerleading. I gave up on trying to keep up with Evvie. I didn't see the point, just concentrated on my homework. Teachers said I was a great student to teach. It was depressing.

At school our junior year we took the SATs in March for practice before we took them for real in the fall. Evvie didn't finish hers. The school guidance counselor told me I should be thinking about college, but I didn't mention it because I knew Gramps's financial situation was bad. I planned to get a job and help out.

It soon became clear that my grandparents weren't going to let me do that. They were dead set on my going to college. In fact, it felt like they'd staked everything on it, as if it were the sure way to keep me from ending up like Mama. The summer after my junior year, Gramps was invited to make the commencement address at a small women's college near Bristol. It was one of those old-fashioned, exclusive southern schools with a pretty campus and high academic standards that was kept running by rich protective parents of bright girls who didn't want their daughters running wild at more liberal institutions. He'd had lunch with the college president and the head of the alumnae association after his speech, and came home with the news it offered a single full, all-inclusive scholarship every year, awarded on academic merit. I ought to apply for it.

It was the last thing in the world I wanted to do. Evvie had been allowed to attend the spring break parties at the University of Tennessee with two of her cousins on her mother's side that year and had had the time of her life. The prospect of doing something similar, having a little fun, began to seem like a possibility. But this college near Bristol didn't sound like somewhere you'd have the time of your life. It sounded like an earnest place where a good time was an evening of classical music followed by a cup of cocoa.

But to please my grandparents, I sent for the scholarship application form in September of my senior year. When it arrived, I opened it and my heart sank. It had many blank pages because applicants had to write a lot of essays. Gramps said not to be discouraged, he knew what the college was looking for and we'd discuss it after dinner before I started writing.

Dinner had been waiting on the stove for an hour when Granny told me to call him in, said he was probably watching the sunset the way he liked to do and lost track of time. Instead I found him collapsed from a heart attack. I ran back to the house yelling to Granny to call 911, then we both rushed back to Gramps's side. He couldn't talk by then.

It seemed like forever before the ambulance got up to Wildwood, though Granny said it was only ten minutes before we heard the siren at the bottom of the mountain, and they must have driven up the mountain like a bat out of hell because minutes later the flashing lights came through the gate and the paramedics jumped out with the stretcher.

But it was too late. Gramps died in the ambulance, holding Granny's hand.

Later that night we sat in shock at the hospital, in Dr. Read's office. He told us Gramps had suffered from heart problems for years. It was hereditary. "Eugene never told me," Granny quavered. I'd never seen Granny cry before.

"The stress of keeping the *Messenger* from going under was probably the last straw," Dr. Read said.

"Oh, Rose-Linda, what am I going to do?" Granny wept.

I had no answer.

CHAPTER 35

The *Grafton Messenger*, October 3, 1998

> *EUGENE MARSHALL, OWNER OF THE* GRAFTON MESSENGER, *DIES AT HOME*
>
> *The* Grafton Messenger *regrets to report the death of its proprietor and editor, Eugene Marshall, who died on Tuesday evening, age 78, at his home, "Wildwood," on Frog Mountain. He was of the seventh generation of the family, and the grandson of the* Messenger*'s founder, Ben Marshall, who started the paper in 1883 . . .*
>
> *Funeral arrangements are in the hands of Drumheller Funeral Home. Visitation will take place on Saturday at Wildwood between 11:00 a.m. and 4:00 p.m. The funeral will be held on Sunday afternoon at the Methodist Church, followed by interment at Orchard Grove Cemetery.*

The family requests that in lieu of flowers, donations be made to Grafton Memorial Hospital's neonatal unit.

A lady from Granny's Bible study group had Gramps's obituary framed in time to bring it to her at the visitation, and I hung it on the nail I hammered into the kitchen wall to keep it from getting greasy or lost among the food people were bringing. Granny, who studied Latin at her fancy school in Richmond, called it a "memento mori"—a reminder that we all die.

The day of the visitation was strange. Wildwood smelled different. It was hot fall weather so the doors and windows were open, but flowers, lilies especially, too much greenery, face powder, and aftershave wafting off the crowd of people made everything smell too sweet until burning chilies and vinegar from a forgotten pot of barbecue somebody had left scorching on the back of the stove drowned the sweetness some.

Within a day of Gramps's death, the kitchen was filling up with food people had brought or left on the porch—casserole dishes covered in foil, chicken salad in Tupperware, a whole ham, platters of cold cuts, bowls of potato salad, and sheet cakes wrapped in plastic. I was supposed to be putting it all somewhere, but it was like my mind wouldn't work right. I was wandering around forgetting what I was supposed to be doing, saying thank you so much when people handed me a platter or bowl but incapable of thinking where it ought to go. Things were stacking up in the kitchen where the tea tray, sticky with the sugar I'd spilled, was dumped in the sink, and last night's pans of uneaten dinner were cold on the stove and attracting flies. Normally Granny couldn't abide mess in her kitchen, but I kept picking up a sponge and then putting it down again. Like I wasn't sure what to do with it.

News of Gramps's death spread. Before long women from our church who appointed themselves to step in and take over in a crisis were arriving to get dug in in the kitchen. Evvie called them Death Angels.

The Death Angels came bringing their own aprons, platters of cold cuts from the Winn-Dixie, and grocery sacks of basic things like ground coffee, milk and sugar, bread and Hellmann's, lemons for the iced tea, and a big bottle of detergent for the dishes. They got to work, organizing what had to go in the refrigerator and what could be left in the pantry or the pie safe. They washed all the pans and got the coffeepot going, then boiled more water to fix gallons of tea to chill. They made Granny and me sandwiches and told us we had to eat something.

By early evening people were stopping by, and the Angels set out bottles of Gramps's whiskey and clean glasses beside the iced tea pitchers on the sideboard. I could smell casseroles heating up in the oven and saw the Death Angels bustling back and forth to the dining room table, bringing hot ones out to accompany the potato salad and cold cuts and sliced cakes in the dining room and removing the empty dishes. Callers knew to take a paper plate and help themselves. For the next few days somebody always seemed to be coming through the door and somebody was always eating and it wasn't even the actual visitation yet.

The Angels answered the door and the phone, kept the percolator bubbling so there'd be enough strong coffee to keep everybody going, told people which bedroom to leave coats and pocketbooks in, found plates and paper napkins and plastic cups without having to ask which cupboard, and checked to make sure there was spare toilet paper in the bathrooms and that the men remembered to put the toilet seat down.

They found containers for flowers and damp plant pots. Whatever the obituary said about no flowers, people ignored it. There were flowers to fill every vase, jelly glass, and bucket, and potted plants were lined up on the stairs where they were in the way. Coming downstairs in her black dress, Granny accidentally kicked one over and swore. I could tell she'd like to kick the rest as far as she could, but she thought better of it, and I got the dustpan and brush and cleaned up.

Then florist arrangements—what Granny scornfully called "*florial* tributes"—started coming from miles as more people learned Gramps had died. There were funeral basket arrangements from high schools and colleges where Gramps had given commencement addresses over the years, floral crosses from civic organizations across the state, and wreaths from the chamber of commerce; the governor; Senator Cy Charbonneau; our local congressman, Charles "Call me Chuck" Drumheller; and various state officials. As if the house wasn't crowded enough.

The wreaths from the politicians were kind of a pissing contest—huge, big, and bigger, with ribbons saying "Eugene Marshall," "In Memoriam," or "RIP" in black letters. There was even a big flat American flag, made of red, white, and blue carnations, from some politician I'd never heard of. The blue was horrible, kind of neon.

It made your eyes hurt. I just looked at it, thinking it was so awful somebody made a mistake at the florist. Granny shuddered. "So *common*," she said witheringly. But Granny hated all funeral flowers, especially the lilies that came accompanied by cards with black crosses. She said flowers belonged in the garden, on dinner tables, or on the altar at weddings. Maybe that was what people thought in Richmond, but in Grafton, the obituary could say "no flowers" till the cows came home, and it didn't make any difference. You might as well ask people not to bring food.

It was my job to keep track of everything, write down who sent what in a notebook so we could return dishes and platters to the people who'd brought food in them. Granny said she had to write a note thanking whoever had sent what food in what dish, when we took the things back.

If there were a lot of people drifting in and out the week before the funeral, it was nothing compared to Saturday, the official visitation before Sunday's funeral. Wildwood was packed. There were friends, neighbors, distant relatives, some total strangers, the Methodist minister who was the latest Reverend Merriman in a long line of Merriman ministers, the Baptist minister, even the preacher and some elders from the

Holiness Church of the Nazarene way down the valley. Nice of them, considering Gramps wasn't a churchgoer and the *Messenger* sometimes took potshots at the churches.

Around the house the men from Drumheller Funeral Home hovered like fat black flies, greeting people at the open door in hushed tones, directing ladies carrying food to the kitchen and everyone else to "the widow" in the living room, where Granny sat in an armchair looking wan and irritated and half-dead herself in her black dress, trying to ignore the flower arrangements that were piling up and surrounded by callers all wanting to talk to her at once.

Delivery trucks came and went in the driveway, and the undertakers kept busy rearranging baskets and wreaths in a way that kept the flag arrangement central. From time to time they stepped back with their hands folded to admire their work, which then had to be shifted around when a new tribute arrived. From time to time Granny looked around the room impatiently, as if it were on the tip of her tongue to say "Where has Eugene *got* to?" like Gramps had momentarily disappeared into the kitchen to taste the barbecue when he ought to be out here playing host, saying hello, kissing ladies and shaking hands, being the life and soul of the party.

There was a Gramps-shaped hole in the house, a weird sense *everybody* was expecting him, he'd be there any minute to join the party. I kept talking to him in my head.

Around noon the thrum of funeral conversation ground to a halt as two of the undertakers carried the latest delivery in and propped it against the fireplace. It was a huge cross made of black flowers and a sign that said "EUGENE MARSHALL, See how the evildoers lie fallen, Psalm 36:12" in red letters, like blood.

People gasped, "Who on earth sent *that*?"

Granny held out her hand for the card and shocked everyone by laughing. "An old enemy of Eugene's. One of those segregationists, never forgave Eugene for supporting integrated schools and betraying white civilization. Eugene would have been delighted to know he'd provoked the damn fool enough to send this. Oh, how I wish he could see it!"

People stared at Granny. You could tell from their expressions they were making allowances for Granny swearing at such a time. One of the ladies from church stepped into the breach. "Oh, he can see it, darlin', rest assured he can." She leaned over and patted Granny's arm. "He's sittin' in glory with the blessed, looking down on you and all of us here, lookin' at that . . . that thing . . . from the right hand of Jesus and forgiving his enemy . . ."

The look on Granny's face said that, considering Gramps's views on religion, no, he probably wasn't doing anything of the kind, but she wasn't up to arguing about it.

Gramps's friends Mitch and Curtis and Randall, the other three Hog Callers, and wives Alice and Lurene—Randall wasn't married—came in together. They all gave me a hug, said how sorry they were, that we were in their prayers, and what did I think about them singing at the graveside?

"Gramps would . . . h-have l-liked that," I choked. "So Granny would too." Alice and Lurene handed me Kleenex and patted my shoulder and said how proud he'd been of me.

They headed over to Granny, and I hovered near the open door, wishing this nightmare day would end, when I heard Granny's voice raised high and shrill over the hushed conversation, like she'd had all she could stand. She was pointing at the wreaths and crosses and the flag. "Will *somebody please* take those things outside!" The funeral home people in their black suits obliged, carrying them out and lining them till the porch was full of floral tributes starting to wilt in the sun. The men from the funeral home talked among themselves about taking them down to the church for the funeral next day.

I piped up and said it would be better not to have them there, but the men insisted, "They'll comfort the widow during the service."

Something snapped in me. "No, they won't! You don't *know* the widow, dammit! She hates them!" I yelled.

But the undertakers just looked at me with bland understanding faces. One said, "Now, now."

Gramps once remarked undertakers had professional "taking-the-deceased-softly-to-Jesus expressions, like pious marshmallows." They had those expressions now, and they would have looked the same way if I'd set them on fire. Gramps would have laughed if he'd heard me say that.

I was on the verge of picking up every last one of the stupid wreaths and crosses and the horrible flag and tossing them into the yard and stamping them to smithereens, and I didn't only because just then Evvie and her mother drove up. "Hey, honey," Mrs. Stuart said, hugging me hard, before retrieving a big foil-covered dish from the back seat.

"Macaroni and cheese," said Evvie, following her mother to the porch. "I helped make it because it's your favorite."

The black flower cross stopped Mrs. Stuart dead in her tracks. "Dear *Lord*! As if Primrose doesn't have enough to cope with . . ." Shaking her head, she took her casserole on into the kitchen. Evvie and I sat down on the porch steps.

For a minute Evvie didn't say anything. I guessed her mother read her the riot act before they came, warned her to behave herself and not to go running off at the mouth about Death Angels.

Evvie slipped off her shoes. "Look." She'd painted her toenails gold, and they glittered in the sun. "If you like it, I'll do yours," she offered.

"Cool. Just . . . not now."

"Next time you sleep over," she said. "That flag thing"—she squinted at it up on the porch—"is it supposed to be patriotic? Like, on account of he was in the war?"

"Yes, some politician sent it. Granny hates it."

"I bet she does. Didn't know carnations came in blue. Tacky as sin."

"Granny thinks so too. She said they use white ones and put blue food coloring in the water. Ink for the black ones, in the big cross. And the funeral men want to put them in the church tomorrow smack in front of where Granny'll sit."

"That'll make everything worse. Black flowers! It looks like vampires sent it. 'Resssst in peeeeace vile I sooock your blooood,'" she hissed, baring her teeth at me. "Just the right thing at a funeral."

And suddenly vampires were so funny. I couldn't help it—I was wrung out with feeling sad—and I snickered, "That's what the man who sent it meant. He hated Gramps. I think he would have sucked Gramps's blood if he could have." Then we both got the giggles about vampires, gasping, "Vampires . . . suck your blood . . . black flowers! . . . Suck your blood . . . ha, ha, ha, *rest in peace!*"

When the giggles ran their course, the undertakers were frowning down at us. Evvie flipped them the bird. "Sit still," she said, and disappeared into the house. A minute later she was back with her mother's casserole and two forks. We ate the whole thing, just the two of us. "I'll make Mom come early tomorrow, then I can help you move those monstrosities before the funeral starts," said Evvie, scraping up the last brown bits around the sides. "We'll scoot in ahead of your grandma and push them behind the Sunday school blackboard! OK?"

"OK."

For a few minutes, on the porch with Evvie, the sun hot on our backs, an autumn leaf floating onto the grass every so often, a buzz of conversation in the house, and an empty dish of macaroni between us, everything almost felt OK. We just sat there, Evvie and me, until the sun sank and people started coming out to go home, asking if we two girls were all right and didn't we want to get a sweater because the fall evenings were chilly.

We're fine, we said, getting up when Evvie's mom came out last to take her home. I was cold by now. I said goodbye to Evvie and went in feeling the heaviness of the day. The Angels had cleaned everything up, washed all the dishes, swept the floor, and laid out plates and stuff to be ready for after the funeral next day. Granny was straightening the furniture.

"I'm glad to have a little peace and quiet." She looked drained. "I told Randall they could sing."

"Good," I said.

"I'm going to bed. You should too, Rose-Linda. We have a long day ahead of us tomorrow. A long day."

I dreaded tomorrow. I dreaded the next day and the day after that.

As I got ready for bed, everything about the day felt wrong. It would take months to sink in that it marked the end of a whole period of my life.

CHAPTER 36

1998–2000

The next day, at the funeral, I reached out and held Granny's cold hand under her pocketbook, relieved Evvie and I had hid the worst of the floral tributes. It was bad enough without those in our faces. There was a long eulogy about Gramps's distinguished career as a newspaperman and civic leader, testimonials from professors he'd known, something from the Smithsonian praising the *Messenger* as a historical record of the region.

Reverend Merriman preached a sermon about the power of unseen things, like the power of conviction, of words, how Gramps's legacy was the way he'd used that power of words for good, facilitating school integration, raising money for good causes. Everybody sang with the choir while they carried the coffin out. At the cemetery the jug band played "Just a Closer Walk with Thee," and the three of them harmonized on "I'll Fly Away" at the graveside. Granny closed her eyes. Gramps used to hum "I'll Fly Away" every morning while he shaved.

There was a military salute at the graveside because Gramps was a veteran who'd been in the army during the war. Every time they fired a volley, Granny winced like they'd shot her.

And of course we sang "Guide Me, O Thou Great Jehovah," and Granny and I threw roses from the flower arrangements in after the coffin, and for a minute I thought Granny might just jump in the grave and get buried with Gramps. I held her arm tight.

Afterward, the flowers and food and people gradually stopped coming through the door at Wildwood. People kept talking about "finding closure," whatever that meant. Everything was falling apart. The *Messenger* closed down, and there were a lot of bills coming in. Granny was distracted with grief, unable to concentrate on anything, and suddenly there was no money for even basic necessities like food or gas. Her inheritance was long gone. She'd never had a job other than writing stories for the paper, but of course she didn't get paid for those. Gramps had always dealt with the finances, run the *Messenger*, and managed the land the family owned and rented out to farmers, taken care of everything.

There was still a lot of Marshall land, of course, but she didn't know how to deal with the logging companies or the big farms wanting to lease acreage, which had been a big source of Marshall income. So she dithered about renewing contracts or leases.

The one thing she did was sell the old Vann house that had been turned into apartments but needed repairs. There were a lot of back taxes due on it, and Freeman Hanover Stuart advised that getting it off her hands was probably the best option. One of the Drumhellers bought it, to turn into an old people's home. But then the back taxes still had to be paid, so in the end she didn't get much money out of the sale.

She tried to pull herself together and cope, but Gramps's death had hit her hard. She'd always been a handsome woman, even as she got older. She'd been fastidious about her clothes, elegant, her thick white hair gathered in a loose French twist that became her and showed her earrings. Now she looked old and tired most of the time. She dressed carelessly, her clothes were stained, her slip sometimes showed beneath her hem, and her hair was straggled. Her voice had gotten sharp too. I didn't protest anymore about going to an all-girls college. At Christmas I filled out the scholarship application before she could get irritated that I hadn't.

"Your grandmother looks awful," Evvie said bluntly. "My mom's worried about her."

I tried to ask Granny if she was OK, but she snapped, "Never mind my looks, Rose-Linda. I hate fuss! I'm fine as I can be in the circumstances." Her talking to me like that made me go outside to cry.

It wasn't until Mrs. Stuart came by and said bluntly, "Primrose, you're going to see Stillman Read if I have to drag you there myself!" that Granny agreed she'd go ask about getting some iron pills after Christmas. She was just as grouchy with Evvie's mom as she'd been with me. Rude even. And Granny had been outspoken but never rude before.

I took to wearing Gramps's shirts with the sleeves rolled up and his old tweed jackets on top. They reminded me of him and looked OK with my jeans. Not that I really cared how I looked anymore. But the shirts and jackets were sort of comforting to wear, when everything else was such a mess.

That winter Mitch and Curtis and Randall pitched in and kept us from going under. They came with dinners Alice and Lurene cooked for us, took our old Ford to get filled up at the Pines' gas station and wouldn't let us pay them back, saying we could "put it on the bill." They brought us sacks of corn to feed the chickens, fixed the chicken house, and mended our roof after half the shingles were torn off by a big storm. They persuaded a couple of local farmers from the American Legion to rent grazing land the Marshalls owned down in the valley. They told Granny where to apply for veterans' widow benefits and helped her fill out the forms. Time and again Granny tried to tell them how much she appreciated their help, but they brushed her thanks off, saying they were all three younger than Eugene; it had been a standing joke among the Hog Callers that Eugene was the old man of the group. They still had their get-up-and-go, the least they could do was help out the family. He would have done the same for them.

We were able to afford gas and groceries again, but not much else. I tried to keep the house swept and carried in wood for the fireplace, like Gramps used to do. The sun came up in the morning and set in the evening. By spring Gramps's garden was taken over by weeds. Life felt half-restarted and half not.

In January Evvie had gotten a job after school working in Loretta's café attached to the motel, and I was set to get a job too, but Granny wouldn't let me. She'd gotten really strict. Evvie dated like crazy and kept wanting to fix me up, but Granny wouldn't let me go out. She insisted I use all my time to study. I listened enviously to Evvie talk about parties and going to the drive-in and illicit beers and boyfriends, but I was more scared of not getting the scholarship now. Granny had her heart set on it and kept reminding me Gramps had too. "Plenty of time for boys later, Rose-Linda. That scholarship's your one chance," she warned. "Grab it! Don't you dare let it get away!"

Evvie said Granny was probably going hard on me because she hadn't gone hard on my mother. I was turning into the school nerd, but the thought I'd wind up drifting through life like my mother had scared me too—enough that I didn't try to fight Granny.

Worrying about the scholarship kept me awake at night.

A week before the class of 1999 graduated from high school, I came home to find a letter from the college in Bristol waiting for me after school. I ripped it open and screamed "I got it! I got it!" and punched the air. *"Yes!"* I didn't see Granny asleep on the sofa with a quilt thrown over her, despite the May heat. I should have remembered that she often took afternoon naps these days.

"Sorry," I whispered, afraid she'd say something scathing now. She woke, rubbed her eyes, and shifted upright to a sitting position. "What? Who got what?"

"The scholarship! I got it! The whole thing! Tuition *and* room and board *and* an allowance for books!" It was the first good thing that had happened in a long time. Granny smiled and congratulated me, but it was a strange smile that looked sort of sad, actually. Her hair had come out of its bun, and there were dark circles under her eyes.

"Well, that's wonderful, Rose-Linda. I'm proud of you. Your grandfather would have been too. Now, it's time we had a little talk. Come here." She patted the sofa for me to sit down and folded the quilt. Her hands shook slightly.

"An education equips you for life, and you'll need it. You have to think about your future."

"What?" The furthest I'd got thinking about the future was joining Evvie for weekends of fraternity parties.

"You'll need a good head on your shoulders, child. There're some big decisions coming up, and you'll have to deal with them yourself when they do."

"I thought this scholarship was what you wanted—I'll study hard so I can get a good job when I graduate, and that will keep us going. Don't worry, Granny. I'll look after you."

She patted my hand. "You're a sweet girl, Rose-Linda! But something's happened that we have to grapple with soon. The company that bought the land from Gramps all those years ago and built that awful Cherokee Ridge kept the big piece along the river vacant. It turns out they now have plans to build one of those country club and resort places, with tennis and fishing, and places to do weddings. That's a big business these days, I hear.

"They'd like to buy more of Frog Mountain, even wrote to me, asking if Wildwood was for sale. They want to turn it into a honeymoon cabin or, what did they call it? A romantic getaway. They'd promise not to tear it down, just make a few improvements. They'd redo the bathrooms and put in a Jacuzzi and a big new kitchen, knock down some of the walls. I keep telling them no, but they're persistent, Rose-Linda." Granny sighed. "And look at the state of the place. Shingles are coming off the roof, floorboards are coming loose, and there're a couple of leaking pipes under the kitchen. Randall managed to fix those for the time being, but he says they're old and the joints are going. An old house is a liability. We have to be realistic and think about selling while we can."

"Sell *Wildwood*? You can't! It's been in the family since . . . since forever!" I felt a sudden wave of panic. Wildwood had been my anchor most of my life, and without it I'd be adrift. I'd leave temporarily for college, but *selling* it! Where would Granny and I go?

"The thing is, you may have to fight that battle, decide whether or not to sell it all by yourself."

"I'd never sell Wildwood!"

"You might have to, or let it fall down. It costs a lot to keep it standing. Eventually you'll be on your own here. You'll inherit Wildwood and all the Marshall property when I die. You might get married and move away and kick yourself you didn't sell this old place while you could."

"Don't talk about dying, Granny! Please! And I'll never, never want to leave Wildwood. The thought makes me feel sick."

"Rose-Linda, you have to think about the future. And while we're on the subject of the future, I was hard on you about that scholarship for a reason. I wanted you to get it real bad. There's something I put off telling you, but it can't wait any longer."

Then she told me she had cancer. I sat feeling the room spin around me while she explained the kind she had was too far gone to be treated by the time it was diagnosed. That had been just after Christmas, when

Evvie's mom made her go to the doctor. I burst into tears and threw my arms around her, feeling her bones. She'd grown so thin!

She patted my back. "The doctors think I had it before Gramps died, and when I felt so bad afterward I put it down to grieving, and it just got left too long. I'm thankful Eugene didn't know, that's one blessing. He couldn't have stood it. Now, stop crying. I don't want a fuss, Rose-Linda. I hate fuss. Just promise me that, no matter what, you'll take that scholarship. Randall promised to keep an eye on the place when you went off to college. When you get finished . . . well, then you'll have to figure out what to do."

"How much time did they give you?"

"Not long, Rose-Linda, maybe a year."

The bottom dropped out of my world. Granny was all I had. I sat with my arm around her until Granny said she felt tired and dozed off again.

I covered her up, went to my room, and wrapped up tight in Gramps's favorite jacket. It was a hot afternoon, but I was shivering, rocking back and forth. I picked up a pillow and cried and screamed into it "No, no, no!" until I was hoarse.

A week later, pale and sitting stiffly upright in her best summer hat and pearls, Granny heard me give the valedictorian address at graduation. She smiled graciously when people congratulated her on my achievements, not giving away how bad she felt or what a strain the noise and excitement of the big graduation picnic afterward were for her. She insisted we attend it, wouldn't hear of my driving her home early. "I have to brag a little about my smart granddaughter," she said, "while I can." I think she enjoyed it, people made a fuss over her and me, and I was glad she'd had something pleasant to do for a change.

By the end of the summer, she was spending more and more time in bed. By then I'd managed to get a deferral on taking up the scholarship, and she was mad I'd done that, but by now she was too sick to argue much. I called old Dr. Stillman Read Sr.—who was eighty and retired but still made house calls for certain patients like Granny—and his son, young Dr. Stillman Read Jr., who was fifty and had been on duty when Gramps died. She'd been adamant she didn't want to see either one, but I was desperate. I needed to know how I could look after her, so I asked one of them to visit and tell me what to do. They came up to Wildwood together to try to persuade her to go into the hospital, where they said they could do more for her.

"What for? I've got some time left and I'll spend it where I please! I'd as lief die in my own home in my own bed." They remonstrated, listed all their reasons, but she kept saying no, and finally old Dr. Read snapped. He banged his walking stick on the floor and shouted she was stubborn as a mule and he could see what Eugene had had to put up with.

"I'll be waiting in the car," he said abruptly, and stormed out.

Outside Granny's room, young Dr. Read sighed. "Don't mind Dad," he said to me. "He and Eugene were good friends. If it weren't for the *Messenger*, we'd never have raised enough money for the hospital's neonatal unit. I guess you know the story—your grandparents lost three babies before your mother was born."

"What? They never said anything about that. I thought my mother was the only child. I didn't know about the others . . . how terrible!"

"Sure, that's why your grandpa raised money for the neonatal unit. Said his own grandmother, one of the Vanns, I believe, had lost a number of young children too, and he wanted to support a special unit to help save babies and young kids. Dad says they could probably have saved two of Primrose's pregnancies if there'd been a specialist unit back then. Can't tell you how many babies it's saved since—they come miles by ambulance sometimes."

"Oh, poor Granny," I whispered. I hadn't known about the lost babies. My aunts or uncles. God, everything was horrible!

"I'll have my nurse stop by with medicines and instructions on how to give them to Primrose. God knows you'll need 'em, Rose-Linda. You call me whenever you need to, you hear?"

I couldn't think about college. I did my best, nursing Granny through the winter. I called Dr. Read a lot. He'd give me advice over the phone, and a couple of times he came up to pay her a visit and check for himself that I was doing what could be done. Spring came, then summer, and I was exhausted. It was getting harder and harder. Granny didn't have any health insurance—that was one of the things that fell by the wayside even before Gramps died—and we couldn't hire a part-time nurse. Nursing is hard work, and I was terrified I'd do something wrong with the medicine. I called young Dr. Read more and more often for advice. I made lots of Jell-O and kept a pitcher of ice water with mint from the old springhouse on her bedside table, gave her medicine at shorter and shorter intervals because of the pain. After she took it, we'd have a few good hours, and she liked to look through old scrapbooks I'd hauled down from the attic. Propped up on her pillows, she'd pat the bed and I'd sit beside her. She enjoyed telling me about the people and places, pointing out relatives. "I'd like you to know who these folks were."

She meant so I wouldn't feel so without a family when she died.

There were photos of the old Rehoboth Springs Hotel on Little Frog Mountain in its heyday. There were pictures of young women in white blouses with high necks and muttonchop sleeves, their hair done up in that puffy fashion on top of their heads. Young men with straw hats playing croquet or banjos or posed with tennis rackets. She pointed to a very pretty laughing girl who seemed to be at the center of everything. "That was Bella Drumheller. Your great-granny Horatia's best friend. They say all the boys were in love with her, but she was in love with Gramps's uncle Calvert, who went off to fly airplanes in the First World War and never came back. They think he got shot down at Verdun. Bella never knew because she died in an accident herself.

"This picture is Horatia just before she and Frank got married. You take after her."

The old brownish photo showed a serious dark-haired young woman in a high-waisted dress and pearls, posed with a parasol and wearing glasses.

"Horatia was blind as a bat, I recall. She read all the time and supposedly 'put her eyes out.' Back in those days, girls were supposed to have feeble brains that got strained if they thought too hard! She was active in the Votes for Women campaign."

There were photos of a woman named Aunt Teeny at the newspaper with her two daughters and pictures of Gramps as a young man in his army uniform and of him and Mitch and Randall and Curtis as teenagers playing their jug band, pictures of him giving speeches and getting awards. We both laughed as we'd done many times at the photo where she and Gramps were cutting the wedding cake with Granny's mother glowering beside her, dressed in black from head to toe.

I took the picture of Horatia Vann out of the scrapbook and tried to see the resemblance in the mirror. She'd been very pretty, in spite of the incongruous spectacles. Maybe I looked like her. A little.

But worrying about how I looked wasn't important. Granny slept most of the time, and her breathing sounded harder. I hardly left her side, slept on a chair by her bed in case she wanted a drink of water or another pill.

"Don't grieve too hard when I'm gone," said Granny one day when she was too poorly even to look at the scrapbook. "I had what I wanted—mostly—in life. And it's life that counts, more than death. Just promise me, you'll go on to college like you planned after I go. You'll think you feel too bad to go, but it'll be a distraction from all this." She waved a hand at the medicine bottles and the potty. Her face looked sunken in, and her nose had a sharpness. "Do that for your grandfather and me."

I promised to go when college started, knowing perfectly well I was lying—how could I leave her?

By June, Granny was bad. She couldn't keep food down.

She died quietly one morning early in July. I was straightening her covers, and I realized all I could hear were the cicadas humming in the crepe myrtle bush outside the bedroom window. No sound of her breathing. I could tell she was gone. Her face had changed, the worry and pain were smoothed out, and I knew there was no point calling Dr. Read for an ambulance. I stopped what I was doing and sat down. I had been mostly up for several nights in a row, and was too numb with exhaustion to cry, not yet. I don't know how much time passed, just Granny and me together, little puffs of hot breeze stirring the curtains, and the sound of cicadas, and the room full of . . . peace.

Then I heard a car outside, and I saw Evvie and her mom had just driven up. "Goodbye, Granny," I whispered. The car doors slammed outside, and a minute later Mrs. Stuart was at the bedroom door, taking in what had happened. "Granny died," I said.

She came over and put her arms around me. "She's with your grandfather and Sophy now. Oh, honey, I'm so sorry . . ." It broke the spell. Everything hit me and I started to cry. Mrs. Stuart went to call young Dr. Read, who drove up to Wildwood fast, but of course he couldn't do anything. He pulled the sheet over Granny's face and left me to sit with her a little longer. Mrs. Stuart made phone calls in the living room. I heard her saying something about collecting the body. Evvie came in with a box of Kleenex.

I tried to recover the peaceful feeling, but the moment had passed, and I heard myself sobbing that it was good Granny was dead because she wasn't in pain anymore, and it was horrible of me but I was too tired to stay awake all through another night to give her her medicine. Evvie patted my arm. "It's OK, Rose-Linda," she kept saying. "It's OK." But by now I was crying so hard I couldn't stop or breathe. I was gasping and hiccuping about Granny's babies and the scholarship and my mother, and then Evvie's mom was shouting, "Give her something, Stillman, for God's sake! The child hasn't slept a wink in days." Then I was screaming "No, no!" and fighting off Dr. Read, who was trying to give me a shot.

I woke up in my clothes in my own bed next morning. I could hear people and smelled coffee. I brushed my teeth and splashed my face, then wandered into the kitchen, where the Death Angels were busy. There was a rack full of wet dishes. Automatically I picked up a dish towel and started drying plates.

Conversation stopped, and a lady with her hands in the sink told another one to fix me some toast and a cup of coffee with plenty of sugar. Someone steered me back to the living room and took the dish towel out of my hands. "Here's your toast and coffee, honey," somebody else said, handing me a plate and putting a cup on the coffee table. "Get that down. Then you can see what hymns you want."

I put stuff in my mouth. Toast with blackberry preserves. The coffee was really sweet and had too much cream. I drank it in one gulp.

They gave me a hymnbook and told me to pick out Granny's favorite hymns for the funeral.

Funeral. I heard myself make a moaning sound. The room spun.

"Put her head between her knees," said somebody.

When I could sit back up, I was hemmed in by concerned ladies talking about hymns. I asked what hymns would they sing in Richmond. It wasn't funny, but I started to giggle. I saw the ladies raise their eyebrows at each other, shaking their heads. "Sorry," I snickered, and they patted my shoulders and somebody brought more coffee. I stopped laughing. My hand shook and I got coffee all over my shirt. "Better change," I mumbled. I went to my room and fell back on the bed. Maybe I wouldn't get up after all.

I think Mrs. Stuart chose the hymns in the end.

I hardly remember the time leading up to the visitation or the funeral, just that the Drumheller funeral men were in the house and the Angels were everywhere and it must have been the shot Dr. Read gave me, but I kept falling asleep. Then we were down at the church with the casket, and then we were in the cemetery. Mitch and Randall and Curtis led everyone in "Amazing Grace" at the graveside before she was buried beside Gramps and Mama. Granny liked "Amazing Grace."

I went through the next weeks in a daze. When people asked if I was OK, I said I was fine. I ate funeral leftovers without tasting a thing until even I realized food had gone off and had to be thrown away. I slept in my clothes, forgot what day it was. Wildwood was very quiet except for the sound of the chickens. Evvie came up most days. She reminded me to feed them. She brought leftover meatloaf from Loretta and threw out wilted flowers and their smelly water. She reminded me college was due to start the third week in September. She reminded me I'd promised to go. At least if I went, I wouldn't have to face everyone at the Blackberry Picnic.

The Hog Callers helped me get a gravestone put up next to Gramps's and my mother's graves.

PRIMROSE MURRAY MARSHALL
BELOVED WIFE OF EUGENE MARSHALL
JUNE 2, 1931–JULY 7, 2000

All my family lying there.

I tried not to think about going to college. I tried to keep moving, like it would help anything. Instead I cleaned and swept and stuffed things in boxes, and put the boxes in the attic and got rid of the last of Granny's medicines. I shooed the chickens into burlap bags and took them and the sack of chicken feed to Miss Nettie, who had an old chicken house behind the beehives.

I was a maniac. I was getting sick in my stomach every time I thought about college. I couldn't sleep.

When Evvie finally dragged me to young Dr. Read, he said shock and bereavement did all kinds of things to people, we'd all had a big dose of that. But the way he saw it, Granny would have wanted me to go on and get to college, just try it. I could always come home. He gave me some pills.

I shut my eyes and heard Gramps say, *Just go, Rose-Linda. Go. It's your chance.*

Halfway through September, two days before the term started, Evvie came between shifts to help me pack. The pills Dr. Read had given me made me feel numb and dozy, and sort of half-alive. That helped. A little. But they also meant I didn't focus very well on things, even something as simple as packing. I was moving around my room, taking things out of the closet and drawers and tossing them into open suitcases. Evvie groaned and dumped it all out. She separated stuff into piles, folded things, remembered socks and shampoo, and stuffed the most horrible old T-shirts and odd socks into a plastic bag to throw away. She insisted we load everything into Granny's old Ford right then, so I could make an early start next day.

She brought store-bought macaroni and cheese to heat up for my dinner and a box of doughnuts for my breakfast. She checked to make sure the icebox was cleaned out. She lugged the block of ice Harold Pine had delivered five days earlier out the back door to melt, reminded me to prop the icebox doors open so they didn't slam shut and make the icebox moldy. She hugged me hard and said, "You can do this, don't let your grandma down. It'll be all right, Rose-Linda. Remember, one day at a time. Call me when you get there." Then she went off for her evening shift. I opened the cap on the bottle of pills and flushed them down the toilet. I was going to have to feel whatever I felt, because I owed it to Granny and Gramps not to mess up my chance by being too dopey to concentrate.

Next morning I ate some doughnuts and filled up a thermos with water. The kitchen looked like the emptiest place on earth. I propped the four doors of the icebox open, locked everything, locked the double doors to the dogtrot behind me. When I got behind the wheel of the loaded-up car, I was shaking and my palms were sweaty. I wished I hadn't thrown away the pills. Wildwood filled the rearview mirror.

I opened the door and threw up the doughnuts. I *couldn't* leave. I had to stay here . . . I gulped air and rested my head on the steering wheel.

You don't have to actually go, just turn the ignition on, I reasoned, straightening up. That didn't commit me to actually going.

One day at a time.

I started the car. *Now take off the hand brake, now drive through the gate, imagine you're just going to the store . . .* Fighting panic, I did that. Halfway down Frog Mountain I was nearly overwhelmed by the urge to make a U-turn and run back to my room and pull a quilt over my head. I think I was hyperventilating, because I got light-headed all of a sudden and had to pull over and breathe into my cupped hands. I'd promised Granny. Somehow, I kept going. I made it to the highway, saying "One day at a time" over and over, real loud. I joined the traffic and headed for Bristol.

CHAPTER 37

2000–2002

I finished my first year of college somehow. I didn't really fit in, but I didn't care. The other girls all seemed to come from rich families—some had arrived at college on private planes. They had lots of clothes and expensive coffee makers and cushions for their rooms. Many had been to boarding school, and all of them had been to Europe. They were friendly enough, but I didn't feel like socializing and refused invitations to come drink coffee in this or that girl's room. After a while they left me alone.

I got a job in the college coffee shop to fill in spare time when I wasn't in class or working in the library or at my desk. I didn't make friends or date, even though a couple of girls offered to fix me up with their friends or brothers.

I think a professor came on to me. He was young and unmarried, good-looking in a floppy-haired, tortoiseshell-glasses way, and even seemed nice, but I ignored him. I wasn't happy or unhappy. I was on automatic pilot, and there's no room for a boyfriend on that.

I kept the photo of Horatia Vann with her spectacles and parasol and stuck it in my mirror. Every once in a while I couldn't resist looking in the mirror and lifting my hair up to imitate the way Horatia's framed her face, looking for a resemblance. I'd started to bring photos of Granny and Gramps, but somehow in the end it felt like their photos belonged at Wildwood, not in a strange dorm room. So Horatia's picture was the closest thing to family I had now.

Randall called a couple of times to let me know everything was OK at Wildwood. Evvie and I called each other a lot, but I didn't go back to Grafton that first summer. News of the resort plan had gotten around, and people felt strongly for or against it. I didn't want to talk about it. Really I just couldn't face all the people asking me if I planned to sell Wildwood. Instead I took a summer course for credits and got a waitressing job and a tutoring job, which left me just enough time to sleep.

I planned to get through the second year like I got through the first, studying hard and working every campus job I could find. The scholarship covered most things, but I still needed money. I'd made a few quick trips back to Wildwood to check on things and discovered Randall had been paying for some repairs—a tree had fallen on the roof in a storm and he'd paid to fix that, plus some broken windows and a fence that had come down.

September 11 happened. Like everyone, I was in shock. The whole damn world was falling apart in the months that followed. I wondered what the *Messenger* would have reported about it, what editorials Gramps would have written about America invading Afghanistan.

The following spring, Evvie told me the old Rehoboth Springs Hotel that'd been going to rack and ruin for many years got sold. It had been a dance hall during the Prohibition era, and they were still selling cocktails made with leftover bootleg whiskey when Gramps and his high school friends went whooping it up there. It was kind of a speakeasy by then; they turned a blind eye to the fact that the boys were teenagers. Turned a blind eye to a lot of things, according to Gramps.

Probably why it got closed down. During World War II it got taken over by the government and used as a convalescent home for injured servicemen. Now, said Evvie, a Christian college had bought it.

I'd just finished my end-of-the-year exams in May when Evvie called me all excited. Guess who was back in town? Ricky Pine! He'd finished a tour in Afghanistan and had come swaggering home on leave in his uniform, and it just drove Evvie wild. And I gathered he was smitten by Evvie.

Men usually were. She'd been to see me a couple of times to check I was still alive, and she looked amazing. In the year and a half I'd been away, she'd morphed into an auburn-haired beauty with a little waist, big green eyes, big boobs, and a sassier mouth than ever who could trade raunchy backchat with the truck drivers while looking like an angel. Big good-looking Ricky landed on Evvie like a June bug, by the sound of it. Evvie couldn't believe her luck.

"Remember how we used to be in love with Guy and Ricky?" she bubbled.

"So embarrassing, don't remind me! How is he? Are they still in the army?"

"Yeah, Ricky is. Guy's in the Special Forces or something. He always was kind of gung ho, and guess what, they both got sent to Afghanistan. Ricky got wounded, but he's OK."

Evvie and Ricky drove to Bristol to see me one summer night, and we went out for pizza and beer. Ricky looked good, tan and muscular, maybe a little jittery. He talked a lot, told us stories about Afghanistan that were sort of funny and sort of terrible at the same time. He kept his arm around Evvie like he was hanging on to her, so he had to eat his pizza one-handed. Like she was his anchor. He filled us in on Guy. He and Guy had both tried to join the Green Berets, but only Guy made it. "He always did better at school than me," said Ricky. Guy had turned out to be good at languages, was doing all kinds of specialist training, learning about Afghan customs, how to get down with the "towel heads," stuff like that.

I flinched, hoping no one had heard. His injured leg kept jiggling the table.

Afterward in the ladies' room, I asked Evvie if he was OK. Evvie said Ricky'd been medevaced out before his tour of duty ended; he was having rehab but needed painkillers because his injuries still bothered him. The painkillers acted like a dozen cups of coffee all at once. "But I have a surefire way to calm him down." She smiled wickedly.

"I bet you do, girl. I bet you do."

"How's college?" she asked. "Are you finally dating?"

"No. Campus jobs and classes don't leave me time to socialize."

Evvie groaned. "Come back to Grafton for Thanksgiving, at least. I'll fix us up a double date. You can have Thanksgiving dinner at my house. And I'm not taking no for an answer."

It had been dismal being on my own for the holidays last year, so I went, telling myself I had to check that everything was OK at Wildwood. It wasn't fair to leave everything to Randall.

When I opened the front door, I half expected Granny or Gramps to shout *Hey, darlin'*, to feel wrapped in the embrace of the old house, to smell dinner cooking. Instead, in November Wildwood was freezing cold and smelled musty. I brought in an armload of kindling and logs from the stack on the porch and sat by the fireplace wrapped in a quilt, watching the flames and eating canned tomato soup, thinking about the term paper due before Christmas.

Next day I spruced myself up as best I could and went to Thanksgiving dinner with Evvie and a houseful of her relatives. When the turkey had been carved, Evvie tapped her water glass with a spoon and stood up. "I have an announcement. I'm pregnant, and Ricky Pine and I are getting married at Christmas, before he ships out again to Afghanistan," she bubbled to a suddenly silent, startled table. "Y'all are all invited to the wedding." She turned to me. "Rose-Linda, you have to be my maid of honor. And guess what? Guy Charbonneau's coming to be the best man!"

That sure gave everybody something to talk about, all the way through dinner and into the pie. Mrs. Stuart looked stunned—this was the first she'd heard about Evvie being pregnant—and Evvie avoided her eye and answered questions from her cousins about when Ricky would be sent back overseas and when she would know whether the baby was a girl or a boy. I saw several surreptitiously counting on their fingers, working out when Evvie must have gotten pregnant. About five minutes after Ricky got home on his last leave, by my reckoning.

Evvie launched into the wedding plans with her usual enthusiasm. She wanted an evening wedding, with Tabernacle Baptist Church blazing with red candles amid lots of holly and poinsettias. Her mom came around to the idea fast and started organizing, begging me to come back to Grafton as soon as I could.

Last year I'd spent the Christmas holiday waitressing, sleeping at the Y until the dormitory reopened after the holiday. This year I went back to Grafton the minute my classes finished to help with the wedding. Preparations were in full swing, and I spent most of my time at Evvie's.

Right away Mrs. Stuart measured me for the bridesmaid's dress that she was making me. Then I was given the job of keeping track of who had sent what wedding present in a card index, and giving Mrs. Stuart my opinion about this or that fabric swatch for the curtains she was making for the run-down little house by the river Evvie and Ricky had bought to fix up. I relayed messages from Mrs. Stuart to Evvie's cousins about the shoes to match their dresses. I was sent on errands—like traveling forty miles to an outlet store that had two hundred fat red candles for sale on a special, or to wheedle the use of somebody's crystal punch bowl and cups for the reception. I went to a bridal shower.

It was chaos. To my surprise, it was fun.

CHAPTER 38

On the night of the wedding I stood in the church vestibule listening to the organ and waiting to hand Evvie her bouquet, then to signal the organist to stop playing "Jesu, Joy of Man's Desiring" and start on the bridesmaids' marching music. Evvie kept disappearing, having to go for what she called a "pregnant pee." Waiting at the altar, Ricky and Guy looked handsome in their dress uniforms, though after a few minutes Ricky was shifting around.

Mrs. Stuart was escorted to her seat by her brother-in-law, and I remembered Granny had told me it was a rule, no one could be seated after the bride's mother. We have Richmond to thank for that information, Gramps would have said. Finally I saw Evvie was back from the john in the vestibule. I waved and the processional started.

I went down the aisle behind Evvie's six cousins who were the other bridesmaids. They wore green, but I had a red-ruffled dress Evvie thought would make a nice contrast. She'd chosen the pattern, and I felt self-conscious how low-cut it was. I was teetering on high heels, dyed to match, that made my ankles wobble dangerously. Evvie had spent an hour fixing my hair into one of those loose buns with a few locks teased out to fall down the sides. Kind of done but messy. When Evvie finally let me look in the mirror, all I could say was "Looks like I got dragged through the bushes and caught a bird's nest on the way."

"No, idiot! It's called the bed-head look!" She giggled. "I saw it in a magazine. Who knew you could look so sexy. It suits you. See, you should dress up more." Evvie had also insisted on doing my makeup in the church's powder room, just before she got dressed herself. She said I hadn't had enough practice to do it on my own. This was true. I rarely bothered with makeup. I didn't *own* any makeup. "If they can make penicillin out of moldy cheese, we can make something out of you, hoo-hoo," she sang as she layered on the blusher and the eye shadow. She helped me fasten Granny's pearl-and-garnet necklace, handed me the single long-stemmed red rose I was to carry, sprayed me heavily with Shalimar, and told me to check myself out in the full-length mirror in the vestibule. "Lookin' good!" she exclaimed.

A startled person looked back at me. A startled person who actually did look pretty good. Smelled good too. I must've been wearing half a bottle of expensive perfume. I smiled at myself.

The church was packed. Walking carefully, I made it up the aisle, following the bridesmaids, like we'd practiced at the rehearsal the previous evening. Then everybody except Evvie was at the altar. When we got to the altar, the organist was supposed to sort of crash into "Here Comes the Bride" so Evvie could make a grand entrance.

In fact, after a dramatic *da-DAH-da-da!* from the start of the wedding march, the organist segued into "What a Friend We Have in Jesus." No Evvie. Was she back in the john?

Finally the organ burst into *da-DAH-da-da* again, and this time Evvie came down the aisle on her uncle's arm, smiling behind a shoulder-length veil and looking beautiful in a short white dress with a lace overskirt and a high waist. She carried white roses and wore white satin high heels. Evvie walked like she'd been born in high heels.

Ricky was shifting his weight like his leg was killing him while the preacher read from the Bible, then gave a long homily about marriage before finally getting to the vows and the rings. Both mothers cried when the I dos were said. I think Loretta was crying with relief that Ricky wasn't marrying a barroom hooker or lap dancer—Loretta's no fool—but a nice local girl who'd keep him steady, and who was obviously in love with her son.

Evvie's mom was crying because, I'd gathered by now, Mrs. Stuart wasn't convinced Ricky was such a prize, grandchild on the way or not. He had a lot to live down. Plus, he was getting sent back to Afghanistan shortly, and however stabilizing family life might be, it wouldn't have a chance to take hold for a while yet.

I held Evvie's flowers and watched Guy out of the corner of my eye to see if he was looking at me—he wasn't. He was hunting in his pockets for where he'd put the wedding ring. Reverend Jones pronounced them man and wife, and the choir started up with a sort of sprightly rendition of "Blest Be the Tie That Binds." And it hit me all of a sudden—Evvie was married and everything would be different. She was going to have babies and cook her husband's dinner. There wouldn't be any more of our silly sleepovers where we'd stay up late with a bottle of wine and laugh our heads off. My best friend! Thinking of this, I suddenly got emotional, with not a scrap of Kleenex tucked into my glove. I sniffed a little louder than was ladylike, snorted actually, because tears make my nose run, and snot is not an attractive accessory. Guy passed me a handkerchief with a deadpan expression on his face as the couple kissed and turned to go back down the aisle.

As the best man, it was Guy's job to escort the maid of honor out of the church. I turned to join him, and my ankle twisted. I staggered and practically fell into his arms. He caught me. "Feels like we're at sea and you're going down for the third time," Guy muttered out of the side of his mouth, bracing himself to steady my full weight.

"I wish men had to wear high heels!" I hissed, my face flaming with embarrassment. So much for making a good impression on Guy.

At the reception in the fellowship hall—no alcohol allowed—I stood behind the punch bowl filled with pink stuff and fruit, smiling and ladling it into cut-glass cups. No one could see I'd slipped my shoes off. People kept saying things like "Why, Rose-Linda! Never seen you look so pretty, honey!" "Looks like college suits you." "Love that color on you." "Guess you'll be next." I felt my face getting hot from the compliments. I wasn't used to compliments.

Then Guy was standing at the punch table, and I grabbed a little cup and scooped up punch, but he said no punch, it was always awful and sweet, weddings made him nervous, and would I go have a drink at Jayjay's tavern with him.

I hesitated. Was this a date? "Umm." I was taken aback. I hadn't dated much, and somehow you get to be the girl nobody asks out and you don't feel blazing with confidence. Or even know what to say. So you don't exactly sparkle. So no one asks you out. It was a vicious cycle.

Guy must have thought I was being coy. "Oh come on, Rose-Linda. We went to school together. You've turned out OK. You're much better looking than I remembered."

"You are too," I said without thinking, like I was fourteen again. I felt my face get red. I missed the cup I was holding and ladled sticky liquid over my hand. "Dammit!"

Guy grinned. "Besides, you've got that come-hither perfume on. I can't resist. Soon as Evvie and Ricky leave—I know you want to throw rice—I'll get your coat. And you might want to put your shoes back on. It's cold."

When Evvie went to throw her bouquet, her cousins and the other girls pushed forward, giggling, yelling, "Over here, Evvie!"

"No, throw it to *me*, baby!"

"No, throw it here. I *need* it more'n she does!"

Evvie looked at me standing over by the side and called, "Catch, Rose-Linda!" And she lobbed it straight at me. Instinctively I put up my hands and caught it.

"What am *I* supposed to do with this?" I laughed.

I threw rice, handed the bouquet to Mrs. Stuart to keep, and managed to walk to the tavern without falling over. Guy was hanging up my coat on one of the hooks Jayjay has by the door, and I walked in ahead where it was warm. Right away I sensed trouble. My red flounces and hooker heels were sending a message to the work-shirt-wearing clientele gathered at the bar.

They whistled and leered. "Well, well, look what just walked in! My lucky day! Hey, sweet thing, that guy your boyfriend?" drawled one guy in a baseball cap with a boilermaker in front of him, not taking his eyes off me long enough to focus on Guy. He jerked a thumb at Guy. "A uniform? He's a loser, babe. Come over here close to me."

"Special Forces." Guy stepped in front of me, face to face with Prince Charming. "So I know ten ways to kill you. With my bare hands." And smiled. The guy looked at him, clocked the uniform and Guy's size. He looked away, shifted on his barstool, and tried to decide if I was worth a fight. His friends studied their beers intently. They weren't going to be any help.

Jayjay leaned across the bar to slap one of those male handshakes on Guy. "Good to see you back, Guy! Heard you'd joined the Green Berets! Afghanistan's a tough one."

The beer drinkers muttered, "Green Berets! Damn, Billy, back off!" and concentrated even harder on their beers.

"This here's on the house." Jayjay pulled an unlabeled bottle from under the bar and poured us both a generous drink before I could protest that whiskey was too strong for me. Plus, you'd be crazy to drink anything from an unmarked bottle around here. It would likely make you go blind.

Jayjay added ice and said, "Drink that slow, and tell me if you ever tasted anything like it." Guy sniffed at it. I could tell he was worried about going blind too. "Go on," Jayjay urged, "taste it! Then I'll tell you where it came from. You won't believe it."

Guy took a cautious sip, and his dubious expression vanished. "Where on earth did you get this? Dad had some good whiskey, some of the best stuff you could get, but this is . . . !"

"Fine stuff, ain't it? Smooth as anything. I got no idea how old it is, but you recall the youngest Vann boy, Casey? Little runty guy, always up to something nobody else had thought of. People always said he was sorta crazy, but turns out his problem is he's real smart. And he found it."

I laughed. "Casey? He was two years ahead of Evvie and me at school. Smart all right, always reading, always figuring out ways he could make money. Gramps put a story in the paper about him once. He'd dug up an Indian mound, sold some pots and a skull to a museum. Think he found where the Drumhellers buried silver during the Civil War and dug that up too. The Drumhellers gave him a reward to get it back, before he could sell it."

Jayjay nodded. "That's how he found the whiskey. Diggin' around where he wasn't s'posed to. You recall that old falling-down cabin in the woods kids say's haunted? Was a story, the old man who'd built it was a freed slave who got rich, either from workin' at the Drumhellers' iron-works or from bein' a bootlegger. Anyhow, he didn't have a family, was supposed to have buried a lot of money somewhere. Remember when we were kids, Guy, you and me and Ricky always said we'd go digging one day and find the money, 'course we never did. But old Casey, he went pokin' around the ruins, trying to work out where he'd bury his money if he was a old man. What he found was a old still fallen down, and underneath was half a dozen bottles sealed up.

"He brought 'em in here, told me where he'd got it, and asked me to taste it. I said no way, whatever that stuff is, keep it away from matches and pour it out, but Casey, he told me he'd pried one bottle open and drunk some to see if it'd kill him, but it hadn't. It tasted fine to him, and if I didn't want it, he could sell it to some boys at the high school. Little runt took a drink on the spot, looked me in the eye, dared me to try it."

Jayjay shook his head. "I dunno why I rose to the bait, but you know how it is, now I had to try it. I said a prayer it wouldn't do something terrible, took a little sip, and damn, Casey was right! Best whiskey I ever tasted. I bought what he had, cleaned out the till. Smart aleck went swaggering off with the money, said he'd found his calling. 'Stead of archaeology at college he's switching to chemistry, to figure out how it was made, so he can go into the whiskey business. He'll be rich one day. Crazy, but rich."

"That sounds like Casey," I agreed.

Then Jayjay went to settle an argument between the guys in the work shirts, and I took a cautious sip of whiskey. It sort of burned, but I managed not to choke. It left a strong taste and a nice warm feeling afterward. "Casey used to have a crush on Evvie," I said, "but she wouldn't go out with him. She thought he was too weird."

Guy and I both remembered the cabin overgrown with creeper and empty windows behind it, like eyes. Mostly kids looked at it through the trees but didn't want to get closer, let alone go poking around the bushes and all the stuff growing next to it. We drank a little more, reminisced about high school, stuff we'd done growing up in Grafton, Eskimo Pies at the gas station, the time Ricky thought a run-over rattlesnake in the road was dead and picked it up to chase a girl with it, swinging it by the tail. Only it wasn't dead and bit him, and he had to get rushed to the hospital. How in high school Ricky and Guy had snuck out at night and gone on moonshine runs with Vann Drumheller.

Guy told me stories about the trouble he and Ricky had gotten into during their short college careers, how when they got expelled for shooting up their dorm rooms Guy's father had made a big donation to the college to keep them from pressing charges. Then when they went into the army, Guy had quickly observed that wise guys didn't do too well, tended to get the shit knocked out of them, and the safest thing to do was to just straighten up, but Ricky kept doing crazy stuff, nearly got court-martialed. Now, Ricky a father? He shook his head.

"Well, Evvie being a mother is a turnaround," I said. "She used to be Miss Fun, but pregnant, she's with the program. Doesn't drink, takes her vitamins. People grow up."

Guy sighed. "Yeah, wish I'd done it sooner, before my dad was dying. He was sick for years, so the family was used to it. Dad was tough. He hid it pretty well, insisted on carrying on like normal. Then the time came when he had to go to the hospital, and all of a sudden it hit us, this was the end. It was right when I got expelled from college.

"Sick as he was, Dad was furious, said I was too old and too smart for such a dumb stunt, that he should have let them arrest us, and he'd only bought the college off so my mother didn't have another thing to distress her. He warned me that if I was determined to act like a rich entitled bum, I'd never see a cent of inheritance. My mother was taken care of, but he'd tied up everything my sisters and I would inherit in a trust fund, and the trustees wouldn't release a penny of it until the girls and I proved we could stand on our own two feet without it. The girls were in college, both of them studying to be teachers, which he approved of, but it hit me, if I didn't fix this quick, he'd die before I had the chance to prove I was as good a man as he was.

"Right then I decided what I'd do. I told him I was going to enlist in the army. He said he'd believe it when he saw it. I signed up next day and Ricky did too. Glad I could show him the papers before he died. His last words to me were 'Stick with it. Make me proud.'"

He drained his glass. "It's stayed with me. Always wished I could have known if I did."

"He'd be proud. I mean, you've been to Afghanistan."

"Later, when the war started, they didn't send me right away. I took some tests, got assigned to a psych-ops course first. Ricky's unit went straight over. A couple of months later they were out on patrol and got caught in a shitstorm, killed half of them. Ricky got messed up pretty bad, and for someone who already kind of has a screw loose, I wonder if the army's the right career. Him getting married surprised me, is all. I hope Evvie'll be all right with him. She's a sweet girl, and Ricky . . . He's getting shipped back over, swears he's ready to go . . . but I don't know. It's bad over there—the heat, insurgents, land mines. Don't know who you can trust. Messes with your head. And his leg gives him more trouble than he lets on. You saw how he was jigging around during the wedding."

We were quiet for a minute, Guy worrying about Ricky in Afghanistan, me worrying now about Evvie and a husband with a war injury and possibly PTSD.

"Are you going back soon?"

"Not for another five months. They assigned me to a language course. I'm learning Pashtun."

"So, is the military your career choice?" I asked, adding water to my whiskey when Jayjay's back was turned.

"Nah." He grinned. "I'm getting in touch with my inner mature adult. I'll finish college, then maybe law school. Law's a family tradition. My uncle, Senator Cy Charbonneau, told me to get in touch when I pass the Bar, and in his words, I'm 'good to go.' He's been in Washington for more than forty years, dropped some hints about needing an up-and-coming younger man to follow in his shoes, talked about laying some groundwork first. He says being a lawyer familiar with local people, local problems, some pro bono work, stuff to do with the environment, sets you up."

"You're interested in politics?"

"I might be. Dad would have approved." Guy changed the subject. "That's enough about me. What are you doing besides giving those fellas at the bar a heart attack?"

I told him about my scholarship and college and that Granny had died. "I heard," he said. "I'm sorry. She was a smart woman, disapproved of Ricky and me."

"She thought you'd both end up in prison. She didn't cut me any slack either, was always telling me I had to make something of myself. My own mother didn't go to college—she just . . . left me with them and ran off when I was little—so Granny and Gramps were determined that I would. She made me apply for my scholarship. Knowing that I was doing what they'd wanted me to do kept me going after Granny died, so I understand how you feel about doing what your father wanted."

"Funny how the dead stay with you like that. I took my father for granted when he was alive. Now he's gone, I think about him every day, what a decent person he was, how much time he spent with my sisters and me, how brave he was about his cancer, how important he thought it was to do the right thing. Since he died, people who worked for him, or did business with him, people we never knew he'd helped have told me that's what he did. I wish I hadn't disappointed him for so many years. I've tried to live up to him ever since. I can almost feel him looking over my shoulder."

"I know what you mean," I said. "Sometimes I can imagine so clearly what Gramps would say about something—it's kind of weird, like he tunes in to my mind. But in a good way."

Guy put his hand on mine, gave it a squeeze. "We're both lucky."

"I wish he'd speak up and tell me what to do about Wildwood," I said. "I've inherited a big responsibility—Wildwood and what's left of the Marshall land. Some of it's rented out to farmers, and that about pays the taxes, but I'll either have to find a way to make it pay for itself or sell it. It's falling down. But it's been in the family so long . . . you know, it's home." My voice quivered a little. The idea of selling

Wildwood still made me feel physically sick. *Shut up, Rose-Linda,* my inner voice said. *You're out with Guy Charbonneau. Don't get intense. Just shut up.*

Jayjay poured us another round. I gulped half of it. By now it tasted fine.

"Changing the subject, aren't we related? Around here everybody's related," Guy said.

"Mmm . . . from way back. Granny and Gramps knew all that stuff."

"I want to be sure sitting here with you isn't like dating my sister."

"Please!" I dug my elbow in his side.

"Distant kin's permissible, though . . . Who do we have in common? . . . Let's see, my great-great—lotta greats—grandfather was Lafayette. I think his father came from Europe. A Charbonneau married one of the Marshalls a long time ago."

"How on earth do you know all this?"

"My mother's big on genealogy. You know, bloodlines. I kid her it's because she's from Baltimore. She has ancestors who fled there because they supported Bonnie Prince Charlie. Her family claimed they were related."

Somewhat befuddled with alcohol, we tried counting back generations on our fingers, trying to remember names. "Granny said I had a Charbonneau great-something-grandmother. She must have been the one you're talking about. I had a Comfort somewhere along the line, and . . . Granny said there was a Sophia Marshall way back. That's why Mama was Sophy. There was somebody who communed with spirits."

"Yeah, Dad said one of the Marshalls married a woman who talked to the dead."

"My great-great-grandma. Prob'ly crazy." Had Mama inherited the same craziness? Did she talk to the dead? "And then there was Horatia, my great-grandmother. I think she was a Vann."

"Lessee, in my line I had a Magdalena and Aimée," Guy said. "And there's a Caitlin somewhere in there? Whose relative is Caitlin? Yours or mine?"

"Dunno." I hiccuped and exploded into inebriated giggles.

"I give up. We're probably sixteenth cousins, or something," said Guy. "Let's dance." He pushed a quarter into the old jukebox that had been in the bar since Jayjay's dad ran it. "In the Still of the Night," the old fifties version by the Five Satins, came on, and Guy pulled me off my barstool to slow dance. I kicked off the heels for safety. "You've got shorter all of a sudden," he said. "Hold on tight."

I did. The material of his uniform felt rough against my cheek, and he had on some nice aftershave that smelled of fresh limes. When the song ended, he leaned over without letting go of me and dropped another quarter in. The jukebox played "A Whiter Shade of Pale," and we were slow dancing again. It's a long song. Fine by me.

Afterward we went back to the bar with our arms around each other and had another round of Casey Vann's whiskey. We played every slow song on the jukebox, Guy and me hugging, just moving our feet a little. Then we were the last people in the bar, and Jayjay was wiping things down. Guy said something about my coat. Coat appeared. On. Shoes. On. Then we were outside, kissing. Very nice. I felt like every part of me was supercharged. "Guy, take me home. You can spend the night."

"I'll get you home but no way am I staying."

"Why not? Aren't I attractive?"

"You're gorgeous, and you're jailbait!"

"Jailbait my ass! I'm twenty-two! Besides, you were kissing me."

"Was I? Blood kin and all." He shook his head.

"Don't be an idiot. We're hardly related at all. Let's go!" But we were plainly too drunk to drive, especially up the curves to Wildwood.

I kicked off the shoes again. "Leave the car," I said. "We can go this way." I actually started up the old path through the orchard, me in stocking feet in the cold. Waving my shoes gaily over my head.

"You're nuts," Guy laughed, coming up behind me and slinging me over his shoulder like a sack of potatoes, "and drunk." I shrieked and protested, but he told me to quit squirming, carrying a wounded buddy was part of their training. Laughing like fools, we actually made it up the old path to Wildwood. He swung me over the fence, carried me across the yard and into the house. There was more kissing, and one thing led to another. Wildwood was cold, but my bed was a mattress and a pile of quilts I'd dragged in front of the big living room fireplace. And I'd brought in wood that morning. Guy got a fire going real fast, and we fell onto the mattress. We each had freezing-cold hands.

It didn't matter.

Later, buried under the quilts, I said sleepily, "The good thing about sex is it keeps you warm." I felt warm. Inside and out. It was getting light outside.

"Not the best thing, though," Guy muttered into my shoulder.

"Your hands aren't cold anymore," I told him.

It was nearly dark again when we finally got up.

Guy took me to one Christmas party after another, and it made me laugh seeing how people's heads turned when we came in together, and after a few parties they were exchanging these *Hmm, look who's dating* looks. I wished Evvie could have been there to see, but she and Ricky were in Hawaii on their honeymoon.

It snowed and Guy found an old sleigh in the Charbonneaus' barn. He greased the runners, hitched up some of their horses, and a bunch of us went for a sleigh ride and built a bonfire and cooked hot dogs on sticks and ate leftover Christmas fruitcake for dessert.

He made his mother invite me to Christmas dinner at Chiaramonte with his sisters and their families. I wore my flouncy bridesmaid's dress with one of Granny's old cashmere sweaters, a black one, buttoned up for decency, and her garnet-and-pearl necklace. With the red satin high heels. Guy brought me a huge bunch of red roses when he picked me up, wolf whistled, and said I looked like his Christmas present.

It was lovely at the Charbonneaus'. The house was warm, for one thing, which was heavenly after freezing Wildwood. There was a huge tree, we had champagne and oysters, and I had a third helping of turkey. It was a change from canned soup.

Afterward there were coffee and liqueurs in the living room, and Guy said I had to try Grand Marnier because it tasted like oranges and that was Christmassy. Guy's mother, Claire, was gracious but a bit of a snob, talking about Baltimore and interior decorating and the magazines she'd worked for and the "old" Grafton families like the Marshalls and Vanns and Stuarts.

I got the impression my being a Marshall was what she liked best about me.

Having spent nearly every waking minute and most of my sleeping minutes with Guy, it was a shock when the Christmas holiday came to an end. All of a sudden Guy was going back to Fort Bragg and I had to pack up to go back to college.

Guy went, and Evvie came back from Hawaii with a tan. I told her I'd had a thing with Guy, but it was just for the holidays. She gave me the fish eye and said everybody was talking about us being a couple. I burst into tears and asked, "What am I supposed to do now?"

"Stay cool," she said. "He'll be in touch."

I went back to college and tried to stop thinking about Guy and be clearheaded because I couldn't afford to be anything else. I had an overdue term paper and a bank balance of $68.97 after splurging on my wedding shoes. I couldn't afford to act like a soppy teenager about a soldier who'd be going off to Afghanistan soon. I had to keep my grades up to hang on to the scholarship. I was miserable.

Then Guy called. He'd been out of touch because he'd been on training maneuvers. He missed me, and would I come see him at Fort Bragg if he sent me a plane ticket? I said yes and next weekend found myself on a small plane bouncing through air pockets in the mountains of North Carolina, praying we wouldn't crash. It was terrifying, but over the next months I did it most weekends. Anything to be with Guy.

CHAPTER 39

2003

Ricky went back to Afghanistan when Evvie was seven months along. Her phone calls were cheerful; to keep the blues at bay she was busy, painting the baby's room and her kitchen cupboards and everything else she could think of, hanging the curtains her mom had made. I tried not to think about the fact that in two months Guy would be gone too.

I was a little in awe of my situation—Guy Charbonneau was dating *me*! As in, Officially Dating. A couple of girls at college knew the Charbonneaus and mentioned it. I could tell they were impressed—I had more going for me than they'd realized.

But I was increasingly worried. How had Guy and I got to . . . wherever we were? And more to the point, where exactly were we going? This had begun to matter. He occasionally talked about the future after the Green Berets but not in a way that hinted I was part of the plan. On one hand, we were close—I even told him about how Evvie and I had had terrible crushes on him and Ricky in junior high, about the makeup and stalking and everything, and of course he roared with laughter—but on the other, I was uncertain. Since we didn't have much time left and I had no idea what to do in this situation, I kept quiet. I mustn't seem clingy or needy and ruin . . . whatever this was.

At Christmas, I'd come across a daguerreotype of Guy's ancestress Aimée Charbonneau—a lovely creature with big dark eyes and a tiny waist—in Gramps's desk drawer, together with her obituary from the *Messenger* that Ben Marshall had written. Remembering how we'd talked about how we were related that first night in the bar, I brought it back to college to keep the photo of Horatia company. On impulse I took it to Guy at Fort Bragg that spring.

"Aimée, hunh?" Guy whistled appreciatively. "She was a looker, even in that old picture. That reminds me. I need to ask my mom about something . . ."

Our last weekend before Guy left for Afghanistan we took a hike in the mountains. It was mid-May and the rhododendrons were out everywhere. We'd stopped to sit at an overlook to rest and admire the view and the explosion of color. "Won't see this in Afghanistan, it's mostly deserts," Guy said. "I want to remember seeing it with you." My heart felt heavy as lead, and my face ached from the effort of holding a smile in place. I stood and went to the railing with my back turned, trying to will tears away before he saw them.

He came up behind me and put his arms around my waist. He put his mouth on my ear and whispered something that sounded like "Will you marry me when I get home next year?"

He hadn't said it very loud.

"What?"

"What about what?"

"What did you say just now?"

"Did I say something?"

"About . . . next year."

"Next year?"

"You said something else!"

"Did I?"

I turned to stare at him. Had he had second thoughts in the space of five seconds? I took a deep breath. "Guy Charbonneau, don't mess around with me. Did you just propose? Or were you just mumbling to yourself?"

"Oh, that. I guess I did." He was grinning.

My heart was pounding. "If you're teasing me, I'll kill you."

"I was about to get to the 'I love you' part, but you started saying 'what' . . ."

I just stared at him. I'd been scared to make an issue of it, and been so cool about everything, though the effort tied my stomach up in knots, and now . . . Guy wanted to marry me! I was so overwhelmed I could hardly breathe. I didn't dare breathe. My eyes filled with tears.

"You're being a little cryptic here, Rose-Linda. Are you trying to say yes? Nod once for yes, twice for no. So I'll know whether to go on."

I nodded. Once.

"Good, you had me worried there for a minute." He took a small box out of his pocket. "Let's get down to business. Make it official. When you gave me Aimée's obituary, I checked with my mother. If I remembered right, she had Aimée's ring. Aimée's husband, Lafayette Charbonneau, gave it to her. They had three children. The eldest was a girl, married one of the Drumhellers before the Civil War, and then Aimée had two younger boys, Virginius and West. West came to no good and died in a boardinghouse brawl somewhere in California, and Aimée left this ring to Virginius, my great-great-great-grandfather. It's a family tradition that the eldest Charbonneau son inherits it to give to his fiancée when he gets engaged. It was my mother's engagement ring, and now it's yours."

It was a very large diamond in an old-fashioned gold setting, and I held my breath while he slipped it on my finger. It didn't quite fit. "I'll get it fixed for you. You get to wear it until it's time to pass it on to our oldest son for his fiancée. When that happens, I'll buy you another one."

Our oldest son. A life together. He loved me! How had *this* happened? Guy began telling me we'd think of a way to manage Wildwood—he promised we'd keep it, we could live there some of the time or all the time or it could be our vacation home, we'd fix it up. He knew what it meant to me, we'd figure out something. He'd call his mother and sisters right away and tell them the good news and I needed to stop crying and talk about a wedding date when he came home next year.

A year! He'd be gone for a year, and it would be horrible and I was afraid for him, but then we'd get married. All I could do was laugh and cry and kiss him. Happiness and sadness so mixed up, I wasn't sure which was which.

CHAPTER 40

When Guy went to Afghanistan, it was horrible. I followed the news of what was going on over there and it scared me. Where Guy was stationed, email and calls were impossible, so I wrote every day and kept busy filling in for Evvie at the Pines' café that summer so she could stay home with the baby, Ricky Scott.

I drove over to see Evvie and her mom, who were painting the porch of Evvie and Ricky's little house. I took a set of rompers for Ricky Scott and to show them my ring, which Guy had had adjusted to fit and delivered back to me at Wildwood by special courier.

I went to see the Hog Callers and Alice and Lurene, and they all exclaimed over the exciting news, and Randall said Guy was a good ol' boy like his father, and Mitch said he'd always thought Guy had more than a single brain cell, and if he was marrying me that proved it. Curtis shook his head in mock sorrow, said poor Guy, he's about to join the henpecked club. Alice and Lurene both said I had the prettiest ring they'd ever seen and that my grandparents would have been thrilled.

"Which of us gon' give you away, Rose-Linda?" Curtis asked.

"All three of you, of course. It's like having three bridesmaids."

Word got around. People kept congratulating me, saying my grandparents would have been so happy. Old ladies Granny had known stopped me in the street to congratulate me—they'd heard the Charbonneau boy and I'd been keeping company, they said, giving me knowing looks. In September I went back to college, on track to graduate the following June if I took some extra courses. I managed to land a part-time job as a professor's assistant and was grateful to be busy.

Claire Charbonneau kept phoning me about things like china patterns. The last thing I needed was more china. There were loads of it at Wildwood. Granny said one of Gramps's spinster ancestors collected it. Nevertheless, Claire had promised to see that my choice got onto the wedding registries in the main stores in Bristol and Kingsport and Richmond.

Wedding registries? In those places? I didn't know anybody there, I said faintly. Claire brushed that aside, saying that didn't matter, the Charbonneaus did, in an "I'll take care of it" voice.

Claire wanted to help me with the wedding. She meant well, but I was juggling my teaching assistant job and extra coursework, and had no time or money to do much of anything about a wedding. But when I tried to refuse, she "helped" anyway, taking over little by little. She insisted she'd see to flower arrangements, the photographer, and the wedding cake. And why not have the wedding at Chiaramonte? she wondered. There were so many of their friends who'd be invited. She was making a guest list. They could have a tent in their garden. She'd ask the bishop to officiate. She sent a photo of me to the Engagements section of the Richmond, Kingsport, and Bristol papers. It took me by surprise when some of my classmates pointed it out. I hadn't known it was going to be there. The announcements focused on how old a family the Marshalls were and said that Granny's Murray ancestors had fought in the Revolution.

Guess who'd written the announcements?

I wrote Guy that this was starting to drive me crazy—all I wanted to do was marry him—and he wrote back that as soon as he got home, we'd find a JP and get married the minute we got our license. His mother could have a reception for us afterward.

I thought Claire would have a fit, but I was willing to risk it if Guy was. Evvie was going to be our witness. I couldn't get married without Evvie.

That spring, when dogwoods turned the mountains white, I went home for spring vacation. I wrote Guy the last letter I expected to reach him before he came home, telling him how when I first saw dogwoods in the dark when I was little I thought they were ghosts and now they made me think of white weddings. And I was making my wedding dress.

Even if there'd just be me and Guy and Evvie and Mrs. Stuart, I was into the wedding thing enough by now to have my heart set on a white dress and a bridesmaid in a bridesmaid dress. That sort of went with my engagement ring.

Evvie left Ricky Scott with her mother for a weekend and stayed at Wildwood, where we stayed up late cutting out the Simplicity patterns for my wedding dress in white linen and Evvie's bridesmaid's one in pink linen. Thanks to a bottle of wine Evvie brought, white in case we spilled some on the material, both of us were tipsy, and Evvie had pinned the zipper in crooked down the side of my dress. She was fooling with it, trying to get it straight and muttering "Zippers are a bitch," when the phone rang. "Stand still, don't you dare move," Evvie ordered, and answered it. "Hey, Miz Charbonneau." She made a face at me across the room, mouthing "What now?"

"What's wrong, you sound so . . . *what?* Slow down, I can't understand you . . . Who came to see you? They said . . . He *what?*"

The blood drained out of her face. She screamed "No!" then slammed down the phone and turned to me. In a shaky voice she said, "Rose-Linda, Rose-Linda, sit down."

Evvie started to cry. "Claire called to tell you . . . she said . . . I can't even say it . . . Guy stepped on a land mine . . . Guy got killed."

Afterward, over and over and over, I relived that last moment before the phone rang when Evvie and I were making my wedding dress and laughing and everything was still OK because Guy was coming home. Thinking if only I could get back there, maybe he would.

Evvie and the baby pulled me through a time so bad I don't remember much of it. There was no body to bury—I don't know whether it would have been better if there had been. *Better* isn't a word you use in those circumstances. There was a service with no body, no coffin. Just an absence . . . of Guy. A void. The whole world was a void. Empty. People spoke to me, and I watched their lips moving and didn't hear what they said. The Charbonneaus' friend who was a bishop came to officiate in a black robe. There was a service chaplain and people in uniform. A flag got folded up. They gave it to Claire standing with her daughters and their families. Claire clutched it to her chest for a minute, then turned and tried to give it to me, unable to stop her face from crumpling in anguish.

Evvie told me I just stared at it and pushed it back into her hands. What good was a flag? I don't remember much else, except that Evvie was standing on one side of me with Loretta on the other. Like anchors, keeping me upright, with Harold behind us holding Ricky Scott, who cried when the military salute got fired.

And those damn dogwood trees and their white flowers looking like ghosts.

Ricky wasn't there, he'd gone back for a third tour in Afghanistan, God knows why. I couldn't think much, couldn't pray for anything except please don't let Ricky get killed too. He's got a family.

Claire sent me a note thanking me for letting her have the flag. She wanted me to keep the ring.

CHAPTER 41

I was a mess all summer. I'd missed my final exams at college, but Mrs. Stuart had called them and gotten an extension for me to take them in the fall. I took them, numb to the core, but I passed. They sent my diploma.

When Ricky finally finished his tour of duty and came home, Ricky Scott had several teeth and was walking. Evvie had taught him to say *Dada*. They came to see me one afternoon soon after Ricky got back. Ricky was no longer devil-may-care funny, just sort of wild-eyed, talking too fast about Guy. Evvie had a bruise on her face, said it was because she'd fallen out of bed and hit her head. I tried hard to remember the sweet boy Ricky'd been when he helped me make my first s'mores, the good-looking young man who'd married Evvie.

Weeks later Evvie called and said could she come over, she was going out of her mind. She broke down and told me Ricky had gotten a dishonorable discharge. Now he kept going off in the car and coming back in a weird mood with his eyes looking strange. He was in pain all the time unless he took pills, and she was afraid he was addicted, but he refused to go to the veterans' hospital for help. They were arguing most of the time, he didn't have a job, and he didn't care about fixing up their house anymore. Loretta and Evvie's mother were taking turns helping with Ricky Scott, and Evvie had gone back to waitressing because she needed the money. She couldn't count on Ricky. And she had to hide the money she made or he'd go off with it. Nobody knew what to do.

I wanted to comfort her, but the best I could do was say "I'm so sorry, I'm so sorry" over and over.

Evvie and me, way back in the eighth grade, we'd wanted Ricky and Guy to fall in love with us. Granny had said be careful what you wish for.

I'm not sure how I wound up applying for another scholarship and starting a master's. History. I remember filling out applications, automatically. It was the way I did everything. I opened books and took courses and buried myself in academic stuff, like an automaton, so I couldn't think of anything or feel anything. I decided somewhere along the line that the topic of my thesis would be the *Messenger*—a study in small-town journalism. I had an entire archive in the attic. The thesis committee approved it. They'd heard of Gramps. Bingo.

I kept getting letters from the property developer. I threw them away. I wasn't selling Wildwood.

But I was going to have to figure out how to keep it up. It was falling apart, like me.

Evvie called me at the university to see how I was doing, and to tell me Ricky was better. He had some new medicine and counseling. Hopefully they could settle down and be a family now. She was pregnant again and still waitressing but Ricky had calmed down and had a job at Jayjay's tavern. It wasn't ideal because Ricky drank a lot, but it was a job.

I was working late at my desk one night in my bare campus apartment when my phone rang. It was after midnight and I thought it was a wrong number. There were some hiccups on the other end, and then someone with a hoarse, croaky voice said my name four or five times—Rose-Linda. Rose-Linda. A weird prank call.

I was about to hang up when I realized it was Harold Pine. He was so incoherent I thought he was drunk and laughing. It wasn't like Harold to get drunk, and anyway, why call me? I caught the word "Ricky," and I figured something had gotten out of hand at Jayjay's. Loretta wouldn't have alcohol in the house. Then I realized he could hardly talk because he was sobbing and gasping for breath. Ricky had smashed the car he was driving, plowing through a barrier on a mountain road. He was dead. Evvie and Ricky Scott had been with him. Ricky Scott was strapped in his car seat in the back, and they pulled him out without a scratch, but Evvie was barely alive and had lost the baby.

I threw on my clothes. By the time I got back to Grafton, they'd done a postmortem and found drugs and alcohol in Ricky's blood. A lot of both. Evvie was unconscious and on every prayer list Loretta knew of. Mrs. Stuart took Ricky Scott home to look after, and I waited with the Pines at the hospital for four long days, while Loretta and Evvie's mom alternated looking after Ricky Scott, taking turns to go talk to her, hoping she could hear us telling her to live, watching the machines beeping. Finally Evvie opened her eyes and asked for Ricky Scott. We got shooed out while the doctors took over.

Later a tired-looking doctor came out to say Evvie would live, but she'd be in a wheelchair for the rest of her life.

Loretta still feels guilty, she blames herself that Ricky had the accident, it happened because she hadn't been a good enough mother. I don't think that's right. I thought back to what my mother's odd behavior and death must have done to my grandparents. How they must have wondered what they should have done, what they could have done. Had Granny been a bad mother? Gramps a bad father? From my experience with my grandparents, that seemed impossible. From what I knew of Harold and Loretta Pine, that seemed impossible too. Maybe no matter what people did, a child developed problems. Still, it's a heavy burden for parents to carry.

Afterward, if anybody mentioned the tragedy around the Pines, trying to be sympathetic but maybe not thinking straight about who they were talking to, Loretta's face went hard and her eyes got this fierce look. She'd snap that Ricky was safe in the arms of Jesus, like it's the best place for him. In private she still reminds the Lord every chance she gets to help Evvie and Ricky Scott, even though it got to the point where if Loretta even mentioned they were praying for Evvie and Ricky Scott at church it set Evvie off something terrible. She had a real short fuse now. She said "Butt out" a lot if you tried to help her too much.

Right from the start I knew I had to pull myself together if I was going to help Evvie. When she finally got out of the hospital, her mother and the Pines fussed over her until she got ratty and swore at everybody, insisting she could roll her own wheelchair, thank you.

Right away she wanted to make it plain she wasn't a charity case. And she had a son to raise.

Being in a wheelchair, Evvie was limited in what she could do to earn money. She couldn't waitress anymore, which was a shame because the truck drivers were good tippers, but she was independent-minded and she always had a gift for making stuff.

When her mother tried to get her to come back home to live where she could look after Ricky Scott, Evvie refused. Crippled or not, she said she was damn well going to raise her child in her own home, and if her mother wanted to help, buy her a sewing machine. She had a plan. She went back to her little house and started in right away making cushions and patchwork things to sell to tourists at the motel.

She was good at that—her mother had taught her to sew when she was young—and she was onto something. People bought her stuff. She kept raising her prices, but they still bought stuff. She made cushions and quilts and rag rugs out of any scraps she could lay her hands on, same way people made them in Grafton for over two hundred years.

Word got around, and people brought her spare material they'd never found time to make into a skirt or curtains, old clothes and bedspreads they didn't want anymore, and Evvie used everything, turned them into works of art. There's nothing prettier than a patterned quilt or an appliquéd cushion. But the motel office was small, and there wasn't a lot of room to show off Evvie's handiwork.

So I suggested Evvie display her stock at Wildwood until she could afford to rent a little shop in Grafton. You know, just sort of drape it around so it showed off. She'd sell more if people could see how nice all her things looked when put together, like a showroom, better than piled into the motel office. Predictably she said no at first. For someone so pretty in spite of the accident, Evvie's got a cussed streak that comes out if anyone goes too far in the helping department. So I asked if she had a better idea, and she turned her wheelchair so I couldn't see her face and after a minute said "No" in a small voice.

"Think of the extra money for Ricky Scott. And it would hide how shabby Wildwood is. I'd really appreciate that just now, Evvie."

Evvie finally agreed. I got Loretta and Evvie's mom to come up and help me. I suddenly realized Wildwood was a mess, cleaning house not being high on my list of things I needed to do. Once it was clean and the dust of ages gone—housework is thought to be therapeutic—I felt better than I had in a while. We spent an afternoon draping quilts on the beds and hanging them on walls, patchwork cushions all over the place, braided rugs on the floor. Wildwood was worn around the edges and looked its age. But dusted and cleaned up, windows washed, furniture rubbed with Miss Nettie's polish, and all Evvie's handiwork hiding the shabby parts, it looked like a different place by the time Harold drove her up. The thing is, while all that stuff looked good on its own, Loretta and Evvie's mom and I agreed when you saw it all together, it looked really amazing. The patterns and colors played off each other in a way that'd make any space look warm and homey.

When she saw what we'd done, Evvie gasped. "I don't believe it!" Her face lit up and she grinned like her old self, kept spinning her wheelchair around to admire everything. "I feel like a fancy interior decorator with a showroom!" Then she started to cry, and instead of saying butt out, for once she said thank you.

When her mom and Loretta left, she turned to me and said we had to talk business, that we'd split the money from sales. I said no way, and we had an argument. Finally I bargained her down to where I'd take fifteen percent. Evvie didn't know that went into a bank account for Ricky Scott's college education. It would only set her off if she did.

That was eight years ago. Since then Harold finally finished building a "Trading Post" next to the motel, so she could sell her work down there where it's more convenient, and Ricky Scott can come after school. Thanks to the interstate, the motel gets people on vacation going between places like Williamsburg in Virginia and Rock City and Ruby Falls farther south. There are signs urging people to pay a visit to the historic river town of Grafton in the heart of the scenic Bowjay Valley, but other than a riverwalk, there's nothing much left that's historic except the little local museum at the back of the post office. It has cases of arrowheads and old rifles and Indian baskets, a few gold Spanish coins from the days of the conquistadors—they say de Soto explored as far as the Bowjay Valley—and Miss Vesta Conway's interpretive paintings of local historical scenes. These are violently colorful, with Indian maidens and grizzled long hunters and Civil War soldiers, but the museum will only entertain people for so long. So they drift over to the Trading Post to buy mountain crafts. Seeing that Evvie's in a wheelchair is good for business, especially when she lets it drop in the conversation she's a veteran's widow. People buy enough quilts and cushions and braided rugs and homemade pralines, which she makes and puts in little cellophane bags tied up with ribbon, to keep Evvie and Ricky Scott going.

She left a bunch of things at Wildwood as a thank-you for the help in the early days of her business. Lord knows it transforms the place. I'd hate to see it go.

Last year Evvie took some samples of her work to a big home-furnishing store in the shopping mall in Enterprise, and they took a few things that sold out right away. Now she's getting regular orders for so much stuff she's had to farm out some of the sewing to older women who do it at home. "It's a living." Evvie shrugs every time I point out she's started a business. But I think she's a little bit proud. Evvie's never been one to hide her light under a bushel. And I say let it shine.

CHAPTER 42

May 2014

So we're hanging on, getting by, Evvie and I. Ricky Scott is doing fine at school. I finished my master's degree and got a job teaching history at Rehoboth Springs Christian College, where the old hotel used to be. They call me a "professor," because it sounds good, though strictly speaking I'm not. I still live at Wildwood. Along with two dogs. Guy's mother, Claire, dropped by one day with two of their hunting dog puppies in one of those dog boxes with mesh sides, saying if I was going to live up here on Frog Mountain by myself I needed dogs for company and protection. She still has the Charbonneau kennels because they were one of the few places that bred the hunting dogs, who are white with brown and blue-black markings, that came from Europe a long time ago. People call them "trikklers," which Claire says comes from their original French name, *tricolore*. The puppies were cute. Dumb but cute. Now they're huge, big as small ponies and still dumb. Expensive to feed, and I pray they don't need the vet. But they bark like mad if anyone comes around.

I do my job and just get by. It means I can live at Wildwood. The college doesn't pay much. It keeps tuition and staff salaries as low as possible. Most of the students have part-time jobs, aware their parents make sacrifices to send them there to arm them with a sound Christian education and guide them along the straight-and-narrow path to salvation through a sinful world. It's pretty strict. Students have to sign a pledge to Jesus not to indulge in alcohol, drugs, or sex before marriage for the duration of college. There are prayer breakfasts in the cafeteria. Bible study nights twice a week in the dorm lounges.

Most of my students wait like earnest baby birds to be spoon-fed predigested American history so they can tick it off the humanities requirement for their college diploma. I try to shake them up, persuade them history isn't as dead and gone as they think, but my attempts to interest them in things that happened before they were born make them look at me funny.

Here it was May, with graduation less than two weeks away, the time all the teachers at the college dread because we have to deal with an avalanche of term papers and evaluation reports and then have to figure out a way to pass everybody. You can't justify failing students trying so earnestly to be good Christians, but sometimes you have to look deep.

So I pulled into Harold Pine's gas station Friday afternoon, with the pickup's gas gauge arrow pushing the bottom of the red line and five cardboard boxes of term papers that had to be graded by Monday, along with evaluation forms for each student, in the back. Randall, Mitch, and Curtis—who pass most of their time at the gas station now, though Harold doesn't actually employ them—came out when I stopped.

They are in their nineties now, but you'd never know it. They're pretty spry, pretty sharp, still get around. I tell them anybody'd think they're mere spring chickens of eighty, and I'm only half joking. At the gas station, they sit and talk about old times until a customer pulls in. Then they set their baseball caps on straight, spit out any tobacco they happen to be chewing, and stroll outside. A regular welcoming committee, and not in a hurry either. If it's a woman driver, they tip their hats. Then they lean on the car to visit for a while, talk about rising gas prices or the incompetence of the federal government, then one of the guys will ask "Fill 'er up?" and go unhook the gas pump while the other two clean the windshield and check the oil.

They're lonely, have too much time on their hands. Randall doesn't have a family because he never married anybody, which always struck me as surprising. In the old snapshots he was the best-looking one of the four young men. Mitch and Curtis both have kids, but the kids moved away. Mitch's wife, Alice, is dead, and Curtis's poor wife, Lurene, has dementia so bad he had to move her to the special unit they built onto the old folks' home.

They don't sing or play together anymore. Life's beaten the music out of them. It isn't much help, I know, but I visit Lurene when I can, make cookies or a cake sometimes, and bring them down to the gas station for Curtis to take when he visits. I nag them every year till they get their flu shots. They say I'm getting too bossy.

Now all three were gesturing and talking before I switched the engine off. Curtis, who's usually half-asleep, was yelling. "Hey, Rose-Linda, you heard the news? They wanta make a TV show here! The fella makin' it says he might put us in it!"

"The Hog Callers?"

"Yeah, he's here lookin' around. Investigatin'. Asked can he hear us play Sunday before he leaves town."

"The Hog Callers on TV!" I exclaimed.

"Might be! If it goes good Sunday."

"Is that so?" I like the jug band just fine, but this is the land of the Carter Family, and so full of musical talent you can hardly hear yourself think for old-time music conventions, the picking and singing, the flatfoot dancing, dulcimers and mandolins, and pedal steel guitars. And that's not counting the hymn singing in the country churches, some of it still using old shape-note hymnals, five-part harmony, and call-and-response. There's likely a very small niche market for a three-old-man jug band. "Who said?"

"That's what I'm tryin' to tell you. Guy stops for gas yesterday, turns out he's staying at the mo-tel. Drove some kind of old sports car, low down on the road, funny-lookin' thing, had a belt on it to hold it together, engine making a racket, like he'd lost his muffler—"

"Never seen no car like it before," interrupted Mitch. "Kind of beat up, but it had nice leather seats. I asked him how she drives, and he says good but her gas pedal sticks, say's you got to downshift before it'll unstick."

"That's right! Wouldn't catch me driving that thing! No sirree! It'd flat run away with you," said Curtis.

"Car's called a Morton . . . something like that."

"A Morgan? That's a fancy English sports car."

"Is that a fact! Said he'd come from New York." The three were interrupting each other, and tugging the gas hose back and forth, talking about the guy who'd stopped to fill up his car and asked more questions about Grafton than anyone ever asked before. I thought to myself that he asked the right three guys. I bet they bent his ear for a long time.

"He's in TV! He said he was making a program."

"A *series*, Curtis!"

"Well, it'll be on TV anyhow. So we just kind of mentioned the jug band. And Randall, winding him up, said he should use us as background music . . ."

"And he said maybe! Maybe! He's at the mo-tel till Sunday, and would we come and audition. But Loretta likes her Sundays peaceful, so we said can we play for him over at the Legion hall, and he said that'd be fine. Two o'clock Sunday!"

I hadn't seen them so excited about anything in a long time.

"Look, I'm about to die of thirst. I need a Coke. Y'all want one?" I pictured a cigar-smoking fool in sunglasses in his sports car lording it over three of the nicest guys in the world, pretending he wanted to hear their jug band. So he could feel important. It made my blood boil as I dug into my bag for change. What a prick, winding up old men with not a lot to go home to.

"Actually," said Mitch, cleaning dead bugs off my windshield, his eyes inches from mine and, I suddenly thought, oh-so-slightly shifty under the brim of his baseball cap. "He mentioned your name."

"Did he?" I ran my hand into the gap between the seat and the backrest, where my spare change goes to find a home. Sure enough, dimes, nickels, and quarters. A few pennies. I stuffed the pennies back. "Why? Does he want me to sing? Maybe clog dance while y'all play?"

Through the windshield Mitch avoided my eye. "Yeah, he asked did we know a Professor Hamilton Marshall."

"If it's anything to do with music, he's not looking for me, Mitch. Even in church, when I go, I sing hymns flat and real quiet so's not to upset anybody." I swung myself out of the truck with my handful of change, walked over to the drinks cooler, and got four Cokes. "What'd he say exactly?"

"Said he'd heard they's a Professor Marshall teaches history up at the college, knows everything about Grafton and the valley," Randall chimed in, washing the rear windshield like his life depended on it.

Everybody here knows the title "professor" is sort of honorary at the college, to make the students and their parents think they're getting their money's worth.

"Did he say what he wanted?"

"Wasn't anything to do with music. Just some bidness," said Mitch vaguely.

"Oh," I said. The only thing in the way of "bidness" I do is genealogy research. Over the years I've looked for "Lamarr Hamilton" on genealogy websites, and once somebody saw where I was from and got in touch. They didn't know anything about Lamarr Hamilton but wanted to know about the Bowjay Valley and offered to pay for lookups. There was a story in their family that they were related to an aristocratic

English woman who came to the Bowjay Valley before the Revolution. And did I know anything about who that might have been.

I figured they meant my Marshall ancestor Sophia Grafton, who married Henri de Marechal and is buried in the cemetery. I took photos of her grave and their children's graves and the original patent of land from King George II and sent them on. Since then other people have gotten in touch, wanting to know if they might be related to the Vanns because they believed they were part Cherokee, or people who wanted to know if their ancestors could have passed through on a flatboat traveling to Kentucky or farther west to find a homestead. I have trunks full of old papers and documents in the attic, plus all the copies of the *Messenger*, which is sometimes helpful.

There's the cemetery too, though not all the graves have markers, and the older ones that do are hard to read. But if I find anything about anybody's ancestors, or more likely people who might be related, or even any of the names they're looking for, I draw a little genealogy chart to go with my report. Makes me a little extra money.

If this jerk wanted me to look for his relatives, I'd do it but charge him double.

I handed the Cokes around. "Curtis told him, if he went over to Jayjay's tavern about six he'd find Hamilton Marshall there, havin' a beer. You know, the way you do most nights. And it'd be a surprise you're a girl. Break the ice, so to speak."

"Still, wouldn't hurt if you could fix up a little before you do, 'stead of lookin' like you been hoein' corn in a cyclone," muttered Randall, eyeing my faded jeans and the shirt that had wilted in the heat. And was possibly a little sweaty under the arms. "Ain't you got a dress somewheres?"

A dress? I began to smell a rat. We'd been down this road before, them trying to fix me up. Over the years they've sprung one prize turkey after the other on me.

"Wouldn't kill you to have a beer with him, just while you talk bidness. It's not a *date*, like you'd go out with a fella. Bidness is bidness." All three gave me sheepish looks.

"No. No, no, no, no. Sorry, guys, I'm not going to Jayjay's tonight, it's that time of year. The Weekend from Hell, remember? I've got a pile of term papers I have to grade or my students won't graduate and I'll be out of a job. Good luck with the audition if it happens, but you can't rely on these directors and producers and talent scouts who promise everybody the moon but hardly ever deliver. If I were you, I'd forget show business and go fishing on Sunday instead. I hear the bass are up out at the cove. Got to go," I added, counting out the amount the gas pump showed I owed Harold, and shoving it in the window where Harold sometimes sits but mostly doesn't because he trusts people will pay him, and if they're short, they'll come back later with the money.

"Come on, Rose-Linda, just go act nice and . . ."

I slammed the truck door hard. "No!" I said firmly. "That guy with the sports car's shining you on. He's not for you. He's not for me. He can take his 'bidness' and stick it where the sun don't shine. Just no!"

"You can be so pigheaded," Mitch muttered. "They shoulda just called you Ham, 'steada Hamilton, suited you better'n a pretty name like Rose-Linda."

"Ham. Got a nice ring to it. Porky. Heh, heh, heh!" This was Randall.

"It wouldn't kill you to have a beer with him, Rose-Linda."

I waved and pulled onto the road.

Mitch cupped his hands to shout, "WHAT'RE YOU MAD ABOUT? WE WEREN'T SETTIN' YOU UP ON A DATE!"

Oh yes they were! "I'm not mad," I snarled through gritted teeth, then gunned the motor. The truck fishtailed when I hit the road.

Sometimes I'm a little oversensitive, Evvie says. But of course I'm not.

CHAPTER 43

What greeted me when I got home didn't improve my mood. Water was leaking across my kitchen floor where a big section of pipe under the old stone sink had come apart—just another thing broken around here. I got Gramps's tool kit and pulled up old oak floorboards trying to find the problem. It's a no-man's-land of plumbing and dust down there, and by the time I'd found the joint that had come apart and fixed it, it was 10:00 p.m. and I was too filthy and grumpy to do anything but feed the dogs and scrub myself in the bath, resigning myself to the purgatory of wading through the term papers in a hurry by Monday's deadline.

Next morning I forced myself up and into yesterday's clothes. They needed washing but so what. I filled Granny's battered old percolator with water and ground coffee and put it on to boil. People say my coffee tastes like rocket fuel. I fed the dogs and let them out of the dog run, took the phone off the hook till bedtime, made toast, poured more coffee, and stacked the term papers into a pile. Sighing, I attacked the first one.

By midafternoon the grading had brought on a headache. Poor sentence structure, woolly reasoning, and worst of all, a number of handwritten papers that took forever to decipher. We have computers and word processors in the library for students who don't have their own to use, but the library closes at six. I wrote notes in the margins, put question marks where needed, and tried hard to be charitable about grades.

By 9:00 p.m. I was less than a quarter of the way through the pile and had lost the will to live. I was also starving. I gave up for the day and made a plate of what Granny used to call a "wet sandwich," three layers of bread with tomato and green pepper slices and lots of mayonnaise. I spiked it up with Tabasco, pulled a cold beer from the icebox, and went to sit on the porch swing in the dark. I ate my dinner with my bare feet resting on the dogs' backs.

Lightning bugs flicked across the dark yard, and the sleeping dogs made huffy noises as I massaged their backs with my feet. Down by the river it's hot and muggy, but the evening air is fresh up at Wildwood. Something to do with the trees and the way Frog Mountain catches the wind. I finished my beer and put the dogs in their pen, noticing as I bolted it that the heavy gate was dragging off its hinges. Another thing to fix. If I don't shut them in at night, they'll go chasing a deer or raccoon halfway to Alabama.

Term papers—I went to bed feeling like the Ancient Mariner with the albatross hanging around his neck. Sometimes I think I'll find a different job. But I don't.

I forgot to set my alarm, and next morning I woke up and for a minute it was as if a quarter of a century hadn't passed and I was a kid again. I lay wrapped in the same faded quilt on the same creaky oak-framed rope bed, relieved to see the washstand and the lamps with the shepherd and shepherdess. I was half-convinced I could smell sausage frying on the cool early-morning air, Granny calling "Rose-Linda! Breakfast's on the table! Get up this minute!"

I was jolted out of this comforting memory by the phone ringing in the kitchen. It's still on the wall, like when it was installed many years ago. I squinted at the radio clock. The few people who would call me in an emergency, like Evvie or Loretta or Curtis or Mitch, have my cell phone number. Others, like the college, only have the landline number because I don't want them contacting me at all hours of the day and night on my cell phone, but the college calling at 7:00 a.m. on Sunday? Nah! Wrong number. I pulled the covers over my head.

But I was awake now, remembering how the leaking kitchen pipe was just the latest thing to need fixing at Wildwood. I might have to call a plumber, and plumbers are expensive. Property taxes are overdue, and the rail fence that separates the yard from the woods is falling down. And the college is looking for ways to cut back on staff. If I didn't get those papers graded and those evaluations written, I wouldn't have a job.

I threw off the covers, brushed my teeth, splashed my face with cold water, and pulled on my clothes. Jeans, yesterday's shirt—and the day before's, come to that, which *really* needed washing—and a man's tweed vest I'd spotted at the church rummage sale. Twenty-five cents. I wear it over a shirt first thing in the morning when it's still cool. It was the kind of thing Gramps wore. I was twisting my unruly mop of hair up out of the way when the phone rang again. I ignored it and finally it stopped. Then rang some more. Stopped and rang again. Really irritating. Whatever the college wanted me to do, I didn't want to know.

I took it off the hook again and tidied up the term papers spread all over the kitchen table.

After teaching at the college a couple of years, I feel like I'm settling into dusty old-maidhood. I'm thirty-four and still sleeping in my childhood bed, wearing dirty shirts, and living in a house that's slowly turning into the kind of dilapidated wreck Jackie Kennedy's eccentric old Bouvier relatives lived in called Grey Gardens, unless I can find a way to make enough money to prevent it. Which I'm not doing. I start most days worrying about that, and there's never any answer.

This was beginning the day on a depressing note, but coffee usually improves my outlook. I waited for Granny's battered coffeepot to start perking. Nothing lifts your heart more than the smell of hot coffee in the morning. Unless it's bacon. Bacon frying will raise the dead. Suddenly I needed a big breakfast, strength for the task ahead. I needed bacon. I sliced some off the last side I'd bought from Harold Pine and put it on to fry.

I turned on the old radio and got the news that came on just before the first preacher's Sunday-morning broadcast.

There was a police bulletin. Two convicts, dangerous and possibly armed, had escaped from Lee Penitentiary. They say Lee's hard to break out of, but anybody who escapes into these mountains and finds the caves, Lord, they're safe. Caves all over these mountains to hide in, full of roosting bats, so police tracker dogs can't pick up a scent. Bat droppings contain ammonia and confuse the dogs' sense of smell. If dogs breathe in bat shit spores, they can get a fatal lung infection.

Anybody who escaped prison and had survival skills—a lot of people born and bred in these Virginia mountains do—could hide forever. Or you could get lost and die in the caves. There've been human bones found in the old bear cave higher up Frog Mountain.

I was turning down the heat under the bacon skillet when my dogs went crazy. I'd forgotten to let them out of their pen. I went to the door. "Hush, Dixie. Hush up, Buddy!" I yelled. "I'm coming." The screen door slammed behind me. But the hounds were ignoring me, barking and snarling fit to raise the dead and lunging hard at the fence in the opposite direction, dying to go after something in the overgrown orchard. I figured a possum or a raccoon, maybe a polecat, was somewhere nearby, though polecats usually came out at night. I didn't want the dogs sprayed by a polecat—it stinks something awful, and I'd have to catch them and give them a bath, and I just didn't have the time or energy today.

"Hush up!" I said in my don't-mess-with-me voice the dogs know to mind. The barking became growling, letting me know they'd go after whatever it was the second they got the chance.

I was wrestling with the latch on the gate when I realized something *was* moving between the trees, big enough to make branches shake. Deer don't do that . . . And then I saw what was moving in the trees was a man, and he'd nearly reached my fence. Shit! I ran in and grabbed Gramps's Winchester from over the stone fireplace and loaded two shells, then raised it to my shoulder as he got one leg over the fence. Then he stopped. He seemed to have the other one caught in the blackberry vines.

It had to be one of the escaped convicts, because nobody in his right mind around here would come through the orchard these days. Although you'd think somebody who escaped from a high-security prison facility like Lee would be smart enough not to get snagged up in plants.

A long time ago people from Grafton came up Frog Mountain to Wildwood by a path through the apple and peach trees. It was steep but the shortest way from the river landing where a trading post operated. When Granny was first married, she used to go up and down the old path herself if she needed something from the store. It was quicker to walk than wait for Gramps to drive her down the old potholed dirt road to the bottom of Frog Mountain.

The orchard path hasn't been cleared since Gramps died. I don't know how Guy managed to navigate it carrying me on his shoulder all those years ago, but it was winter, so I guess the vines had died back and the snakes were hibernating. In summer, grass grows high as your waist now, poison ivy in it. Rattlesnakes and copperheads living under the blackberry vines tangled up everywhere.

The intruder was still stuck at the fence, snagged good on a blackberry vine by the looks of it. The chiggers would get him before I could. I lowered the heavy gun, waiting for the fool to extract himself. Too bad he wasn't snakebit, because it would have saved me the trouble of shooting him. But at least he'd have *chiggers*. It was almost funny.

CHAPTER 44

Gramps had taught me how to hold the shotgun steady and shoot straight, had me practice until I could hit a tin can he threw in the air. So I'm a pretty good shot, which I feel is handy, considering I live alone up here.

The intruder finally released himself, swinging his other leg over the fence and dropping into my yard. He looked up to see me aiming at him.

"Hey!" he shouted. "Don't shoot! I just want a word with . . ." He started toward the cabin.

"Hold it right there!" I yelled.

"I'm not dangerous enough to shoot!" he yelled back. But he stopped, hands on his hips. "OK, I surrender. Put the gun down, thing makes me nervous."

I looked for the other escapee but didn't see him. This man had hair too long for a convict's, and what he was wearing wasn't prison issue. His denim shirt wasn't prison blue, and he had pants with pockets on the front. Like the hunting pants men order by catalog from some fancy store in Maine. You can get them insect-proof, supposedly. His clothes were probably stolen. I didn't see any sign of a gun or a sheath knife, but that didn't mean he wasn't armed. Or that his friend wasn't lurking out of sight.

"Depends how you explain what you're doing on my property, whether I put the gun down." I held the shotgun trained on him and edged down the porch steps to the dog pen. I groped for the bolt on the gate, keeping my eyes and gun on the intruder. I'd let the dogs get him. What was I going to do? If I sent him back into the woods, he'd hang around. I had to get to my phone to call the police, keep him in my sight till they got here. Or shoot him.

The dog run gate was really stuck. Needed oiling. I kicked it and the dogs barked, leaping at it and getting in the way so I couldn't open it. I couldn't hear what the man was yelling. "Dixie, Buddy, dammit, sit!" The two big hounds growled and circled the dog run impatiently, then started up again and drowned him out. "SIT!" I screamed. They did, keeping up a low growl, and I yelled back at the man, "What?" I had to keep him where he was and talking until the dogs were out.

He was still standing with his hands on his hips. "Didn't you hear me?"

"No!"

"I said what I'm doing here is . . . I've come to raise the dead."

Uh-hunh. I lowered the gun. A nutcase. I hoped I wouldn't have to shoot somebody with mental problems.

Unless . . . maybe he was one of the con men we get through here sometimes—faith healers mostly, who get money from gullible folks who hope they can do what they say. The main market for raising the dead, if you can call it a market, are the old communities deeper in the mountains, into old-time religion, where people handle snakes as part of their beliefs—something to do with the part of the Bible that says if people are saved and believe right they can handle serpents and won't get bit. You'd think from the number who die they'd get the message God doesn't have much time for folks who play with snakes.

Maybe the guy thought anyone dumb enough to pick up a copperhead with bare hands would be dumb enough to think someone like him could pray you back to life—if you paid him.

"Well, we don't have any dead need raising here." My cell phone was inside on the kitchen table—how was I going to get to it so I could call the police? The man walked a couple of steps closer. I raised the gun again. He stopped.

"Want to know how I raise the dead?"

"Not particularly."

"I make documentaries, historical ones. I raise the dead by bringing history to life. I'm a director. I've been hired to make a TV series about the Bowjay Valley, and I've been trying to get in touch with Professor Hamilton Marshall. But he doesn't pick up at his office, and his home number's always busy like the phone's off the hook. I have to head back to New York later tonight and want to talk to him before I go."

"You *walked* up here to do that?" I was incredulous.

"I had car trouble, gas pedal jamming again, left it at the gas station yesterday to see if they could unjam it, asked the men who work there if this Marshall guy they'd told me about had gone away. They told me he'd be at the tavern Friday night, but he wasn't, so the fellas said I should go on up to Hamilton Marshall's house, because the car wasn't going to be ready till this afternoon. Didn't mention I'd need a machete." He wiped his shirtsleeve across his brow. "Sorry for scaring you, but is that his house?"

"Mmm, you could say that."

"Are you, er, Mrs. Marshall?"

"Nope."

"His daughter?"

"No."

"Girlfriend?"

I sighed.

"I'm Hamilton Marshall."

"*You?* But the way everybody talked I assumed Professor Marshall was older . . . and male. I wasn't expecting . . ."

He was about to say "a girl." Not a woman, a girl. I just knew it.

"A girl. Name like Hamilton, it's gotta be a man. Sorry, that just slipped out." I waited while he tried to dig himself out of a hole. I do not look young for thirty-four. I look middle-aged and worried, often irritated. Like when I haven't had my coffee yet.

"Hamilton's my middle name. First name's Rose-Linda. I use Hamilton because . . . never mind. Who're you?"

"Jackson Lamarr. You might have seen my stuff on TV?"

Lamarr? I suddenly took an interest. His last name was my father's first name. I hadn't heard it said out loud in years. It's not a name you hear often. Ever, even.

"Don't watch TV much." I didn't actually own a TV anymore. Granny's old set had died and I couldn't afford to replace it.

"I'm always less famous than I think. Please, put the gun down. I want to hire you. Can we talk about that?"

I could tell by the smell the bacon was nearly done, and if I didn't have my coffee soon, I'd shoot him for the hell of it. I weighed up my chances. The guys at the gas station knew he was looking for me. They had his car. If he was staying at the motel, then Harold and Loretta knew who he was. I had the dogs, who'd go for him if he laid a finger on me. If I was murdered, the police would know who to look for. But above all, if he really was offering a paying job, I needed to risk it.

And what was with the Lamarr name? Probably nothing.

"Look, you want breakfast?"

"Breakfast would be great. I'm starving. Only place to get dinner last two nights was the motel. That was so early I was ready to eat again by nine."

Loretta serves supper at five thirty sharp—a choice of meat loaf or fried chicken, three vegetables, hot rolls, prize-winning pie, and coffee or iced tea. Between her regular clientele of truck drivers off the interstate and motel guests, her small restaurant's packed most nights. The food's good and she serves plenty of it, but there's no hanging around. By six thirty she's been on her feet for fourteen hours, by a quarter to seven she's got a first load of plates in the dishwasher, and she's rushing everybody through dessert in time for her to settle down on the sofa with a glass of iced tea and a package of Fritos with her feet up when *Twilight Gospel Hour with Brother Jimmy Wills and the Whip-Poor-Wills Family Choir* comes on at seven thirty every night.

Once a month Loretta sends in a ten-dollar donation to *Twilight Gospel Hour* so they'll sing her favorite hymn, "The Old Rugged Cross," accompanied by a request for Brother Wills and the viewers to keep holding Evvie up in prayer.

Evvie has blotted this knowledge out of her mind.

"Come on up," I said. I popped the shells out of the shotgun, put them in my pocket. A final kick unjammed the kennel gate. The dogs would be my protection if I needed any. They raced toward Jackson, who stood still and let the dogs sniff at him, then he bent and rough-housed and rubbed their ears and under their jaws until their tails were wagging. It was so irritating to see the dogs trot along beside him as he crossed the yard to where I was standing. Like I said, the dogs are dumb. No loyalty.

He stuck out his hand to shake mine. "Jackson. Nice to meet you, Professor," he said. "Great dogs. Bacon smells good too."

"Uh-huh, nice to meet you too," I said. "And it's Rose-Linda. Go ahead in."

Watching him walking up the porch steps ahead of me, I was still wary. Way he looked at everything, touching stuff, I would have said he was casing the joint, fixing to rob it. I was being crabby. Maybe historical documentary makers would notice things? Like I would know. His feet echoed on the porch with the three rocking chairs and the swing. He nodded at the porch swing with its rusty chain. "That hold if I sit on it? May I?"

"Go ahead."

My unwanted visitor sat and stared at the view down over the valley and whistled. "Takes your breath away." Jackson ran his hands over a porch rocker, then turned it upside down. "Those hand-hewn shingles on the roof? Original?"

"Well, no, but there's an old guy who still knows how to make them. He made replacements when my grandparents needed them. Go on in."

"Incredible." He was looking at the fireplace now, peering up the chimney. Next thing I knew he had his head in the bread oven. "You still use this?"

I said, "You can and I have." I hoped he wouldn't ask for a demonstration.

Now he was looking at the floorboards. "Oak, aren't they?" He sort of bounced up and down.

It would be next week before we got any coffee, which by now would have perked so long it would kill us to drink it.

"Big old cabin. You must have six, seven rooms. How old is it?"

"Eight rooms plus the kitchen. First part of it built about 1750, I think. Added to since then."

"Never saw a porch open straight on into the house like this," he said, pacing it back and forth.

"It's called a dogtrot, and before you ask, it's for dogs to trot in and out of the house when they feel like it. See, they've followed us in. In the winter those double doors close to keep out the wind and the cold. Kitchen's *this* way . . ." I had to keep Jackson moving or we'd never eat.

"A dogtrot? Wish my house had one. We've got three kids, and three dogs—everybody trots in and out all day long."

I wanted to shout *sit* like I do to the dogs. I restrained myself. "Have a seat. There." I pointed to the chair in the kitchen, invitingly full of Evvie's patchwork cushions.

Now he was examining the chair like it had been made by Joseph the Carpenter. Then he was inspecting the cushions. "Did you make these? Looks like real patchwork."

He was getting on my nerves. "Of course it's real patchwork! What other kind would there be?" I snapped. And realized I'd better make an effort to sound like a nicer person. Remember he had paying work. "A friend makes them, supplies interior decorators, sells to these big stores in Chicago, New York, Dallas—Neiman Marcus. Fast as she can make them. Everything's handmade. And for sale."

Evvie didn't sell beyond Enterprise, but he wouldn't know. If he wanted me to work for him, he was damn well going to buy a *lot* of Evvie's stuff for his wife.

I poured coffee and set the cracked sugar bowl and the bottle of milk out on the pine table a little harder than necessary. "Here. Help yourself." *And please shut up for a minute! Please!* I thought, taking a pull of coffee. Feeling better, I took a bowl of eggs, butter, a carton of buttermilk, and a mayonnaise jar full of bacon grease out of the four-door icebox.

He was talking again.

"Didn't know there were any of those four-door iceboxes from the thirties still in use. That's quite an antique. Can you still get ice?"

"Oh yeah, that's been in this kitchen, must be eighty years or more. My grandfather's family got it when he was a boy, and even when he married my grandmother he insisted on keeping it, said it was part of the house. Harold Pine gets ice for the gas station and the motel restaurant, orders a few blocks of it every week for me."

"You still use it? Incredible."

No, not incredible. I just ran short of money for a new refrigerator.

"This place is amazing. You can feel the old."

I put the bacon on a flattened brown paper grocery bag to drain and poured off most of the grease into the mayonnaise jar, already half-full of brown-flecked fat. "It *is* old. It's on the original patent of land owned by one of my ancestors, Henry de Marechal, before the Revolution. He was French. It was actually his wife Sophia's property, but at the time the law was that a married woman's property automatically became her husband's when she married." I got down baking powder, flour, and cornmeal and Granny's old mixing bowl with the blue stripe around the middle and hoped he wouldn't need to know how old that was, keeping a close eye on my visitor in case he turned weird or violent after all. "This was their house, where they raised their children. Sophia died here in an Indian raid during the Revolution. They think the Americans believed she was a Tory and got their Indian allies to kill her. The de Marechals changed their name to Marshall at some point, and Marshalls have lived here ever since."

He drank some coffee, winced, added milk. "I need to get my bearings . . . Are we near that Indian reservation the freeway signs advertise?"

"No. That's way far southeast, over the North Carolina state line. But a lot of this area was Indian land before they drove the Cherokees west in the 1830s. You heard of the Trail of Tears? Before that, there was a lot of intermarriage between the settlers and the Cherokees. There was a big mission school, and the kids grew up and married people they'd been at school with. Most of the old families here have Indian blood."

I sifted flour and cornmeal into the bowl, pinched some baking soda on top, beat in two eggs and some sugar, and added salt and buttermilk.

"Don't you measure stuff?"

"I can tell when it's right."

"You actually *keep* bacon grease?"

"Of course! Harold Pine's brother smokes the best bacon you ever tasted, uses hickory and corncobs, fattens the pigs himself. I'd never waste the grease." I spooned batter into the big hot frying pan, then flipped the corncakes over. When they were done, I poured in more bacon fat, then more batter.

Jackson must drive his wife crazy wanting to know everything, I thought. I piled corncakes and brown slices of bacon on two plates, then plonked them and the butter and an earthenware jug down. Jackson looked at the jug. "Will I go blind?"

"Syrup, so probably not," I said. "Blackberry. Made it last fall. You thought it was moonshine?"

He nodded, pouring a purple trickle over his corncakes. "I'm from New York, remember?" He left the butter alone.

Suit yourself, I thought, slapping on butter and flooding my plate with syrup so dark it was practically black. I like it when the butter and syrup soak the corncakes to where you practically have to use a spoon. It may not be ladylike but who cares. Jackson stared at my plate, looked down at his own, said, "I've never seen a woman do that before."

"Guess that's New York for you," I said.

"Hell with it," said Jackson, and followed my example. He stopped talking. He ate seconds. To be polite I offered him thirds. He said no, he couldn't eat another thing, and passed me his empty plate. I filled it again.

"Cholesterol's my favorite thing." He sighed, finishing the last bite. "My wife won't have it in the house."

"Nobody here bothers about cholesterol," I told him, dumping the dishes into a pan of soapy water at the sink. I refilled our coffee cups and sat down.

"Now. What exactly do you want?" I looked at the pile of term papers waiting for me.

"Did you see the PBS miniseries about the American Revolution? *Liberty*, it was called." That dragged my attention back from the papers, and I nodded. My classes had watched it. Actors impersonating figures like Jefferson and John Adams were talking heads from time to time, bringing it to life.

"Did you direct that?" I asked. I was ready to be a little more impressed.

"No, but it's the kind of documentaries I make." He started telling me about them.

I snuck a look at my watch. He stopped telling me about them.

"OK, we'll get down to business. I work for Far Horizons Production Company, which is making a four-part TV miniseries about the Bowjay Valley for *American Crossroads*. You heard of it?" I nodded. "OK, then you know *American Crossroads* has programs about the histories of old communities and towns. Grafton's a good example of an early settlement that grew up around a trading post on the river in Indian territory, and became a town, got wealthy, then declined, and now you have a whole new town, Enterprise, to the east of Frog Mountain, with the industrial parks and the housing developments, and it's booming. We like the historical contrast."

Pity he couldn't hear Gramps's opinion on Cherokee Ridge.

"I'm the director. In a nutshell, my job is putting it together. And what I need, aside from the local history, is the human-interest angle, stories about real people who lived here. Here we've got the drama of Old World meets New World, the civilized English Virginia colony east of the mountains, but this part of the colony was the frontier, inhabited mainly by Native Americans. Who were the Native Americans, who were the incoming settlers? Names and faces.

"That's why, when people ask what I do, I say I raise the dead. Historical narrative's one thing, but it has to be fleshed out with what happened to the people. People's stories, that's the real history."

According to Gramps, Ben Marshall had thought much the same thing, wanted the *Messenger* to record the lives of people who lived here, what they did, their day-to-day concerns, how things that happened out in the wider world—stuff like wars and the Depression—impacted folks in Grafton. I thought again about all those old copies of the *Messenger* in the attic.

Mustn't look too eager. I pretended to think hard. "I might have access to some local archives. Take some digging, though, a lot of time. Don't know how much time I've got to spare."

I racked my brains to think what else was up there. Those old trunks stuffed with papers. The original land-grant map was still up there—he'd love that—no telling what else.

Jackson nodded. "Let's talk business and see how much time you'd have."

"Sure." I poured us more coffee, and instead of talking business Jackson talked some more about his project, so while I waited for the business part I started calculating how much of Evvie's stuff I could sell him. I'd even offer to drive him and the stuff back down to the motel.

"So," he was saying, "could you do it?"

"What?"

I tried to arrange my face in an expression that said I'd been paying close attention.

"Have you got a hangover or something?"

"Not yet," I said.

"What I said was, first we need a pre-script outline. Think of it as a blueprint for the documentary, a timeline that we can hang stories and visuals on. The problem is that the person we'd originally hired to do this quit, and everything's urgent. Once we have a draft, we fine-tune it so . . ."

"So you found me and you haven't got enough time to go looking for another historian, right?"

Jackson shrugged. "You're used to teaching, so all this should be right up your alley. Isn't college about to break up for the summer? So you'd have the time."

"Um, yes. Maybe. I might. How much does the job pay?" I tried to be casual.

"Ballpark, if you can start right away and do it fast," and he named a sum that was twice what I make in a year at the college.

"*What?*" I gasped, then tried to recover my cool. "Seriously?" I said, giving him a level look. He must have thought I was refusing, because real quick he was saying there was room to negotiate up a little. I said that would be a good idea. Mentally, I victory-punched the air.

We discussed the series concept in greater detail. He asked me a lot of questions about the valley, seemed really interested. He kept stressing it wouldn't exactly be like working up a lecture for a college class. I had to think about the drama element—colorful characters, mysteries, ghosts, legends.

Oh boy, I thought, *you have no idea.*

And were there any local people who'd be willing to appear on camera?

"Oh yeah, probably half the folks in Grafton. There's an old folks' home down by the river full of, well, old folks who remember things that happened, who was who in all the old families. And the local artist Miss Vesta Conway lives there now. She's a character, the oldest person in Grafton, but she still has all her marbles. The first Conway was an itinerant portrait painter, no idea how he wound up here. But all the Conways have been artists; some of them were kind of famous. One of them was an early impressionist; they say he has a painting or two in a New Orleans museum, and I think there are a couple of Conway portraits in Congress. Miss Vesta's the last of the line. Her specialty is interpretive historical paintings. The paintings are kind of lurid, but she knows a lot of history, can talk the hind leg off a donkey telling you about it. Then there's a jug band called the Hog Callers, who think you're auditioning them this afternoon."

Before I could give him a piece of my mind for leading harmless old men on, he checked his watch. "Damn! The Hog Callers! I lost track of the time. Promised the old guys I'd meet them at two. Gotta go fight my way back through the jungle. Thanks for breakfast," he said, standing up.

"Hang on a sec," I said, and went out on a limb, told him if he wanted my services, then the jug band was part of the deal. They had to be in the series. Jackson looked at his watch again and muttered it was blackmail, he couldn't promise.

"In the contract," I said firmly. "I'm not doing anything till I have one and my lawyer's had a look at it. And something else. Remember I said these cushions and the quilts are for sale? A veteran's widow makes 'em. What she's raising her boy on. And she's in a wheelchair. So . . ."

"I have to buy some, right?"

I grabbed an armful, calculated the price. "We'll call it eight hundred dollars even. A check is fine." He called me shameless, took out his wallet, and peeled off eight hundred dollars, just like that. How many people carry around eight hundred dollars?

"Your wife will love them," I said. "Traditional mountain craftwork. Handmade." His sour expression said patchwork wasn't the wife's thing. Too bad, but not my problem.

I drove him and his purchases down to the motel in the pickup. Loretta was sweeping outside his room, and I could tell from her expression she was waiting to remind him checkout time had been 10:00 a.m., and it was now almost two. But she shut her mouth when she saw the load of Evvie's stuff he pulled out of the pickup, changed her mind about charging him for another night.

"You want to leave that in the room till you're ready to go. Let me use the passkey and open the door."

She took her broom back to the office. Jackson came back out, handed me a copy of the contract signed by him, with a large sum of money filled in for what I'd get paid, told me to sign it—I said not till my lawyer had seen it. He said fine, he'd pick it up and get copies made when he came back the weekend after next. Then he went off toward the gas station in a hurry, where Mitch and Randall and Curtis were hovering over his car, rubbing at this and polishing that, waiting for him.

I followed Loretta into the office and gave her the money to pass on to Evvie. Evvie wouldn't argue with Loretta, but she sure as hell would argue with me, plus she'd be mad I'd sold a lot of the things she'd left behind at Wildwood to say thank you when she finally got her own shop.

I drove home wondering if this job Jackson was offering was for me. I had no idea how to write a pre-script outline, but I was used to doing course outlines, so maybe I could fake it. And as much as I needed the money, I also wanted to keep Jackson in the picture until I found out why his last name was Lamarr.

But I still had to get the damn papers graded and assessments written first. I was in for a long night.

CHAPTER 45

Next day, soon as I'd dropped off the assessments in the office, I went to the library computer, and woozy from lack of sleep, I looked up Jackson Lamarr. Half an hour on Google convinced me he was legit, famous, and had won a lot of awards for his historical programs. There were plenty of pictures online with his TV actress wife, all glossy and blond and thin, obviously not someone who'd have cholesterol in the house.

My classes met for the last time before the summer break, and I handed out their term papers, saying anyone who wanted to discuss grades could stop by my office later. With a few minutes left in class, I couldn't resist telling them that a TV production company was going to make a miniseries about Grafton's history. Grafton was going to be famous. That got their attention.

"Say *what?*"

"Here?"

I told them history wasn't as dead as they thought. The director, Jackson Lamarr, had been in touch with me about it.

To my surprise, Donnalise Ozment, whose sole purpose on earth seemed to be looking good, wearing tight jeans, and tossing her hair flirtatiously when the football players were around, sat up and exclaimed, "Jackson Lamarr?" Her big blue eyes opened wide with surprise. And . . . awe?

"Yes."

What was that all about?

The bell went.

Donnalise came over. "Professor Marshall, hope you don't mind me asking, but . . . Jackson Lamarr! You really met him? I mean, he's sooo famous! And sooo cute!" She wrinkled her nose and gave a little squeal of excitement.

"Donnalise, what do you know about Jackson Lamarr? Are you a fan of history documentaries?" I tried to keep the sarcasm out of my voice. If she were, she'd always hidden it well.

It turned out she'd seen his picture all over those trashy tabloid magazines at the Winn-Dixie checkout and read the article while she waited for the woman ahead of her to finish bagging her groceries. The story had really been about Jackson's actress wife, who was described as "temperamental" and "highly strung."

"That's media talk for 'pain in the ass,' Professor Marshall. Jackson's wife made a terrible scene at an awards dinner, accusing the chef of trying to kill her. You know, with gluten, or no, I remember, it was because there was parsley and she's allergic to parsley. I mean, *parsley*? And on top of that, she got her picture taken knocking a tray out of a waiter's hands, screaming he was a clumsy wetback who should go back to Mexico. Jackson threw her over his shoulder, carried her out with her shouting and hitting him with her pocketbook and kicking her high heels in the air, and there's a picture of him shoving her in a limousine. He was just carrying her around like a big, hulking caveman!" Donnalise finished breathlessly, "Do you guess, if he's gonna be making his documentary here, I could, like, maybe meet him?"

"You never know." I was noncommittal.

When I got home there was a big envelope with a Washington law firm's return address. I opened it and found a letter announcing some company I'd never heard of, Royal Grant, had acquired the rest of the land Gramps had sold to the Richmond developer. Royal Grant wanted to bring their new plans to build a resort there to my attention. There was a brochure featuring happy smiley families hiking and playing in the pool, ladies having spa facials, men fishing in the river. The brochure also promised a "private honeymoon cottage with breathtaking views" in a secluded location on Frog Mountain, with a Jacuzzi, for those seeking the ultimate luxury retreat.

It would bring new jobs and exciting commercial possibilities to Grafton, so long neglected in the march to progress achieved by nearby Enterprise, blah, blah. The lawyers enclosed a personal letter to me from the owner of Royal Grant.

They wanted to reopen negotiations with the owner of Wildwood over a possible sale. Since their last approach, they had learned the elderly property owner who'd refused to sell earlier was sadly deceased, they were reaching out to me as the heir, to discuss a purchase of the property, blah, blah, blah, which could be given a new lease on life as the resort's private honeymoon cottage, blah, blah . . . The signature was a big scrawl I didn't bother trying to make out.

I threw the letters and the brochure in the trash. Wildwood wasn't for sale, was never going to be for sale, and they could damn well build their honeymoon cottage elsewhere.

I should have deciphered the signature. Instead I fed the dogs and fell into bed.

CHAPTER 46

Next day I slept late and was prying at the dogs' gate with the screwdriver, trying to fix it before it came off the hinges, when Freeman Hanover Stuart drove up. Freeman had been a highly successful single practitioner for fifty years, and people said that between him and his secretary, Inez, they knew everybody's secrets in southern Virginia. There's a saying that someone "knows where the bodies are buried." That's Freeman.

He's supposed to be retired but he says Inez won't let him. What he really means is he can't stand not to be in the thick of something. And he's still driving his silver 1968 Mustang convertible with the top down. He says when he was a younger man, he needed a flashy car because it made him look successful so people would hire him. Now he says it's to match his gray hair and attract women.

Back in the 1960s, right after the big segregation battle, Freeman came to Grafton after getting his law degree from UVA. His grandmother had been Miss Willa Hanover Freeman, who'd had a successful dressmaking business here. Freeman and his mom, who'd married a distant Stuart cousin, used to come back to Grafton to visit her in the summer. Miss Willa had gotten rich enough to pay his tuition at law school and persuaded him it was time one of her family came back to live here, and anyway Grafton needed a black lawyer and he was going to be it. He started using Hanover as his middle name. There was a big Hanover clan in the valley—all related to him one way or another—and he thought it would help him get their business. It did. He and Gramps struck up a friendship.

Life magazine did a story on "New Blacks in the New South" in the late 1980s and used Freeman as one of their examples. By that time he was hugely successful. Gramps thought the piece was patronizing, and Freeman agreed, said the way the article read they might as well have photographed the doctors and teachers and politicians and professors featured in it barefoot and eating watermelon, but he shrugged his shoulders and said maybe the young people would look beyond the crap and see examples.

Freeman started with divorces and petty crime, but since the Hanovers owned a lot of land in the valley, they had a lot of property transactions that required a lawyer. There's often a problem because old deeds—two hundred years old sometimes—often aren't very clear. You have to locate other documents that clarify what the boundaries are, or the records are incomplete about who inherited what piece of land, whether or not they can buy a piece of property at all, and if so, from whom, and how big is it exactly and are there any restrictions or covenants or rights of way that a buyer needs to know about. Freeman was good at ferreting out stuff like that. Unraveling who'd inherited titles, easements, or could sue a future owner who breached an obscure but existing right.

Over time he became an expert in all the complicated issues to do with property around here. Little by little he expanded his practice so that anything to do with land in the Bowjay Valley, you wanted Freeman Hanover Stuart, the one-man law firm.

"Hey, Rose-Linda," he said.

"Well, hey, Freeman, nice to see you." I oiled the bolt and gave the dog run gate a final kick. "Come on up to the porch and sit down. Can I get you some iced tea?"

"No thanks, I'll just take a seat. I'm here on bidness. Got something I need to discuss with you." He was dressed for work in a lightweight suit, a pinstriped shirt, and a tie and had his monogrammed briefcase with him. He looked sharp, cool, and comfortable. Expensive, in other words. Which he was.

"Who's paying you to talk business with me?" I asked as we went up the porch steps.

"You'd be surprised," Freeman said, sitting down and opening his fancy briefcase. He slid a thick batch of papers on the old pine table I keep on the porch. Among them I spotted the same brochure I'd been sent. Uh-hunh.

"What you got there, Freeman?" I asked suspiciously.

He peered at me over his glasses. "You got a letter from the Royal Grant company, didn't you? With their brochure outlining their plans for a resort?"

"I threw it away . . . Oh no, don't tell me you're representing them!"

"I am. They needed a local lawyer on the team. Me, naturally. More to the point, the company's owner knows the Marshall family has owned Wildwood for over two hundred years and that previous attempts to buy it, when your grandmother was alive, were rebuffed. Knowing your grandmother, I suspect the rebuff would have been couched in terms that left no doubt in the mind that she wasn't selling."

"Granny would have cut off her own head before she let the people who built Cherokee Ridge buy another inch of Marshall land. And before you go any further, the answer is still no. If that's what you've come up here for. Just no."

"Rose-Linda, just look around you. The roof has holes, this porch we're sitting on is sagging. I happen to know the property taxes are in arrears. Look at that fence by the orchard. It's collapsed, and those dogs of yours are damned expensive animals. I bought one from the Charbonneaus after John died, and the vet bills . . . whooee!"

Well, yes, I'd had several eye-watering vet bills myself.

"These folks have got money to spend, and you could drive a hard bargain. I bet you don't know who the owner of Royal Grant is?"

"I bet you're going to tell me."

"You remember Casey Vann?"

"What? The weird kid from high school?" His name brought back my first date with Guy, going to Jayjay's tavern after Evvie's wedding, and Casey Vann had sold the whiskey that we drank to Jayjay, and . . . I mustn't go there. "What I remember about Casey is people said he'd wind up either rich or in prison. Maybe both."

"Well, he's not in prison yet, but he's rich all right. As soon as he graduated from college, he started making whiskey. Fact is, he went to college to learn how to make whiskey. In Virginia he couldn't buy the liquor stores to sell it in, but he bought liquor stores in a couple of other states. Then he got into buying the property they were on, which got him into other retail property, and then he started buying property to turn into high-class leisure complexes. He's got a string of those from here to Maine now. And his company Royal Grant owns that big stretch along the river where the new resort complex will be. He doesn't take no for an answer. He just figures out ways to get things."

"He sounds like a megalomaniac."

Freeman grinned and shrugged. "Enterprising. He's retained me because he's got zoning approval for this resort in Grafton, and he wants to make sure no old covenant or easement crops up to bite him. He's got a lot invested, says it will bring new life to the town, and I think he's right. Grafton's dying on its feet, while Enterprise is thriving. He's kind of a control freak, down there right now with the architects and engineers, got a temporary office and a temporary building to show the plans to anyone who wants to see them, and you could go take a—"

"Oh hell! No, I don't want to see them!"

"The money you could make, Rose-Linda, you wouldn't have to worry about keeping this place going. He'd see it got fixed up. He's making you a good offer. I have the papers here, and I bet I could negotiate for Casey to build you a new house—hell, I bet he'd be willing to give you the land for it down there, guest privileges at the resort, use the facilities and spa anytime you want as part of any deal. But his heart's set on Wildwood being part of the resort, and he'll pay to get it."

"His heart can just set on it till the cows come home. I'm not leaving Wildwood. And that's final."

Freeman sighed. "Look, think about it. I've known you most of your life, Rose-Linda, and I may be acting for Casey, but I wouldn't mislead you. We'd both hate to see Wildwood fall down. Your grandparents loved this place and you grew up here, but they probably would have agreed with me that this was the best way to preserve it."

"With a Jacuzzi? Come on!"

"A time comes when we all need to move on." Freeman looked at me sternly over the top of his spectacles. "You're still too young to turn into Miss Havisham in a broken-down house." He gathered the papers back into his briefcase. "I'll leave the copy of the agreement with you. Think it over. You should even get advice from another lawyer. I'll call you in a couple of days."

I watched his car disappear out of the gate, feeling depressed. Freeman had always been someone my grandparents trusted, and I trusted him too. So I couldn't dismiss what he said about Wildwood going to pieces. Or Miss Havisham. Damn Casey Vann! Upsetting as this was, it galvanized me. I should have had Freeman look at Jackson's contract while he was here. Because Jackson was offering a lot of money, I'd better stop dithering and sign the contract. Then do some research and put together a précis. Fast.

For the rest of the day I was dragging dusty boxes of the *Messenger* down from the attic, arranged in chronological order in the living room. Next morning I was dragging down boxes of papers and old trunks of more papers and clothes and schoolbooks and who knew what. I was trying to figure out where to start when I got interrupted by a phone call from Evvie.

"You know that resort place supposed to get built on the river? Well, taking Ricky Scott to school this morning, I saw they put a fence up and a gate, and there's this prefab building there now and some men in hard hats, and a big sign with an arrow pointing at the office says everybody's welcome to come in and look at the plans and see how it's going to look. And guess what? The company building it, Royal Grant or whatever it's called, is owned by Casey Vann! Casey Vann, can you believe that? He was the strangest kid!"

"I heard."

"I couldn't go in, had to get to work, but I called my mom and she went to have a look and said it's going to be something else—they've got pictures of everything, right down to how the guest rooms in the lodges will look, sort of old-fashioned and country-style but in a really expensive way, you know, and there'll be concessions for local people who want to use the pool and tennis courts. Mama suggested I go over there, take a couple of cushions and bedspreads and rugs and see if they'd want to buy some, you know, add a little local flavor to the decor. Do you think I should? They'll probably have fancy decorators from New York or somewhere, better stuff than mine, but all they can say is no, right? What do I have to lose, right?"

It wasn't like Evvie to ask for reinforcement, about selling the things she made, about anything. She makes a plan and does it. Period. She's got a lot of self-confidence most of the time, and people in town are so used to her and her wheelchair now, they forget she's in one.

But back when Ricky Scott started school, she heard he was getting bullied and made fun of because his mom couldn't walk. I could tell that cut her to the quick when she told me about it, trying to laugh it off and not succeeding. She still gets anxious about meeting new people, like the buyer in the Enterprise department store who turned out to be a nice lady.

But wheeling herself into a roomful of strange men in hard hats to sell her stuff without sounding like she was begging, well, that was going to make her nervous. Evvie would rather die than have people think she was begging, or buying her things because they felt sorry for her.

"Great idea," I said. "They've got to furnish the place. They'll want a local touch. A quilt and a rag rug for every bedroom."

"That'd be nice, but I'd settle for cushions in the lounges or the bar. I'll leave my card and hope Casey doesn't hear about it or realize Mrs. Pine is me. He might remember back in high school I wouldn't date him. He kept asking me and asking me and finally I told him he was like a fly, you know how they buzz around and drive you nuts and you just want to swat them. Guess he'll remember that?"

"For Pete's sake, Evvie! That was years ago. And Casey won't be anywhere around, he's too big a deal. Plus he's probably married, rich guy like him. He's probably been divorced and is on his third trophy wife by now. Probably has six disturbed kids, gets chased for alimony and child psychiatrist bills. He's not going to hit on you!"

"He's just been divorced twice. He's dating some talk show host. Hostess, I guess you have to call her. She's a lot taller than he is. From the pictures. He's still sort of runty. No kids. But you're right, a crippled single mom's not worth getting even with." Evvie sighed.

"Did you look him up on the internet?" I was incredulous. "Look, Evvie, just take your stuff over and give it your best shot. Hopefully they'll keep you in mind when they call in the decorator. Like you say, the worst they can do is say no."

"OK. I will. This afternoon."

"Let me know how it goes. Talk to you later. I have to go to work now."

"But the college year just finished. Are you teaching summer school?"

“No.” I told her about Jackson Lamarr and the program and how he wanted an outline in a week and they’d be filming this summer and maybe on and off into the fall, and how this felt like an overdue term paper, and a lot of pressure, and Jackson talked so much and so fast it was hard to keep up with his ideas but at least I’d make some money.

Evvie’s response was “Lamarr? How’d he get that name?”

CHAPTER 47

My living room looked like an archaeological dig. That weekend before graduation, when I should have been attending the president's reception for the graduating class or the chaplain's commencement prayer service, I was going through the attic, hauling down trunk after trunk, box after box, of old clothes, papers, letters, and junk, including the set of encyclopedias that had been left to Gramps by Evaline May Vann. I spread the contents around in vaguely chronological order, talking to myself, covered in dust and cobwebs, and sneezing. There were spiders, big spiders, crawling all over those boxes. I had misgivings about what I'd taken on.

By Sunday night I'd separated a pile of things I thought might inspire me or interest Jackson—a really old prayer book, with "Duty Before Inclination" written on the frontispiece in old-fashioned handwriting. There was the old handwritten yellowed deed of land, brittle now, that said "Grafton Patent" with those *s*'s that look like *f*'s, with a map that showed the Grafton patent with the river—it had little waves and a tiny fish—running through the middle of it, and if I'm right, the king's signature at the bottom. There was an old shawl and a mashed-up bonnet and a lock of some long-dead person's hair and a Bible and a book with the title in gold letters: *An Inquiry into the Better Preventing of Clandestine Marriages*. Go figure what that was doing there.

There were shoe buckles and a battered man's hat and a Williamsburg broadsheet from 1756 with ads for runaway slaves. There were a lot of papers, many of them old and cracked where they'd been folded, but I didn't have time to decipher what all of them were.

And then I realized a box I'd just ripped open was the one of my mother's things Gramps had brought home when she died.

I was going to have to do this sometime. I took a deep breath and dug in.

There were mostly old clothes. A few pairs of worn jeans, and a leather jacket and some boots, kind of workmen's boots. I dimly remembered how we used to shop in charity stores and secondhand shops. A flashlight that didn't work. A bedroll. A stained pillow. A couple of plates and glasses.

A picture of Granny and Gramps with Wildwood in the background.

A picture of a baby. Written on the back: "Rose-Linda Hamilton b. to Sophia Catherine Marshall and Lamarr Hamilton 8th October 1980."

It was a long time ago. Mama was dead and gone, and God only knew what had become of Lamarr Hamilton. Granny told me he'd just disappeared while hitchhiking. She never heard whether my mother found him or if he'd died. This awful bleak feeling seized me, and I just sat there with my hand on the box for a long time. Why did she just leave me? Why hadn't she come back?

When I went to toss everything back in, I saw a cheap notebook at the bottom. I picked it up and opened it. It looked like she'd written a story. Then I noticed it said on the front page she was writing something as part of her therapy . . . It started with why she'd left her daughter.

Oh God! Thinking about Mama had made me angry ever since she died. I'd been angry when Guy died too. Dead people and anger. I couldn't go there, not now. I was exhausted. It was 2:00 a.m., and I had to attend graduation in a few hours. It was no time to dredge up past sorrows and have an emotional crisis. I'd read it when I could handle whatever revelations I was going to discover.

Next morning in a desperate attempt to get myself together respectably for commencement, I found a slightly faded blue-and-white flowery dress of Granny's that had sort of come back into fashion and a straw hat and one of her nice old white leather pocketbooks. Granny had taken good care of her clothes, and I thought vintage was supposed to be cool now. Not that I spent any time worrying about fashion. But looking in the mirror, I liked the effect.

Donnalise Ozment sashayed up to me after graduation and exclaimed she loved my dress, and it was real interesting about the TV program, and not to take it the wrong way, but if I was going to be on TV, she and her girlfriends would love to fix my hair, maybe even try a little makeup. Donnalise said when I knew when the filming would start, I should call her and she'd round up her girls and they'd come over.

"Sure, thanks, that'd be nice, Donnalise," I said. Not that I was planning to take her up on it. She just wanted to meet Jackson Lamarr.

That afternoon, while I was still dressed up, I went by Freeman's house with my contract from Far Horizons. Freeman read it carefully, said it sounded like a big job, and what did I know about pre-script outlines?

"Nothing, but the money's good enough to make me learn. So I won't need to sell Wildwood."

Freeman shook his head. "Good luck."

Back home I changed into my jeans and an old shirt and tried not to think about Mama's notebook, because I'd signed the contract and was committed now, and I had too much to do before Jackson came back.

I hit the internet on my old computer to get some idea of how to write a pre-script outline. Episodes. Beginning, middle, and end. Characters. Events. Visually driven.

I started by making a note of some of the old folklore like the stories about the shape-shifter and the Uktena and the dead people under the river surface that got told year after year around the campfire at the Blackberry Picnic.

Then I went through the *Messengers* looking for stories. I made notes about legends and ghost stories and missionaries and put Post-its on old photographs of the mission school and the Spiritualist Campground that's just marked now with a National Park Service metal sign, and Rehoboth Springs Hotel when it had dances and was decorated with Chinese lanterns and people in old-fashioned clothes whose photos I could identify, and shuffled them and the *Messenger* stories around, and above all, I looked hard for drama.

I was living on coffee and adrenaline by the time Jackson came back, but I had a pre-script outline. But before I'd let him see it, I insisted on giving him a tour.

I started with the old river path you can still make out that they say Indians used to travel when they migrated back and forth because of wars or the seasons. I showed him the old Vann house that's now called Riverbend Assisted Living, where my great-grandmother, who inherited Cherokee blood from both her parents, had grown up, and where he needed to talk to old people like Miss Vesta Conway, a local celebrity as a "lady artist" descended from a long-ago itinerant portrait painter. I showed him where the old Vann river landing and trading post had been once, the hub around which Grafton grew, which became Vann's Emporium and later burned down.

The post office is located there today, and I showed him the museum at the back with some pieces of old Indian pottery and baskets and fishing nets, and a gold Spanish dubloon that somebody had found up near the Old Man of the Mountain. It supposedly proved Spanish explorers had come through here centuries ago.

We looked across the river to Chiaramonte, the Charbonneaus' property, and you can still see the little landing where they say a girl named Stefania, who married the first Charbonneau, used to keep a canoe, so she could paddle over to see her friends in Grafton.

"Why'd they name the place Chiaramonte?" asked Jackson.

"No idea." I shrugged. And suppressed the thought that Guy might have known . . .

Then we went up to the Old Man of the Mountain and had a drink of water from the spring, and I told him about the schoolchildren who'd disappeared. I led him up to the old bear cave and said there are supposed to be human handprints on the wall, and the legend was that they were made by a creature who was part man and part eagle, which they called a shape-shifter.

I shouldn't have told him that. Being Jackson, he just had to go in to see for himself, which is a dangerous thing to do. But the gate the Park Service had put up had a rusty lock, and he pried it open with his state-of-the-art Swiss Army knife that had some kind of super-strong little flashlight and went in by himself.

He was gone so long I got scared and was imagining him fallen down a hole or dead when he came out looking puzzled. "I'm no archaeologist, but a guy we worked with on another series is. I'll fly him in to have a look. Those handprints could be thousands of years old."

"The Indians must have made them."

"Unless it was your shape-shifter, it must have been Indians. Just thousands of years ago. I've seen similar handprints on cave walls in Europe."

We made our way down from the cave, and Jackson sat down on the Old Man of the Mountain's head and got out his phone and started dictating notes into it. When he finished he said sorry, he had to make some calls, and so I got up and walked away to give him some privacy.

I stretched and admired the view. It's hard not to admire the view.

"I'm finished; you can come back now. What's the story behind the Old Man of the Mountain?"

I started pacing around in front of him like I do when I'm lecturing—it's like my feet and my brain are connected—and recited what I'd put in my pre-script outline.

"Legend says it's because the rock holds the spirit of a real man who lived here nearly three hundred years ago. His name was Gideon Wolfpaw Vann, the son of a white long hunter who was probably Scottish and a Cherokee woman, what they called a half-blood back in the eighteenth century. If you were looking for a pivotal character, it would be him, a product of two worlds, the old Cherokee one with its magic and shamans and the new one that would come with the European settlers. Gideon could read and write English—they say his father taught him from a Bible. His mother had special powers that made her respected in her tribe. A sort of shamaness. Or what they called a 'beloved woman.' They say he inherited special powers from her, that he could speak with animals and see the future.

"Gideon married a white woman, the daughter of Welsh settlers who had a trading post farther up the river. Gideon and his wife came south to make a trading post here. They built the mill that still grinds corn today, and their trading post supplied pioneers traveling west on the river with cornmeal and iron pots and plows from the forge at Rattlesnake Springs.

"But Gideon wasn't just an early frontier entrepreneur. He used to come here to this spot on Frog Mountain where I'm standing, build a fire, and make offerings and ask for guidance from the spirits. They say he foresaw the Cherokee removals would happen, and tried to warn people. Then he disappeared. By that time he would have been very old, so he probably died. His wife is buried in the graveyard in Grafton, and his descendants were living near the site of the first Vann cabin until the early 1950s. The legend says that the Old Man of the Mountain is

Gideon looking west, waiting for the Cherokees to come home so his spirit can finally be released from the rock and he can join his wife in the Darkening Land."

I just blabbed on, the way you do when you're in front of twenty students you're trying to interest with something from the past, when I noticed Jackson was watching me with an expression I hadn't seen before. Sort of intent. "Let's do that on camera."

"What?"

"I've been thinking. The plan was to have various narrators, but the structure would be better if we had a single narrator for the whole series. You."

"No way, Jackson. That wasn't in the contract!"

"Why not you? You're used to speaking in front of a class, the Marshall family is the focus, you know your stuff, and if anybody's going to bring the history of this place to life, it's you. Charisma. Some people have it, some don't. You'd be great."

"In front of a class of dozy students is one thing. National TV is another thing."

"We'd pay you more. A lot."

"I'll have to think about it." The thought of being in front of a TV camera made me want to throw up.

CHAPTER 48

I went home and was sitting down with a beer and wishing Jackson and everything to do with him would just go away when my phone rang.

Evvie said, "Hey, Rose-Linda. Got to tell you what happened when I went to the Royal Grant site." She didn't sound like herself. "After we talked last time, I took some stuff over there and talked to the foreman, before I lost my nerve. He took my card and said come back in two days. So I did. And there was this big black Mercedes parked in front, and when I rolled into the prefab office, who was there but Casey himself, with his sleeves rolled up, surrounded by men in suits and hard hats, and a table full of architects' drawings. He turned around and said, 'Hello, Mrs. Pine,' and started introducing me to the other men, and like an idiot I got all flustered and wished I hadn't gone, and so I said he looked busy and I'd come back another time, and I was heading for the exit as fast as I could roll. He said 'Wait,' told the other men he'd get back to them later, and when they'd gone he asked if I'd have dinner with him.

"I was surprised and embarrassed and he said I owed him for not going out with him in high school, and anyway, I was a woman with her own business and he wanted to talk business. I said sure, OK, thinking we'd have a hamburger at Jayjay's. He said no, we'd go out of town.

"'Oh, Enterprise,' I said, and my heart kind of sank—I had on an old sweatshirt—but hey, whatever. It wasn't like I had to impress him, he's still little and runty. I called my mother to look after Ricky Scott, and we got in his Mercedes—it took the wheelchair—and instead of Enterprise we got on the freeway and went to Bristol! To a French restaurant! With candles on the table and champagne and dinner that cost as much as two weeks of groceries for me and Ricky Scott.

"He poured me most of the champagne—he doesn't drink much, as a whiskey maker he said it was better not to. And, Rose-Linda, we just talked and talked. We didn't realize everybody else had left, and they seem to know Casey because the manager came over and made a fuss and said stay as long as you need to and lit more candles because ours had burned down. He told me about his divorces and said he couldn't believe he was talking so much because he didn't usually but we'd known each other since we were kids, and by then I was tipsy and telling him, you know, about everything and Ricky Scott, what had happened and the business and how you helped me, and then—oh, I'm so embarrassed! I started crying and talking about raising Ricky Scott right so he didn't end up like his father.

"He drove me home. Next day I woke up hungover and so mortified I'd made a drunken fool of myself that I didn't answer the phone all day in case it was Casey. So . . . next day, that black Mercedes is standing in front of my house when I came back from work . . . Well, he wants to order all my stock! Everything! And all the stuff I can make. The decorator will be in touch."

She sounded a little breathless.

"Good going, Evvie!"

"And the thing is . . . he wants me to have dinner with him again. Even though we had dinner two more times after the first night. You know, just to discuss my ideas."

"Hmm, really? Is he getting taller and better-looking all of a sudden?"

"And he promised Ricky Scott a ride in his plane."

"Did he?"

Evvie's voice sounded sort of small when she said yes. It sounded even smaller when she said, "I might have been wrong about Casey. He's nice." And hung up before I could comment.

I kept working on the outline, and a bossy young woman edited things and asked questions, and I got harassed by Jackson, who told me to hurry it up. Teams of people seemed to be involved. Jackson's archaeologist friend flew down on a Far Horizons plane to have a look at the cave. Then more people came to have a look, because the archaeologist pulled some political strings and got permission from the Park Service to go in with a professional caving team. The film crew kept swearing at them and yelling at them to get out of the way. Loretta's café was packed every night. Jayjay's too. The Hog Callers were doing gigs at the tavern most nights and having a whale of a time.

My first filming day was coming up. I was a nervous wreck.

So nervous that I called Donnalise and her posse. The girls arrived late in the afternoon. I'd gotten pizza and soft drinks, and the girls unzipped their plastic flowered bags and unloaded an entire drugstore of lotions and hot rollers, some green goo they said was a face mask, and a startling amount of makeup for Christian young women who'd signed a pledge not to have sex before marriage.

They set up next to the bathroom sink and got down to business, with shampoo and conditioner and cold water for a shine. My wet head was slathered in pink stuff and wrapped in a towel, and then there was a lot of giggling as they slapped green stuff on my face.

They washed off the pink goo and I washed off the green goo and a girl named Jenny got out her haircutting scissors and said she was going to give me a good trim. Then she plugged in her hair dryer and blasted my head, then stuck hot rollers in my hair. A girl named Sally Ray got started on my face, toner and moisturizer first—*"OK?"* she said, like I was going to argue with her. Then Donnalise whipped out big fluffy brushes and little bottles and tubes of this and that, told me not to say one word till they'd finished.

They took out the rollers, and another brush whisked over my face, the towel came off my shoulders, and I had a good look at myself in the mirror. My hair kind of bounced—I threw my head around and looked at my reflection from this side and that side, and it kept bouncing and catching the light. With liner and eye shadow my eyes looked really big, and blusher showed up my cheekbones.

Was that really me? "Thank you," I quavered, so touched that the girls had taken so much trouble over me.

"You look hot!" exclaimed Donnalise. There was a chorus of "Oh boy!" and "Sure do!"

I hugged them all and said, "Thank you!"

"Don't you dare cry and ruin all our hard work!" ordered Sally Ray.

They packed up, said they had to go.

Getting into their car at dusk, the girls were high-fiving each other. When I went to clean up the bathroom, I saw they'd left a bag of makeup, brushes, face cream, and the hot rollers with a little note that said Jenny had a spare set, and Donnalise wrote a PS to say thanks for the pizza, and Sally Ray wrote, "Remember, eyes are your most important feature. Go heavy on the eyeliner."

It was just so sweet I did cry. Just a little.

Next morning I got up early and carefully re-created last night's makeup session. It made sense people called it war paint. I was surprised how much it boosted my confidence in front of the TV camera for the first time. I managed not to throw up.

"Let me tell you about this part of Virginia. From where I'm standing now, on Frog Mountain, you can see all the way to Tennessee, watch the Bowjay River snaking through the Appalachians until it reaches our valley and the little old town of Grafton down there, on the west side of the mountain. After it passes Grafton, you can see where the Bowjay doglegs and disappears west into a kind of blue haze that hangs over these mountains. I like to imagine it's that color to remind us that millions of years ago all this was covered by a sea." I babbled woodenly. "Just an ordinary small southern town. But look close and it has a story all its own."

It was strange to be talking and pointing with the camera right there on me like the Eye of God, but Jackson said everybody felt like that at first and not to worry, I'd get used to it and loosen up. Donnalise and her posse hung around on the sidelines to watch the filming. Eyeing Jackson. He didn't seem to mind, but he didn't seem to care much either when I introduced them at the end of the day.

And he was right about getting used to it. After a while it didn't feel any different from teaching. "You've got authority in your voice now. Good," said Jackson. "You're on a roll."

"After the sea retreated, underground rivers honeycombed the limestone mountains with caves. Nobody knows how deep this cave is, but these caves are dangerous, they often have hidden passages and underground water and drop-offs. There's an iron gate bolted across this one for safety. They say bears hibernated in it when there were still bears in the mountains. The Indians who lived here called it the breathing cave because if you stand in front of the gate, there's air coming out, sometimes in puffs, like breath. That may be because there's another entrance that lets in the wind, but no one's ever found it."

This was where they were supposed to cut from my segment to the archaeologist, who was supposed to stand at the cave entrance and talk about handprints on cave walls all over the world, made by the same technique of blowing colored earth around hands. Weird and strange and sort of awesome.

But then Jackson decided he wanted to film *in* the cave—I thought it was more a case of him being gung ho, some kind of testosterone-fueled competition with the archaeologist—and they went in to test for the kind of lights they need when filming. They were in for a couple of hours, then the team, the archaeologist, and Jackson came out looking stunned and having a loud argument.

"Now what," muttered Jackson's assistant. "I wish the shape-shifter had bit them."

After a while it became clear they weren't arguing about the hand-prints like we thought, they were arguing about some clay figurines they'd found inside on a rock ledge. My first thought was they were probably souvenirs left behind by tourists who hiked up the mountain, maybe on their honeymoon or something. Probably left their initials in a big heart on the cave wall . . .

Jackson was yelling, of course they were made by the Indians, who else. The archaeologist was shouting they were fucking Greek and not just Greek, but Greek from Sicily, and he could tell because they were votive figures to Demeter, the Goddess of Many Crowns, and her daughter, Kore, made in a way they were only made in Sicily and were thousands of years old. Jackson argued he was damn sure the ancient Greeks never got to the mountains of southern Virginia. The archaeologist shouted louder, and Jackson told him not to be a fool. After that the archaeologist stormed off, saying he was calling a professor of antiquities to come have a look. Jackson hollered that he wouldn't interrupt the filming schedule for some academic, and everybody heard the archaeologist say, to hell with his damn schedule, this was *important*.

"Egos! Back to you, Rose-Linda," said a cameraman wearily.

"But the script isn't finished for the next part," I protested.

"Improvise," he ordered. "We can't waste the time. We'll keep doing takes, and the editing will come later. Let's see if we can get any usable film, delay's costing money."

"OK."

Rattled, I started blabbing on about bears and buffalo and mountain lions being long gone from the valley, same as the Native American tribes that lived here for hundreds, maybe thousands of years, hunting and planting their crops and going to war. Their encampments and fields and hunting grounds formally became the town of Grafton when the last of the Native American tribes, the Cherokees, were mostly carried off in the "removals" of 1836.

"Ethnic cleansing wasn't invented in the twentieth century. The whites wanted the Cherokees' land. The local people were arrested, dragged from the fields they were planting and the cabins they were sweeping, the clothes they were washing in the river, children from their classes at the mission school. Soldiers and their local henchmen roped everyone together and forced them at gunpoint onto flatboats that would take them part of the way west, to Arizona. It was the first stage of a deathly journey known as the Trail of Tears.

"They say some Cherokees hid in the mountains to avoid being taken. One of them was supposed to be a little Cherokee girl from the mission school. After the removals, a strange thing happened on Frog Mountain. Children from the mission school came up here for a picnic with their teacher and vanished while she was setting out their lunch. There was an odd theory—who knows where it came from—that eagles took the children, but of course an eagle couldn't fly away with a child, let alone nineteen of them. The only possible explanation seemed to be that they'd wandered into a cave and got lost. But parents were strict in those days, and going in a cave meant a whipping. And even if one or two naughty ones had done it anyway, what about all the others? It didn't seem a likely explanation, but search parties roped themselves together and looked in all the caves they could find. Still, no trace of those children.

"For a long time after that, the only people to go up to the Old Man, the last place their children had been seen, were some of the mothers. They came back saying they'd heard a little girl's voice up there, but they were told they were just out of their minds with grief. And then a child who hadn't gone on the picnic because her mother needed her at home told people that after the children disappeared, she'd seen a little Cherokee girl who said her name was Dancing Rabbit. Dancing Rabbit begged the child to come fly away with her, like the eagles, but when the child refused, Dancing Rabbit vanished into thin air.

"The Park Service put up this metal sign that tells the story of those disappearing children, and Dancing Rabbit. But you know what they say about time healing all wounds. Old sorrows don't outlast the folks involved, and people don't take so much note later."

I was about to get started on the shape-shifter that was supposed to live on Frog Mountain and the Thunder Beings when Jackson came back, looking like he wanted to kill somebody.

"It's nearly sunset. Let's shoot a take on the sunset windup," he ordered. "Go on, Rose-Linda."

"Sure," I said, trying to remember what the sunset windup was.

"A change . . . ," prompted the assistant.

"A change comes at sunset in the mountains. The birds go quiet, and something sets dogs barking one after the other, you can hear it echoing down the valley. Hikers coming down the trail at dusk will swear they heard animal noises, a bobcat, a wolf howling, or the scream of wild pigs fighting. Curious, because all these animals are long gone from the valley.

"But as darkness approaches, the valley fills with returning spirits, the souls set free of whatever lived and died among these mountains for thousands of years: wolves, possums, bears, wild pigs, polecats, mountain lions, deer, badgers, foxes, raccoons, great herds of buffalo, and the people who hunted them—the Meherrins and Chickasaws and Saponi and Creeks, the Cherokees, the settlers who drove them out. They say that the night breeze around the Old Man of the Mountain carries their stories, smells of buffalo and campfires, echoes of war songs and death chants, the crack of long rifles, call-and-response hymns, long-dead girls sighing for their lovers, riverboat whistles, a train in the distance, phantom hounds treeing ghost bears, chasing ghost deer across the ridge.

"One day we'll all go to our rest, and the little stories of those of us who're here for the moment will get swept away in the same eternal cycle. One story ends, another begins. That's history for you."

There was a silence. Maybe I'd been too dramatic and messed it up. Oh shit! Then Jackson started to clap and the others joined in.

CHAPTER 49

It went on like this the entire summer, me talking, rewriting, and filming take after take until Jackson was satisfied. At the end of most days, he'd come back to Wildwood with me because it was the only place in Grafton we could have some peace and quiet to go over the day's filming, edit or tweak the script. We sat working on either side of the double desk Gramps had given Granny, me making script notes and Jackson pre-editing on his laptop. Jackson would pick up groceries—whatever he wanted to eat, which was mostly steak—and we'd have dinner while we worked.

He put butter on his steak for the extra cholesterol.

It seemed like somebody was overreacting to the no-cholesterol rule at home, but of course I didn't say anything.

But I got used to him being there. Mostly he was quiet company, concentrating. Sometimes we'd bounce ideas off each other. I told him my grandparents had done that when Gramps had the *Messenger*. Some afternoons he'd send one of his assistants to the liquor store in Enterprise to get wine, and over dinner we'd finish a bottle and talk a little, unwinding before he went back to the motel. He wanted to hear how it was growing up at Wildwood, and I told him how Mama had left me here and never come back, and about the family and Ben Marshall starting the *Messenger*, and all the old copies I'd dredged for stories. How my grandparents made sure I went for a scholarship so I could go to college. I even told him about Guy, and how I'd come back to Wildwood to live.

He was a good listener.

He told me about his family in Boston, where his father had been a successful obstetrician, but had given up a month's lucrative practice every year to donate his time to a clinic on an Indian reservation in Oklahoma, where a lot of the residents were addicted to drugs and alcohol, and there was a high infant-mortality rate because health care on the reservation was poor. "He saved so many babies that mothers on the reservation often named their children Lamarr. He was proud of that."

"*What?*" I stared at him. "I can't believe this. My father might have been one of them! His name was Lamarr Hamilton, and I think he had some connection with a reservation in Oklahoma. He was hitchhiking there. I think my mother told Granny he was in some sort of VISTA program that was running a clinic on the reservation. But I can't remember exactly. Coming from medical school, he passed through Grafton hitchhiking, and my mother picked him up. She kept on going with him, I was born, and he went hitchhiking somewhere else. I think it might have been another reservation. He was some kind of health worker . . . Anyway, he disappeared, and my mother took me and went looking for him. And brought me here, like I told you. Far as I know, she never found him."

"That's weird." Jackson shook his head. After a while he paraphrased the old line from *Casablanca*, "Of all the yards in all the world, I hadda walk into yours."

"Glad you did," I said. We just looked at each other for a moment and . . . I don't know, there was sort of this feeling in the air. Electric. Then he left like he did every night to go back to the Pines' motel.

What did I expect? He was married. Had kids. He took weekends off to go home and be with his family. I started to think what I'd do if he made a pass, realized it was much better if he didn't. The last thing I needed in my life was a married man.

But I kept using the makeup every day. Tried to pull myself together in a way I hadn't before. You can't let yourself go in front of a whole film crew.

I called Evvie next day to tell her about the Lamarr thing and how unbelievable it was to think my father might have been named after his father. Evvie asked if I was sleeping with him. "Of course not!"

Then we didn't talk for a while. Evvie was swamped with work, busy with decorating schemes and mood boards for the resort. I was busy sifting through the old stuff from the attic for inspiration, and one way or another, the summer passed in a hurry.

Jackson came and went.

But he was good as his word and got the Hog Callers doing the background music for the credits, and he even filmed them playing at the American Legion's Fourth of July barbecue in one episode. He recorded some call-and-response singing at the churches. The last of the filming was interviews of the old folks in Riverbend, and he sweet-talked Miss Vesta Conway, Grafton's oldest person—she must be nearly a hundred—who describes herself as a "paintress" and thinks that makes her more important than anybody, into being filmed while she told the stories behind her "interpretive" history paintings. He was good with people, good at listening to Miss Vesta. Miss Vesta drives most people nuts.

Then Jackson went back to New York just before the Blackberry Picnic came around. I almost asked him to stick around for it. It was as historical as anything. He'd love it. But of course I didn't.

"You seem like you're moping," Evvie said, over a big plate of barbecue at the picnic.

"I am not moping!" I snapped, piling coleslaw on my paper plate. I hate coleslaw.

There was a quiet week before college started, and I decided since I'd eventually have to read my mother's therapy notebook I might as well get it over with. I felt out of sorts and blue anyway. I braced myself for something rambling and crazy.

It said, "For Rose-Linda." To my surprise.

It started with Mama's early memory of picking blackberries with other children at a Blackberry Picnic and looking up to see a little girl watching her, half-hidden behind a tree. She wasn't picking blackberries. Just staring at Mama. Mama didn't like her. She whispered her name was Dancing Rabbit. And when Mama got closer, she saw the eyes staring at her were red, and Mama was scared all of a sudden and ran back to Granny and Gramps.

After that Dancing Rabbit was always near Mama. Like she followed Mama home. Other people couldn't see her. She would appear, then disappear for a time, and then my mother would wake in the night to see the red eyes. They would shine, shine, shine in the dark. Mama would scream, and her parents would come and say it was her imagination and Vann Drumheller ought to be shot for scaring children with his ghost stories.

Dancing Rabbit went to school with Mama and was there when she went to birthday parties or played with other children. Sometimes she went away, but she always came back.

Mama tried to tell the child psychiatrist in Atlanta the time her parents took her there.

He gave her some tests and agreed with her parents, it was her imagination. Bright children often had lively imaginations. Mama was bright but perfectly normal.

Dancing Rabbit was sitting beside Mama the whole time she was in the psychiatrist's office. He couldn't see her any more than her parents could. But Mama was tired of trying to explain.

After that Mama concentrated on playing "normal." She did well in school and copied the other girls, dressing the same way, cheerleading, and taking her college entrance exams. It was a strain and she cracked sometimes, acted awful. She argued with Granny.

Then she'd met Lamarr Hamilton. He was hitchhiking and she picked him up. He told her he'd wanted to see the place the Cherokees had been driven out of, and she told him all about growing up in Grafton and the Bowjay Valley and how her family had been some of the first settlers, so maybe they were partly responsible for the Cherokees being eventually removed. They'd hit it off at once.

He was a medical student on his way to volunteer at a clinic on one of the reservations in Oklahoma. He'd been born in the clinic, nearly didn't survive because his mother was addicted to alcohol and he was born with fetal alcohol syndrome. A white obstetrician who volunteered in the clinic every year saved him, and when his mother died a few years later he was adopted by the Hamiltons, a family in Vermont, who'd given him a comfortable New England upbringing. He'd kept the name Lamarr and gone to medical school so that when the time came he could help people too poor to get medical care, give something back for the good life he'd had with his adoptive family.

I was reading faster and faster, almost dizzy with what I was finding.

Lamarr said he'd managed to learn something about his Cherokee ancestors and their ways before he was adopted. Mama told him about Dancing Rabbit, and he'd believed her. He was the first person to do that. He thought about it for a while and said Dancing Rabbit's spirit probably wanted revenge because the Marshalls had brought the first settlers to the valley. In the old days, if a clan member was killed, the clan would avenge the death by killing a member of the killer's clan. Dancing Rabbit couldn't go to the spirit world, the Darkening Land, until she had done that. He told her what he knew about the removals and what life was like on the reservations now, that many people like his mother were addicted to alcohol.

She and Lamarr had fallen in love. And when Lamarr was there, Dancing Rabbit kept away from Mama. When the summer ended they stayed near the reservation. Lamarr kept working at the clinic, and in time I was born.

Then Lamarr got a call from another reservation. There was an outbreak of measles, few people had been immunized, and the clinic was shorthanded, could he help? He left, hitchhiking again, but never reached the other reservation. Dancing Rabbit came back. Mama tried to leave her behind, moving from place to place, looking for Lamarr. And Dancing Rabbit would disappear for a while, then Mama would see her again. She'd taken me back to Wildwood, thinking maybe Dancing Rabbit wouldn't follow us, but she saw her watching me in the night. She left Wildwood, hoping Dancing Rabbit would follow her and leave me alone.

Dancing Rabbit did follow Mama. I could tell from the way her writing grew disjointed and incoherent. Dancing Rabbit was making her life harder, wouldn't let her sleep, made her write at the end that she was ready to go to the Darkening Land herself, perhaps Lamarr was there.

Dancing Rabbit would follow her. And then Rose-Linda would be safe. Her only wish was to keep Rose-Linda safe.

I was too stunned to cry for a long time. I just sat holding the notebook while many years of misunderstanding between Granny and Mama, and Mama and me, unraveled. Then I unraveled.

After a sleepless night, early the next morning I went down to the cemetery with a bunch of wildflowers. I laid them on Mama's grave, said I was sorry for being angry and I hoped she'd found Lamarr and was with him now. He sounded like a wonderful man, just as wonderful as she was.

And I was proud to be her daughter. Their daughter.

CHAPTER 50

The series aired on prime time after Christmas, and the entire college, plus the Hog Callers and Miss Vesta Conway in her wheelchair and the other local people who'd been in it, watched every week's episode in the college gym. My students cheered and stomped and whistled when I came on.

Evvie said, "I never thought history could be glamorous. But look at you! It's like you're flirting with the camera. Was that aimed at Jackson? I mean, you were spending a lot of time together in the evening, you couldn't just have been working. And you've been looking, well, sort of hot lately. So I figured you two had to be . . ."

"For God's sake, Evvie! I was just the voice of the documentary! Between the singing at the bar and Loretta's place full of people wanting dinner, the film crew drinking like fish every night, not to mention archaeologists and graduate students and caving teams getting in the way of the filming and pissing everybody off, Donnalise and her girlfriends slavering over Jackson, there was no peace anywhere. And Jackson was on edge, pissed off about the archaeologists underfoot causing delays. He was ready to slug somebody. His assistant said he's done it before. Wildwood was the only place in the entire Bowjay Valley that was quiet, and there was nobody there he felt like arguing with. Plus how cute is carrying on with a married man? Granny would turn in her grave."

"If you'll let me get a word in edgewise, Rose-Linda, I have news for you. Jackson got divorced."

"How do you know that?"

"One of those trashy magazines at the Winn-Dixie checkout. I was waiting in line and his picture was on the cover. I'm just sayin' we think you two look like you're together. For cryin' out loud, Rose-Linda, are you blind?"

"We?"

"Casey and I."

After that I thought about Jackson a lot more than I intended to, but you know the saying, once burned, twice shy.

Anyway, why hadn't Jackson mentioned he was getting divorced? We talked about so many personal things. I looked in the mirror and told myself, "You got it wrong. He's just not that into you." I wasn't going to miss him. I've missed enough people in my life. My bank account was in good shape now, that's what mattered.

I also had enough money for an application fee for conveying an easement over Wildwood to the Virginia Board of Historic Resources. Freeman had let slip something about this, and I pressed him for more information. Developers hate easements because they prevent inappropriate changes to a historic property. So I applied, and eight months later, the easement was approved. Wildwood was safe from Casey and his Jacuzzis.

There was talk of another TV special because of Greek artifacts in the old bear cave. Big mystery, a lot of academics investigating. That's kept Grafton in the news and the Pines' motel busier than ever.

We heard the Bowjay series and Jackson were up for a big award.

Evvie was disappointed when I didn't go to the award ceremony in New York, like I was invited to. Jackson sent me a plane ticket and called and called to argue with me until I stopped answering the phone. Jackson and the series won, and he made a little speech of thanks, saying he owed a lot to his star presenter, Rose-Linda Hamilton Marshall, and how he was sorry I wasn't there to share the limelight. I felt terrible, like I'd made a huge mistake not going. But I can't do this mating game. Flirting and retreating and wondering what it all means and it hits you all over again . . . somebody might step on another land mine and then . . . it's all over. I've got past all that. For company and companionship, give me dogs any day.

That's what I told Curtis and Mitch and Randall, who kept asking me how Jackson was and when he was coming back.

"Say what?" They nudged each other and grinned at me.

That's what I told Evvie when I stopped by her shop to say hi and she asked me what I'd heard from Jackson.

"Dogs? Really?"

"Really. What's new with you?"

"Weeelll." Evvie sort of drew the word out and got this funny look on her face. Something was up. Like Casey had fired her?

"Casey signed me up for this new treatment with stem cells, or something. I don't understand it really, in fact I try not to think about it, you know, to avoid disappointment, but there've been trials and some paralyzed people have been able to walk again . . ."

I stared at her. "What? That's great news! Incredible!"

"There's a because."

"I'm waiting."

"Because he wants me to have a shot at walking down the aisle when . . . I marry him. He wants a big wedding." Evvie blushed. She actually blushed. And stuck out her hand to show me her big new diamond ring.

I was speechless.

"I got real mad at him when he started talking about the treatment—you know the accident didn't sweeten my temper, and I hate, hate, hate it when people think I'm so pitiful I need charity—and when he suggested it, I kind of shouted at him. But he just stood there and said calm down, you don't have to fight every battle to the death, try fighting for happiness sometimes. Like now. I ought to give him a chance, he's been in love with me since high school and now he admires me too, for the way I didn't let myself get beaten down. He's made a success of his businesses by never taking no for an answer, so he wasn't taking no from me now. That's when he said the bit about walking down the aisle to marry him, and pulled out the ring."

She started to cry. "And I was so mean to him in school! And now he's my best friend and I love him and I hate it if he goes away just for a couple of days, and Ricky Scott, he's so good with Ricky Scott. My mother thinks he hung the moon. Loretta says he's the answer to her prayers."

"So, Evvie, that's just . . . wonderful! Why are you crying?"

"Because"—she sniffed into a Kleenex—"I care that he's happy and, like . . . I'm no bargain, the wheelchair and all, I mean, who wants a wife in a wheelchair, and I said if the treatment didn't work I wouldn't let him marry an invalid, and he said he wasn't marrying an invalid, he was marrying me, and if I tried to back out, he'd find a lawyer who'd figure out a way to sue me for breach of promise, so . . ."

"So?"

"The treatment will take about five months, lots of physical therapy too. If it works, we'll know by Thanksgiving. I'm thinking about a Christmas wedding. Do you think it would be bad luck? I mean, Christmas still seems perfect for weddings, and I want it to be perfect. This time. Casey said we'll do it so big it'll lay the ghost of my first wedding."

"Casey sounds like a keeper."

Evvie blew her nose. "I know!"

"Christmas will be ideal. All those poinsettias and evergreens."

"Red candles."

"Miniature lights."

"Big red ribbon bows on the pews."

"And maybe a bride on her own two feet. What kind of dress, Evvie? Something with a fur trim at the neck?"

"Yeah." She gave a little smile. "Ermine."

CHAPTER 51

Of course I was happy for Evvie. Who wouldn't be? And I agreed to be her maid of honor again when she asked me, though it reopened old wounds. I wished I had someone. Like Casey. No, I definitely didn't want Casey—someone like Jackson. But Jackson wasn't coming back. He was divorced. If he'd wanted to get in touch, there wasn't anything stopping him.

I wasn't going to think about him anymore.

I tried hard not to.

Evvie had her treatment that spring and summer and the intense physiotherapy started and Evvie acquired a whole new set of swear words to express her feelings about what she was being put through. In October she took a few slow steps out of her wheelchair.

Just before college started in the fall, the college president called me in to say they had funding for a living history project recording the old people at Riverbend, and they wanted me to run it alongside my classes. I'd get a salary increase.

I said yes, and learned how to use the recording equipment.

It turned out to star Miss Vesta the Paintress, who is the most talkative person I ever met, as well as the oldest, but she has all her marbles and was thrilled to have another star turn. As we'd seen when Jackson interviewed her, she couldn't get enough of talking into the microphone, about anything and everything, not necessarily connected, wouldn't let the other residents get a word in edgewise. Especially Mary Ann O'Malley, eighty-four. Apparently Miss Vesta and Mary Ann have "had words" in the past.

Miss Vesta viewed the living history project as her own. "It's all about *her*!" Mary Ann O'Malley kept complaining. Ignoring her, Vesta kept talking about *her* childhood, *her* art training at her father's knee, how she'd been a prodigy, according to her mother, Euphemia, who recognized her child's talent right away, her particular gift for interpreting historical events and people on canvas, following in the footsteps of her distinguished Conway ancestors. On and on she talked, and when I finally tried to wind up the session, she didn't pause for breath. "What happened to that nice boy who made the TV shows? With you in 'em? He was sweet on you."

"He had to go back where he came from," I said.

"Looked to me like he was willing to stay *here*. Been what, eight months since he went?"

"A year," I said right away. You'd think you could forget practically anything in a year. Except Guy, I reminded myself.

"He told me he was divorced, and I told him if I was seventy years younger, I'd be his next wife."

"Did you?" I said, winding up cable. "I bet he was flattered. What did you do then?"

"I said I was going to give him some advice."

"That was . . . brave of you."

"It wasn't brave at all, honey. When you're my age you can give anybody advice who needs it. You do it as a favor."

"She never stops," muttered Mary Ann. "Bossy's what I call it."

Miss Vesta ignored Mary Ann. "I told him there's a younger candidate for the second Mrs. Lamarr. We had a long talk and he confided in me, said you didn't seem to have room in your life or your heart for anybody but your dead fiancé. Said he'd never been worried before about going too fast, but he was afraid of scaring you off. He was trying to figure out what to do next. Didn't want to do something that'd make you come over all pigheaded and stubborn . . ."

"Pigheaded and *stubborn*?"

"He'd been talking to the Hog Callers about you, honey."

My mouth was hanging open.

"Gave me his card," said Miss Vesta. "So I could call him up. When you wouldn't go to New York with him for that big to-do they threw for his series, this living history thing was his idea so he could come back and maybe persuade you. He roped the college in. Wants to make another TV program about it when it's done. Says if he could get you working on it, he'd have another try. I'm s'posed to call him when it's a good time to come back and see how my project's going."

"Ha!" Mary Ann O'Malley chimed in. "Your project! My hind foot! Always meddlin', Vesta is. She shouts on the phone in case the person at the other end is deaf as she is. Yesterday morning Vesta's shouting down the telephone at him, 'Rose-Linda still doesn't know you're behind this. Her friend's gettin' married again, and every time the wedding comes up she gets touchy as a cat, thinks a thunderstorm's coming. Get back here and strike while the iron's hot.'"

"You're an eavesdropping sneak," said Miss Vesta tartly, "with no judgment about what needs sayin'. Sometimes you have a responsibility to say what needs sayin'. Otherwise people get stuck. They have to be pried loose. Now listen, Rose-Linda, Jackson tried every which way to raise your feelings for him, everybody saw it but you, 'cause you're still thinkin' about the Charbonneau boy. But he's gone and you're still in life. So be in life. Broken hearts can heal, the right person comes along. Which they don't every five minutes. I'm telling you, Rose-Linda, you got to grab happiness before it runs past. It won't come sit on your lap uninvited."

Mary Ann O'Malley piped up, "She told him, 'Don't give up! She just needed to miss you some, she misses you some now. How soon can you get here?'"

"Oh, Miss Vesta, you didn't!" I groaned.

Miss Vesta looked at her watch. "I told him you'd be here recording this afternoon. He said he'd drive all night and get here today."

I was hurrying to get my equipment packed up and get out of there. "I made it," said a voice. I looked up and Jackson was standing in the doorway. Looking tired. This was really embarrassing.

"We should talk, Rose-Linda," he said.

"Yes, you should," said Miss Vesta.

"Thanks for getting me on this project, Jackson, but I'm going."

Jackson put his arm across the doorway to block the entrance. "Please, Rose-Linda."

Miss Vesta waded in again. "The visiting parlor's empty—shut the door."

Jackson said, "Come on, five minutes," like he wasn't taking no for an answer.

I took a deep breath, like I was about to jump off the high-diving board and I didn't like heights.

"OK," I said.

EPILOGUE

Mary Ann O'Malley, 84

Rose-Linda and Jackson went in the parlor and the door slammed shut. Vesta and I waited. Five minutes passed. Then ten. Then a half hour. "I expect they're kissing!" Vesta exclaimed, and rubbed her hands with glee. In my day, sneaking off to the parlor so a young man could act familiar was considered fast, and I don't care who knows it.

Vesta's hogged the limelight on this living history thing. Well, I'm history too! I was born in 1931. My granmaw Ida O'Malley was a housekeeper at a men's boardinghouse out past the town limits. In those days male travelers, salesmen and the like, well, they had their own rooming houses. They liked to smoke, take their whiskey and their rum, take snuff, even play cards. And spit. Lord, my granmaw used to say the spitting was the worst of it, you know, what with the chewing tobacco and the snuff. Spittoons all over the place, but she recalled none of 'em had a good aim.

But it wasn't just drink and gambling, and it wasn't just a rooming house. There were girls upstairs! The woman Granmaw worked for was a bad woman. Of course, the girls got pregnant a lot. And if they were expecting, they weren't much use for the men. Granmaw would do what they called "taking care" of the problem. Until the house closed down. Then she got religion, got saved, and repented of what she'd done getting rid of babies.

She brought me up Christian, and I'm against getting rid of babies. It's a sin.

But Granmaw said she knew how to do it so the girls were all right after. The woman she worked for never did it, left everything to Granmaw.

Except for one night. Granmaw answered a knock at the back door. It was snowing hard outside and she opened it, thinking maybe a customer was taking the short way in. It was two rich girls from town. It was plain what one of them wanted, wouldn't have been there for any other reason, and Granmaw was wondering what she ought to do, when the owner came in and told her she'd take care of it and told my granmaw to go refill the men's drinks.

And it was the owner who got rid of a baby that night! Granmaw heard the girl was poorly for a long time after and then got drowned when her car went into the river.

Well, years later that bawdy house burned down, and the owner and the girls left town, went to St. Louis. Granmaw stayed behind, bought a little piece of land with a little house on it, started going to church, and took in sewing work to make ends meet. And the woman she worked for sewing was colored, a Miss Willa somebody, made all the clothes for the town ladies, had more work than she could do. Granmaw resented having to work for a colored woman but she did it, said she had to accept it was God's punishment for her years spent helping wickedness and vice to flourish.

Granmaw took a strict Christian view of men and women and taught me to have one too. These days wickedness and vice are right out there in the open, couples living in sin and no one bats an eye.

Those two couples getting married next month—way they act, you can tell *they* haven't walked the straight-and-narrow path to the altar. You see 'em in Grafton, looking at each other with calf eyes, like they jumped the gun and are already one flesh. For a wedding present I'm giving each pair a Bible with some special passages about lust and the wages of sin marked with those little yellow sticky note things. It's for their own good.

Mrs. Anna Louise Drumheller, 50, matron at Riverbend Assisted Living

You'd think all the old people would have had enough excitement with the carol concert put on by the elementary school and my husband playing Santa Claus and giving out presents and the turkey dinner. I ran myself ragged cooking, but oh no! All that's nothing compared to the wedding tomorrow. The double wedding.

The Marshall girl's intended is a big TV director and acts like this is one of his productions. He's arranged a minibus for all of us here and special seats on the first couple of rows where we can see good. The church is being decorated something wonderful, red candles and little white lights everywhere and a big Christmas tree at the back with a manger scene underneath. I hear they've bought up every poinsettia in fifty miles.

The reception's going to be at the old hotel in town. It's got big rooms to fit everybody in, and it's been cleaned up and spruced up and repainted inside. Now with two days to go before the wedding, there's caterers' trucks all the way from Richmond blocking everything and everybody, and people in white aprons running around and shouting.

Miss Vesta's painting an interpretive portrait of both couples as local historical figures as a wedding present, and now she's gotten oil paint all over her room. Casey Vann said not to worry, he'll redecorate it afterward. His wife-to-be's in the business.

You see her walking around town every day now, that Evvie Stuart as was, before she married that wild Pine boy who like to killed her, getting exercise with two walking sticks after spending years in a wheelchair. Casey's usually with her, but if he tries to take her arm, help a little, she snatches her arm back like she'll do this on her own, thank you. But then she smiles at him. They say she'll go down the aisle without the sticks on the day.

Ricky Scott's giving his mother away. He's almost tall as her now. Casey Vann's filled up my refrigerator with orchid corsages for our ladies and buttonhole carnations for the men to wear at the ceremony. The Marshall girl's intended wants her two big dogs at the wedding! Whoever heard of dogs at a wedding! I warned him to give those dogs a tranquilizer first.

In fact I'm planning to give us all one. There's only so much happiness you can stand before you give out, only so much, I told Miss Vesta.

Miss Vesta said old people could stand as much happiness as it took to attend anything that wasn't their own funerals. "It's the young people who have a hard time with happiness," she said. "You have to help them along sometimes."

"Amen," said Mary Ann O'Malley. "Amen to that."

ACKNOWLEDGMENTS

A book is always a team effort. The solitary process of turning out a manuscript suits me, but a finished manuscript requires a good deal of transforming by other people before it becomes an actual book on the shelves.

As always, I want to thank the literary agency that represents me—Dystel, Goderich & Bourret LLC—and in particular Jane Dystel, the agency's president, who represents my work. I am grateful for her unstinting support and encouragement for my career, as well as for her professionalism and knowledge of the industry, which not only make my life easy but seem to smooth the whole publishing process. Jane takes my rashly optimistic approach to deadlines with a grain of salt and a reminder that "it takes as long as it takes" just when I begin to flag and feel there's no end in sight. She is always available to consult or advise, and is unfailingly generous with her time and attention to the writers she represents. As someone who works in conditions of what I call peace and quiet and my family calls lockdown, I spend perhaps far too much time in a state of detachment, hence in need of Jane's calm good sense and pragmatic advice about practicalities.

Also at Dystel, Goderich & Bourret, thanks are due to Miriam Goderich, who oversees contracts and scrutinizes everything before I sign. I want to express my appreciation to Kemi Faderin, who oversees royalty payments, for the help she has given me over the years in compiling calculations for different tax jurisdictions.

As ever, Amazon Publishing and their imprint Lake Union are hugely supportive of their authors and it's wonderful to work with them. Huge thanks especially are due to Jodi Warshaw, executive editor at Lake Union. I greatly appreciated her patience and unfailing good humor when my manuscript was, first, late and then very late indeed, given my tendency to rewrite and rewrite. I would be driven to despair if I had to deal with an author like me, but fortunately Jodi is made of sterner stuff and remained a constant source of encouragement and support.

Thanks also to Amazon production editor Laura Barrett for her oversight in the production process.

Once again I was fortunate to work with developmental editor Charlotte Herscher. It is always with great relief that I turn a manuscript over to Charlotte, who has an unerring ability to get straight to the heart of a manuscript and provide the kind of editorial advice that transforms it into a much better version of itself.

Thanks are due to Michael Trudeau for his painstaking work as copyeditor. When I say no detail, and I do mean *no* detail, escapes his eagle eye, that is meant as a compliment.

My appreciation to Phyllis DeBlanche, who has done an expert job of proofreading.

It is typical of Lake Union that much thought and attention goes into finding the perfect cover art. Thanks are due to art director Rosanna Brockley and her team for tracking down a series of striking images, and to Shasti O'Leary Soudant for devising a stunning cover around the image we chose.

Special thanks are due to marketing manager Erin Mooney and her team for their robust efforts in marketing my books.

I would like to express my appreciation to author relations manager Gabriella Dumpit. She is always contactable to respond to any queries, and though Amazon's publishing process appears seamlessly problem-free from my perspective, I know that if there were problems, Gabriella would see they were fixed.

Finally I want to thank my family. Immersed as I often am in imaginary worlds, they draw me back into the real one. My husband, Roger Low, is a constant source of companionship and encouragement and makes it possible for me to write in the first place, keeping interruptions at bay when I'm working. He deserves a medal for bearing with me when my concentration on plots, characters, timelines, and geography delays dinner yet again. When I become a little too wound up in details and mutter darkly that "my brain is too full and it hurts," he makes me laugh and think of something else. He and the rest of my family—Cassell, Jonny, Jake, Heath, Niels, Poppy, Bo, and Lucinda—support me in lovely, cheerful ways, both large and small, that lift my heart every day.

Whatever the world may say about my books, my family remain my greatest fans and most loyal supporters, and everything I write, I write for them.

ABOUT THE AUTHOR

Photo © 2020 Cassell Bryan-Low

Helen Bryan is a Virginia native who grew up in Tennessee. After graduating from Barnard College, she moved to England, where she studied law and was a barrister for ten years before devoting herself to writing full-time. A member of the Inner Temple, Bryan is the international bestselling author of the World War II novel *War Brides*; the historical novel *The Sisterhood*; the biography *Martha Washington: First Lady of Liberty*, which won an award of merit from the Colonial Dames of America; and the Valley Trilogy, featuring *The Valley, The Mountain*, and *The River*, which are based on Bryan's childhood stories of ancestors who settled in Virginia and Maryland before Tennessee became a state. She is also the author of the legal handbook *Planning Applications and Appeals*.

Made in the USA
Las Vegas, NV
02 August 2021